# CARL VINE

## *Piano Sonata No.3*

(2007)

*Piano Sonata No.3* was commissioned by The Gilmore International Keyboard Festival
and the Colburn School, assisted by the Australian Government through
the Australia Council, its arts funding and advisory body.

The recipient of the 2004 Gilmore Young Artist Award, Elizabeth Schumann,
gave the world premiere performance at Zipper Hall,
Los Angeles, California on 11 May 2007.

Duration: *c*.22 minutes

*Piano Sonata No.3* is recorded by Adam Herd on Master Performers MP004
and by Benjamin Boren on Enharmonic Records ENCD11-021

## PROGRAMME NOTE

This work is constructed in four movements to be played, generally, without breaks
between them: *fantasia – rondo – variations – presto.*

The *Fantasia* introduces several ideas which reappear in various guises in all of the
other movements, but also includes some isolated and undeveloped declamatory material. The *Rondo* explores a simple rhythmic motive while the *Variations* develop the
chordal theme from the opening of the work. The *Presto* is a self-contained ternary
structure that echoes thematic components from much that preceded it.

C.V.

To buy Faber Music publications or to find out about the full range of titles available
please contact your local music retailer or Faber Music sales enquiries:

Faber Music Limited, Burnt Mill, Elizabeth Way, Harlow, CM20 2HX England
Tel +44 (0)1279 82 89 82   Fax: +44 (0)1279 82 89 83
sales@fabermusic.com   fabermusicstore.com

# Piano Sonata No.3

CARL VINE

senza rall.

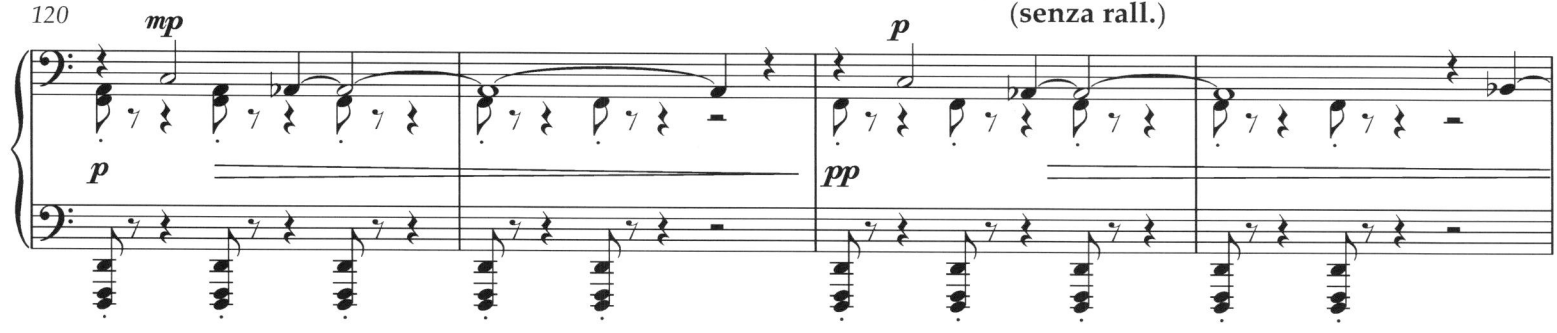

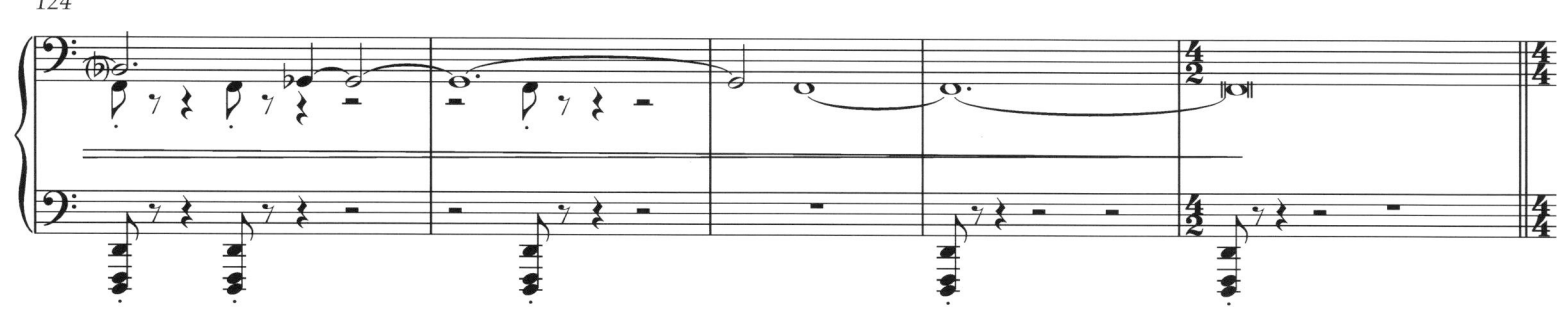

**Rondo** ♩ = 90

poco morendo

277
ppp
8
6
(loco)
Presto ♪. = 192
281
p
285
289
mp
293

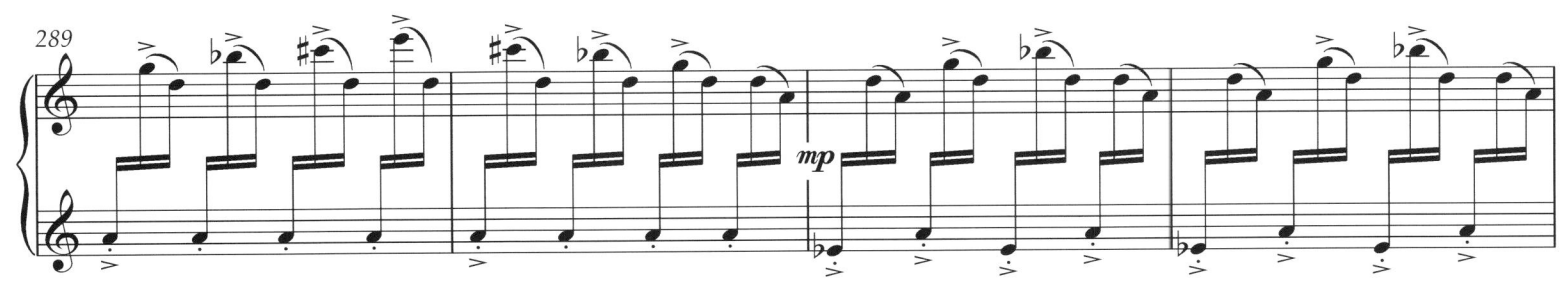

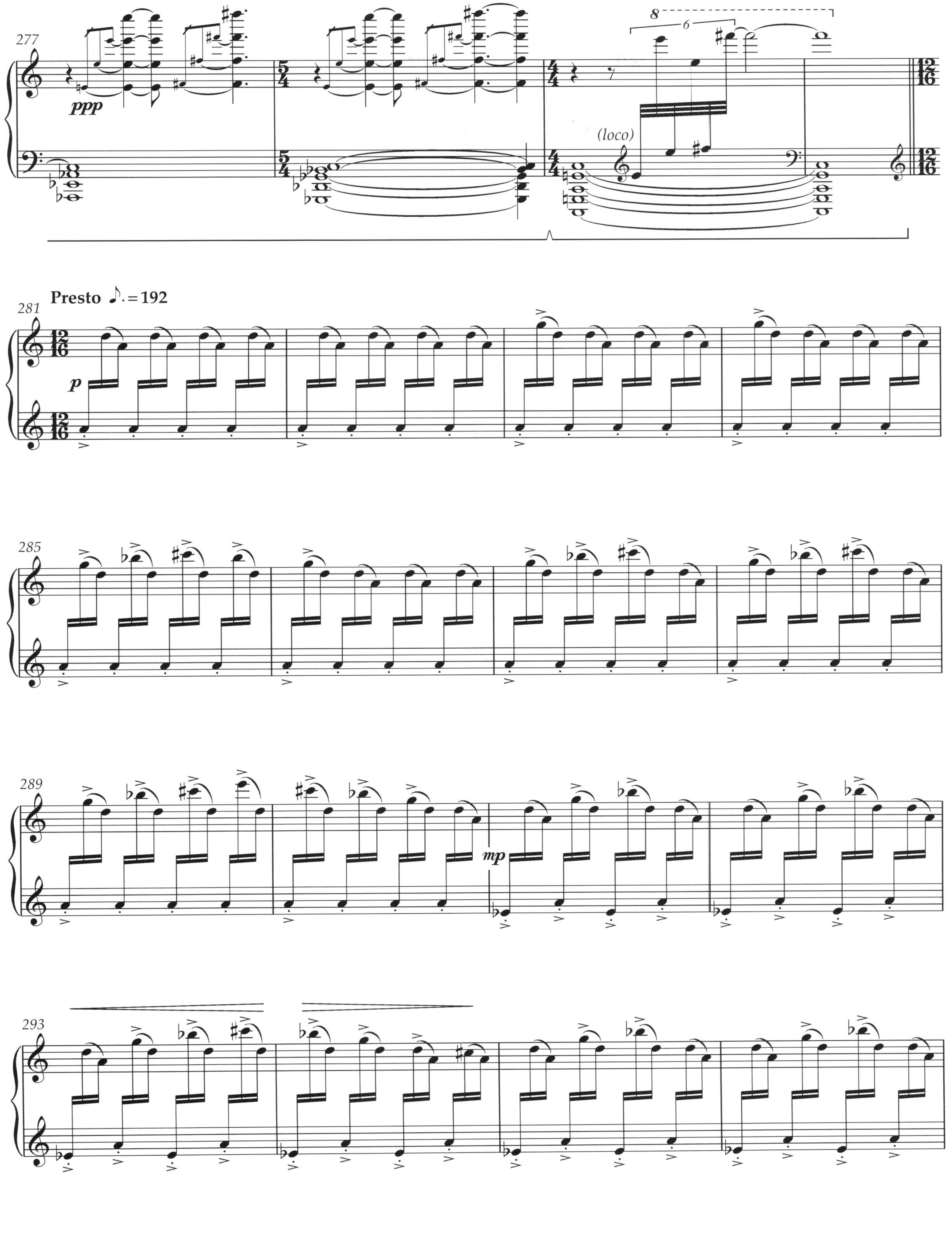

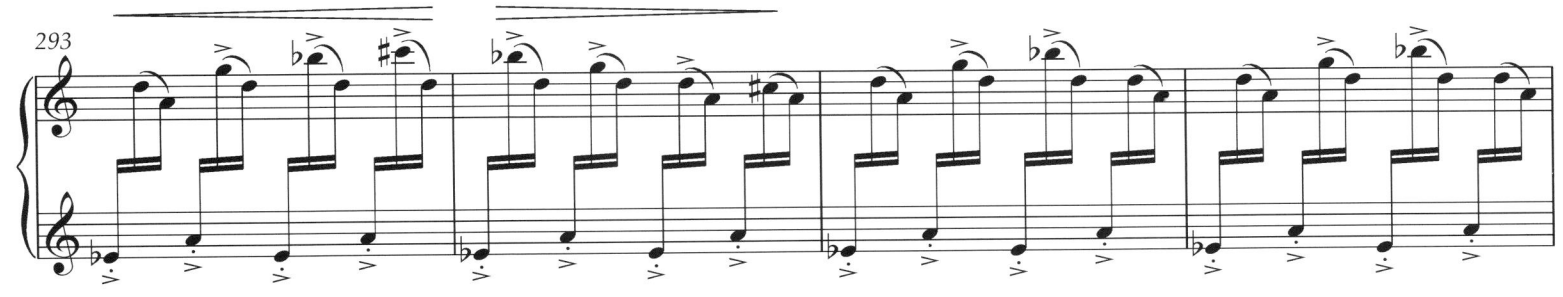

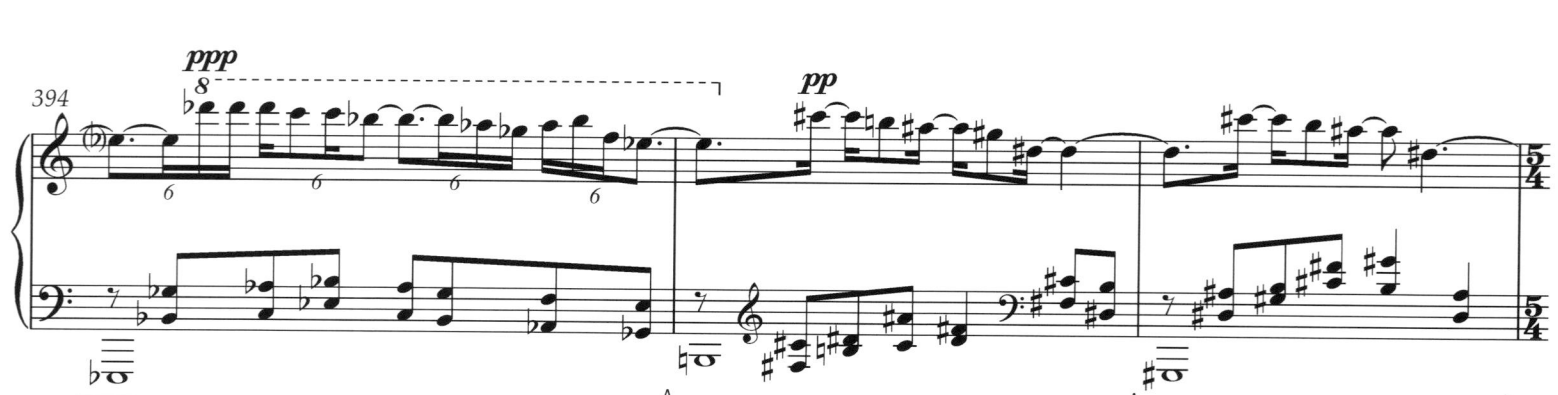

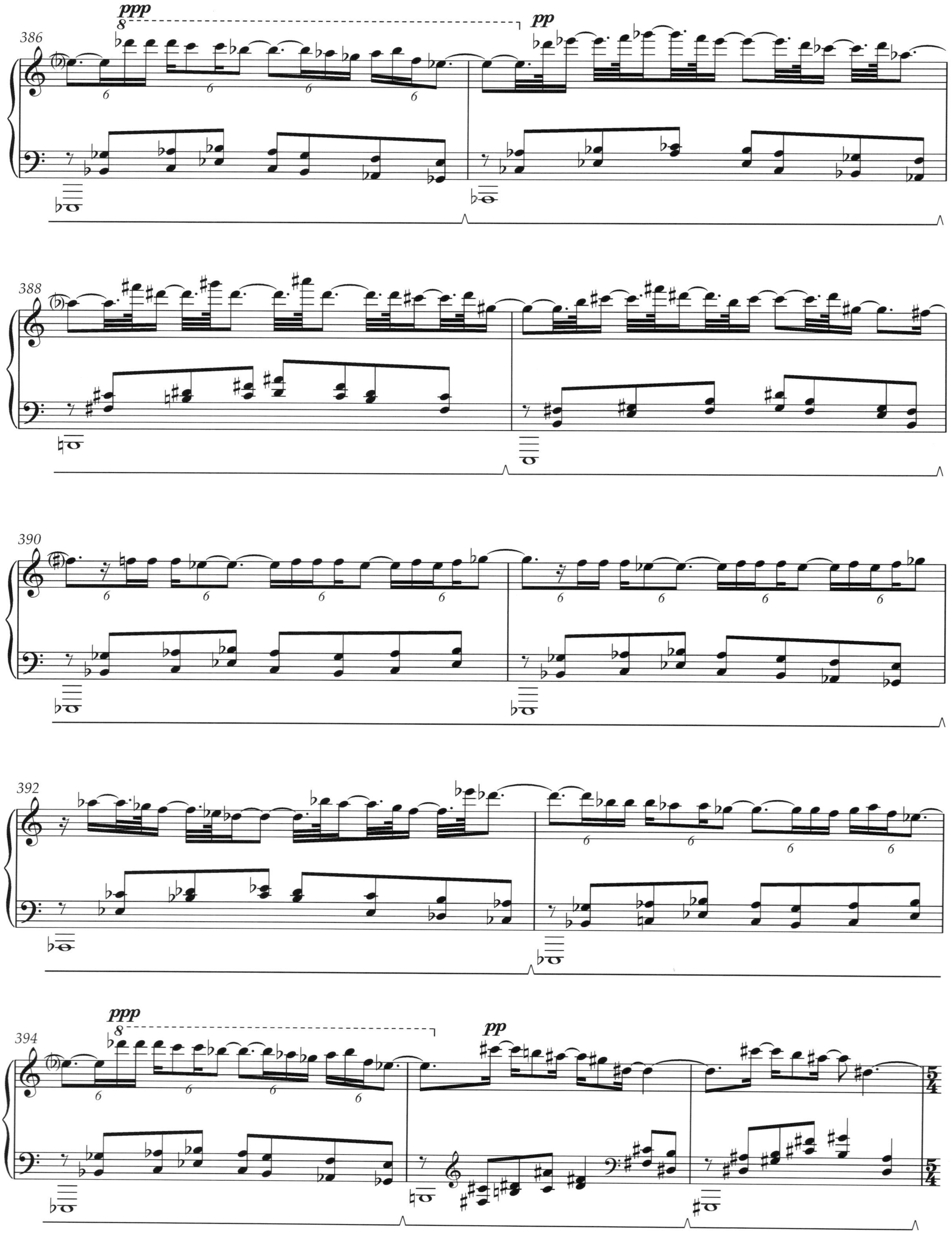
386
ppp
pp
388
390
392
394
ppp
pp

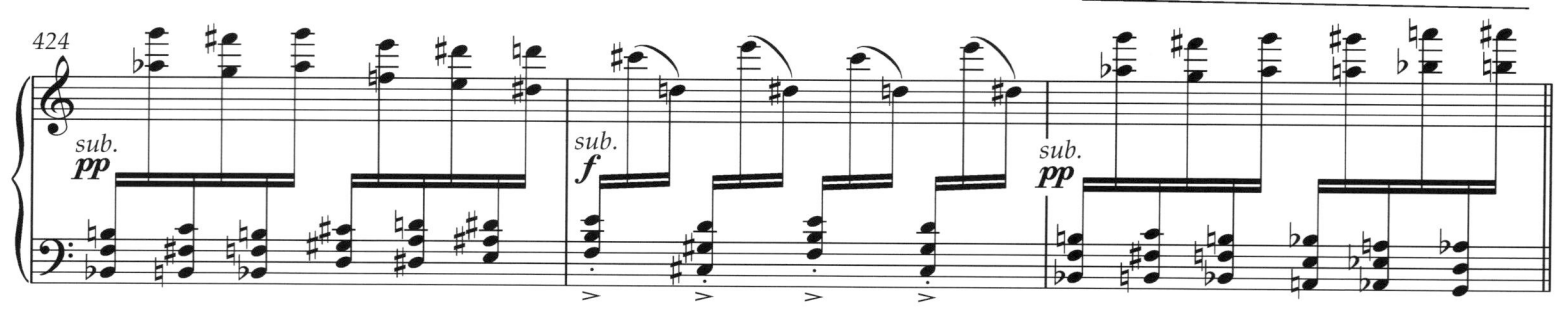

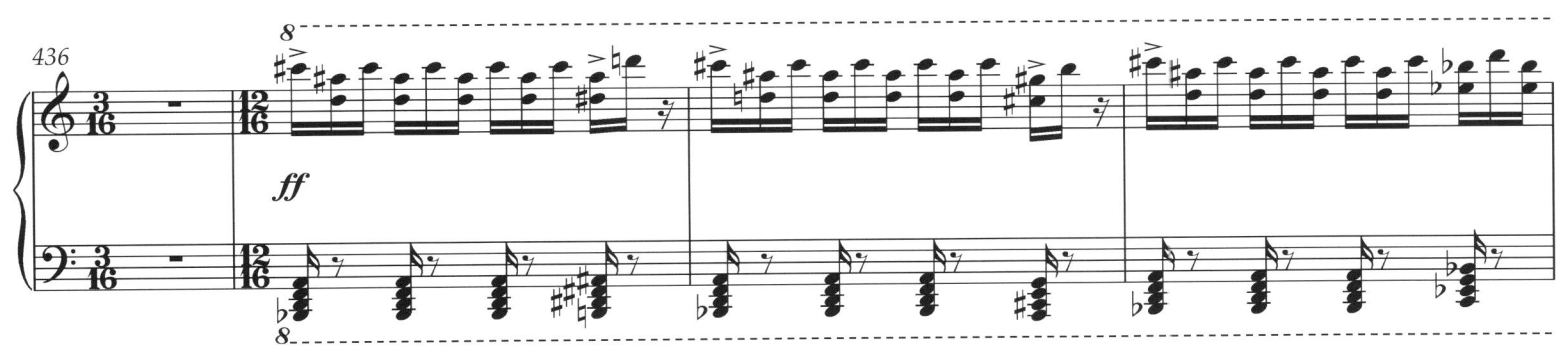

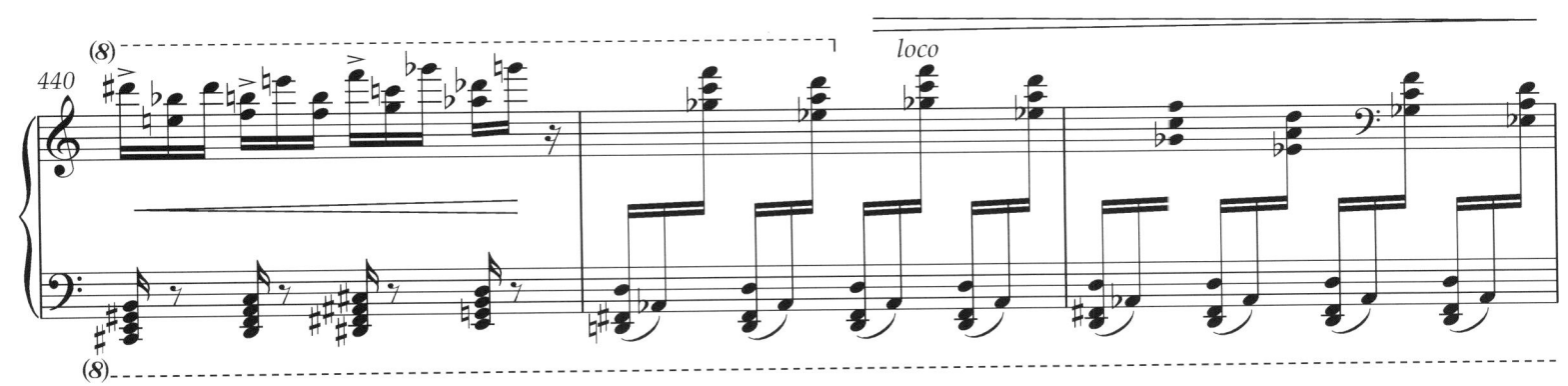

19 January 2007
Revised 11 July, 15 December 2007 & 21 May 2009
Sydney, Australia

COOP 2016: Proceedings of the 12th International Conference on the Design of Cooperative Systems, 23–27 May 2016, Trento, Italy

Antonella De Angeli • Liam Bannon • Patrizia Marti
Silvia Bordin
Editors

# COOP 2016: Proceedings of the 12th International Conference on the Design of Cooperative Systems, 23–27 May 2016, Trento, Italy

 Springer

*Editors*
Antonella De Angeli
InterAction Laboratory
Department of Information Engineering
and Computer Science
University of Trento
Trento, Italy

Patrizia Marti
Department of Communication Science
University of Siena
Siena, Italy

Liam Bannon
LERO Department of Computer
Science & Information Systems
University of Limerick
Limerick, Ireland

Silvia Bordin
Department of Information Engineering
and Computer Science
University of Trento
Trento, Italy

ISBN 978-3-319-33463-9      ISBN 978-3-319-33464-6   (eBook)
DOI 10.1007/978-3-319-33464-6

Library of Congress Control Number: 2016949411

Printed on acid-free paper

This Springer imprint is published by Springer Nature
The registered company is Springer International Publishing AG Switzerland

# Preface

This volume presents the proceedings of COOP 2016, the 12th International Conference on the Design of Cooperative Systems. COOP 2016 has marked an important milestone for the European community of researchers who embrace the idea that the design of cooperative systems requires a deep and contextualised understanding of collective activities, involving both artefacts and social practices. While moving to Italy, COOP 2016 opened up to the topic of collaborative design, with a special emphasis on "Making Together". This widening interest from research to design is evident in this volume.

The book is articulated in three main sessions. The papers were selected from 40 submissions following a process of blind review. They cover various and interconnected themes: grounding reflections in CSCW, research in the workplace, studies of collaborative working practices and analysis of formal and informal care relationships. The emphasis towards design increases towards the end of the book with studies on collaboration in design and design as reflective practice. The focus on design becomes central in the Interactive Experiences section.

The programme was supplemented by four thought-provoking workshops organised by leading experts in their fields and a symposium. The first workshop "Contextual Collaboration Where Automation and People Meet" investigated the emerging challenges of collaboration with autonomous systems and in automated environments. The second workshop "Infrastructuring Collaboration" addressed the issue of how to support collaboration in design. The third workshop "Exploring Data-Work in Healthcare: Making Sense of Data Across Boundaries" discussed how to increase the reuse of data for clinical, governance and research purposes. The fourth workshop "Making Laboratories" focused on the topic of "Workshopology", engaging experts from different fields of research and practice – from academia to fablabs – in the co-creation of guidelines for workshops and physical prototypes of educational activities. Finally, the symposium was titled "Challenges and Experiences in Designing for an Ageing Society. Reflecting on Concepts of Age(ing) and Communication Practices": it addressed issues of design for an ageing population in two parallel tracks that reflected on images of age and ageing from a meta-perspective and focused on communication practices in UCD and PD projects.

COOP 2016 was possible thanks to the help and enthusiasm of many people whom we would like to briefly acknowledge: all the authors who submitted high-quality papers, the participants to the workshops and the doctoral colloquium, the artists who submitted their interactive exhibitions, the members of the conference and programme committees, the student volunteers who provided support to the event and the sponsors.

Trento, Italy                                              Antonella De Angeli
Siena, Italy                                                    Patrizia Marti
Limerick, Ireland                                              Liam Bannon

# Contents

# Contributors

**Khuloud Abou Amsha** Troyes University of Technology, ICD, Tech-CICO, Troyes, France

**Jørgen Bansler** Department of Computer Science, University of Copenhagen, Denmark

**Klaus Bengler** Technical University of Munich, Munich, Germany

**Olav W. Bertelsen** Department of Computer Science, Center for Participatory-IT, Aarhus University, Aarhus, Denmark

**Pernille Bjørn** Department of Computer Science, University of Copenhagen, Copenhagen, Denmark

**Claus Bossen** Aarhus University, Aarhus, Denmark

**Tone Bratteteig** University of Oslo, Oslo, Norway

**Morten Breinbjerg** School of Culture and Communication, Aarhus University, Aarhus N, Denmark

**Federico Cabitza** Università degli Studi di Milano-Bicocca, Milano, Italy

**Melissa Cate Christ** School of Design, Hong Kong Polytechnic University, HKSAR, China

**Lars Rune Christensen** IT-University of Copenhagen, Copenhagen S, Denmark

**Tommaso Colombino** Xerox Research Centre Europe, Meylan, France

**Andrea Conci** InterAction Laboratory, Department of Information Engineering and Computer Science, University of Trento, Trento, Italy

**Michela Cozza** Department of Engineering and Computer Science, University of Trento, Trento, Italy

**Antonella De Angeli** InterAction Laboratory, Department of Information Engineering and Computer Science, University of Trento, Trento, Italy

**Aparecido Fabiano Pinatti de Carvalho** Institute of Design and Assessment of Technology, Multidisciplinary Design Group, Vienna University of Technology, Vienna, Austria

**Vincenzo Del Fatto** Faculty of Computer Science, Free University of Bozen-Bolzano, Bolzano, Italy

**Gunnar Ellingsen** Arctic University of Norway, Tromsø, Norway

**Jonas Fritsch** IT University of Copenhagen, Copenhagen S, Denmark

**Verena Fuchsberger** University of Salzburg, Salzburg, Austria

**Markus Garschall** AIT Austrian Institute of Technology, Innovation Systems Department, Business Unit Technology Experience, Vienna, Austria

**Edona Gashi** Faculty of Computer Science, Free University of Bozen-Bolzano, Bolzano, Italy

**Rosella Gennari** Faculty of Computer Science, Free University of Bozen-Bolzano, Bolzano, Italy

**Antonietta Grasso** Xerox Research Centre Europe, Meylan, France

**Erik Grönvall** IT University of Copenhagen, Copenhagen S, Denmark

**Michael Habiger** Institute of Design and Assessment of Technology, Multidisciplinary Design Group, Vienna University of Technology, Vienna, Austria

**Theo Hamm** IT for the Ageing Society, University of Siegen, Siegen, Germany

**Richard H.R. Harper** Social Shaping Research, Cambridge, UK

**Susanne Hensely-Schinkinger** Institute of Design and Assessment of Technology, Multidisciplinary Design Group, Vienna University of Technology, Vienna, Austria

**Thomas Herrmann** Department Information and Technology Management, Institute for Applied Work Science, University of Bochum, Bochum, Germany

**Marie Koldkjær Højlund** School of Culture and Communication, Aarhus University, Aarhus N, Denmark

**Yves Hoppenot** Xerox Research Centre Europe, Meylan, France

**Dominik Hornung** IT for the Ageing Society, University of Siegen, Siegen, Germany

**Netta Iivari** INTERACT Research Unit, Faculty of Information Technology and Electrical Engineering, University of Oulu, Oulu, Finland

**Jonas R. Kirkegaard** Sonic College, University College Southern Denmark, Haderslev, Denmark

**Arto Lanamäki** INTERACT Research Unit, University of Oulu, Oulu, Finland

**Myriam Lewkowicz**  Troyes University of Technology, ICD, Tech-CICO, Troyes, France

**Angela Locoro**  Università degli Studi di Milano-Bicocca, Milano, Italy

**David Martin**  Xerox Research Centre Europe, Meylan, France

**Cécile Boulard Masson**  Xerox Research Centre Europe, Meylan, France

**Raul Masu**  InterAction Laboratory, Department of Information Engineering and Computer Science, University of Trento, Trento, Italy

**Stina Matthiesen**  Department of Computer Science, University of Copenhagen, Copenhagen, Denmark

**Matthieu Mazzega**  Xerox Research Centre Europe, Meylan, France

**María Menéndez-Blanco**  InterAction Laboratory, Department of Information Engineering and Computer Science, University of Trento, Trento, Italy

**Zeno Menestrina**  InterAction Laboratory, Department of Information Engineering and Computer Science, University of Trento, Trento, Italy

**Naja L. Holten Møller**  Department of Computer Science, University of Copenhagen, Copenhagen, Denmark

**Fabio Morreale**  InterAction Laboratory, Department of Information Engineering and Computer Science, University of Trento, Trento, Italy

Centre for Digital Music, School of EECS, Queen Mary University of London, London, UK

**Claudia Müller**  IT for the Ageing Society, University of Siegen, Siegen, Germany

**Katja Neureiter**  Center for Human Computer Interaction, University of Salzburg, Austria

**Alexander Nolte**  Department Information and Technology Management, Institute for Applied Work Science, University of Bochum, Bochum, Germany

**Yushan Pan**  Norwegian University of Science and Technology, Trondheim, Norway

**Nicole Perterer**  University of Salzburg, Salzburg, Austria

**Katie Pine**  University California, California, USA

**Enrico Maria Piras**  Fondazione Bruno Kessler, Trento, Italy

**Giacomo Poderi**  Department of Engineering and Computer Science, University of Trento, Trento, Italy

**Morten Riis**  School of Culture and Communication, Aarhus University, Aarhus N, Denmark

**Ole Kristian Rolstad** University of Oslo, Oslo, Norway

**Julian Sanin** Faculty of Computer Science, Free University of Bozen-Bolzano, Bolzano, Italy

**Kjeld Schmidt** Department of Organization, Copenhagen Business School, Denmark

**Marén Schorch** Information Systems and New Media, University of Siegen, Siegen, Germany

**Carla Simone** Università degli Studi di Milano-Bicocca, Milano, Italy

**Hilda Tellioğlu** Institute of Design and Assessment of Technology, Multidisciplinary Design Group, Vienna University of Technology, Vienna, Austria

**Manfred Tscheligi** University of Salzburg, Salzburg, Austria

**Karin Väyrynen** INTERACT Research Unit, University of Oulu, Oulu, Finland

**Lex van Velsen** Roessingh Research and Development, Telemedicine Cluster, Enschede, The Netherlands

**Angelo Ventura** Faculty of Computer Science, Free University of Bozen-Bolzano, Bolzano, Italy

**Ina Wagner** University of Oslo, Oslo, Norway

**Astrid Weiss** Vienna University of Technology, Vienna, Austria

**Jutta Willamowski** Xerox Research Centre Europe, Meylan, France

**Max Willis** Semantics and Knowledge Innovation Lab (SKIL) Telecom Italia, Trento, Italy

**Volker Wulf** University of Siegen, Siegen, Germany

**Alberto Zanutto** Dipartimento di Sociologia e Ricerca Sociale, Università di Trento, Trento, Italy

# Conference Committee

*Conference Chair*: Antonella De Angeli (University of Trento)
*Programme Co-chairs*: Liam Bannon (University of Limerick, Ireland; Aarhus University, Denmark), Patrizia Marti (University of Siena; Eindhoven University of Technology)
*Local Chair*: Massimo Zancanaro (FBK)
*Workshops and Panels Co-chairs*: Myriam Lewkowicz (Université de Technologie de Troyes), Madhu Reddy (Northwestern University)
*Making Laboratories Co-chairs*: Shaowen Bardzell (Indiana University), Jeffrey Bardzell (Indiana University), Sabina Barcucci (FabLab, MUSE)
*Doctoral Colloquium Co-chairs*: David Hakken (Indiana University), Luigina Ciolfi (Sheffield Hallam University)
*Interactive Experiences*: Jonas Fritsch (IT University of Copenhagen), Maria Menendez Blanco (University of Trento)
*Proceedings Chair*: Silvia Bordin (University of Trento)
*Student Volunteers Chair*: Fabio Morreale (University of Trento)

## Programme Committee

- Monica Divitini – IDI-NTNU
- David Martin – Xerox Research Centre Europe
- Catherine Letondal – ENAC
- Carla Simone – University of Milano-Bicocca
- Giorgio De Michelis – University of Milano-Bicocca
- Keiichi Nakata – University of Reading
- Pascal Salembier – Université de Technologie de Troyes
- Myriam Fréjus – EDF
- Maria Normark – Södertörn University
- Marc Relieu – CNRS Télecom ParisTech
- Michael Prilla – Ruhr University of Bochum

- Kari Kuutti – University of Oulu
- Kjeld Schmidt – Copenhagen Business School
- Markus Rohde – University of Siegen
- Claudia Müller-Birn – Freie Universität Berlin
- Mark Ackerman – University of Michigan
- Chiara Rossitto – Department of Computer and Systems Sciences
- Wolfgang Prinz – Fraunhofer FIT
- John Rooksby – University of Glasgow
- Hilda Tellioglu – Vienna University of Technology
- Karine Lan – Université de Technologie de Troyes
- Béatrice Cahour – CNRS Telecom ParisTech
- Flore Barcellini – CNAM
- Tone Bratteteig – University of Oslo
- Lars Rune Christensen – IT University of Copenhagen
- Jacki O'Neill – Microsoft Research India
- Gabriela Avram – Interaction Design Centre, University of Limerick
- Antonietta Grasso – Xerox Research Centre Europe
- Nina Boulus-Rødje – IT University of Copenhagen
- Marcin Sikorski – Gdansk University of Technology
- Bernhard Nett – University of Siegen
- Alain Giboin – INRIA Sophia Antipolis-Méditerranée
- Janet Mcdonnell – Central Saint Martins, University of the Arts London
- Christian Licoppe – CNRS Télecom ParisTech
- Volker Wulf – University of Siegen
- Dagny Stuedahl – University of Oslo
- Madhu Reddy – Penn State University
- David Randall – University of Siegen
- Carmelo Ardito – University of Bari Aldo Moro
- Volkmar Pipek – University of Siegen
- Anders Morch – University of Oslo
- Susanne Bødker – Aarhus University
- Barry Brown – Mobile Life Research Centre
- Michael Baker – CNRS Telecom ParisTech
- Julie Dugdale – LIG
- Silvia Lindtner – University of Michigan
- Francoise Detienne – CNRS Telecom ParisTech
- Vincenzo D'Andrea – University of Trento
- Preben Hansen – Stockholm University
- Antonio Piccinno – University of Bari
- Maurizio Teli – University of Trento
- Federico Cabitza – University of Milano-Bicocca
- Angela Locoro – University of Milano-Bicocca
- Pernille Bjorn – University of Copenhagen
- Ina Wagner – Vienna University of Technology

# Part I
# Papers

# Chapter 1
# Six Issues in Which IS and CSCW Research Communities Differ

Arto Lanamäki and Karin Väyrynen

**Abstract** Computer-Supported Collaborative Work (CSCW) has become increasingly positioned as a subfield of human-computer interaction (HCI). Earlier, CSCW has had a closer connection to the Information Systems (IS) field, but this relationship has seemed to become more distant. In this paper we reflect on the distinct characteristics of the research communities of CSCW and IS. We identify similarities, but also stark differences between the two. The six identified issues of difference are the roles of theory, context, methodology, organizational layer, sociotechnicality, and power-alignment. Our contribution is in making these differences visible. We hope this paper will promote diplomacy and understanding between these research communities, so that scholars may consider cross-disciplinary IS-CSCW publication strategies.

## 1.1 Introduction

In its 30 years of history, Computer Supported Cooperative Work (CSCW) has been positioned in several different ways. First, it has been viewed as a unique, self-standing research community. Greif [1], who coined the CSCW moniker in mid-1980s, provided a vision for CSCW as "distinct from any of the fields on which it draws" (p. 9). Twenty-five years later, Schmidt and Bannon [2] assessed that CSCW had indeed become "an established field of research" (p. 345).

Another way of positioning has been the paradigmatic view. Here, CSCW is neither a discipline nor a field. Instead, CSCW is seen as tentacles spread in several existing fields simultaneously. In 1991, Hughes, Randall, and Shapiro [3] envisioned how "CSCW can be placed on the boundaries of computer science, sociology, organisational and management studies, perhaps even anthropology; not to mention older HCI concerns which already place it on the boundaries of psychology, linguistics and ergonomics" (p. 310). Similar view was held by Grudin in 1994 [4] (p. 25).

A. Lanamäki (✉) • K. Väyrynen
INTERACT Research Unit, University of Oulu, Oulu, Finland
e-mail: arto.lanamaki@oulu.fi; karin.vayrynen@oulu.fi

© Springer International Publishing Switzerland 2016
A. De Angeli et al. (eds.), *COOP 2016: Proceedings of the 12th International Conference on the Design of Cooperative Systems, 23–27 May 2016, Trento, Italy,*
DOI 10.1007/978-3-319-33464-6_1

The third position is to label CSCW as a subfield to human-computer interaction (HCI). This interpretation has seemed to become a dominant view during the last 15 years [5–7]. For instance, Rogers [8] has stated that HCI is now "generally accepted as the umbrella term" for various subfields, including CSCW (p. 2).

In this essay, we argue that CSCW and Information Systems (IS) have had a close relationship, but somehow the mutual comradeship has withered. Between these two communities, we identify common history and mutual interests. Our core message is that six differences separate these communities. However, once the differences are acknowledged, these can be bridged. We encourage agility between the communities, to make use of each other's findings, with researchers traveling back and forth.

This article is structured as follows. Section 1.2 presents methodological notes, in which we discuss the approach we took in this article. In Sect. 1.3 we discuss the common ground between the two. Subsequently, we elaborate on the six differences we have identified. We discuss the implications in Sect. 1.5, and finally conclude the article in Sect. 1.6.

## 1.2   Methodological Notes

This essay was initiated from our personal interest in trying to understand the European CSCW community in more depth. Both of us authors come from an Information Systems background. While we have read some CSCW studies, we had never participated in any CSCW forums. As we participated in the EUSSET CSCW Summer School in August 2015 in Como, Italy, we saw that as an opportunity to increase our own understanding of the positioning between the IS and CSCW communities. The foundation of this essay is the coursework that each of the summer school participants had to write. In this exercise, both of us authors chose to reflect on the differences we noticed between IS and CSCW based on the glimpse into the European CSCW field that we gained during the summer school.

Eventually, we realized this is a possibility to be develop a more carefully examined analysis of the two research communities. We started elaborating on our coursework and reviewed much literature. We figured out that if we write a publication out of this, others can read it. That way, this would not remain as our proprietary learning exercise. The present paper is a result of this process.

We acknowledge that our comparative discussion between the two research communities has required some stereotyping. Both of these research communities are quite large, have a long history, and have their internal tensions of what constitutes proper research and what does not. Our depictions of both of these communities thus reflect a *version* of them. Not everyone will agree with these versions we have offered. However, we think and hope that these characterizations will help both camps to understand the other's point of view. Additionally, we hope that our analysis will facilitate a fruitful discussion in and between both camps.

## 1.3 The Common Ground Between CSCW and IS

CSCW and IS had a close comradeship before the turn of the millennium. In this section we prove examples to demonstrate how several prominent researchers had a strong foothold in both camps. For example, Liam Bannon published his "CSCW: An Initial Exploration" article in the *Scandinavian Journal of Information Systems* in 1992 [9]. In that same year, Wanda Orlikowski won the best paper award at the CSCW conference with her paper *Learning from Notes* [10]. She later published that paper in *The Information Society* journal [11]. Star and Ruhleder published the initial version of "Steps Towards an Ecology of Infrastructure" in the CSCW conference [12]. Two years later in 1996, an improved version of that paper got published in *Information Systems Research* [13]. In early 1990s, Kalle Lyytinen was writing about CSCW topics in journals such as *Computer Supported Collaborative Work* [14] and in *Accounting, Management and Information Technologies* (now *Information and Organization*) [15]. Another prominent dual-contributing scholar was Rob Kling [16, 17]. Similarly in 1993, Heinz Klein – an influential IS scholar [18] – coauthored an article for the CSCW journal [19].

We could provide numerous other examples, but we think our point is made clear. IS and CSCW had close unity back then, and for good reasons. Both IS and CSCW emphasize the use of computer applications. In contrast to computer science, both share an interest on the *social* aspects related to technology. For instance, communication, cooperation, and coordination are mutually relevant keywords. However, there are areas in which IS and CSCW clearly differ. CSCW focuses, among other topics, on the integrity of work situations, mediation between tools, the worker, and the object of the work. IS has developed to focus on the macro level, on the organizational level, with less consideration for actual work processes, whereas CSCW specifically focuses on the moment-by-moment work processes [20].

One central uniting notion is *practice*. Many CSCW scholars consider 'practice' as a central concept in CSCW research [21, 22], and the CSCW journal nowadays wears the tagline "*The Journal of Collaborative Computing and Work Practices*". Similarly in IS, practice approaches have a long history and a strong position [23–26].

We have observed that several institutional developments have made these communities more distant from each other. For example, the ACM CSCW conference was rebranded as "CSCW and Social Computing" [27]. As a consequence, the conference attendance has grown tremendously, while at the same time it has assimilated a similar profile as many HCI conferences. Meanwhile in IS, from 2007 onwards the field has featured a shared journal publication standard of "basket of eight" e.g. [28]. Eight elite journals have become central in tenure and promotion decisions in the IS field [29]. As a consequence, there are now less incentives for IS researchers to publish outside these eight journals. As an additional example of this division, Group Support Systems (GSS) researchers had close ties with CSCW in the 1980s, but divergent views caused a chasm in early 1990s [30]. GSS later transformed into an IS orientation called Collaboration Engineering [31]. In sum, many contributing factors have caused separation between IS and CSCW.

We will next discuss six areas of difference between IS and CSCW in more detail.

## 1.4 The Six Areas of Difference

In this section, we will present the six areas of difference between IS and CSCW research. These differences root in our observations during the EUSSET summer school, and in our reflections afterwards. We outline these differences with help of supporting literature from IS and CSCW.

### 1.4.1 Theory

The role of theory is a major difference between the two communities. IS is very theory-obsessed, and has been characterized to have a "theory fetish" [32]. The top journals in IS devote much space for conceptualizations of theory [33, 34]. For example, in a central IS design science article, Gregor and Jones [35] call for a "more rigorous" approach to design, aiming towards "cumulative design theory ... raising our discipline above the craft-level" (p. 331).

To us it seems that CSCW is perfectly happy with the craft-level, and is not concerned with high abstractions, and boxes and arrows. CSCW researchers are committed to the particular level instead of the abstract. Meanwhile, Seddon and Scheepers [36] outline how IS research "actually has very little interest in the samples studied, per se", but in "lessons that are applicable in other settings" (p. 6).

While IS has been questioned for its obsession with theory [32, 37], some commentators have seen CSCW as under-committed to theory [38]. Yet, as the 2004 CSCW theory panel [38] outlined, assessments of over/under-commitment depend on what is counted as theory. In addition, it also depends whether we are satisfied that theory works as a tool in a particular study, or if we also wish to work towards a cumulative theory that has been tested and had predictive power. The famous Kurt Lewin quote "nothing so practical as a good theory" is often quoted in these kinds of discourses, though the truth value of this anecdotal one-liner largely relies on what we mean with "practical", "good", and "theory" [39].

CSCW clearly puts more emphasis on descriptive accounts of how practice looks like in a specific context, without much attempt to generalize. In the information systems field there are numerous papers that are concerned with the nature of theory in IS (e.g., [33, 35]) and the development of theory in IS (e.g., [40, 41]). Meanwhile, the CSCW field has theoretical concepts that are applied in research. For instance, Blomberg and Karasti [42] conducted a literature review of 25 years of ethnography in CSCW. They identified the concepts of situated action, situated awareness, articulation work, invisible work, and so on.

One of the more widely used theories in CSCW is the activity theory [43, 44]. Activity theory is a descriptive framework, or a sensitizing lens, instead of a causal model. This theory helps consider the entire work and activity system beyond individual users. To us it seems that the key theoretical difference between IS and CSCW is the ideal of causality. This is strongly present in IS in statistical and theoretical causal models. In turn, Christensen and Bertelsen [45] recently argued that the CSCW view of causation concerns manipulation as accomplished in work practices. For instance in chemotherapy, manipulation of causal relationships occurs "between drugs and cancer cells in an effort to destroy the latter" (p. 168).

IS is fascinated with theorizing theory, for example through propositions of taxonomies [33, 46]. In the words of Kincheloe and Tobin [47], IS has adopted a somewhat "crypto-positivist" ethos, signaling the values of positivism in the post-positivist era. However, critique towards theory-obsession and lack of practical relevance has emerged in IS [37, 48]. Iivari [49] states that "the dominant research philosophy has been to develop cumulative, theory-based research to be able to make prescriptions. It seems that this 'theory-with-practical-implications' research strategy has seriously failed to produce results that are of real interest in practice." (p. 40)

One difference between CSCW and IS seems to be the role the existing body of knowledge and the type of contribution sought in the different disciplines. In IS one has to show the contribution by first arguing what the existing body of knowledge is (so, what is known so far about this), and how one's own research extends, confirms, and/or disputes previous findings. This requires one to be familiar with what has been done before, and implicitly assumes that what has been found before is also relevant and applicable to what one wants to study in a maybe different context (as studying the same thing in the same context is not seen to give new insights). Then, in order to show that one actually has made a contribution, the findings of one's own study have to be critically analyzed in the light of previous research, and it has to be clearly indicated how ones findings differ from or build on previous research and theory. New research has to be novel, and novelty can be shown towards the existing body of knowledge. In CSCW, however, the building on existing theory and findings seem to play a smaller role. Already in 1995, Plowman et al. [50] discussed "the tension between providing explanatory accounts and usable design recommendations" in workplace studies in the CSCW field. They discussed how many of the CSCW studies they reviewed did not offer clear design recommendations, thus not translating the descriptions of field studies into something that designers of IT systems could make use of.

## 1.4.2 Context

Related to the discussion of theory, we arrive to the topic of context. As mentioned in Sect. 1.2, IS research is seen to levitate in abstractions that are detached from any practical relevance. In European CSCW, the focus of interest seems to be on work practices mostly in a very local context, on the micro-context, on body language, interaction order and the coordination of action. In IS research, the context often is somewhere in the background, not receiving much attention.

When reviewing previous research, we found support for this impression both in IS and CSCW research. In a recent IS paper by Davison and Martinsons [51], the authors problematize how IS research often falsely implies universalism, relies on convenient samples, or ignores indigenous constructs. As a solution, they call to pay more attention to the context at hand. On the other hand, Monteiro et al. [52] argue that CSCW is too focused on "localist studies" which are restricted to particular settings and timeframes. There are also several studies in the IS field where the context plays a strong role in the analysis of the results and development of implications. For example, work by Schultze [53] and Alvarez [54], provide thick descriptions of the study context. However, admittedly these are the exception, not the rule. The majority of IS research is rather detached, and prefers to employ survey research designs and large samples [55]. As such, the focus or non-focus on context is also strongly related to the prevalent research methods in the two research fields, where certain types of research methodologies on purpose abstract the context away (e.g., quantitative research), and other types of research methods put specific emphasis on the context (e.g., ethnography). We will discuss these research methods in more detail next.

### 1.4.3   Methodology

A clear difference between IS and CSCW research are the research methods employed. Many of the CSCW classics adopt ethnographic fieldwork as the preferred method [42]. The researchers are interested in how things actually work in the real world. In other words, the study concerns actual practices. In Information Systems there are fieldworkers as well, but they are in the minority. The IS mainstream – particularly in North America – is oriented towards quantitative variables-centric research that is based on survey responses. Ethnographic fieldwork can provide a deeper floor-level moment-by-moment insight of the role of technology in actual use settings.

This impression is supported when studying the CSCW and IS literature. Chen and Hirschheim [56] conducted a methodological examination of information systems research from 1991 to 2001. They studied eight major IS outlets and distinguished between positivist and interpretive research paradigms. They classified those studies as interpretive articles that do not involve any positivist indicators, no deterministic perspectives imposed by the researchers), where participants' perspectives are the primary sources of understanding and investigating the phenomena, and where the phenomena are examined with respect to cultural and contextual circumstances. Therefore, we see that interpretive studies in IS research are very close to the research methods preferred by CSCW research. In their analysis of IS outlets, Chen and Hirschheim [56] found that US outlets are dominated by positivist, quantitative studies (58 % positivist vs. 7 % interpretive), whereas the difference in Europe is less striking (23 % positivist vs. 12 % interpretive). Later, Palvia et al. [55] conducted a meta-review of around 2400 papers published in 8 major IS journals between 2004 and 2013. They found that 72.3 % of the studies were positivist, and only 21.7 % were interpretive. Survey research was the dominating research methodology in IS research between 2004 and 2013.

In turn, Jacovi et al. [6] conducted a citation graph analysis of all papers published at the CSCW conference between 1986 and 2004. They wanted to find out which were the main topics or trends at the CSCW conference, and identified eight main clusters, each of which contained 5–83 papers. One of these smaller clusters (five papers) is "management of computing and information systems". On the other hand, the two biggest clusters, "theory and methods ethnography, user studies" (83 papers) and "computer science papers" (82 papers) represent the majority of CSCW papers.

In an interview Liam Bannon gave recently for the Italian *Tecnoscienza* journal [57], he commented on the "ecological validity" that is strong in ethnographic field studies. He argued for the importance to study "the world of work in which these systems are used" (p. 138). In his view, participatory design has become a somewhat devalued concept, seen as just people "participating in our surveys" (p. 143). Instead, Bannon called for an emphasis on the "very issue of participation: what do we mean by it, what are we participating in, and under what conditions?" (p. 146).

Generally, IS prefers a broader view and uses a lot of survey studies. Meanwhile, CSCW is adopting a deeper analytic interest in which surveys do not fit.

### 1.4.4 Organizational Layer

As mentioned in Sect. 1.3 when discussing the historical roots of IS and CSCW, one major difference between CSCW and IS research concerns the organizational layer that is studied. CSCW seems to focus on workers and work groups on the "end user" level. IS has been traditionally concerned with Management Information Systems, engaged with Chief Information Officers (CIOs) and Chief Executive Officers (CEOs), and is detached from the factory floor activities.

However, Neale et al. [58] point out that "the individual, group (team), organization, and industry are common levels of analysis for CSCW systems". One example for CSCWs interests in organization-level issues is Pipek and Wulf's [59] paper on Infrastructuring, where they look at organizational IT as work infrastructure and describe the challenges of designing within and for this type of infrastructure.

When talking about the organizational layer and focusing on different layers, it also implies looking at interdependencies from different perspectives. Both CSCW and IS look at interdependences. CSCW looks at interdependence of work (Schmidt and Bannon [60], p. 13): "at the core of this conception of cooperative work is the notion of interdependence in work". CSCW also focuses on interdependence between single persons when doing the work, some examples being the application of conversion and interaction analysis, studying gestures and body configurations (e.g., [61]). This perspective was applied by, for example, by the CSCW senior scholar Ina Wagner. Analysis on this level is rather uncommon in IS research. On the other hand, also IS research look at interdependencies, but with a stronger focus on interdependencies between different organizations and departments: how do departments cooperate and how does an IT system support that (e.g., [62]), and how do different companies cooperate (and how do IT systems support that) (e.g., [63]).

Of course the difference between IS and CSCW research is not black and white. Some of the IS research also focuses on interdependence between different groups of workers (e.g., [64]), whereas we can also find examples of CSCW studies of cooperation and interdependence between different organizations. One such example is Pipek's [65–67] studies of a crisis management system prototype, which was built to help coordination in situations of crisis between different governmental organizations (e.g., firemen, police, hospital, etc.). Fitzpatrick and Ellingsen [68] argue that in the past 25 years of CSCW in healthcare, the majority design prototypes focused on smaller-scale interactions, which is problematic because also Western European healthcare-systems are moving towards large-scale integrated systems.

### 1.4.5 Socio-technicality

Even though both IS and CSCW research have a common interest in social aspects related to technology [20], there still exist differences in how both communities approach the issue. In the CSCW community, IS research is confronted with the critique that IS researchers tend to be oriented towards technological determinist thinking. In other words, that IS seems to assume that IT artifacts have certain consequences, and the role of users is just to "accept" technology. We somewhat agree that this tends to be the underlying assumption in much of the technology acceptance studies [69, 70]. CSCW research, on the other hand, is seen to emphasize that the user will use *local rationality* when using IT. The user will appropriate the IT artifact in a way that the artifact fits the actual practices of the user, or disregard the technology when it does not support local practices. When trying to pinpoint the difference between IS and CSCW concerning socio-technicality, which is rather difficult, we came to the conclusion that the main difference seems to be the way IS and CSCW look at the relationship between IT (systems) and humans. Here, we make a broad generalization of "what is seen as the problem" in each of these camps.

In CSCW, the attitude seems to be that the problem is in the technology, and therefore technology has to be developed in a way that supports the current work practices of real-life people. In IS, in contrast, a large stream of research seems to have the general attitude that the problem are the people who use IT systems, and therefore we have to find out how to make people adapt to the IT. This point of view is also known in CSCW research. Ackerman [71] argues that this view of humans having to adapt themselves efficiently and effectively to the machine can be seen as new-Taylorism. A prime example for this view in the IS community is the technology acceptance model (TAM) [69]. TAM proposes that a technology's perceived usefulness and perceived ease of use positively affect attitude towards using the technology, which positively affects behavioral intention to use the technology, which in turn affects actual system use. In this line of research, the focus is on what things affect a person's behavior in an IT use setting. In addition, packaged software applications require the user to adapt to the system, as Strong and Volkoff [72] pointed out: "Packaged software applications such as enterprise systems are designed to support generic rather than specific requirements, and hence are likely to be an imperfect fit in any particular instance." However, also within the IS field there has been critique towards predictive models, particularly towards TAM (e.g., [73, 74]).

Ackerman [71] discusses the gap between social requirements and technical feasibility. He argues that much of CSCW research argued that one problem is that system designers do not sufficiently understand the social world. This is then taken as a reason for the fact that IT systems are not supporting real work efficiently. Cabitza and Simone [75] discuss computational coordination mechanisms and discuss the need for control the system keeps about how work is coordinated, versus the flexibility the system can give to the users in making adaptations of the system to their own needs, to create deviations from how the system designer originally intended the system to be used. They introduce seven levels of flexibility and argue that most systems combine several levels of flexibility in different parts of the system. Also Cabitza and Simone's [75] paper concerns this struggle between the user following exactly the work process the system has outlined, versus the system being adaptable to different users and different situations of use.

In summary, it seems that whereas IS has a focus on "processes will follow IT", CSCW puts more emphasis on "IT need to adapt to social practices".

## 1.4.6 Power-Alignment

Those aspects of computer science that are concerned with designing systems for users have also an ideology of service: contributing to the capacity for creation and production (and sometimes – in terms of funding rather often – for destruction). For HCI such a notion is necessarily central. Sometimes that involves a more critical notion of service which is concerned about *who* benefits from systems and what uses they are put to; others are content to follow a market-led notion of utility. When systems seem to be failing, that is a problem for either version. (Hughes et al. [3], p. 317–318)

We have observed that the European CSCW community has a strong sensitivity to emancipatory and even contrarian discourses. Not only is CSCW research committed to issues of collaborative work, but it is also concerned with the *worker*.

We say this that much of CSCW research shares the acknowledgement that the worker – as the end user of technological systems in organizations – is much affected by those systems while often has little to say about the design and implications of the systems. This has been addressed especially in the participatory design angle of CSCW research, aiming to give users a *voice* in systems development projects.

In turn, IS research tends to be more conformist towards power [20]. Management Information Systems – as the field used to be called – traditionally takes an organization-level focus rather than that of the worker. As such, IS research tends to adopt the management's perspective. Competitive advantage and profit thinking is a major feature of IS research. In turn, this is fairly absent in CSCW research. Strategic thinking is also not present in CSCW research, while in IS research it is. There is, for example, a whole journal dedicated to strategy among the top 8 journals in the IS field – the *Journal of Strategic Information Systems*.

In Europe, IS is located in many kinds of faculties and schools (for example, engineering, information, social sciences, etc.), while in North America it is mostly within business schools. The institutional positioning of CSCW is trickier, as it is a smaller and more scattered movement. CSCW seems to be a loose network of intrinsically motivated scholars who have found unity with likeminded scholars. This unity seems to be founded partly on what CSCW is not. It seems that a driving force of CSCW has often been to act as an opposition to a common "enemy". For example, the social psychological experiment research in HCI seems to be one such target.

In addition, it seems CSCW scholars, and particularly those oriented towards activity theory, seem to be influenced by Marx. That is a rare source of inspiration in North American business schools where IS departments are located.

## 1.5   Discussion

In this paper, we have presented six aspects in which CSCW research and IS research differ. These six aspects are theory, context, methodology, organizational layer, socio-technicality, and power-alignment. While the presentation of these six issues has required some stereotyping – a necessary precondition needed in talking about a whole research community as a single unit –, we have grounded our arguments in examples from literature.

In this analysis, we have attempted to promote interdisciplinarity between IS and CSCW. Regardless of interdisciplinary intent, all research communities struggle to balance between two dynamics: how to strengthen its own identity, versus how to interact outside of its boundaries. In the contemporary academia where researchers are pressured to publish constantly, the first dynamic tends to get served rather than the second [76]. For example, Barley [77] recalled how he received early-career advice to "establish a solid stream of research that built on itself" (p. 67).

Alvesson and Sandberg [78] name this mindset as "boxed-in research", in which specialization in one topic, method, and/or theory, within a single research community, is seen to provide the best ROI, return-on-investment. In a quest to serve a single audience with an abundance of "ROI-search" [79], research communities tend to become self-serving and inbred. Alvesson and Sandberg [78] present several guidelines for conducting and assessing box breaking research and present three possible versions of box-breaking research: box changing, box jumping, and box transcendence. We will discuss each of these versions in the light of differences between CSCW and IS research, and what each of these strategies would mean for a box-breaking CSCW researcher and a box-breaking IS researcher.

Box changing means that a researcher's primary reference point is a specific box, but that the box changer "reaches outwards for new ideas, theories or methods that can be used to change the box in some significant way." [78] For an IS researcher who would want to employ in box changing making use of CSCW, for example a focus on the specific work practices employed in the use of a specific MIS could be a possible approach. For a CSCW researcher, box changing could mean, for example, to write a meta-analysis of the research methods and paradigms prevalent in CSCW and publish is in a CSCW outlet. As we pointed out in Sect. 1.4.3, this type of studies is common in the IS field, but rather rare in the CSCW field.

Box jumping, on the other hand, means that a researcher is able to embrace a number of different research identities, and involves some significant thematic, methodological or theoretical variation. For a CSCW researcher, box jumping could mean, for example, that s/he conducts a positivist comparative case study, employing an ethnographic field study as data collection method, but trying to compare several different of these field studies to make some generalization. For an IS researcher it could mean to conduct an ethnographic field study on, for example, cooperative work activities between outsourcer and service provider. As Fitzpatrick and Ellingsen [68] argue, it would be important for CSCW to move into the direction of large-scale systems as well.

Box transcendence means that a researcher has a commitment to more than one box with distinct characteristics, and aims to make broader connections and framings of phenomena, opening up new ways of seeing things and acting. One way of achieving this in the context of IS and CSCW research could be to aim at the intersection between the management and user perspectives, which to date is largely missing in both IS and CSCW research. Let us take as an example a company that produces IT systems to support collaboration. From an IS perspective, the purpose is to deliver some added value to a customer (which in fact is the purpose of any business), and the focus might be on how to organize and manage the processes that enable the delivery of that added value. For CSCW, the focus in this example would be to design the system in a way so that it would support the collaboration practices of the workers, of those who actually use the system, in the best possible way. This, again, can be seen as the added value to the customer (or worker). Thus, both IS and CSCW actually look at the same thing (added value to the customer – and this customer can be the future user of the system), but from different perspectives. In order to be able to develop the system in a way that maximizes both the added value the customer will gain through the system and the profit the organization will gain with this system, it requires an understanding of strategic/management/organizational requirements, user requirements, and system designer requirements. Thus, the focus of such box transcending research could be the intersection in which the management's strategy and requirements, and the work practices of those who actually develop and use the systems meet.

Another approach would be to choose a research topic that is common to both research communities. We now discuss two research themes that have strong foothold in both communities: *engaged research* and *information infrastructures*. These two topics are just some of the potential ones that are accepted among both fields. With engaged research, we refer to approaches in which the researcher has a proactive role in affecting change in a real-life context; for example, participatory design and action research. These approaches have a long history in Scandinavian research in IS [80, 81], as well as in CSCW [82], and is still a thriving research stream [83, 84]. Similarly, information infrastructures is a central topic in CSCW [85, 86] as well as in IS [87, 88]. The recent interest in *infrastructuring* originates from participatory design in CSCW [89, 90], and has informed recent research in top IS outlets [59, 91, 92]. We also note that infrastructure researchers at University of Oslo have been able to build a successful research stream that contributes in both communities [52, 88, 93].

Overall we feel that the differences between IS and CSCW are bigger in North America than what they are in Europe. The European IS community is well familiar with qualitative and interpretive research methods which take the context into account, even though the main source of data still seems to be interviews. The CSCW way of data collection and analysis is not as "strange" for European IS researchers as they most likely are for quantitative-oriented US researchers in the IS field. Our observation is also that the North American CSCW scene, particularly when observed from the studies published in the ACM CSCW conference, is more similar to those published in HCI venues such as the premier CHI conference.

In this paper, we have presented differences between IS and CSCW. In addition, we have provided examples of research that bridges gaps between IS and CSCW. We believe there is even more potential to combine "the best of both worlds", by building on research topics that are relevant in both research communities. Thus we encourage researchers to engage in both the IS and CSCW communities. In that task, we believe the identified six differences will be revelatory.

## 1.6   Conclusion

In this paper, we discussed similarities between IS and CSCW, but more importantly, six areas of difference between the two. We hope that this will help researchers in understanding the perspectives of both of these communities. The differences should not be barriers to participation, but seen as strengths of pluralism. These are the characteristics to be taken into account when making publication roadmaps, and drafting individual manuscripts. In such, this is a practical contribution that supports CSCW's foundational ethos of interdisciplinarity [3].

Finally, let's take a *railway station* metaphor to consider the positioning between an individual researcher and a research community. At first glance it seems that one can either enter a station, stay in it, or leave it. We suggest a fourth option: *scholarly commuting*. We encourage scholarly diplomacy and mutual informing. A win-win situation will be reached when researchers travel back and forth, in our case between IS and CSCW.

**Acknowledgements** This article is a result of mutual cooperation in which both authors have contributed equally. We want to thank the participants and organizers of the EUSSET summer school for all the inspiring discussions, and the reviewers and editor for their valuable comments.

# References

1. Greif I (1988) Computer-supported cooperative work: a book of readings. Morgan Kaufmann Publishers, San Mateo
2. Schmidt K, Bannon L (2013) Constructing CSCW: the first quarter century. Comput Support Coop Work (CSCW) 22:345–372
3. Hughes J, Randall D, Shapiro D (1991) CSCW: discipline or paradigm? a sociological perspective. In: Proceedings of the second conference on European conference on computer-supported cooperative work, pp 309–323. Kluwer Academic Publishers, Amsterdam
4. Grudin J (1994) Computer-supported cooperative work: history and focus. Computer 27:19–26
5. Horn DB, Finholt TA, Birnholtz JP, Motwani D, Jayaraman S (2004) Six degrees of jonathan grudin: a social network analysis of the evolution and impact of CSCW research. In: Proceedings of the 2004 ACM conference on computer supported cooperative work, pp 582–591. ACM, Chicago
6. Jacovi M, Soroka V, Gilboa-Freedman G, Ur S, Shahar E, Marmasse N (2006) The chasms of CSCW: a citation graph analysis of the CSCW conference. In: Proceedings of the 2006 20th anniversary conference on computer supported cooperative work, pp 289–298. ACM, Banff
7. Grudin J (2006) Is HCI homeless?: in search of inter-disciplinary status. Interactions 13:54–59
8. Rogers Y (2012) HCI theory: classical, modern, and contemporary. Synth Lect Hum Centered Inform 5:1–129
9. Bannon LJ (1993) CSCW: an initial exploration. Scand J Inf Syst 5:3–24
10. Orlikowski WJ (1992) Learning from notes: organizational issues in groupware implementation. In: Proceedings of the 1992 ACM conference on computer-supported cooperative work, pp 362–369. ACM, Toronto
11. Orlikowski WJ (1993) Learning from notes: organizational issues in groupware implementation. Inf Soc 9:237–250
12. Star SL, Ruhleder K (1994) Steps towards an ecology of infrastructure: complex problems in design and access for large-scale collaborative systems. In: Proceedings of the 1994 ACM conference on computer supported cooperative work, pp 253–264. ACM, Chapel Hill
13. Star SL, Ruhleder K (1996) Steps toward an ecology of infrastructure: design and access for large information spaces. Inf Syst Res 7:111–134
14. Lyytinen K, Maaranen P, Knuuttila J (1993) Groups are not always the same. Comput Support Coop Work (CSCW) 2:261–284
15. Lyytinen KJ, Ngwenyama OK (1992) What does computer support for cooperative work mean? A structurational analysis of computer supported cooperative work. Account Manag Inform Technol 2:19–37
16. Lamb R, Kling R (2003) Reconceptualizing users as social actors in information systems research. MIS Q 27:197–236

17. Kling R (1991) Cooperation, coordination and control in computer-supported work. Commun ACM 34:83–88
18. Truex D, Cuellar M, Takeda H, Vidgen R (2011) The scholarly influence of Heinz Klein: ideational and social measures of his impact on IS research and IS scholars. Eur J Inf Syst 20:422–439
19. Klein HK, Kraft P (1993) Social control and social contract in networking. Comput Supported Coop Work 2:89–108
20. Kuutti K (1996) Debates in IS and CSCW research: anticipating system design for post-fordist work. In: Orlikowski WJ, Walsham G, Jones MR, Degross JI (eds) Information technology and changes in organizational work: proceedings of the IFIP WG8.2 working conference on information technology and changes in organizational work, December 1995. Springer US, Boston, pp 177–196
21. Schmidt K (2014) The concept of 'Practice': what's the point? In: Rossitto C, Ciolfi L, Martin D, Conein B (eds) COOP 2014 – Proceedings of the 11th international conference on the design of cooperative systems, 27–30 May 2014, Nice (France), pp 427–444. Springer International Publishing, Cham
22. Kuutti K, Bannon L (2014) The turn to practice in HCI: towards a research agenda. In: Proceedings of the 32nd annual ACM conference on human factors in computing systems, pp 3543–3552. ACM, Toronto
23. Orlikowski WJ (2011) Practice in research: phenomenon, perspective and philosophy. In: Golsorkhi D, Rouleau L, Seidl D, Vaara E (eds) Cambridge handbook of strategy as practice. Cambridge University Press, Cambridge, pp 23–33
24. Orlikowski WJ (2000) Using technology and constituting structures: a practice lens for studying technology in organizations. Organ Sci 11:404–428
25. Ellway BPW, Walsham G (2015) A doxa-informed practice analysis: reflexivity and representations, technology and action. Inf Syst J 25:133–160
26. Mathiassen L (2002) Collaborative practice research. Inf Technol People 15:321
27. Koch M, Schwabe G (2015) Interview with Jonathan Grudin on "Computer-Supported Cooperative Work and Social Computing". Bus Inf Syst Eng 57:213–215
28. Bernroider EWN, Pilkington A, Cordoba J-R (2013) Research in information systems: a study of diversity and inter-disciplinary discourse in the AIS basket journals between 1995 and 2011. J Inf Technol 28:74–89
29. Lowry PB, Moody GD, Gaskin J, Galletta DF, Humpherys SL, Barlow JB, Wilson DW (2013) Evaluating journal quality and the association for information systems senior scholars' journal basket via bibliometric measures: do expert journal assessments add value? MIS Q 37:993–A921
30. Briggs RO (2015) Interview with Jay Nunamaker on "Computer-Supported Cooperative Work and Social Computing". Bus Inf Syst Eng 57:217–220
31. de Vreede G-J, Briggs RO, Massey AP (2009) Collaboration engineering: foundations and opportunities: editorial to the special issue on the journal of the association of information systems. J Assoc Inf Syst 10:121–137
32. Avison D, Malaurent J (2014) Is theory king?: questioning the theory fetish in information systems. J Inf Technol 29:327–336
33. Gregor S (2006) The nature of theory in information systems. MIS Q 30:611–642
34. Kuechler B, Vaishnavi V (2008) On theory development in design science research: anatomy of a research project. Eur J Inf Syst 17:489–504
35. Gregor S, Jones D (2007) The anatomy of a design theory. J Assoc Inf Syst 8:312–335
36. Seddon PB, Scheepers R (2012) Towards the improved treatment of generalization of knowledge claims in IS research: drawing general conclusions from samples. Eur J Inf Syst 21:6–21
37. Ågerfalk PJ (2014) Insufficient theoretical contribution: a conclusive rationale for rejection? Eur J Inf Syst 23:593–599

38. Barley SR, Dutton WH, Kiesler S, Resnick P, Kraut RE, Yates J (2004) Does CSCW need organization theory? In: Proceedings of the 2004 ACM conference on computer supported cooperative work, pp 122–124. ACM, Chicago
39. Sandelands LE (1990) What is so practical about theory? Lewin Revisited. J Theor Soc Behav 20:235–262
40. Urquhart C, Lehmann H, Myers MD (2010) Putting the 'theory' back into grounded theory: guidelines for grounded theory studies in information systems. Inf Syst J 20:357–381
41. Orlikowski WJ, Iacono CS (2001) Research commentary: desperately seeking the "IT" in IT research – a call to theorizing the IT artifact. Inf Syst Res 12:121–134
42. Blomberg J, Karasti H (2013) Reflections on 25 years of ethnography in CSCW. Comput Support Coop Work (CSCW) 22:373–423
43. Kuutti K, Arvonen T (1992) Identifying potential CSCW applications by means of activity theory concepts: a case example. In: Proceedings of the 1992 ACM conference on computer-supported cooperative work, pp 233–240. ACM, Toronto
44. Halverson CA (2002) Activity theory and distributed cognition: or what does CSCW need to DO with theories? Comput Support Coop Work (CSCW) 11:243–267
45. Christensen LR, Bertelsen OW (2015) A view of causation for CSCW: manipulation and control in the material field of work. In: Wulf V, Schmidt K, Randall D (eds) Designing socially embedded technologies in the real-world. Springer, London, pp 151–169
46. Järvinen P (2011) A new taxonomy for developing and testing theories. In: Carugati A, Rossignoli C (eds) Emerging themes in information systems and organization studies. Springer, Berlin/Heidelberg, pp 21–32
47. Kincheloe JL, Tobin K (2009) The much exaggerated death of positivism. Cult Stud Sci Educ 4:513–528
48. Lanamäki A, Stendal K, Thapa D (2011) Mutual informing between IS academia and practice: insights from KIWISR-5. Commun Assoc Inf Syst 29:123–132
49. Iivari J (2007) A paradigmatic analysis of information systems as a design science. Scand J Inf Syst 19:39–64
50. Plowman L, Rogers Y, Ramage M (1995) What are workplace studies for? In: Marmolin H, Sundblad Y, Schmidt K (eds) Proceedings of the fourth European conference on computer-supported cooperative work ECSCW'95, pp 309–324. Springer Netherlands
51. Davison RM, Martinsons MG (in press) Context is king! Considering particularism in research design and reporting. J Inf Technol
52. Monteiro E, Pollock N, Hanseth O, Williams R (2013) From artefacts to infrastructures. Comput Support Coop Work (CSCW) 22:575–607
53. Schultze U (2000) A confessional account of an ethnography about knowledge work. MIS Q 24:3–41
54. Alvarez R (2001) "It was a great system": face-work and the discursive construction of technology during information systems development. Inf Technol People 14:385–405
55. Palvia P, Daneshvar Kakhki M, Ghoshal T, Uppala V, Wang W (2015) Methodological and topic trends in information systems research: a meta-analysis of IS journals. Commun Assoc Inf Syst 37
56. Chen W, Hirschheim R (2004) A paradigmatic and methodological examination of information systems research from 1991 to 2001. Inf Syst J 14:197–235
57. Mattozzi A (2015) The pilgrimage goes on . . . a conversation with Liam Bannon about humans, machines, and their interactions. Tecnoscienza Ital J Sci Technol Stud 6:133–152
58. Neale DC, Carroll JM, Rosson MB (2004) Evaluating computer-supported cooperative work: models and frameworks. In: Proceedings of the 2004 ACM conference on computer supported cooperative work, pp 112–121. ACM, Chicago
59. Pipek V, Wulf V (2009) Infrastructuring: toward an integrated perspective on the design and use of information technology. J Assoc Inf Syst 10:447–473
60. Schmidt K, Bannon L (1992) Taking CSCW seriously. Comput Support Coop Work (CSCW) 1:7–40

61. Mondada L (2009) Emergent focused interactions in public places: a systematic analysis of the multimodal achievement of a common interactional space. J Prag 41:1977–1997
62. Gattiker TF, Goodhue DL (2005) What happens after ERP implementation: understanding the impact of interdependence and differentiation on plant-level outcomes. MIS Q 29:559–585
63. Bensaou M (1997) Interorganizational cooperation: the role of information technology an empirical comparison of U.S. and Japanese supplier relations. Inf Syst Res 8:107–124
64. Pee LG, Kankanhalli A, Kim H-W (2010) Knowledge sharing in information systems development: a social interdependence perspective. J Assoc Inf Syst 11:550–575
65. Ley B, Pipek V, Reuter C, Wiedenhoefer T (2012) Supporting inter-organizational situation assessment in crisis management. In: Rothkrantz L, Ristvej J, Franco Z (eds) Proceedings of the 9th international ISCRAM conference, pp 1–10, Vancouver, Canada
66. Reuter C, Marx A, Pipek V (2011) Social software as an infrastructure for crisis management – a case study about current practice and potential usage. In: Proceedings of the 8th international ISCRAM conference, pp 1–10, Lisbon, Portugal
67. Reuter C, Marx A, Pipek V (2012) Crisis management 2.0: towards a systematization of social software use in crisis situations. Int J Inform Syst Crisis Response Manag (IJISCRAM) 4:1–16
68. Fitzpatrick G, Ellingsen G (2012) A review of 25 years of CSCW research in healthcare: contributions, challenges and future agendas. Comput Support Coop Work (CSCW) 1–57
69. Davis FD (1989) Perceived usefulness, perceived ease of use, and user acceptance of information technology. MIS Q 13:319–340
70. Venkatesh V, Morris MG, Davis GB, Davis FD (2003) User acceptance of information technology: toward a unified view. MIS Q 27:425–478
71. Ackerman MS (2000) The intellectual challenge of CSCW: the gap between social requirements and technical feasibility. Hum Comput Interact 15:179–203
72. Strong DM, Volkoff O (2010) Understanding organization-enterprise system fit: a path to theorizing the information technology artifact. MIS Q 34:731–756
73. Legris P, Ingham J, Collerette P (2003) Why do people use information technology? A critical review of the technology acceptance model. Inform Manag 40:191–204
74. Hirschheim R (2007) Introduction to the special issue on "Quo Vadis TAM – Issues and Reflections on Technology Acceptance Research". J Assoc Inf Syst 8:203–205
75. Cabitza F, Simone C (2013) Computational coordination mechanisms: a tale of a struggle for flexibility. Comput Support Coop Work (CSCW) 22:475–529
76. De Rond M, Miller AN (2005) Publish or perish: bane or boon of academic life? J Manag Inq 14:321–329
77. Barley SR (2004) Puddle jumping as a career strategy. In: Stablein RE, Frost PJ (eds) Renewing research practice. Stanford University Press, Stanford, pp 67–82
78. Alvesson M, Sandberg J (2014) Habitat and habitus: boxed-in versus box-breaking research. Organ Stud 35:967–987
79. Alvesson M (2013) Do we have something to say? From re-search to roi-search and back again. Organization 20:79–90
80. Bjerknes G, Bratteteig T (1995) User participation and democracy: a discussion of Scandinavian research on systems development. Scand J Inf Syst 7:73–98
81. Mathiassen L, Nielsen PA (2008) Engaged scholarship in IS research: the Scandinavian case. Scand J Inf Syst 20:3–20
82. Kensing F, Blomberg J (1998) Participatory design: issues and concerns. Comput Support Coop Work (CSCW) 7:167–185
83. Bødker K, Kensing F, Simonsen J (2011) Participatory design in information systems development. In: Isomäki H, Pekkola S (eds) Reframing humans in information systems development. Springer, London, pp 115–134
84. Simonsen J, Robertson T (eds) (2013) Routledge international handbook of participatory design. Routledge, London
85. Hanseth O, Lundberg N (2001) Designing work oriented infrastructures. Comput Support Coop Work (CSCW) 10:347–372

86. Turner W, Bowker G, Gasser L, Zacklad M (2006) Information infrastructures for distributed collective practices. Comput Support Coop Work (CSCW) 15:93–110
87. Gal U, Lyytinen K, Yoo Y (2008) The dynamics of IT boundary objects, information infrastructures, and organisational identities: the introduction of 3D modelling technologies into the architecture, engineering, and construction industry. Eur J Inf Syst 17:290–304
88. Hanseth O, Lyytinen K (2010) Design theory for dynamic complexity in information infrastructures: the case of building internet. J Inf Technol 25:1–19
89. Karasti H, Baker KS, Halkola E (2006) Enriching the notion of data curation in E-science: data managing and information infrastructuring in the Long Term Ecological Research (LTER) network. Comput Support Coop Work (CSCW) 15:321–358
90. Karasti H, Syrjänen A-L (2004) Artful infrastructuring in two cases of community PD. Proceedings of the eighth conference on Participatory design: artful integration: interweaving media, materials and practices – volume 1, pp 20–30. ACM, Toronto
91. Aanestad M, Jolliffe B, Mukherjee A, Sahay S (2014) Infrastructuring work: building a state-wide hospital information infrastructure in India. Inf Syst Res 25:834–845
92. Halkola E, Iivari N, Kuure L (2015) Infrastructuring as social action. Thirty Sixth International Conference on Information Systems (ICIS 2015), Fort Worth
93. Grisot M, Vassilakopoulou P (2015) The work of infrastructuring: a study of a National eHealth Project. In: Boulus-Rødje N, Ellingsen G, Bratteteig T, Aanestad M, Bjørn P (eds) ECSCW 2015: Proceedings of the 14th European conference on computer supported cooperative work, 19–23 September 2015, Oslo, Norway, pp 205–221. Springer International Publishing

# Chapter 2
# Computational Artifacts: Interactive and Collaborative Computing as an Integral Feature of Work Practice

**Kjeld Schmidt and Jørgen Bansler**

**Abstract** The key concern of CSCW research is that of understanding computing technologies in the social context of their use, that is, as integral features of our practices and our lives, and to think of their design and implementation under that perspective. However, the question of the nature of that which is actually integrated in our practices is often discussed in confusing ways, if at all. The article aims to try to clarify the issue and in doing so revisits and reconsiders the notion of 'computational artifact'.

## 2.1 Introduction

The key concern of CSCW research (and arguably of HCI too) is that of understanding computing technologies in the social context of their use, that is, as integral features of our practices and our lives, and to think of their design and implementation under that perspective. As Lucy Suchman expressed it in a programmatic article from 1993 to 1994:

> Our efforts to develop a work-oriented design practice are based in the recognition that systems development is not the creation of discrete, intrinsically meaningful objects, but the cultural production of new forms of material practice. Our agenda [ ... ] is to bring developing objects out into the environments of their intended use, such that their appropriability into those environments becomes a central criterion of adequacy for their design. An implication of this agenda is that in place of the vision of a single technology that subsumes all others [ ... ], we assume the continued existence of hybrid systems composed of heterogeneous devices. [39, p. 34]. (Cf. also [36, p. 99]).

K. Schmidt (✉)
Department of Organization, Copenhagen Business School, Denmark
e-mail: schmidt@cscw.dk

J. Bansler
Department of Computer Science, University of Copenhagen, Denmark

© Springer International Publishing Switzerland 2016                                      21
A. De Angeli et al. (eds.), *COOP 2016: Proceedings of the 12th International Conference on the Design of Cooperative Systems, 23–27 May 2016, Trento, Italy,*
DOI 10.1007/978-3-319-33464-6_2

In fact, there has, over many years, been a wide range of attempts to conceptualize, in Suchman's words, the 'appropriability' of such 'objects' into 'the environments of their intended use' so as to facilitate their 'artful integration'. Noteworthy examples of such attempts are notions such as 'artifacts in use' [1], 'appropriation' of interactive artifacts [6, 49], 'coordination mechanisms' [27], 'ordering systems' [28], 'socially embedded technologies' [12], 'artifact ecologies' [2], and 'practice-oriented' or 'practice-based' computing [18, 29, 30]. However, it seems fair to say that the large variety of proposed conceptions, and the obvious fact that nothing even remotely akin to consensus has emerged, indicates that the whole issue is still wide open.

Now, a strong contender in the competition to conceptualize the 'artful integration' of computing is the broad tradition that attempts to conceive of computing from an 'infrastructure' perspective [cf., e.g. 9, 13, 14–17, 21, 24, 34, 35]. But again the conceptions are hugely variegated if not contradictory. On one hand, Rob Kling and others introduced and have used the term 'infrastructure' to denote 'all the resources and practices required to help people adequately carry out their work' [15, 17]. On the other hand, Ole Hanseth and others use the term 'information infrastructures' to denote large-scale 'computer networks with associated services' [13, p. 409], not in the sense of 'some kind of purified technology, but rather in a perspective where the technology cannot be separated from social and other non-technological elements, i.e. as an actor-network' [14, p. 349]. And finally, Leigh Star and Karen Ruhleder have argued that the concept of 'infrastructure' should not simply be understood as a notion of large-scale technical structures but as a 'fundamentally relational concept':'It becomes infrastructure in relation to organized practices', that is, in as much as 'it' from the point of view of a particular 'organized practice' 'sinks into the background' and thus is treated as infrastructure [35]. In line with this rather boundless notion of 'infrastructure', 'information infrastructures', according to Star and Bowker, 'provide the tools – words, categories, information processing procedures – with which we can generate and manipulate knowledge' [34]. While the notion of 'infrastructure', like the range of other notions mentioned above, does serve to frame and focus on the issue of understanding computing technologies in the social context of their use, the disparities in its use are a source of immense confusion: In a given study, what is 'the infrastructure'? A complex of interconnected technical artifacts or the social context in which it functions or even organizational arrangements that make it work? When talking about an 'information infrastructure', what is the 'technology' that 'cannot be separated from social and other non-technological elements'? Is the 'information infrastructure' the underlying system of networked computers with associated software and protocols, or is it the applications or services running on that platform, or is it the network and services *in use*? Is it the artifact or the practice?

Moreover, what are the 'heterogeneous devices' that form the 'hybrid systems' of our work settings? Applications of computer technologies are surely used, often artfully, in conjunction with a host of other kinds of artifact, from pen and paper to tables and chairs, but does it make sense to create an abstract category of 'heterogeneous devices' and conceive of the motley of artifacts and materials of our lives as instances of such an all-encompassing category? While it certainly makes sense to point to the heterogeneity of our settings, distinctions are surely required.[1] In short, in order to overcome our bewilderment, not to mention to be able to compare findings from our studies, we need to be able to talk systematically about the entities that are to be 'appropriated' or 'infrastructured' or 'artfully integrated' into the manifold material settings of our practices.

Now, that is not as trivial a question as one might imagine. And this is probably one of the sources of our embarrassment. A simple question should illustrate our problem: What is it that is an application of the technical knowledge in computing? A 'computer', 'a program', a 'system'? Do users actually 'interact' with a 'computer', and, if so, in which sense of 'interaction'? With the computer 'as a whole', perhaps, but what would that mean? With the 'application program' and only now and then with 'programs' that are part of the operating system? With all these 'programs' as a whole or also with the 'programs' in conjunction with the CPU? With the 'program' as conceived by the developers, with the 'program' as compiled and installed, or with the 'program' as instantiated as live circuits of running code? Or do users rather 'interact' with the objects of their work, whether digitally represented or not? Consider for example an ordinary digital calendar. It provides representations of categories such as 'year', 'month', 'week', 'day', 'hour', 'day type', 'event', and 'event type') as well as a set of operational primitives (e.g., 'create event', 'set alarm'). It may also subscribe to data from services such as weather forecasts, national holidays, etc., just as it will exchange information such as event invitations, contacts, maps, etc. with other application programs. So far, it is straightforward to conceive of it as an application program with its specific data structure (in the form of one or several interconnected files). But when working with multiple devices (laptop, smartphone, tablet), what is displayed as one's calendar may be distributed data structures that are continually and automatically synchronized via some cloud service. It is now no longer simply an identifiable application program with its files. One will nevertheless routinely use 'it' as a unitary calendar by virtue of the dependable and uniform replication of events in their relation to the generic data structure (a set of files, reciprocally synchronized). Now, a 'shared' calendar (shared by members of a project or a department) is not merely a stable set of files replicated across multiple devices. It is rather a composite of multiple individual calendars, partly intersecting, continually changing. And still, while distributed over myriad devices, it is routinely used as a unitary calendar. One is confident that what one sees in one's calendar app is the 'shared' calendar. How do we systematically conceive of this?

These issues are more than technical: they are conceptual. This paper is an attempt to address these issues. We do not aim to develop a conceptual framework; we merely attempt to clarify the issue. In doing so, we are in the fortunate situation that the issue of what it is we 'interact' with when working with digital devices has

---

[1]Similarly, what are the artifacts that make up 'artifact ecologies? Are they devices, or apps, or services, or network protocols, or all of the above [2, p. 457]?

been addressed before, 30 years ago in fact, under the label 'computational artifact' (or 'interactive artifact'). This seems a good place to begin, not because what was achieved then solves our problems, which it does not quite do, but because the issue was raised and addressed squarely.

## 2.2 A Logico-Grammatical Preamble

First, however, in order to steer clear of the metaphysics of computing, let us begin by making the conceptual observation that a bathtub is only a bathtub to a form of life for which taking a bath is an established practice. To an ant it is just a barren surface. Similarly, a technical artifact (a tool, a machine) is only a technical artifact by being a complement of a practice in which it is appropriated and routinely used. Or as Samuel Butler (1835–1902) wrote in his notebooks:

> The very essence of a tool is the being an instrument for the achievement of a purpose. [...]
> Therefore the word "tool", implies also the existence of a living, intelligent being capable of desiring the end for which the tool is used, for this is involved in the idea of a desired end. [4, p. 19].[2]

An artifact such as a calculating machine may be able to perform 'automatically', i.e., proceed causally (for a period of time and under certain operational conditions) and without human intervention, but it does not make sense to say that it 'calculates' in and of itself. In the words of Ludwig Wittgenstein, in critical remarks aimed at Alan Turing:

> Does a calculating machine *calculate*? Imagine that a calculating machine had come into existence by accident; now someone accidentally presses its knobs (or an animal walks over it) and it calculates the product $25 \times 20$.
> I want to say: it is essential to mathematics that its signs are also employed in *mufti*.
> It is the use outside mathematics, and so the *meaning* of the signs, that makes the sign-game into mathematics. [47, V §2].

The point is that *to calculate* is a normatively constituted activity; it is an activity governed by rules of what amounts to correct procedure and correct result: it is *a practice*. Wittgenstein again:

> Turing's "Machines". These machines are *humans* who calculate. [48, §1096].

That is, it is *we* who, by manual control of tools and instruments or by the use of more or less automatic machines, do the work. Sure, the use of automatic machinery as part of our practices may have implications for these practices (educational, organizational, etc.), but they are nevertheless just that: technical complements of our practices. It only makes sense to talk about this *mechanical* (or *causal*) regularity from the point of view and in the context of the *normative* regularity of our practices in which these artifacts are integral technical complements [29, Chap. 13; 30,

---

[2] We are indebted to Bannon and Bødker for bringing Butler's astute remarks to our attention [1].

32, 46]. In other words, it is *we* who engage in normatively constituted practices, *by* using rulers, compasses, and by using machines, computational artifacts included.

This should be clear enough. It is *we* who, in using computational (or interactive) artifacts, do the work. In that respect they are like any other kind of technical artifact: complements of our practices. This is not an issue here. The issue is rather that this class of artifact, computational artifacts, has some very special characteristics that are smothered when we, without further distinction, conflate them with other kinds of artifact or infrastructure.

## 2.3  The Notion of 'Computational Artifact' in Suchman

The notion of 'computational artifact' was originally introduced by Lucy Suchman[3] in 1985 in a PhD-dissertation based on empirical studies at Xerox PARC and published as a technical report by Xerox PARC [37, pp. [iii], 1–12].[4] The notion of 'computational artifact' occupies an important place in the foundations of HCI, CSCW, and related fields of computing technology research, not because it is widely used, far from it, but because it figured prominently in the incontestably most influential attempt to formulate a conceptual foundation for this kind of research, namely, Lucy Suchman's *Plans and Situated Actions: The Problem of Human-Machine Communication*. She introduced and used it in her pathbreaking attempt to give a principled and clear articulation of what was to be addressed and explored in the research program of 'human-machine communication' or 'interaction': it was suggested as the term for *that* with which humans were supposedly 'interacting' or 'communicating'. By virtue of that role, and although the notion quickly all but dropped from circulation in HCI and neighboring fields, it was a cornerstone concept of her argument.

To understand Suchman's notion of 'computational artifact' it is important to keep in mind the context in which it was hatched. From 1979 to 1984, she was employed as a research intern at Xerox Palo Alto Research Center (PARC) in

---

[3]The term 'computational artifact' is of course also used in methodological discourse in the completely different sense of contamination of data caused by the computational procedure. 'Artifact' in this derived sense generally means 'something observed in a scientific investigation or experiment that is not naturally present but occurs as a result of the preparative or investigative procedure' (Oxford Dictionary of English). To make matters even more confusing, the exact same term is also being used in recent literature on the foundations of computer science [e.g., 45], without any reference to Suchman's work whatsoever and in a very different sense, namely 'the entities that computer scientists construct, the artifacts of computer science' (*ibid.*, §1). And computer science is defined as what? The science of computational artifacts?

[4]The dissertation was later published in a revised edition [38]. The two editions differ somewhat, most importantly in that the concluding chapter is greatly elaborated in the 1987 version. In this version the book has become a classic in CSCW and HCI. Suchman later republished the 1987 text with a lengthy introduction and under another title [41]. – The different editions of the book have together received almost 10,000 citations.

California, and upon having received her PhD degree in Social/Cultural Anthropology in 1984 she became a member of PARC's research staff, ultimately to be appointed Principal Scientist.[5] The point of this piece of biographical information is that she was working as a researcher at Xerox PARC when and where the ultimate conceptual development of the 'interactive computing' paradigm took place.

The 'interactive computing' paradigm was initially conceived in the early years of the Cold War in the course of the development of the Whirlwind computer (the key computer system for a new US air defense system, SAGE, which became operational in 1958 [23]). It received important further developments in the following years, with the early development of Computer-Aided Design at MIT [25, 42] and with the NLS ('oN-Line System') created in the 1960s at Douglas Engelbart's Augmentation Research Center at SRI International [11]. But the step that was decisive for establishing the paradigm was taken at Xerox PARC in the development in 1972–1973 of an experimental computer 'workstation' with a 'graphical user interface', dubbed Xerox Alto [19, 43]. Based on the Alto concept, a more viable interactive computer named Xerox Star was developed (at PARC as well as the Xerox lab in El Segundo, California); it was introduced in 1981 [33]. That is, Suchman started working at PARC while the development of the Star was ongoing and finished her PhD dissertation at PARC only months after the ultimate exemplar of the interactive computing paradigm, the Apple Macintosh, was released up the road in Cupertino. Her dissertation was produced in the very epicenter – temporally, spatially, institutionally, culturally, and socially – of a technological upheaval of the first order.

The notion of 'computational artifact' was developed in order to be able to subject the 'interactive computing' paradigm that was then taking shape to critical examination.

Suchman was explicit about the context in which she developed the notion of 'computational artifact' and described it as follows:

> we now have a new technology which has brought with it the idea that rather than just using machines, we interact with them. In particular, the notion of "human-machine interaction" pervades technical and popular discussion of computers, their design and use. Amidst ongoing debate over specific problems in the design and use of interactive machines, however, no question is raised regarding the bases for the idea of human-machine interaction itself. [37, p. 3; cf. 38, p. 1].

She did not cite examples of what she was referring to but did not need to either: she was referring to an idea that had become pervasive. The pioneers of the emerging technological paradigm had used different words to express this idea: 'human-computer team work' or 'conversation' [25], 'man-computer symbiosis' [20], 'human intellect' 'augmentation system' [10], 'man-machine communication system' [42], etc. The terminological variations notwithstanding, the core idea remained the same, namely that of a symmetrical relationship between human and machine.

---

[5] http://www.lancaster.ac.uk/fass/sociology/profiles/lucy-suchman

Suchman's point of departure was that she found the very notion of 'interaction' between computing devices and humans problematic, i.e., in need of clarification. Thus, in examining the relationship between human and machine any preconceived notion of the specific nature of that relationship (such as 'interaction', 'communication', etc.) would anticipate what was to be investigated. In other words, she could not use a term like 'interactive artifact' in a critical investigation of the nature of that 'interaction'. The term 'computational artifact' was accordingly presented as a key term in formulating the research problem:

> The point of departure for this research is [ ... ] the apparent challenge that computational artifacts pose to the longstanding distinction between the physical and the social; in the special sense of those things that one designs, builds, and uses, on the one hand, versus those things with which one communicates, on the other. While this distinction has been relatively non-problematic to date, now for the first time the term interaction – in a sense previously reserved for describing a uniquely interpersonal activity – seems appropriately to characterize what goes on between people and certain machines as well. [37, p. 7; cf. 33, p. 6].[6]

In short, Suchman introduced the notion of 'computational artifact' in the context of her effort to offer a critical corrective to 'the emergence of disciplines dedicated to making [computational] artifacts "intelligent"' and especially 'a practical effort' to subject the 'interaction between people and machines' to engineering [37, p. 9; cf. 38, p. 7].

Central to her concern with the notion of some symmetrical 'interaction' was the then much debated idea that computational artifacts might be able to 'explain themselves' and even give advice. She summarized the target idea as follows:

> Researchers interested in machine intelligence attempt to make [formal representations of plans] the basis for artifacts intended to embody intelligent behavior, including the ability to interact with their human users. The idea that computational artifacts might interact with their users is supported by their reactive, linguistic, and internally opaque properties. Those properties suggest the possibility that computers might explain themselves: thereby providing a solution to the problem of conveying the designer's purposes to the user, and a means of establishing the intelligence of the artifact itself. [37, p. [iii]].

To address this 'problem of human-machine communication' she conducted and reported on 'a case study of people using a machine [a photo copier] designed on the planning model, and intended to be intelligent and interactive' (*ibid.*). From this she concluded that the 'access of user and machine to the situation of action' is 'asymmetrical' in that 'the ordinary collaborative resources of human interaction are

---

[6]Suchman's research problem was articulated in the same terms in 1999 in an article written in collaboration with Jeanette Blomberg, Julian Orr, and Randy Trigg: 'A central aim of Suchman's project was to suggest that the challenge of interactive interface design is actually a more subtle and interesting one than it was assumed to be by her colleagues in the field of human-computer interaction in the 1980s. Basically, their assumption was that *computational artifacts just are interactive*, in roughly the same that way persons are, albeit with some obvious limitations [ ... ]. However ambitious, the problem in this view was a fairly straightforward task of encoding more and more of the cognitive abilities attributed to humans into machines in order to overcome the latter's existing limitations.' [40, p. 393. – Emphasis added].

unavailable' to the machine [37, p. 124]. This insight was elaborated in the extended concluding chapter in the 1987 version of the text:

> Today's machines [ . . . ] rely on a fixed array of sensory inputs, mapped to a predetermined set of internal states and responses. The result is an asymmetry that substantially limits the scope of interaction between people and machines.' [38, p. 181]. 'I have argued that there is a profound and persisting asymmetry in interaction between people and machines, due to a disparity in their relative access to the moment-by-moment contingencies that constitute the conditions of situated interaction. Because of the asymmetry of user and machine, interface design is less a project of simulating human communication than of engineering alternatives to interaction's situated properties. [38, p. 185].

That is, the argument offered is that computational artifacts, in spite of 'their reactive, linguistic, and internally opaque properties', are cut off from ordinary human interaction because the latter is 'situated', i.e., 'essentially *ad hoc*'.[7]

Suchman's conception of 'computational artifact' has obvious merits.

First, by opting for the adjectival form 'computational' of 'computer' she shifted the emphasis from *thing* to *behavior*, from *object* to *functionality*. She thereby did not have to resort to common but notoriously confusing terms such as 'the computer', 'the technology', 'the system', 'software', 'the program', etc. For the problem with 'interactive computing' is the same irrespective of whether the device in question has the form of a permanent 'hardware' circuit, a temporary circuit in the shape of 'firmware', an ephemeral circuit in the shape of running 'software', or all of the above in conjunction, or whether the particular circuit is part of a CPU, the operating system, or some application program running under the control of the operating system, or whether the circuit resides as 'embedded code' in a photocopier or is a transient circuit distributed over multiple devices connected by some network.

Second, by using the term 'artifact' she was implicitly drawing on a century of anthropological work. For anthropology as well as archeology, 'artifact' is the standard term for objects designed, manufactured, and used by human cultures. It suggests that what we have here is comparable to stone axes, earthen pottery, and rattan baskets. The term 'artifact' was used in a similar deflationary way shortly after, by Pelle Ehn ('computer artifacts' [8]) and by Donald Norman and Edwin Hutchins ('cognitive artifacts' [22]).

In sum, the notion of 'computational artifacts' was introduced in order to address, in a principled way, the new phenomenon of humans working with machines that are highly reactive and malleable. It was introduced in the context of an attempt to dispel the mythology this new form of machinery had occasioned: the notion that we now are dealing with material objects imbued with human characteristics ('intelligence', 'language', etc.).

---

[7]The proposition that situated action is 'essentially *ad hoc*' is deeply problematic (it leads to infinite regress) but that is not the issue here (for a critical discussion, cf. [29, Chap. 12]).

## 2.4   Suchman on the Nature of 'Computational Artifacts'

According to Suchman's pioneering analysis, computational artifacts are characterized by having 'reactive, linguistic, and internally opaque properties' [37, p. [iii] and Chap. 2; 38, Chap. 2]. Let us briefly summarize what was meant by this proposition.

*The 'reactivity' of computational artifacts*: The characterization of computational artifacts as *reactive* seems obvious: Electronic computers are several magnitudes faster than any traditional machines and can react virtually instantaneously. However, as argued by Suchman, not all computing devices can be said to be *reactive*. As she emphatically points out, the reactivity of computational artifacts is predicated on 'the availability of interrupt facilities whereby the user can override and modify the operations in progress' [37, p. 10; 38, pp. 10 f.]. By contrast, computer devices used in batch processing modes (for the calculation of payrolls, tax returns, or master production schedules, or for the compilation of source code) are not reactive at all. They run their course. In stressing *reactivity*, that is, Suchman explicitly excluded the large body of computer programs used in mass data-processing from the category 'computational artifact'. The reason is obvious. It was the conceptual issues of the very concept of 'interactive computing' that were the target.

*The 'linguistic properties' of computational artifacts*: In elaborating what she meant by 'linguistic properties', Suchman stated that

> the means for controlling computing machines and the behavior that results are increasingly *linguistic*, rather than mechanistic. That is to say, machine operation becomes less a matter of pushing buttons or pulling levers with some physical result, and more a matter of specifying operations and assessing their effects through the use of a common language. With or without machine intelligence, this fact has contributed to the tendency of designers, in describing what goes on between people and machines, to employ terms borrowed from the description of human interaction – dialogue, conversation, and so forth: terms that carry a largely unarticulated collection of intuitions about properties common to human communication and the use of computer-based machines. [37, p. 10 f.; cf. 38, p. 11].

It is a source of confusion that Suchman in the quoted passage distinguished 'linguistic' from 'mechanistic' means of control. Entering a 'command' ('copy', say) by typing it or by choosing a menu item or a button-like field on the display (whether or not labeled 'Copy') is not a linguistic act any more than pushing a tangible button on a dish washer or pulling a lever. They are simply different ways of activating a mechanism; in the case of computing machinery connecting an electric circuit, 'with some physical result'.

This indicates some deep-seated ambiguity, which is unsurprising given the historical context and the fact that this was a pioneering and hence also tentative effort. The 'tendency', to which Suchman referred, of designers 'to employ terms borrowed from the description of human interaction' that 'carry a largely unarticulated collection of intuitions about properties common to human communication and the use of computer-based machines' was simply not easily overcome.

Anyway, one can certainly say that computational artifacts have 'linguistic' (or, rather, *semiotic*) properties in the very limited sense that we can use them to manipulate signs, where term 'manipulation' is shorthand for various transformative operations on the physical carriers of signs: Boolean operations as well as composite operations such as parsing, adding, subtracting, sorting, rearranging, moving, copying, comparing, etc. such (physical carriers of) signs and collections of signs.

The ability to manipulate (physical carriers of) signs is anyway not at all specific to or defining of computational artifacts. A mechanical typesetter, a traffic light, a time piece, or an electromechanical desktop calculator can also – in their own very limited way – be used to manipulate signs.

*The 'internal opacity' of computational artifacts*: Suchman's third defining characteristic, the computational artifact's being 'internally opaque', is *prima facie* mystifying. The entire argument is mystifying in that it, with references to Daniel Dennett [5] and Sherry Turkle [44], presumes that in order to understand a phenomenon, we have to reduce its behavior to internal mechanisms. But we do not need to understand the internal mechanism of an artifact in order to make rational use of it; nor do we in fact normally do that. One doesn't need, say, to understand the specifics of the lattice structure of steel alloys causing the operational properties of one's damascene kitchen knife: its hardness, its tensile strength, its elasticity. What one needs to understand is its 'functionality'. And in the case of machinery, what one needs to know is the dependable regularity of its behavior. That's all. The computational artifact is just a machine: a complex of elemental mechanisms carefully configured and built to perform with a high degree of predictability and dependability. And in incorporating it into our practice, we incorporate it *as such*: as a complex of causal mechanisms behaving in a highly regular manner which is useful in that practice. As long as the exhibited mechanical regularity can be integrated with the normative regularity of our practices, the internal mechanics is not of interest, except for very specific purposes, such as, for instance, maintenance, where we of course do take internal mechanisms into account.

Anyway, the point Suchman was trying to make by ascribing 'opacity' to computational artifacts was probably that we, in using a computational artifact, routinely treat it as a *functional unity* while disregarding its being an assembly of myriad computing devices:

> The overall behavior of the computer is not describable [ ... ] with reference to any of the simple local events that it comprises [ ... ]. To refer to the behavior of the machine, then, one must speak of "its" functionality. And once reified as an entity, the inclination to ascribe actions to the entity rather than to the parts is irresistible [38, p. 15 f.].

Not only 'irresistible', we would like to add, but quite unproblematic. A computational artifact is indeed 'opaque', but the opacity is the result of deliberate design: mechanisms that are irrelevant to users are carefully hidden from view. That is, what Suchman (with Turkle) calls 'opacity' is what may just as well be called 'transparency'. Something is hidden for others things to be visible. In this case, the mechanism is hidden (opaque) to make visible what is relevant for the work. That is, their 'internal opacity' is what makes computational artifacts *transparent* in *users' terms*. What users need to 'see' are objects and operations pertinent to the practice in which the computational artifact is incorporated, that is, they need to be able to take for granted that the artifact behaves appropriately from the point of view of that practice.

In sum, then, on Suchman's conception, computational artifacts are designed to react in step with the activities in which they are used, to be incorporated in sophisticated semiotic practices, and to exhibit functional unity irrespective of its shifting internal constitution.

The notion of 'computational artifact' was introduced in order to address the nature of the 'interaction' in the then emerging 'interactive computing' technology and to do so in a way that did not subscribe, implicitly, to the then prevailing presumption of some kind of 'symmetry' between human and machine. By doing so, it oriented HCI and CSCW research towards the practices in which the artifacts are incorporated. This makes it an indispensable concept for technological research oriented towards developing applications for our work practice. The notion of 'computational artifact' has considerable merit.

## 2.5 Computational Artifacts: A Reconstruction

Let us first briefly reconstruct the conception of 'computational artifact', that is, try to clarify its rational core while avoiding the ambiguities and logical mistakes that were probably unavoidable birthmarks.

Just as we do not live in the blueprint of a house but in the building specified in the blueprint, when we talk about 'computational artifacts' (e.g., a 'shared calendar') we are not talking about 'computer programs', or the various stages of program specification as expressed in diagrams and code; we are rather talking about programs as running code (in conjunction with one or more CPUs and assorted other computing components), that is, we are talking about programs as *live electronic circuitry*, be it permanent or ephemeral. It is *that* with which we interact when using computing devices.

A key feature of computational artifacts is their capacity to react to and thus be an integral part of unfolding events. Several architectural features are required to afford this.

1. For the reactions of the device to be experienced as immediate and the device to be experienced as 'interacting', reactivity presumes a response-time that is less than (what in the context of a given practice is considered) state-changes in the environment, i.e., they must be able to execute in 'real time'. This is elementary.
2. In the stored-program architecture originally devised by Alan Turing and John von Neumann, programs in the compiled form of binary code are treated as data and, when launched, reside in the computer's storage as – invisible and transient but no less physical – electronic circuits that can be activated virtually instantaneously. The advantage of this architecture was originally that

the program only has to be launched once and that the computing device does not have to spend time to access external input devices to obtain the next command.

3. The reactivity of computational artifacts is not afforded by the stored-program architecture in itself but presumes the very specific mode of operation classically referred to as 'manual intervention' [26] or, in Suchman's words, 'the availability of interrupt facilities whereby the user can override and modify the operations in progress' [37, p. 10; 38, p. 11]. Under this paradigm, the computing device does not simply run through a prespecified set of 'commands' in a prespecified sequence; rather, a program launched into working storage and activated awaits the occurrence of certain external events to execute a 'command' (in source code expressed as, for example, 'on mouse-up, do X').

4. By virtue of their reactivity, as well as high-capacity gigahertz storage media, computational artifacts are used to manipulate signs (letters, numerals, geometric elements, patterns of imagery and sound) in step with external events. They are used as complements of semiotically constituted practices (calculating, computing, drafting, planning, writing, searching, etc.). It is this that occasions some to ascribe normative behavior ('rule-following') to automatic machinery, others to latch on to a mechanical model of the mind to account for rational conduct, and others again to cover-up their embarrassment by conceiving of 'interactive computing' (or 'human-machine systems') as a symmetrical relationship. The source of the befuddlement lies in the confusion of the 'grammatical' or conceptual distinction between normative and mechanical regularity. We should not allow ourselves to be misled by the apparent ability of computing devices to react usefully to written or spoken instructions or provide results in similar modalities.[8] We should remember that computing machines do not use *signs* any more than Tibetan prayer mills engage in *praying*. What makes computational artifacts different from classical-mechanical and electromechanical machinery in regard to their ability to manipulate (physical bearers of) signs is strictly their speed of operation together with the fact that they can manipulate vast amounts of data in real-time, because of related features such as high-speed inexpensive random-access storage technologies (RAM, flash storage, harddisks).

5. A computational artifact is constituted by a structured set of 'object classes' and 'objects' (i.e., data structures with associated elementary operations). Accordingly, a computational artifact is inherently bound to *a practice* from which the categories represented by these objects and classes are derived and to which they are indigenous. It is within such practices, and only there, that the objects of the computational artifact have meaning.

---

[8] It is of course common for computer scientists and engineers to refer to the highly regular patterns of behavior of computational artifacts, that are the hallmark of their art, as 'rules' or 'procedures' (just as they speak of 'programming languages', etc.). This is an unavoidable feature of the natural attitude of these professions. Within the bounds of the practices of devising and building computational devices, it is as harmless as when we in ordinary language use expressions like 'sunrise' and 'sunset'. Damage only arises when this innocently convenient language is incorporated into systematic conceptualizations.

An electronic calendar, for example, is bound to our institutionalized practices of time measurement for purposes of planning and organizing events such as harvesting, meetings, deadlines, travels, and is constituted by object classes such as 'time', 'event', and so forth, as well as the associated operations. The functional unity of the digital calendar is a manifestation of the dependable reproduction of this structure, irrespective of the distribution of objects and operations, and the circuitry in which they are realized, across computer entities and devices. Only the objects are made visible, the internal mechanics are not (they are transparent or opaque).

A CAD system similarly offers a family of elemental object classes (such as, in architecture, 'wall,' 'door', 'window', etc.) and complex object classes (such as 'floor plan', 'elevation', 'cross section', 'building'), and requisite operations on these types (such as 'locate', 'copy', 'move', 'group', etc.). Modern CAD systems furthermore offer the advanced functionality of abstraction called 'overlay drafting' in which the representation of a composition is divided conceptually into layers such that objects and object complexes can be separated according to, for example, the material involved (brick, concrete), the type of object (walls, doors, plumbing), or author, while the geometric projection is rigorously maintained across layers (cf. [7, §2; 28, 31].). This enables architects and engineers to work with discrete digital representations of different aspects of the overall composition in a manner such that the parts created or amended by each of them are immediately available to any other, in various combinations, by direct projection between or superimposition of their respective layers. That is, they interact by making state changes to a set of (digital) representations while at the same time ensuring overall consistency of their distributed activities by means of the functionality of an associated assembly of computational artifacts carefully designed to perform the projection calculus in real time.

Thus, although a computational artifact incorporates the behavior of multitude, physically distinct, elemental entities, perhaps distributed over multiple devices, it exhibits *functional unity* over these myriad events without necessarily involving users in its intricate 'internal affairs', and it does so by virtue of its being bound to a practice. The functional unity exhibited by computational artifacts-in-use is the manifestation of just that – a design feat of the highest magnitude.

6. When a program, under the stored-program paradigm, is compiled and stored in RAM and thus exists as live circuitry, the device can not only react but may – in response to (determinate) environmental conditions, especially to actions users might take – change behavior (within the determinate but vast, in practice perhaps incalculable, solution space constituted by the totality of possible combinations). It may also modify its own 'code' or regular behavior (or that of another running program) and do so in 'real time'.[9] Accordingly, the reactivity of computational artifacts obtained under the interactive computing

---

[9]This is what makes hacking possible.

paradigm is afforded by far more than simple operational speed; computational artifacts may change behavior quasi-dynamically as environmental conditions change. Reactivity thus also implies behavioral flexibility and variability.

7. In an operating environment facilitated by the stored-program architecture, 'programs' no longer necessarily exist and act in splendid isolation. When active, a program may 'call' another program, even a program residing on a remote device, to execute a given 'command' (e.g., perform a specific process and return a data string) before it proceeds, or it may simply, under certain (determinate) conditions, hand over 'control' to another program (which operating systems do all the time). This is of course elementary. The point, however, is that in this environment, running programs may be made to combine and recombine to form large but often ephemeral machine systems. Multiple computational artifacts can be combined and recombined in real time, just as they can form more or less stable machine systems through remote resource calls or linking. Just think of a trivial browser operation involving preference files, java applets, browser extensions, queries to remote database system facilitated by CGIs, etc., and the invocation of other applications to handle special file types (such as PDF) – not to mention the OS level machinery making all this possible.

## 2.6  Computational Artifacts in Practice

The point of the concept of 'computational artifact' is to enable us to conceive of its dynamically accomplished functionality as integral to a work practice.

As with any technical artifact, a hammer, a power loom, or a computational payroll calculation, computational artifacts are complements of our work practices; beyond that, they would be merely evanescent electromagnetic pulses. A computational artifact is bound to the practice of which it is a technical complement by being used – routinely, competently, repeatedly – to process signs (in the form of object classes and objects) inherent to that practice. But computational artifacts are also complements of our practices in a different and stronger sense. As technical accompaniments of *interactive* computing, and even more so as *collaborative* computing applications, their overall behavior is determined in the course of the activities in which they are incorporated. Now, a computational artifact is of course a material artifact, an assembly of live electronic circuitry. It is carefully designed to behave in a highly regular way. When not in use, i.e., in the absence of 'manual intervention', while in the 'wait loop', it is like an idling car engine, and in this state its behavior is well defined: it does nothing but 'wait'. However, *in use* its behavior is determined by the pattern of activity of which the interventions are part. For each intervening act, its behavior (its response to each 'command' or 'mouse-up' or 'swipe': the 'subroutines' activated, the data exchanged, the remote calls, etc.) is of course strictly mechanically determined. For each state in the process of its dynamic execution there is a finite set of possible moves, but once a move has been made (a key is pushed, a button tapped, a dial turned) the artifact undergoes an 'automatic' (highly regular causal) process. And so on. However, the overall pattern of behavior of the artifact-in-use is not one of mechanical regularity (in contrast to a computational payroll calculation); the overall behavior is a manifestation of the normative regularity of the practice in which it is used as a material artifact. When integrated into our practices, the causal regularities of the enacted computational artifacts – the shifting electronic circuitry – are interwoven into the patterns of the normatively regulated activities of these practices. It is this fine-grained interweaving of normatively regulated activities and mechanical regulation that is specific to computational artifacts.

The conception of computational artifacts outlined here may also help clarify the notion of 'infrastructure': (a) There is first 'infrastructure' in the sense of a technical complement of a given cooperative work practice or family of practices: an assembly of computational artifacts constituted by object classes conceptually indigenous to that practice or family of practices. Obvious examples are the 'information infrastructures' provided by what in CSCW is often termed 'coordination technologies': large-scale collaborative applications such as CAD systems, electronic patient records, document management systems, workflow management systems (and of course also group calendar systems). These are assemblies of computational artifacts that exhibit functional unity in use by virtue of the complex of domain-specific object classes (workflows, classification schemes, etc.) they all embody. (b) Then there is 'infrastructure' in the sense of (more or less stable) patterns of live circuitry, established dynamically, typically by cascades of automatic connections unleashed by manual intervention in the use of the practice-bound infrastructures, and facilitated by the 'information super-highway' or 'infrastructure' of the multitude computer devices (servers, laptops, smartphones), network facilities (routers, fiber-optic cables, electromagnetic fields), and the multitude network protocols and APIs by means of which the formation of the former are controlled and mediated. Infrastructures, in this second sense, are facilities that enable 'infrastructures' in the first sense to form; the infrastructure of the infrastructure, if you will. (c) And of course, there is also, to make the picture complete, 'infrastructure' in sense of the 'work to make the network work' [3]: the organized practices through which 'infrastructures' in the second sense are constructed and maintained.

In sum: in the design of computational artifacts for the purpose of serving in a regulating capacity in coordinative practices (a group calendar, a workflow system, a document management system), we construct a repertoire of potential electronic circuitry that can be activated and combined in multiple but determinate ways and that then, in step with the unfolding actions of the cooperating actors, are used in the coordination of interdependent activities. In other words, what is designed are mechanisms that function in a strictly causal manner but interactively: step by step, move by move. A major challenge in this, if not *the* challenge, is the following: (a) to identify, analytically, not only the governing schemes of the coordinative practice in question (categories, principles) but also the spectrum of variations, contingencies, routine troubles, etc. that practitioners have to deal with, as well as the sources of these variations, etc., the probabilities of their occurrence, and the ways in which they deal with these variations: contingency measures, improvisations, and workarounds; (b) to devise computational artifacts with a corresponding space of possible moves – including, of course, a repertoire of means of improvisation enabling workers to temporarily circumvent or respecify the behavior of computational artifacts; and (c) to devise means for workers to express the categories and principles of their coordinative practices in the behavior of computational artifacts, and so on. In short, the real challenge is that of developing machinery designed to be an integral part of our normatively constituted but contingent cooperative work practices: the challenge of meeting the requirements of *normatively* constituted practices by means of *mechanical* machinery while at the same time dealing with the contingencies of our work.

**Acknowledgments** The research reported in this article has been supported by the Velux Foundation under the 'Computational Artifacts' project.

# References

1. Bannon LJ, Bødker S (1991) Beyond the interface: encountering artifacts in use. In: Carroll JM (ed) Designing interaction: psychology at the human-computer interface. Cambridge University Press, Cambridge, pp 227–253
2. Bødker S, Klokmose CN (2012) Dynamics in artifact ecologies, NordiCHI'12. ACM Press, New York, pp 448–457
3. Bowers JM, Graham B, Sharrock WW (1995) Workflow from within and without: technology and cooperative work on the print industry shopfloor, ECSCW'95. Kluwer Academic Publishers, Dordrecht, pp 51–66
4. Butler S (1912) The note-books of Samuel Butler. A. C. Fifield, London
5. Dennett DC (1978) Brainstorms: philosophical essays on mind and psychology. MIT Press, Cambridge, MA
6. Dourish P (2003) The appropriation of interactive technologies: some lessons from placeless documents. Comput Support Coop Work (CSCW) 12(4):465–490
7. Eastman CM (1989) Why we are here and where we are going: the evolution of CAD. In Yessios CI (ed) ACADIA 1989: new ideas and directions for the 1990s: ACADIA conference proceedings, 27–29 October 1989. Gainsville: University of Florida, pp 9–26
8. Ehn P (1988) Work-oriented design of computer artifacts. Arbetslivscentrum, Stockholm
9. Ellingsen G, Røed K (2010) The role of integration in health-based information infrastructures. Comput Support Coop Work (CSCW) 19(6):557–584
10. Engelbart DC (1962) Augmenting human intellect: a conceptual framework. Stanford Research Institute, Menlo Park
11. Engelbart DC, English WK (1968) A research center for augmenting human intellect. In: FJCC'68. Part I, vol 33, AFIPS Press, New York, pp 395–410
12. EUSSET (2013) A position statement, European society for socially embedded technologies. (Originally posted 2009). http://eusset.eu/position-paper/
13. Hanseth O, Monteiro E, Hatling M (1996) Developing information infrastructure: the tension between standardization and flexibility. Sci Technol Hum Values 21(4):407–426
14. Hanseth O, Lundberg N (2001) Designing work oriented infrastructures. Comput Support Coop Work (CSCW) 10(3–4):347–372
15. Jewett T, Kling R (1991) The dynamics of computerization in a social science research team: a case study of infrastructure, strategies, and skills. Social Sci Comput Rev 9:246–275

16. Karasti H, Syrjänen A-L (2004) Artful infrastructuring in two cases of community PD, vol 1, PDC 2004. ACM Press, New York, pp 20–30
17. Kling R (1987) Defining the boundaries of computing across complex organizations. In: Boland RJ Jr, Hirschheim R (eds) Critical issues in information systems research. Wiley, New York, pp 307–362
18. Kuutti K, Bannon LJ (2014) The turn to practice in HCI: towards a research agenda, CHI'14. ACM Press, New York, pp 3543–3552
19. Lampson BW (1972) Why Alto, XEROX inter-office memorandum. Xerox PARC, Palo Alto
20. Licklider JCR (1960) Man-computer symbiosis. IRE transactions on human factors in electronics, vol HFE-1, no 1, March, pp 4–11
21. Monteiro E et al (2013) From artefacts to infrastructures. Comput Support Coop Work (CSCW) 22(4–6):575–607
22. Norman DA, Hutchins EL (1988) Computation via direct manipulation, Institute for cognitive science. University of California, San Diego
23. O'Neill JE (1992) The evolution of interactive computing through time-sharing and networking. PhD dissertation, University of Minnesota
24. Pipek V, Wulf V (2009) Infrastructuring: toward an integrated perspective on the design and use of information technology. J Assoc Inf Syst 10(5):447–473
25. Ross DT (1956) Gestalt programming: a new concept in automatic programming, AIEE-IRE'56 (Western). ACM Press, New York, pp 5–10
26. Ross DT, Ward JE. Investigations in computer-aided design for numerically controlled production: final technical report: 1 December 1959 – 3 May 1967, Electronic Systems Laboratory, MIT, Cambridge, MA, May 1968
27. Schmidt K, Simone C (1996) Coordination mechanisms: towards a conceptual foundation of CSCW systems design. Comput Support Coop Work (CSCW) 5(2–3):155–200
28. Schmidt K, Wagner I (2004) Ordering systems: coordinative practices and artifacts in architectural design and planning. Comput Support Coop Work (CSCW) 13(5–6):349–408
29. Schmidt K (2011) Cooperative work and coordinative practices: contributions to the conceptual foundations of computer-supported cooperative work (CSCW). Springer, London
30. Schmidt K (2014) The concept of 'practice': what's the point?', COOP 2014. Springer, London, pp 427–444
31. Schmidt K. Of humble origins: the practice roots of interactive and collaborative computing, ZfM Online, May 2015. http://www.zfmedienwissenschaft.de/online/humble-origins
32. Shanker SG (1998) Wittgenstein's remarks on the foundation of AI. Routledge, London
33. Smith DC et al (1982) The star user interface: an overview, AFIPS'82. AFIPS Press, Arlington, pp 515–528
34. Star SL, Bowker GC. 'Work and infrastructure'. Communications of the ACM, vol 38, no 9, September 1995, p 41
35. Star SL, Ruhleder K. Steps towards an ecology of infrastructure: complex problems in design and access for large-scale collaborative systems, Inf Syst Res, vol 7, no 1, March 1996, pp 111–134
36. Suchman L (2002) Located accountabilities in technology production. Scand J Inf Syst 14(2):7
37. Suchman LA (1985) Plans and situated actions: the problem of human-machine communication. Xerox Palo Alto Research Center, Palo Alto
38. Suchman LA (1987) Plans and situated actions: the problem of human-machine communication. Cambridge University Press, Cambridge
39. Suchman LA (1993) Working relations of technology production and use. Comput Support Coop Work (CSCW) Int J 2(1–2):21–39 [article dated 1994]
40. Suchman LA et al (1999) Reconstructing technologies as social practice. Am Behav Sci 43:392–408
41. Suchman LA (2007) Human-machine reconfigurations: plans and situated actions, 2nd edn. Cambridge University Press, New York
42. Sutherland IE (1963) Sketchpad: a man-machine graphical communication system. PhD dissertation, Lincoln Laboratory, MIT, Cambridge, MA, 30 January

43. Thacker CP et al (1979) Alto: a personal computer, Xerox PARC, 7 August
44. Turkle S (1984) The second self: computers and the human spirit. Simon & Schuster, New York
45. Turner R (2014) The philosophy of computer science. The stanford encyclopedia of philosophy, 20 August
46. Williams M (2007) Blind obedience: rules, community, and the individual. In: Williams M (ed) Wittgenstein's philosophical investigations: critical essays. Rowman & Littlefield Publishers, Lanham, pp 61–92
47. Wittgenstein L (1978) Remarks on the foundations of mathematics (Manuscript, 1937–44). Transl. from Bemerkungen über die Grundlagen der der Mathematik. Basil Blackwell Publishers, Oxford
48. Wittgenstein L (1980) Remarks on the philosophy of psychology. Volume I (Typescript, Fall 1947). Basil Blackwell Publisher, Oxford [TS 229]
49. Wulf V et al (2011) Engaging with practices: design case studies as a research framework in CSCW, CSCW'11. ACM Press, New York, pp 505–512

# Chapter 3
# "The Device Is Not Well Designed for Me" on the Use of Activity Trackers in the Workplace?

Cécile Boulard Masson, David Martin, Tommaso Colombino, and Antonietta Grasso

**Abstract** The workplace, with its central place in peoples' lives, can be considered as a key site for promoting better health practices. From this perspective, companies are considering providing employees with activity trackers and supportive services aiming at improving employee health. As an initial exploration of possibilities and challenges for activity trackers in the workplace we undertook the following study: a qualitative study of 13 users of activity trackers within our company. Our main findings are that the successful adoption of activity trackers within the workplace is not straightforward, unless for short term intervention, since all participants stopped wearing them within 3 months. In this case we also saw that the use of activity trackers generated various frustrations and raised a number of concerns around end-user configurability, usefulness and privacy and control of data. The findings can have broad implications in designing and developing adequate wellness solutions at the workplace.

## 3.1 Introduction

The on-going progress in technology innovation, especially in the miniaturisation of electronic systems has promoted the growth in development of wearable devices and pervasive technology. In response to this, research into wearable devices and their uses has become a significant area of interest within the HCI and ubiquitous computing communities [e.g. 8]. Wearable devices are also central in other studies characterised as personal informatics [15], quantified-self [3] or even smart devices [13]. All these studies focus on the use of devices for the practice of collecting a great amount of data on oneself for analytical and purposeful reasons.

C. Boulard Masson (✉) • D. Martin • T. Colombino • A. Grasso
Xerox Research Centre Europe, 6 chemin de Maupertuis, 38240 Meylan, France
e-mail: cecile.boulard@xrce.xerox.com; david.martin@xrce.xerox.com;
tommaso.colombino@xrce.xerox.com; antonietta.grasso@xrce.xerox.com

© Springer International Publishing Switzerland 2016
A. De Angeli et al. (eds.), *COOP 2016: Proceedings of the 12th International Conference on the Design of Cooperative Systems, 23–27 May 2016, Trento, Italy*,
DOI 10.1007/978-3-319-33464-6_3

The marketing around activity trackers has clearly identified the health and self-improvement as the positive outcome of their use. The way activity trackers are marketed promotes a set of assumptions/expectations around their use and who is targeted as a user. A first assumption is that everyone should be focusing on their health with the help of this type of tool, meaning that there is a prospective user base of the whole population. *"There's a Fitbit product for everyone"* [7]. Then there is the notion of a common willingness to change towards a better life. And this change should be based on a day after day continuous improvement. Finally activity trackers are good tools to answer those obvious needs. Therefore, to summarise, the image promoted is that the targeted user of activity trackers is everyone and that the proper use of the device is long-term to achieve continuous improvement. These assumptions recall what Morozov describes as "technological solutionism" [23]. As such, these companies both help define and tap into a moral *zeitgeist* for continual self-improvement towards fulfilment, which is questionable, while also clearly referencing quite legitimate concerns over sedentary life-styles and their attendant health dangers. For Morozov *"what's contentious, then, is not [just] their [solutionists] proposed solution but their very definition of the problem itself"* (p6). Is it really always an issue to improve fitness? It might be for some people but not for everyone. In *fact "what many solutionists presume to be problems in need of solving are not problems at all"* (p6). While we might not think this last quote is appropriate in relation to the health aspect, when we consider the self-improvement/fulfilment aspect we might think that the type of discourse around these products is just as likely to create the problem it seeks to solve rather than having alighted on a pre-existing one.

In the field of health, the growing problem of sedentary lifestyles is becoming a real concern. Regular physical activity is valuable for everyone and can help to prevent health problems from heart disease, to diabetes, colon cancer, depression and even anxiety [25]. As there is a growing awareness of the importance of physical activity, people are more aware of a need to nurture healthier habits, and for this purpose, it is suggested in marketing and other materials that activity trackers can provide useful support: *"The Withings Pulse $O_x$ can help you be more active and improve your health"* [33]. The issue of health promotion within the workplace environment is not a new one, but with modern offices environments often considered to be contributory to sedentary life-styles, concerns about the costs for companies of poor employee health and a new range of wearable technologies interest is re-focusing on these as a means for health and fitness promotion [35]. In that context, employers are encouraged to promote "workplace wellness programs" [21]. Activity trackers seem to offer great potential as part of those programs and employers have started to promote their use [1, 17]. Studies have already been conducted in the workplace environment with activity trackers, but the target was more on the medical efficiency of such devices than on the outcome of use of the activity tracker within the specific organizational context of the workplace [5] or providing some initial insight on the way to implement the programs [9].

In this article we want to contribute to this developing body of studies, by examining the use of activity trackers within the organizational context of the workplace, to better understand the real practices around them and discuss the current activity trackers as solutions to health and fitness issues. From this perspective we will first try to understand and describe through the related work the underlying logic of this kind of devices that mainly relies on quantified-self and change management.

## 3.2  Related Work

### 3.2.1  Quantified-Self: A Self-Tracking Practice

"*The quantified self (QS) is any individual engaged in the self-tracking of any kind of biological, physical, behavioural, or environmental information*" [31]. Technological progress provides us with ways of gathering data through lightweight inexpensive technologies. A variety of sensors embedded in technologies make it possible to easily gather a large amount of data automatically. Although, as we will see, configuring and managing these devices and interpreting the data is not 'automatic' nor necessarily simple. These devices represent a major change in the ability of regular consumers and citizens to gather lots of quantified data on their practices, habits and physiological readings. Of course, there has long been an interest amongst various people and groups – such as competitive sportspeople and technophiles – in gathering data, measuring and quantifying things like performance that could be considered as practices of the *quantified self*. However the concept – often traced to Gavin Wolf and Kevin Kelly (2007) of Wired Magazine [26] – very much embodies the modern technically supported incarnation where a lot of data can be gathered very easily. Previously *quantified-selfers* had to gather their data through more manual means using a variety of mundane or specialist devices (some not easily commercially available). Then quantified-self practices required serious engagement and motivation to collect accurate data over time, meaning it was likely heavily purpose and goal driven (why go to all that trouble if you do not want to achieve something in particular?) [6]. Today, with "wearables" gathering data in a simple sense doesn't require such an involvement or cost. People can access data on their own activity easily. This new easy access to data may have an impact on the use of activity trackers and on the quantified-self practices, i.e. it may well promote it widely in the population [18].

Rooksby and colleagues suggest that the use of tracking devices is not always related to a change perspective (i.e. to changing life-style) but also as a means to understand or to satisfy curiosity [27]. It may even be used because of an interest in the technology itself – what can it do, how does it work? Or even for status or fashion. In the uses listed here that are not directed towards self-improvement or better fitness (in fact they are relatively undirected) there is a discrepancy between the way marketing presents activity trackers on how they are meant to be used – that is toward an optimization of the self – and the reality of actual use. The actual use within an organizational context and the issues raised by its use is what we address in our study.

## 3.2.2   Know Thyself and Change Management

The tracking practices are based on the motto "know thyself" (through the collection of data on your habits)[1] in order to identify whether or not things are going well and, if necessary, plan and lead the changes needed to be made [14]. The change is based here on a "holistic engagement" where the user has a whole understanding or awareness of his/her situation [3]. The central position of the "know thyself" in the use of wearable devices raises questions about the accuracy of the data gathered, how well that data may or may not map onto the phenomena it is said to measure/correspond to, and what is it that you might be finding out about or getting to know about yourself. If the users focus on the number of steps he/she might get accurate figures but the estimation of the distance travelled or calories burned is less accurate [10]. This accuracy relates to the device in itself and is not easy to assess [34]. Then the use of the device can lead to inaccuracy, for example when the device is unloaded or when the user forget to wear it. Therefore an on-going engagement from the user is needed to get accurate data. According to Meyer et al. *"There is an inherent trade-off between quality of data – in terms of precision, reliability and availability – on the one hand, and usability and user's effort for data acquisition on the other"* [22].

It is suggested by manufacturers that these are change management devices and that life-style change will be more-or-less a spontaneous outcome of their use as they provide an awareness to the users of their 'to be improved' behaviours. *"There's a better version of you out there. Get UP® and find it"* [11]. This expected outcome is a particularly attractive hook for employers with a financial interest in changing employees' habits towards healthier ones [17]. Can technology provide a fairly cheap and simple to implement route through a thorny social issue? To support and motivate users to adopt better behaviours and change some "bad" habits and also to maintain good new behaviours, a gamification setup is provided with the smart device. This is meant to help the user to achieve his goals. Thus, while using the device, the users receive badges, feedbacks or social support [29].

## 3.2.3   Difficulties Encountered in the Use of Smart Devices

Studies pinpoint the difficulties encountered in the quantified-self practices or in the use of smart devices [6, 13]. Having objective knowledge on oneself is not enough to change in the "right" direction. The use of smart device is strongly impacted at the beginning by the novelty and the curiosity [20]. It is possible to find people that use smart devices over a long period of time [6, 8]. But some others identify

---

[1]Of course 'knowing thyself' through data is something new. Conventionally knowing thyself is all about, qualitative, critical, moral introspection. We might think about what sort of *knowing* is possible through data and measurement on physical activity.

some reasons why users abandon the use of smart devices. Some feel that the device does not fit their conception of themselves, others find the data collection not useful, or the extra work associated too large. The questions raised in this article are the following ones: Are users unanimous in seeking improvement of the self in terms of fitness? Are activity trackers well designed for this purpose? How do people understand and interpret figures provided on their daily activity? The study presented in this paper is broad, explorative and based on qualitative data which are interesting to understand deeply the use of activity trackers, the limits of those devices and the feeling of users [12].

## 3.3    Methods and Settings

We designed and implemented an exploratory study within the context of the workplace with 13 participants who used activity trackers such as Jawbone UP, Pulse or Runtastic, which are all-in-one step, distance, calorie and sleep trackers. Our study involved minimal direction, simply explaining what the device was for and how to use it, how to register on-line to look at their data, and then basically asking the participants to explore usage. After leaving the participants with the devices for a number of months we arranged debrief interviews particularly to try to understand their motivations in signing up for the study and using the activity tracker, how they understood, interpreted and reacted to the device, the data and the feedback and whether and in what way they had achieved the effective use of the device. We were also interested in their opinion on the targeted users by the device. The interviews were semi-structured with a series of topics but the participants were encouraged to share whatever opinions and insights they had. The qualitative set up of the study is particularly appropriate to explore the use of activity tracker as a means of supporting and facilitating change. Interviews are a good means to gather insights on how the device was used and understood and whether and in what ways it enabled change [12]. The study was based on voluntary participation. The participants were recruited in a company performing research and development in information and communication technology (ICT). Thirteen volunteer participants agreed to take part of this study. Among the participants, ten were given a *Pulse* (branded by *Withings*) by their employer within an experimental set-up and were totally free to use it the way they wanted. The three other participants had received as a gift from relatives an activity tracker (*Jawbone* or *Runtastic*).

It's interesting to notice that none of the participants had bought the activity tracker for themselves. Ten were volunteers to try out the device as provided by us and the other three had received their activity trackers as gifts from friends and family. We can therefore consider that the participants are in a situation of *pushed self-tracking* where "the initial incentive for engaging in self-tracking comes from another actor or agency" (p7) [17], although, of course, all volunteered for this study, rather than being strong-armed. Lupton underlines that the workplace is a key site of pushed self-tracking.

Our key purpose was to understand more deeply what such a device would bring to participants who were not interested and motivated enough in the use of an activity tracker to the point of buying one – thus were likely less motivated by specific personal goals and desires – and therefore to see how they were using the device and if it had an impact on their habits and behaviour. Following that goal and in order to not miss interesting aspects of this type of device and its use, impact etc., the questions proposed at the interview were broad.

The interviews lasted between 20 and 50 min and were audio-recorded. All the interviews were entirely transcribed and analysed from an ethno-methodological perspective – we had no theoretical orientation and were interested in how participants expressed their usage, activities, understandings and opinions about the devices in their own words. The main themes that came out of the analysis centre around the effective use of the device and the frustrations experienced in its use.

## 3.4   Findings

### 3.4.1   The Use of the Device: Adoption and Disappointment

A first result on the use of the device is that for all participants it was a short-term engagement, less than 3 months. We were able to distinguish two distinct phases in the use of the device that shows a difference in the involvement of the participants in the use of the device – a period of discovery marked by curiosity and a period of attempted instrumental use often marked by some disappointment. The Table 3.1 presents for each participant the type of activity tracker used and the length of use.

The first phase is a period of adoption of the device: participants start to use the device, the gathering of this type of data is relatively new for all participants and they demonstrate a strong interest for exploring and using the various features of the device. For example participant 11 used the feature that calculates the amount of calories ingested. So each time he ate something, he noted the type of food and then used the app to calculate the amount of calories. Another participant was really attracted by the calculation of the amount of steps taken during the day and also

**Table 3.1** Length of use of the activity tracker

| Id | G. | Activity tracker | Length of use | Id | G. | Activity tracker | Length of use |
|----|----|------------------|---------------|-----|----|------------------|---------------|
| P1 | M | Pulse *Withings* | 3 weeks | P8 | M | Pulse *Withings* | 8 weeks |
| P2 | F | Pulse *Withings* | 4 weeks | P9 | F | Pulse *Withings* | 12 weeks |
| P3 | M | Pulse *Withings* | 4 weeks | P10 | M | Pulse *Withings* | 5 weeks |
| P4 | M | Pulse *Withings* | 8 weeks | P11 | M | Jawbone UP | 4 weeks |
| P5 | M | Pulse *Withings* | 12 weeks | P12 | M | Jawbone UP | 3 weeks |
| P6 | F | Pulse *Withings* | 4 weeks | P13 | M | Orbit *Runtastic* | 6 weeks |
| P7 | M | Pulse *Withings* | 8 weeks | | | | |

by the sleep analysis, so during this period he carefully notified the device the time when he was going to bed and when he woke up in the morning so that the device could identify the periods of different activity and provide accurate data. During this first period, participants were engaged in discovery, trying out and configuring in order to "maximize" the use of the device to their own personal preferences and concerns.

"*At the beginning it was motivation. I could walk instead of waiting for the bus to the next bus stop. But it was at the beginning. Now I don't care about the steps I did during the day*" (P13). The second time period is marked by disappointment, frustration or loss of interest, where participants experience the limitations of the technology and also the limitations of the tracking itself. "*The figures in themselves, it's not that interesting*" (P11). The beginning of that second phase often starts with a break in the routine. Participants who managed to develop a consistent routine with the smart device over a number of weeks did not come back to a regular use of the device after breaking that routine for some reason. Other studies are consistent with that result [13].

There is also a broad feeling coming out of the interviews that "*the device is not well designed for me*" (P4), it cannot represent participants own specific situation in the right way, with the right granularity, and so it generates frustration. This result is explained in details in the following part of the paper. In fact this feeling can be explained by the gap between the actual physical activities undertaken by people and the figures or models used purported to measure those activities that necessarily simplifies and abstracts from reality.

All participants stopped using the device within 3 months. This shows that after a while the users don't find much of interest promoting further use after approximately 3 months. These results are close to those obtained on the FitBit device [19]. The core result here is that activity trackers do not seem to be used as long term and even where they can support any behaviour or habit change this is also of limited duration.

### 3.4.2  Outcomes of Using Activity Trackers: Awareness and Frustration

The use of an activity tracker provides the user with a rough understanding and awareness of their daily activity in terms of their movements (particularly their steps and exertion) during the day and duration and quality of sleep during the night. For 5 participants out of the 13, the use of the device encouraged some change in their habits. P12 expressed that the device helped him to balance his physical activities more over the week such that he did some physical activity every day. This planning of his physical activities was still effective, as a legacy of using the device, even though he didn't use his tracker anymore. P13 found an interesting use of the device to help him to follow a precise training regime in preparation for participating to a half marathon race. Combined with the device, P13 had a specific application on the smartphone to plan the training week by week. The wearable device helped him during his runs to check the distance and the time in order to achieve the proposed training. P2 declared that the use of the activity tracker made her more conscious of exercise such that from time-to-time she was motivated to walk instead of taking the bus, acting as an *aide memoire* and prompt.

Most participants expressed that they were curious about the amount of steps they had taken during the day and were pleased to have a broad understanding about their exercise thanks to the activity tracker. They could compare a "normal" working day to a non-working day, and they could have a comparison between days when they use public transport or their car to travel to their workplace. They could identify a rough baseline of how much they walked on particular 'types' of days. However, some questions were raised around the accuracy of the data, the default milestones of 10,000 steps and 8 h of sleep, the models undertaken to represent their activity, the finiteness of the data, the privacy concerns and the change management.

**Involvement Required to Get Accurate Data** Even though the new wearable technologies make it easier to track some personal activities such as steps or sleep, it still requires some degree of involvement from the user to get accurate data. According to the interviewees this involvement is hard to maintain day after day. "The worst thing is that I have to activate it and when you wake up you have to deactivate" (P13). Participant 11 who recorded all his food intake during the first period stopped because it was highly time-consuming, only approximate in accuracy, and apparently he did not find any tangible benefits from this, particularly in trade-off to effort.[2] Other participants expressed that when they forgot to charge the battery, they lost a few hours or even days of activity recorded on their app and therefore lost accuracy in the figures they obtained. The level of involvement to get accurate data appears to be an obstacle to use the device "properly" over a long period of time, particularly when this is off-set against the perceived value that is produced.

**Default Milestones and Side-Effects of Gamification Set-Up** All the devices used in the study suggest default milestones of 10,000 steps per day or 8 h sleep per night. These milestones are like goals and are bound to a gamification set-up which aims at supporting change behaviors toward a "better" direction. The initial impact of the set-up is that participants feel really motivated, at least at the beginning. After a while, there are some side-effects that in the end discourage participants from using the device longer. For example, two participants claimed to be bored by the mechanistic gamification. "*Rapidly I got fed up that the device always relaunch me like you did 10,000 [steps] now your goal is 12,000 and then you did 12,000 now your goal is 14,000*" (P5). This type of mechanistic gamification setup seems to never consider a limit in the activity users can achieve in a day and in the end participants lost the motivation. It is also clearly very simplistic and does not take

---

[2] The device can access calorie counts through product barcodes and doing rough calculations based on input of self-prepared meals.

into account user preferences and goals. Another side-effect is for participants who do a lot of physical activity that the device can't measure. "*I was doing a lot of workout that the device doesn't take into account. In the end it demotivated me because I couldn't reach the goal proposed even though I was doing far enough physical activity*" (P6). The device sends back to the participant a "bad" image of her/his physical activity that is further more incoherent with what the participant feels. This bad experience tends to demotivate them.

Finally there are the participants for who the milestones proposed is too far from their practices. Some participants were really below the milestones and felt that these 10,000 steps were completely arbitrary. Others were very close to that goal of 10,000 steps: "*my activity was somehow good enough, actually this is one of the reason why I didn't use it [the device] much*" (P12) and so didn't need any motivation to change something. This feedback questions the meaning of that milestone and the fact that the milestone is the same for everyone.

**Simplistic Models, Limits of Technology and Finiteness of the Data** Several participants expressed that they were disappointed by the simplistic models, especially with the sleep analysis. For example, P4 had to wake up at night several times to take care of his children and the device considered that the night ended as the participant stood up, so it didn't count the sleeping hours after the brief wake-up at night. P2 was falling asleep on the sofa before going to bed, "*my sleeping hours in the sofa are not recorded by the pulse, I slept but it's not recorded*". Before using the device P3 had strong expectations toward the sleep analysis, "*But the device doesn't analyse the sleep, only your movements during the sleep*". That is, you need to tell the device when you are going to sleep and it measures sleep through a crude indication of deep sleep – the lack of significant bodily movement. The measure can easily fail to differentiate between sleep and non-sleep and any duration is very approximate. It cannot tell you in any meaningful way whether you got a good or bad nights' sleep, and it certainly can't help you sleep better.

Participants also realize the limits of the devices through using them. The activity trackers are sold as devices that can help people in improving their life but "*in fact it's only a pedometer*" (P1).

The distorted picture creates disappointment because it is very far from the marketing presentation of activity trackers. "*When I go to the swimming-pool with the kids, the device doesn't consider the activity of swimming. So in the end the device doesn't reflect reality*" (P9), or we could emphasize that it doesn't reflect "my" reality. Here we understand a need for the users to get accurate and personalized data in a more holistic way that can provide a full account and assessment of a user's life or life-style. This need can't be provided by the device in its current version.

**Privacy Concerns on Fitness Data** Another issue addressed in the study is a set of privacy concerns about the generated data. On this topic we consider nine users of the Pulse because one participant had to use the pulse for technical reasons. We discount the other users we interviewed because they were not part of the official trial. There was an implicit deal (i.e. specified in the conditions of the trial) that participants using the Pulse device, in exchange of being lent the activity tracker, would give the researchers access to their data. A few weeks after having received the Pulse the participants received an email to asking them to provide access to the data through a web link. Three of them did this, the six others didn't. An interesting point here is that during the interviews, the nine users were asked if they were willing or reluctant to give access to their data to researchers that are employees of their company. Seven of them reported that they were willing to give access to their data. To go deeper in the analysis of the privacy issue in this study, we will examine the responses of the participants to the question: *"Was it an issue for you to share your data for the experiment?"*

P7 and P9 expressed that the data collected through the pulse were private and they felt reluctant to share them. So when P7 was asked to give the access, he preferred to end the study and gave back the device. In this case we can see that the data collected by the pulse was considered as particularly sensitive and private. P9 agreed to provide access to the data in order to support scientific research, but she expressed that if she had bought one for herself, she wouldn't have liked to share the data, which is interesting in itself because although sharing data with your employer is clearly a special case, users don't seem to count sharing the data with the manufacturer as *sharing* in the same way. The six other participants expressed various answers explaining why they agreed to share the data. Interestingly all of these contain caveats, justifications, or some kind of indication of concern. The first explanation is that the data is not for them considered really private, *"the data are very limited"* (P3), *"I had no privacy problem because I didn't use it for the sleep analysis, I feel that the sleep analysis is more private than the step numbers"* (P1). It seems that for P1 the data collected during his sleep are more private than the amount of steps walked in the day, which is not exactly surprising. Another point relates to the fact that participants already share a lot of private data *"I have no matter of principle on the data, because I already unwittingly share so much data that I judge more sensitive"* (P2). This last type of answer shows a comparative and somewhat *fatalistic* position concerning the sharing of data. These various types of answers reveal diverse degrees of agreement for data sharing according to the type data. The use of personal data within an organizational context also raises this kind of concern, as seen in the fact that participants didn't share their data or were reluctant to do so.

Now we can consider the reasons why five participants – even if they felt willing to share the data – didn't carry out the task to allow it. P8 had technical issue in trying to do the task. The four other participants expressed that they were lacking time or just forgot to do it. The interpretation of this data is not easy or straightforward. There are several options. The first one is that the email to give access to the data was sent 5 weeks after the beginning of the study. At that time of the study, five users had already stopped to use the device, so they might feel less concerned by the experiment. A second option might be that only one email was addressed without reminders, so some of them might simply forget to do it. Moreover there was no explicit explanation of the aim of the study, so the participants might not find it made sense to share the data. Another option is that they were not in a hurry to share the data, because even if they declare that they had few concerns on that point, it is still problematic in some way to share data. Whatever the reason, this suggests sizeable barriers for the use of this type of device and data sharing in the workplace.

**Change Management** Five participants claim that the use of the device had an impact on their behaviour and at least it provides them a good awareness of their daily physical activities. Three participants changed some of their habits when they started to use the device but after a while returned to their previous habits. The five other participants said that they didn't change any of their habits due to using an activity tracker. Even though some participants changed some of their practices, it seems that room for improvements are limited as all participants ended their use of the device within a period of 3 months.

**Targeted Users: Who Are They?** A last question during the interviews related to the targeted users for this type of devices. For some "sporty" participants the answer was "*for people who are not really sports people*" (P3) or those trying to do a diet. P5 said "*for people who walk a lot or like running*". P7 and P9 targeted the very sporty people. Finally P4 and P10 identified as target users those who are convinced by the device or those who lack motivation. What is interesting in the answer is that even though the participants has self-identified as interested potential users they now disqualified themselves. However, they maintained a position that it was useful but now to a type of user group that most of the time didn't include them. It underlines the broad feeling that "*the device is not well designed for me*" (P4). Were they just being polite? We refer here to studies showing that users adjust their behaviour and responses to fit the expectations of those running the study, of what they think the experimenters want [2].

## 3.5 Limitations

**Missing Social Dimension of the Devices** In this study, we do not really integrate a social dimension into the use of the activity trackers. So we cannot really assess if social features would play a role in motivating people to use the device longer or in creating a shared motivating environment between colleagues. Rooksby et al. show in their study that the social features of apps or device are not used [27]. However, even though participants state they did not publish the data on Facebook or Twitter, they can get "friends" through using the social feature of the app with whom they like to compete or share practices. Other studies show a positive social impact on the use of self-monitoring device [4, 16].

## 3.6    Design Implications

This study raises a number of issues related to design that should be examined in depth and that could help to improve the design of smart devices such as activity trackers to fit better the needs of users. We will only touch on a few of these here and intend to examine them properly in future work.

Firstly, most obviously smart devices allowing automatic tracking of data should allow the manual input of data in the case of break in the tracking, for example when the device is running out of battery or when the user forgets to wear it. This would overcome some frustrations of the users when the data gathered does not match the reality and then they can't rely on it.

The more challenging aspects relate to the sensitivity and accuracy of the measurement of various activities as well as configuration to particular needs and preferences. It seems clear that the devices can be adapted to provide input from a greater range of activities, and the conception, modelling and measuring of those activities could be improved. For example, it would be relatively straightforward to incorporate (with some user input) other types of activities. One key point to stress on this matter, though, is that it is important that expanding the range and quality of functionality always needs to be traded off against effort or work on the part of the user. Users may be relatively enthusiastic about the idea of quantifying and recording their activities, particularly when it is useful and straightforward. When it becomes a bureaucratic drudge with little value it has little to recommend it.

## 3.7    Discussion

**What About Needs or Goals Associated to Personal Life?** A core question related to devices supporting Quantified-self practices is: Is there any need that people experience and that may be filled with such devices? We can reasonably assume that some people want to change their daily activity for health or other reasons, but that maybe not everyone is concerned by a continuous self-improvement in fitness. The results of the study on these potential users for activity trackers show that while participants counted themselves out as consumers they are reluctant to question the real need for this kind of device in any paradigmatic sense, nor to consider that it might only be a high-tech gadget without any deep usefulness. We suggest that it demonstrates how strong technological solutionism is an accepted way of thinking about things in our society. The way participants of the study discuss the targeted user recalls the habit of "solutionists" talking about other people in simplistic and mechanistic ways that they are somehow exempt from [23]. The interesting point in the study is that the participants do not seem to take into account their own use of the device, the frustration related to it and the fact that they all stopped using it to answer the question of the targeted user but, rather, exempt themselves from the set of relevant users.

**Short Term Use of the Device** This study is not the first one to describe a short term use of smart devices [13, 30]. This statement is out of line with the way marketing tends to promote continuous self-improvement over long period. However it could be interesting to reconsider the "proper use" of smart devices as a means for limited short-term use before frustration sets in. It is reasonable that change occurs on a limited period of time and that after the change, the need of tracking and incentives disappears. This still raises a question of cost-benefit both in terms of effort and money.

**Do Figures Really Fit a Global Assessment of Fitness?** In this part we want to discuss the type of data produced and their appropriateness for judging fitness. Sacks' work on measurement systems may offer some insight into why the quantification of the self that is supported by fitness devices may not be useful or relevant to users over sustained periods of use [28]. In his analysis of conversations between patients and doctors (or therapist) Sacks noted how when people establish what might be thought of a "baseline" for some lay diagnostic assessment of general health, if not fitness – so for example, sleeping or eating "well", they do so with respect to what is normal for them, and can monitor change or directional differences as significant without reference to what that 'normal' actually amounts to by any standardized mean or median measure. And the virtue of a diagnostic category that has an "empty" baseline (i.e. it is your own judgement of normal rather than, for example, a median measure in a population) is that anyone can tell you (or a doctor) if they are sleeping or eating well or not without ambiguity. And this is precisely the 'definition' that is required for this purpose – your sleep has been disturbed because you have not been getting your usual 5, 7, 8 or whatever hours. That is to say that according to Sacks these lay measuring categories do not operate as "rough versions of something that is mathematicalizable" – there is no need in many situations, and it is certainly not a reference to statistics in a general population.

The overall point Sacks is trying to make is that the reason lay measurement systems operate with a measure of vagueness is precisely that it makes them intelligible without reference to a baseline. He explains this with reference to the notion of what it means to be "driving fast", where what is interesting to him about that assertion is that we do not require a measurement from a speedometer to understand what it means. We can say that someone is driving fast or slow with respect to traffic, with respect to the state of a particular road, with respect to some specific individual's general driving habits and these are not statements that need to be validated with specific measurements. It is often a case of a figure-ground relation where the ground is, for example, the relative speed of the rest of the traffic and other aspects of context. None of this means that a baseline shouldn't be established for measurable phenomena, when it is relevant to do so. But in the case of fitness trackers, and perhaps more generally the quantification of the self, it is legitimate to ask whether these measurement systems actually make sense, as well as quite simply, are they useful?

In the case of fitness devices, what we have is a standardized measurement system (steps/calorie consumption calculation) that is typically used to measure specific or discrete physical activities (e.g. going for a run, or training), turned into a generalized tracking system that aims to provide a measure of general fitness. But what these devices are giving to users, along with the standardized measurement system is an arbitrary baseline of 10,000 steps a day which is even not really well-suited for everyone [32], and an arbitrary set of objectives to measure directional differences as constituting progress. Fitness is a vague category and fitness trackers are not diagnostic devices, so when the users don't buy into specific objectives as part of a training regime with serious purposes and goals (as an athlete or serious amateur might do – e.g. running 10 miles under a specific time) the game mechanisms that are overlaid onto the basic step/calorie count run the risk of coming across as unfair, confusing or arbitrary because they may contradict an individual's own perception of a what good effort or progress might be with respect to their own "normal" [13].

**There Is No Magic in the Device** Smart device are sometimes marketed as *magic devices* that user just has to wear in order to appreciate their benefits. They are ready to go out-of-the-box, require little work on the part of the consumer and will somehow share some the burden of life-style change with the user. Instead we find that the motivation toward change has to come from the user (and potentially their social support network) and that the technology can then support the change with measures and records whereby progress can be easily viewed. Our study, with others, supports that without any initial motivation or will for change, and personal goals the device doesn't bring anything else than raw data and badges.

**Collaborative and Organizational Issues Related to the Use of Activity Trackers Within the Workplace** If we were to consider the use of activity trackers in organizational environments as has been done in other studies [9, 24], many issues would have to be considered first. Our study pinpoints many of them such as the privacy concerns, the length of use and involvement, the extra-work associated or the reward mechanisms. There are obvious reasons why the activity tracking ecosystems offered by these kinds of devices would be attractive to an organization (and in particular, to Human Resources departments within organizations). They claim to offer a solution to the hitherto largely unaddressed issue of providing incentives to raise the overall baseline for health and fitness in the workplace. And they come with a ready-made measurement system which on the surfaces of it fits the requirements for standardization and accountability of any large organizational bureaucracy. On this latter point, what we learned from our study is that the measurement system offered by these activity trackers perhaps fits the organizational bureaucracy too well. It reduces a socially complex and hard to define concept like "fitness" to an easily measurable baseline (step-counting), it gives an illusion of accuracy and accountability by producing visualizations and reports, and holds individual performance unfairly up against arbitrary goals which suit the collective (the organization), but don't necessarily constitute a fair assessment of individual efforts and improvements. It is also often envisaged that there would be a direct collaborative dimension to these trackers involving employee comparisons, leader boards, buddy systems and so forth. Given the weaknesses and ambiguities in the data along with privacy concerns and reluctance to share, we question the viability, acceptability and even the ethics of this proposal. For all these reasons, even if all privacy issues were to be properly addressed, we would still recommend extreme caution in formally introducing activity trackers in the workplace and tying the activity tracking ecosystem to financial or any other kind of organizational incentives.

Finally, our study show the complexity of such programs including smart devices and the socio-technical aspects of them, in terms of skills, program definition, and management engagement.

## 3.8  Conclusion

In this paper we explored and assessed the use of activity trackers within the workplace. We set up a study where we focused on a situation of pushed self-tracking where the users engaged in self-tracking practices with the initial incentive coming from their company or a relative. The finding reveals that the use of activity trackers in that context is neither straightforward nor long-term. Users experienced many kinds of frustrations that are based on the engagement required to get accurate data, on the limits of the device, the limited value of the data, and on the gamification set-up based on simplistic models – in summary the accuracy and relevance of the device and data for particular personal needs and circumstances. Another core finding that relates to the pushed self-tracking in the workplace is the issue of privacy and related issues of ownership and control. This study shows various concerns relating to the accuracy of the data, who may access the data and the purpose of collecting data. Pushing activity trackers onto employees without addressing these issues is unlikely to be the best way to engage users or employees in a health oriented change management process. To conclude our findings highlight the limits in using current activity trackers in workplace wellness programs.

## References

1. Arena R, Guazzi M, Briggs PD et al (2013) Promoting health and wellness in the workplace: a unique opportunity to establish primary and extended secondary cardiovascular risk reduction programs. In: Mayo clinic proceedings. Elsevier, Amsterdam, pp 605–617
2. Brown B, Reeves S, Sherwood S (2011) Into the wild: challenges and opportunities for field trial methods. In Proceedings of the SIGCHI conference on human factors in computing systems ACM, New York, 2011, May. pp 1657–1666
3. Calvo RA, Peters D (2013) The irony and re-interpretation of our quantified self. In: Proceedings of the 25th Australian computer-human interaction conference: augmentation, application, innovation, collaboration, ACM, New York, November. pp 367–370

4. Cercos R, Mueller FF (2013) Watch your steps: designing a semi-public display to promote physical activity. In: Proceedings of the 9th Australasian conference on interactive entertainment: matters of life and death, ACM, New York, September. p 2

5. Chan CB, Ryan DAJ, Tudor-Locke C (2004) Health benefits of a pedometer-based physical activity intervention in sedentary workers. Prev Med 39(6):1215–1222

6. Choe EK, Lee NB, Lee B, Pratt W, Kientz JA (2014) Understanding quantified-selfers' practices in collecting and exploring personal data. In: Proceedings of the SIGCHI conference on human factors in computing systems, ACM, New York. pp 1143–1152

7. Fitbit. https://www.fitbit.com/

8. Fritz T, Huang EM, Murphy GC, Zimmermann T (2014) Persuasive technology in the real world: a study of long-term use of activity sensing devices for fitness. In: Proceedings of the SIGCHI conference on human factors in computing systems, ACM, New York. pp 487–496

9. Goldberg L, Lockwood C, Garg B, Kuehl SK (2015) Healthy team healthy U: a prospective validation of an evidence-based worksite health promotion and wellness platform. Front Publ Health 3

10. Guo F, Li Y, Kankanhalli MS, Brown MS (2013) An evaluation of wearable activity monitoring devices. In Proceedings of the 1st ACM international workshop on personal data meets distributed multimedia, ACM, New York, October. pp 31–34

11. Jawbone. https://jawbone.com/up

12. Klasnja P, Consolvo S, Pratt W (2011) How to evaluate technologies for health behavior change in HCI research. Proc CHI'11

13. Lazar A, Koehler C, Tanenbaum J, Nguyen DH (2015) Why we use and abandon smart devices. UbiComp '15 Adjunct, September 07–11, 2015, Osaka, Japan

14. Li I, Forlizzi J, Dey A (2010) Know thyself: monitoring and reflecting on facets of one's life. In: CHI'10 extended abstracts on human factors in computing systems, ACM, New York, April. pp 4489–4492

15. Li I, Medynskiy Y, Froehlich J, Larsen J (2012) Personal informatics in practice: improving quality of life through data. In: CHI'12 extended abstracts on human factors in computing systems, ACM, New York, May. pp 2799–2802

16. Lim BY, Shick A, Harrison C, Hudson SE (2011) Pediluma: motivating physical activity through contextual information and social influence. In: Proceedings of the fifth international conference on Tangible, embedded, and embodied interaction, ACM, New York, January. pp 173–180

17. Lupton D (2014) Self-tracking modes: reflexive self-monitoring and data practices. Paper for the 'Imminent Citizenships: Personhood and Identity Politics in the Informatic Age' workshop. ANU, Canberra

18. Lupton D (2014) Self-tracking cultures: towards a sociology of personal informatics. In: Proceedings of the 26th Australian computer-human interaction conference on designing futures: the future of design, ACM, New York, December. pp 77–86

19. Mackinlay MZ (2013) Phases of accuracy diagnosis: (in)visibility of system status in the FitBit. Intersect Stanford J Sci Technol Soc 6(2):1–9

20. Macvean A, Robertson J (2013) Understanding exergame users' physical activity, motivation and behavior over time. In: Proceedings of the SIGCHI conference on human factors in computing systems, ACM, New York, April. pp 1251–1260

21. Mattke S, Liu H, Caloyeras JP, Huang CY, Van Busum KR, Khodyakov D, Shier V (2013) Workplace wellness programs study. Rand Corporation

22. Meyer J, Simske S, Siek KAGurrin CG, Hermens H (2014) Beyond quantified self: data for wellbeing. In: CHI'14 extended abstracts on human factors in computing systems. ACM, April 2014, pp 95–98

23. Morozov E (2014) To save everything, click here: technology, solutionism and the urge to fix problems that don't exist. Penguin Books, London

24. Norman GJ, Heltemes KJ, Heck D, Osmick MJ (2015) Employee use of a wireless physical activity tracker within two incentive designs at one company. Popul Health Manag 19(2): 88–94

25. Proper KI, Singh AS, Van Mechelen W, Chinapaw MJ (2011) Sedentary behaviors and health outcomes among adults: a systematic review of prospective studies. Am J Prev Med 40(2): 174–182
26. Quantified Self. http://quantifiedself.com
27. Rooksby J, Rost M, Morrison A, Chalmers MC (2014) Personal tracking as lived informatics. In: Proceedings of the 32nd annual ACM conference on human factors in computing systems (CHI'14). ACM, New York, pp 1163–1172
28. Sacks H (1995) Lectures on conversation, vol 1 and 2. Blackwell, Malden
29. Shih PC, Han K, Poole ES, Rosson MB, Carroll JM (2015) Use and adoption challenges of wearable activity trackers. In: Proceedings of the iConference 2015
30. Swan M (2012) Sensor mania! The internet of things, wearable computing, objective metrics, and the quantified self 2.0. J Sens Actuat Net 1(3):217–253
31. Swan M (2013) The quantified self: fundamental disruption in big data science and biological discovery. Big Data 1(2):85–99
32. Tudor-Locke C, Hatano Y, Pangrazi RP, Kang M (2008) Revisiting "how many steps are enough?". Med Sci Sports Exerc 40(7):S537
33. Withings. http://www2.withings.com/us/en/products/pulse/
34. Yang R, Shin E, Newman MW, Ackerman MS (2015) When fitness trackers don't 'Fit': end-user difficulties in the assessment of personal tracking device accuracy. UbiComp '15 Adjunct, September 07–11, 2015, Osaka, Japan
35. Young JM (2006) Promoting health at the workplace: challenges of prevention, productivity, and program implementation. NC Med J 67(6):417–424

# Chapter 4
# "You Cannot Grow Viscum on Soil": The "Good" Corporate Social Media Also Fail

**Federico Cabitza, Angela Locoro, and Carla Simone**

**Abstract** The paper illustrates the adoption of an Enterprise Social Media in a multinational corporation: the primary goal was to support the sharing of experiences among its members and to facilitate their collaboration. The paper highlights the outcomes and the problems that have been encountered in the effort to link this initiative to the achievement of the goals mentioned above, and tries to summarize the main reasons of these problems. The study adopted a research design in which an online questionnaire was administered to the corporation employee. By analysing the responses, we distilled the major points raised by the employees, among which lack of interest and use. The discussion focuses on the lessons that we drew from this experience on how an Enterprise Social Media should be introduced within organizations, e.g., by considering integration with other systems and the inadequacies emerged during the pilot experience.

## 4.1 Motivations and Background

In this paper we will report of an acceptance study of an *Enterprise Social Media* (ESM) in a big, multinational corporation counting more than one thousand employees distributed worldwide.[1] The concept of ESM is broad and fuzzy and in the academic literature there is not yet a commonly accepted definition [13]. Besides ESM, scholars also use expressions like *corporate social networking sites* [28], *corporate social tools* [17], and *enterprise social software* [9] to denote in short any "organizational system and tool which utilizes Web 2.0 technologies to stimulate participation through informal interactions" [9, pp. 92–97].

---

[1]The name of the company as well as the name of the ESM will be left voluntarily anonymous due to the non disclosure agreement.

F. Cabitza (✉) • A. Locoro • C. Simone
Università degli Studi di Milano-Bicocca, Viale Sarca 336, 20126 Milano, Italy
e-mail: federico.cabitza@disco.unimib.it; angela.locoro@disco.unimib.it;
carla.simone@disco.unimib.it

© Springer International Publishing Switzerland 2016                                57
A. De Angeli et al. (eds.), *COOP 2016: Proceedings of the 12th International Conference on the Design of Cooperative Systems, 23–27 May 2016, Trento, Italy*,
DOI 10.1007/978-3-319-33464-6_4

The concept of ESM can then subsume a whole ecology of more or less sophisticated tools, which McAfee popularized with the catch-all phrase of "enterprise 2.0" [18] to hint at technologies like message boards, blogs, wikis, friend and contact networks, activity streams and file, photo, and video shares" [29] that are used in an enterprise domain for their potential to "knit together an enterprise and facilitate knowledge work in ways that were simply not possible previously".

The difficulties in framing a precise definition of ESM lies, not so paradoxically, in the simple idea that they are but social media used within an enterprise, that is closed social groups and communities that are organized for and managed toward commercial purposes.

In our case study we focus on a phenomenon that is often overlooked: good technical means, like state-of-the-art technologies, can fall short of achieving the socially-oriented purposes that motivated the necessary investment not because of intrinsic shortcomings or design flaws. But rather because, when these tools are moved from a prototypical dimension to be deployed at a large scale corporate level, the dynamics of participation and care [10] that have been effective "in the small" [4] are difficult to be scaled up: adoption and user satisfaction do not follow the mere validation at the level of functional and non-functional requirements [26], and regard the integration of the technical element [8] (the mistletoe plant mentioned in the title) into an existing social milieu (the tree where usually mistletoe grows), or also the challenge to fill in the gap between the social and the technical in an organization [1].

In reporting a sort of failure story, we will make the case that the social aspects that are inevitably connected with the success of social media in real environments cannot be coped with the traditional approaches of IT product delivery; and that further research is needed to explore new and bolder solutions, like to abandon the traditional approach to the design-development-deployment cycle in favor of a more constructivist one [6], where the tool grows and develops with the users, their expectations and initiatives, also and above all with the contribution of the users themselves. Social media is a paradigmatic case to explore this latter idea, as almost all of the content that they mobilize is produced by the users, and their motivation to contribute cannot be imposed from above.

After a concise review of the pertinent literature (see Sect. 4.2), in Sect. 4.3 the paper presents the antecedent of the case study. As anticipated above, this regards the perception of a full-fledged ESM by the employees of the multinational company mentioned above. While we present the results from the adoption-oriented and survey-based user study in Sect. 4.4, Sect. 4.5 closes the contribution with a discussion of the findings and themes that we extracted from the field.

## 4.2   Framing the Object of Study

As said in the previous section, we focus on the perceived low satisfaction of a technically successful ESM. Before delving into the details of the case study, we need to frame the object of study, by better characterizing the essential elements that can be found in an ESM, generally speaking. To this aim, we performed a literature review, which we briefly report in terms of three main dimensions articulated in the following points:

**For whom** – As said above ESM are social media used in the organizational context. However, a distinction can be done if these tools are used to either foster communication with the company customers (B2C) [24]; with the partners and suppliers (B2B) [14]; among its employees [5, 11]; or – possible in theory but much more difficult in practice –to connect all these stakeholders together, both the internal and the external ones. Moreover, it should be made a distinction between those who create content, i.e., the nodes of the overlapping social networks and the actual users of the ESM, and who monitors the evolution of the networks and the content flow among the nodes, in the wings so to say, to get indications of corporate performance and elements for resource management and strategic planning.

**Why** – The explicit and more direct aim of an ESM is to support and improve the quality of the social interactions within an organizational context in the idea that this would positively impact the business performance [16, 19, 30]. This is usually done by leveraging the (social) networks established for a number of more or less explicit purposes, or enabling the creation of new ones. These purposes and the target communities affect how ESMs are proposed and promoted within an organization, and what functionalities they afford, whether mainly communication-oriented [16], innovation-oriented [3], or collaboration-oriented [7]. In particular ESM can be seen as the enabling tool supporting initiatives of company building and brand identity [23], the continuous training of the employees, the increase of the corporate "social capital" [21], which is also declined in terms of the pragmatic need to find the available experts [5] and tap in existing expertise [2], knowledge sharing [20], and idea generation and circulation [33].

**How** – The complexity of any organizational setting requires that the introduction of an ESM is carefully planned [15] and even more carefully evaluated over time, to conceive and enact the necessary adjustments for its evolution and effective use. In fact, the adoption and success of an ESM, differently from any application that is used in a corporate domain (whose use is not optional but rather mandatory), highly depends on the motives driving the employees to use it. As noted in [11], ESM users usually use it to achieve three concrete individual-level purposes: connecting with co-workers; advancing individuals' careers within the company; and campaigning for projects. Complementarily, Richter and Riemer [25] focus on the *use value* of (participating in a) ESM, which they trace back to the opportunistic value of increasing the number of acquaintances (i.e., the social network) to potentially turn to in case of need (cf. the notion of social capital by Putnam and Lin). Therefore, for the interrelation and intersection of personal and institutional interests, the assessment of the impact of the introduction of ESMs in terms of positive or negative outcomes, return of investment and other measurable business performance indicators has proven to be a difficult task [13, 19]. Benefits are reported anecdotally in terms of social capital development [31], business processes improvement, and faster decision making [27].

In light of these dimensions, we will focus on an ESM designed and established to explicitly foster *intra-organizational* collaboration and communication, but that, in the words of the promoters, was also aimed at addressing a number of results in the broad spectrum mentioned above spanning from internal communication to knowledge management, and in particular to stimulate the active participation of the employees in sharing their work practices and new ways to improve them.

## 4.3   Before the Study: "Think Big, Start Small, Scale Fast!"

About 5 years ago the above mentioned company planned the introduction of an ESM for its employees, who were distributed in a number of branches, a big part of which established abroad. To this aim, the top management commissioned the ICT division to develop a desktop (Web-based) application that had to be state-of-the-art with respect to the typical ESM functionalities, such as profile editing, content sharing, people search and the management of personal contacts.

The decision to make such a complex application in-house as a proprietary asset [16] was motivated by two main needs: to protect the potentially confidential information that was expected to flow through the ESM; and to have the full control and a fine-grained visibility of the development process of its functionalities, so as to prioritize and tailor them to the corporate needs. The requirements collected during the design phase mirrored the top management will to invest on the ESM to get a positive impact on the business performance. For this reason, the ESM was intended to support only the social interactions that directly concerned work-related needs or topics and was endowed with functionalities that could be useful to both socialize and work.

Thus, users could create and edit their personal profiles by specifying many options and providing rich descriptions; on the user perspective, this was clearly a way to richly present oneself to the community but, on the corporate one, it was also a way to get up-to-date information and complement what already stored in the records of the personnel department. Users could also receive notifications about the latest corporate news, so as to enrich and integrate the internal communication memos. Location status updates were generated and dispatched by the platform automatically: this was aimed at increasing a sense of connection and co-presence among colleagues, but also improve the monitoring capabilities of the managers. Users could also upload documents and other resources (videos, pictures) to be shared with specific people; this clear collaboration-oriented feature also allowed the emergence and indexing of lots of content that otherwise would have kept private and local to the personal repositories of single employees. Similarly, the capability to exchange messages within one's network of contacts allowed for both the increase of personal communication, but also for the emergence of interactions that once had been totally oral and hence doomed to oblivion. Lastly, but not less important. the ESM also allowed users to create, or alternatively join, virtual "meeting rooms". These latter ones were intended to be devoted collaborative spaces where interested people could meet virtually for common projects, discuss specific topics, and address circumscribed issues with selected participants. Inspired by how real co-located teams coordinate tasks and how people exchange valuable information also in informal occasions (cf. [22]), these rooms were seen as private group chatting rooms, where also electronic resources could be shared.

The top management decided to identify a small division, part of the ICT department, where the basic functional and usability requirements of the ESM could be collected, deployed incrementally, tested on-the-go, and refined according to the continuous feedback collected from the field and by a dedicated and responsive ticketing service.

Identifying the beta testers of the ESM among the members of the ICT department looked at first a reasonable choice. First, this made the interaction loop between beta users and developers short and tight: the division counted about 50 people and they all shared a common background if not a direct acquaintance; second, the Chief Information Officer (CIO) was genuinely interested in investigating the impact of an ESM in the fostering and management of innovation processes in software production. This was mainly due to his belief that an ESM would facilitate the corporate-level strategic decision to adopt cloud computing services, in order to supply software solutions to the whole company and its customers: in a company where employee turnover was among the lowest ones at national level, the CIO's idea was to foster a company climate where the older employees could want to share their experiences from the field of work while also updating their skills and acquiring new competencies, the young would want to "emerge from the shadow" (to quote his expression), and all of the employees to creatively react to the technological challenges posed by these new strategic directions. In Sect. 4.5 we will see how this choice could have prevented the decision makers from expecting potential problems related to the e-literacy of the average company employee, who differed from the average ICT employee.

The pilot test was perceived as highly successful: first, the ESM was delivered according to the plans, that is within the schedule and the intended budget; second, simple quantitative indicators of voluntary use, like the number of profile updates, uploaded documents, posts, exchanged messages, were considered fair and coherent with the overall engagement of the small community of beta users. Furthermore, the ESM was successfully used to promote and host a series of *contests for ideas*, which exploited the functionality of the "virtual rooms" to keep idea discussion and selection focused and effective. These contests, which were aimed at selecting and awarding the best ideas on how to implement new processes and models to improve the quality of the relationships with both the internal and external customers, had been purposely conceived as sort of "fertilizing seeds", to foster participation and feed the ESM with genuine and valuable content from the beginning.

This makes this experience similar to the case illustrated in [33], where the main goal was similarly to stimulate the collaborative generation of ideas with the strong commitment of the top managers involved (including the CIO). The main difference lies in the explicit role of the adopted ESM itself: in the latter case, the role of the ESM was to improve the transparency of core decision processes that the organization perceived as mysterious and opaque; in the pilot case we are reporting instead, the main role was to raise the awareness of the employees about the opportunities of career advance and professional development created by the strategy of *"going cloud"*, rather than to see this as a threat to established positions and traditional competencies.

After this successful pilot, in 2014, the corporate top management decided to open the ESM to all of the departments and employees. On the strength of the positive feedback during the pilot of the ICT department, the company invested in a multi-channel communication campaign aimed at illustrating the positive impact of the initiative on that branch of the company, the state-of-the-art features of the ESM, the importance of "going social" after the worldwide success of generalist social networking sites like LinkedIn and Facebook, and the projects of either competitors or similarly wide corporates (e.g. [5, 11]).

At the beginning of 2015, after observing low scores associated to the quantitative indicators mentioned above, the company involved us in a small project to collect feedback from the shop floor and try to understand why the ESM seemed to lag in reaching full and widespread adoption.

To this aim, we co-designed with the Internal Communication office of the company an online questionnaire by which to collect the opinions of the ESM users about the perceived value of the ESM and its perceived strengths and weaknesses. The survey was considered a feasible means to reach as many employees as possible, also due to the fact that many of them were located in different places and in different countries. The following sections describe the results and discuss the main themes we could extract from the feedback given by the survey participants.

## 4.4   The User Study

The questionnaire-based survey was advertised through the home page of the corporate portal and left open for 1 month. A hyperlink to the questionnaire was also available in the home page of the ESM, but no personal invitation was sent by email. Participation was voluntary and particular care was paid to assure participants that their answers would be kept anonymous by the platform at any step; consequently, no incentive was associated to participation. This could partly explain the fact that when the survey was closed, only 180 complete questionnaires had been collected. Although this number represented a small portion of the whole corporate personnel, it was considered sufficient by the management to get a first feedback about the ESM and by us to inform our research study.

The questionnaire encompassed items where the respondents had to check one or more options (often yes/no), express a level of agreement or appraisal on a 6-value ordinal scale, or leave a free text comment of any length. This mix of closed-ended and open-ended questions was considered critical to get clear and simple indications to be evaluated through statistical analysis (mainly binomial tests and proportion tests), as well as valuable suggestions and comments to be considered more qualitatively so as to surrogate the lack of structured interviews. Interviews were considered both an unfeasible and unreliable technique to adopt in that company, for its dimension and for confidentiality issues, respectively.

As a first question, the questionnaire included a common and simple measure of user satisfaction, the Net Promoter Score (NPS). This score is obtained by asking the respondents to indicate in a 1–10 scale the likeliness by which they would recommend their colleagues to join and use the ESM if they had not yet done it. The resulting NPS was −68, a very low value obtained by subtracting the proportions of so called promoters, i.e., those indicating 9 or 10 in the scale above mentioned (9 %), the proportion of detractors (77 %), i.e., those giving a value from 1 to 6. In short, very few people would recommend their colleagues to spend time on the ESM for any practical purpose and this alone could explain the poor quantitative indicators of adoption that motivated the user study.

Moreover, when respondents were asked whether the ESM *could become* an effective tool to support work activities in the future, those who were clearly positive were in the same number of the clearly negatives (20 % vs. 20 %). However, the uncertain respondents, i.e., those who chose the middle value in the ordinal scale, showed a slightly positive attitude (.60 vs. .40, p = .048.[2])

This partial opening to a better appraisal of the tool could be explained in terms of a still little knowledge of the potential of the tool. Indeed, the second item confirmed that the self-perceived familiarity with the ESM was reported low by the respondents (.59 vs. .41, p = .014) after approximately 3 months since the go-live. To assess their knowledge of the application, the majority of the respondent sample chose the value '2' in an ordinal scale from 1 (no knowledge at all) to 6 (expert level); the median value was 3.

This little knowledge of the ESM could be only partly traced back to the fact that the campaign of communication about the tool was considered ineffective by the majority of the respondents, since the number of positive opinions and of the negative ones were very close and the difference in the proportions was not statistically significant (.51 vs. .49, p = .8).

This campaign targeted *use value* as the main concept that could drive the use of the ESM among the corporate employees. For this reason, advertisements and presentations were aimed at raising awareness of the multiple purposes that using the ESM would allow to achieve. The questionnaire then recalled those intended

---

[2]Proportions are indicated for negative answers vs. the positive ones, followed by the p-value of the binomial test performed on the null hypothesis that the proportions are equal – the lower the p-value, the more significant the differences.

functions of the ESM and asked the respondents to indicate their level of agreement with the claim that the tool was effective to those respect. This was aimed at a twofold objective: to understand whether the respondents could perceive the use value of the ESM; and also what kind of functions they acknowledged as the most relevant ones.

The respondents expressed a general and clear disagreement in regard to all the intended aims suggested in the questionnaire, except for the items regarding the potential: (a) to promote participation and collaboration in the internal projects of the company (.49 vs. 51, p = .9); (b) to improve the sharing and circulation of innovative ideas, best practices and lessons learnt across even distant corporate branches (.45 vs. .55, p = .27); (c) to improve mutual knowledge among colleagues even of those belonging to distant corporate branches (.45 vs. .55, p = .38); (d) to improve horizontal (peer-to-peer) communication (.46 vs. .54, p = .58); (e) to improve knowledge sharing and problem solving (.46 vs. .54, p = .5); (f) to improve the quality of the information regarding the human resources (e.g., their personal details, interests, competencies) (.49 vs. .51, p = .9); (f) to make the company employees more linked in and connected (.45 vs. 55, p = .27).

Although these findings could seem to represent a substantial agreement of the corporate staff with the ESM tenets advocated by its internal promoters, it should be noted that in no case the response proportions have been found to differ with a statistical level of significance.[3]

Conversely, disagreements were all statistically significant. The strongest disagreements were detected in regard to the claims that the ESM could increase the efficiency of decision making and work processes (.74 vs. .26, p = .000), improve the community resilience (that is the capability to confront unexpected difficulties, .68 vs. .33, p = .002) and help people in recognizing the talented employees or in letting the diligent ones gain due visibility (.69 vs. .31, p = .000). Similarly, the users disagreed on that the ESM could improve productivity (.64 vs. 36, p = .015); getting faster information retrieval (.67 vs. .33, p = .005); stimulating positive competitiveness among the employees (.66 vs. 34, p = .005); as well as to improve vertical (inter-hierarchical) communication (.62 vs. 38, p = .35).

Similarly significant (but lower) disagreements were expressed also for other important functions, that is the improvement of the quality of the information about the company projects and products (.62 vs. .38, p = .05); and the increase of the ability of the single ESM users to solve their daily problems or find the right colleagues to rely on to find effective help (.59 vs. 41, p = .04). This was an important aspect that motivated the initial investment on the ESM: therefore the same question was also reformulated in another item, getting even worse results (.64 vs. .36, p = .017). This is in line with the responses given for a third item that specifically focused on the usual practices of expertise finding. To that aim, using the ESM (e.g., by opening a specific virtual room), was one of the last resources

---

[3]In other words, in those cases it cannot be excluded that other surveys, involving other respondents, would yield different results.

considered by the respondents: only the 4 % used it, at the same level of reliance on emails and other social network sites (like LinkedIn). Conversely, asking to close colleagues (i.e., peer referral), asking to the managers of pertinent functional unities (i.e., hierarchical referral), and relying on personal memory were reported as the ways more often performed to find expert people and look for knowledgeable support.

## 4.5  Insights from the Field and Discussion

The questionnaire also encompassed a series of open-ended questions, which allowed the respondents to leave a free-text comment. In particular, the questionnaire invited the respondents: to leave a general and frank comment on the ESM and the questionnaire itself; and to choose three statements from a predefined list that better represented the ESM. In regard to this latter item, Table 4.1 reports the ranking of the predefined options among which the respondents could choose the most representative ones. Notably, claims of uselessness were chosen almost two times more frequently than those regarding utility (132 vs. 68). Negative statements were chosen more often than the positive ones (187 vs. 142).

In addition to the statistic analysis of the closed-ended items that we reported in the previous Section, we also analyzed the free-text comments by adopting techniques inspired by content analysis and Grounded Theory (GT). In the latter case, open, axial and selective coding were applied to identify parts of the responses that we could find similar in meaning, so that we could extract recurring concepts and then higher level categories characterizing the comments of the participants [32]. All of the coding tasks were performed by two authors iteratively, until a sufficient inter-rater agreement was achieved, and no new code or theme could be generated from the available data.

**Table 4.1** The ranking of the options available for the item "choose at most three statements to define the ESM better". (Only the items chosen by more than 10 % of the respondent sample are shown)

| | |
|---|---|
| It's a fad in the wave of the social networking hype | 31 % |
| It's useless since it is not clear its real application | 24 % |
| It's little intuitive and usable | 22 % |
| It's an Internal Communications project | 21 % |
| It improves the sense of belonging | 15 % |
| It's useful to have a better knowledge of the colleagues | 15 % |
| It's useful to find people to involve in new initiatives and projects | 14 % |
| It gives value to the human and informal factor | 13 % |
| It's not applicable to my work | 13 % |
| It's a waste of my time | 11 % |
| It's useless as similar external services already exist | 11 % |

**Table 4.2** The classification categories and the macro-themes extracted from the comments

| Axial coding | Open coding |
|---|---|
| Use value | Redundancy, usefulness, leisure, idea sharing, knowledge circulation |
| Social evolution | Innovation, care, self-improvement, continuous learning, skills, e-literacy |
| Social media aspects | Collaboration, communication, internal communication, dissemination, participation, self-visibility, netiquette |
| Symbolic value | Sense of belonging, emotions, company building, firm culture, participation |
| Technical evolution | Interoperability, accessibility, timely updates, closure, malfunctioning, usability |
| Obstacles and barriers | Control, censorship, working rhythms, informality |

To this aim, first we identified all of the meaningful statements (76) contained in the 50 comments left by the survey respondents. Then we classified each of them according to two different predefined code sets: whether they were positive, negative or neutral with respect to the ESM; and whether they regarded either social, technical, or socio-technical issues. Like in the case of the predefined statements (see Table 4.1) the negative statements were the majority (33), while we found 21 comments to be positive, and 12 to be neutral. For the others, the authors could not convene on a clear category. We also found that the majority of comments regarded social aspects, whereas 22 of the comments addressed technical questions, and 7 socio-technical matters.

Afterwards, we extracted the codes by which to label the statements identified above (cf. the "open coding" phase of the GT method); then, we gathered codes of similar content that allowed to group the statements together (the so called "axial coding" phase); and, finally, we created broad groups of similar concepts, or themes (the "selective coding" phase). The result of our coding is reported in Table 4.2 where in the columns we report all of the single categories extracted from the content of the comments, and the rows represent the axial codes (themes).

*Use value* and *technical evolution* were the themes that recurred most frequently in the respondents' comments. However, the latter theme was explicitly solicited from the respondents by means of an item that asked for suggestions and ideas for the improvement of the tool. The other recurring themes spanned uniformly in the socio-technical spectrum, from interoperability, usability and accessibility (technical concepts), to innovation, idea sharing and symbolic values, which conversely regard how the community appropriated the tool to improve the existing social dynamics and how the community's members perceive it from the inside. These latter socio-technical aspects were perceived both from the perspective of the opportunities unleashed by the ESM, and from the perspective of the obstacles and barriers that could prejudice the success of the ESM. In what follows we report the main macro-themes that we extracted in the content analysis along these two perspectives.

## 4.5.1 Value of the ESM

Around the 30 % of the comments addressed the issue of the use value of the tool. We define the use value of the ESM as the extent this tool was perceived useful and effective in helping its users achieve their business goals. To this respect the main issues were related to a lack of knowledge and understanding of what could be done with the ESM in concrete terms. In particular, many comments addressed the redundancy and overlap of some of the functions of the ESM with respect to other applications already available to the company employees, like institutional personal pages, synchronous messaging, and the institutional document management systems already in use within the various branches of the company as the main sources of information and contact. In the words of a respondent:

> At the moment it does not solve any real problem, so its use remains marginal. I would cut off some functionalities and I would improve others, such as document sharing and classification [...] Create an interface to the employees which enables to directly see which rooms have been created and which ones can be of interest; furthermore, they should consider to let [the ESM] be used by external collaborators and consultants also, as they are a valuable part and parcel of our working teams!

A similar complaint was raised by many with respect to the vocation of the company ESM to be a full-fledged social networking site. In this case, the overlap was perceived as even greater with other systems, like Facebook (for the management of the contact network) Twitter (for micro-blogging and news dispatch), and LinkedIn (for the similarity between its group discussions and the ESM rooms). The idea that the ESM should integrate different classical features in one single application to be used within the organizational borders was clear; however, the temptation to make comparisons was even stronger: when compared with the level of maturity of the above social media, the ESM was perceived as less user-friendly and appealing, and found to be too rigid in how content had to be structured in the virtual rooms. Still on the usability side, some reported the lack of an advanced search functionality that would make the tool a faster and more reliable source of information. The poor perception of some users could then be traced back to the inadequacy of timely updates, both in regard to the personal profiles and the corporate news, that made the ESM to seem a bare and deserted public square.

In short, the ESM was perceived as if still missing the intended role of trigger of new and complementary ways to socialize with colleagues, and to share with them ideas, advice and knowledge, as well as to make the enterprise culture and the employees' sense of belonging stronger. On the positive side, a few respondents found the ESM useful for continuous learning (especially to improve language skills), and to organize informal meetings and recreational activities in a bottom-up manner. Paradoxically, this latter strength of the ESM, i.e., to enable leisure activities and small talk among colleagues, was also perceived as a drawback for a tool intended to improve organizational practices: for those looking for formal documents, official and reliable information, and useful pieces of knowledge in serious conversations, informality, convivial chatter and other forms of shopfloor sociality were considered a sort of noise "muffling the useful signal".

The thematic rooms where you know that "real stuff" is gonna be shared are restricted access, for confidentiality issues. So you cannot peek at them, unless you ask the manager in charge. On the other hand, the open rooms seldom share serious documents that have been certified by someone, but rather provisional drafts and lots of waffling.

One comment explicitly recognized these two opposite poles, of formality and informality; however it perceived the ESM as "having a tremendous potential to be used as a valuable bridge between the formal organization and the informal communities the company hosts".

Only a few respondents (approximately the 10 %) stressed the importance of initiatives like the new ESM to improve the sense of belonging of the company employees, to enhance related symbolic values such as the company spirit, brand identity and firm culture, and to share lessons learnt and success stories across the corporate. These comments regarded more the value of the ESM at a symbolic and emotional level, leaving the socially functional and the merely technical component out of consideration.

### 4.5.2 Technical Evolution and Socio-Technical Barriers

Coherently with the closed-ended items, many respondents were aware of the problems that the ESM was having in terms of usability and flexibility and mentioned them to the survey promoters. That notwithstanding, we also detected a general awareness that most of the issues were but "sins of youth" and that feedback initiatives like the questionnaire itself and efficient ticketing would soon bring to a better system in line with the expectations of the vast and heterogeneous staff of the company.

I like the ESM very much as a project, much less as an application, and indeed I do not use it. However, even Facebook at the beginning had few users and must have seemed useless to those few trailblazers; today everyone uses it and finds it a convenient tool to communicate.

Rather, the main problem regarded how the ESM could be "inserted" in the existing practices of the many communities within the company, which were not only functionally but also culturally various. To this regard, a comment used the botanic metaphor of grafting.

The ESM does not come out of the blue. They deployed it in a multi-level company that already employs tens of big and small applications for its operating procedures. [...] It is proposed as a one-size-fits-all new application that could be used for disparate aims, but its linkage with other specialized tools is poor or absent. It's like they wanted to grow mistletoe on soil. They do take care of it, so they water it, and also pour fertilizers and nutrients on it; but then are surprised if this do not take root and flourish. Mistletoe needs a strong tree to grow, and there it yields its juicy berries.

Another comment shed light on the gap between perceived utility and potentiality and that probably the people of the company "have not understood what that social media is really for".

The professional nature of the EMS should be strengthened and its valence as an ICT tool for the business. [To this aim] the ESM should be more "evangelized" by proposing and pushing it as a new tool available and usable in the current projects [...] they should make it clear that it can improve communication within a distributed team, and that it can be used to share knowledge about specific project documents and resources, as it allows to talk of them *alongside of them*, in a more contextual manner.

Also the redundancy and interoperability problems with the existing corporate tools were seen as both technical (in terms of batch synchronization, standard exporting formats, and uniformity of fields and codes) and socio-technical barriers to the wider adoption of the tool. On the other hand, exploiting the legacy systems was also seen as a way to make the ESM reach a *critical mass* of users that could make membership and participation more natural and even spread by word-of-mouth and imitation [12].

The ICT people should better explain how to use the ESM and which the differences with respect to other systems of internal communication lie. Why should I use the ESM to write to a colleague if I have her email? Is there any complementariness or advantage? I don't see any. [...] It would be very important to integrate the ESM with [a legacy tool]. Now the systems do not speak to each other. I cannot access the ESM with the credentials of the other system and I should not subscribe anew to any novel tool they conceive of. If only they do both these interventions, the ESM can have a future and get not only niche use for very few aficionados (if this is *not* what they really want...).

### 4.5.3  Social Evolution Fostered by the Tool

Most of the positive comments viewed the ESM as a great tool to improve both the individuals, i.e., their e-literacy and social media skills, and their communities, in terms of mutual acquaintance and communication. Approximately the 15% of comments highlighted this, by appraising the creation of rooms where webinars had been made available and their participants could interact with the teachers, asking for clarifications and further materials. Indeed, the case of the rooms where native speakers had written conversations with other non-native colleagues on both professional topics and current news (both for Italian and English learners) was a success case of the first months of use of the ESM, and inspired further similar uses and experiences. The idea was that the ESM could give the opportunity to actually increase the number of the colleagues, and more importantly, the *kind* of colleague, with whom one could interact. While one's colleagues were usually those working at arm's length, in the same physical room, and hence working on the same things with similar competencies, the ESM rooms were seen as distributed "coffee machines" where to meet different people e.g., IT geeks and administrative officers, rookies and experienced project managers, and start conversations triggered by the room topic or aim.

That notwithstanding, other comments highlighted how distant the theoretical advantages were from being exploited by the shop floor employees. After all the

ESM was conceived and developed within the ICT department and its preliminary tuning involved people that already had a mid-to-high expertise with PCs and Web services.

> The problem is that the degree of readiness of most of the people working here for technological innovation is poor. Having a PC on your desktop does not mean that you know how to take full advantage of it; I personally know colleagues that have been using word processors and spreadsheets for decades without knowing most of their options, like formatting styles and simple formulas, let alone automatic indexes and macros. [...] You have to invest on people first beyond a minimal level, and then on the tools you want them to use. If you do it, then the tools could catch on and help you further invest on the people: it's a virtuous loop.

Approximately one comment out of ten also addressed the obstacles to the acceptance, appropriation and use of the tool. Some related to the sense of being controlled, even censored. This feeling was reported by some respondents who noticed how some of first rooms were closed and deleted "for alleged infringement of the ESM netiquette" which, however, was communicated only after that the first comments had been posted. This gave the impression that some designers or managers behind the ESM project were initially peeking at how the users get accustomed with the concept of room, and worse yet, at what content users used to create to "inhabit" those collaborative venues, and did not like it, deciding soon after to obstruct those habits and practices. The line between acceptable and improper uses of the corporate tool appeared immediately very fine: is speaking at length of the last elections in English for Italian employees indulge in small talk during working hours or time devoted to professional updating? Would the continuous and assiduous updating of one's own profile be considered by the supervisor a sign of professional narcissism or rather of care for the quality of the content available in the ESM?

> Is it legitimate the use of a social network during the working hours, even if it is the corporate one?
> I have begun to use [the tool] to refresh my language skills in a room where an English course was provided. However, this neither preparatory nor immediately related to my job. So I could have given the impression to steal working hours to the company and I quit the room. Maybe even the fact that I quit it could backfire on me. Am I paranoid, or what?

> Soon after the communication campaign pressing for the diffusion of the ESM among us, another campaign started. They called it of "awareness raising" on what should be written on the ESM and what not. I remember the case of one colleague being scolded because he had posted a picture of him at the beach. But he was at a salesperson periodic meeting that was held at a fashionable beach! To be frank, If I have to be afraid of what I write, I'd better not write...

The fear to expose oneself to the judging eye of the managers cannot be underestimated as a factor having the potential to condition participation, both in terms of quantity and quality. Improper use can relate not only to *what* it is shared or published and to *how much* it is (as it is quite obvious), but also to *when* something is shared. This is less obvious, because updates times in a ESM can provide indications of how often and when one employee gets access to work stuff outside her office hours, as well as give hints about one has a break, so to say, within those hours, especially if the current schedule given by the supervisor is very tight (and she knows it).

> It is a social media well done: it is a pity not to have time to use it properly. On the other hand, even if I had time to, I would hardly linger over it. It would be silly...

As said also in regard to the perceived use value, the informal nature that many employees associated the ESM with clashed with the idea of a tool aimed at supporting decision making and problem solving. Even besides the conceptual level, it was the concrete use of the system to disappoint those who seek available expertise and reusable knowledge. On the one hand, there was a general awareness that many conversations could convey useful pieces of information, advice and solutions, what it is commonly denoted as tacit knowledge; on the other hand yet, finding this knowledge when needed without proper functionalities of structured indexing, semantic tagging and effective full-text search could prove to be impossible.

> The idea is good on paper but there looking for usable information in it would be too time demanding. Looking for the right room where some issues could have been discussed and solved is easier said than done, especially if the number of rooms is huge (as the ESM promoters hope it will become soon). [...] if I need an information I know at least where to find it, or whom to ask to. Even in case I were so lost not to know where to turn, I'd hardly want to give this impression on everyone on a corporate level.[...]

As expected, we also found some negative comments regarding the inadequacy of any virtual tool in replacing *de visu* communication, even if the intended aim of the ESM was to complete traditional means and even triggers more encounters and physical interactions.

> I personally think that colleagues should meet in place and have opportunities to socialize in an authentic way [...] this form of communication cannot be replaced by anything else and it's even dangerous to think it can. The direct knowledge of people is always the best thing to attain and I am worried that the more we think of being connected [virtually], the less we are actually.

> I know my opinion could sound silly, but I think that the ESM actually reduces the number of opportunities to discuss in presence. You write someone for help and get a fast reply, which does not satisfy you. But you don't want to seem harassing and quit asking. You actually burnt it. Let alone group chats, the rooms [how the call them]. Would you call it a conversation? The whole thing is reduced to a spurious virtual chattering.

## 4.6 Conclusions

In the light of the themes extracted from our case study, we now wrap things up. Our paper contributes in a still neglected strand of research, which regards the socio-technical failure of apparently good software applications. It is also a contribution into a growing area of CSCW research: the domain of ESM. The most relevant studies in this area, also mentioned in Sect. 4.2, like [5, 11, 25], convene that the adoption of ESM is not specifically depending on the technical functionalities, or the degree they are valid, but rather on the different contexts in which the technology is deployed, that is on the fit between the technical and the social dimensions of the overall socio-technical system.

In [28], the authors claim that "despite the huge potential returns, few managers adequately invest in developing these kinds of networks [. . . and] experiences in real-world companies suggest that these entities can and should be actively managed, *albeit not with conventional forms of management*" (our emphasis). In the same vein, in [25] it is suggested that ESM are open systems, that is it is not possible to precisely define how and for what purposes they can be used. Therefore, understanding their impact requires understanding several factors, including the adoption strategy, the local conditions and the user expectations.

Moreover, the same authors claim that co-evolution is the suitable strategy to make the appropriation required by open technologies possible: co-evolution can be based on the transformation of technologies that users are familiar with, and/or on a strict involvement of the users in the technology design. This is also the idea that the experience we have reported in this work has suggested us. The care paid by the top management, which is a necessary element for the success of complex software applications in organizations [10], and that also in our study proved to be essential for the good impact of the beta version of the EMS in the ICT department, is simply not enough when a "good product" that is fit for a small environment is deployed "into the wild" of a greater organization.

The idea of *product*, and its deployment, must give way to the idea of *project*, and its participatory co-production. More importantly, the idea of care "from the above", which we argued [6] is effective in a paternalistic relationship between the top management and the shop floor, could be overturned in a more dynamic and creative relationship between the content producers (i.e., the EMS users) and the content consumer (both the EMS users and the top managers).

To recall a respondent's comment above, further research must be then performed on how to graft growing *network communities* [7] (the viscum, which incidentally in the flower language means goal achievement, success and prosperity) into already established and firm communities of practice (the tree). If the graft is successful, plant and tree can co-evolve and become a hybrid organism (known in botany as *viscum continuum*) that can thrive and yield innovative fruit and outcomes.

# References

1. Ackerman MS (2000) The intellectual challenge of CSCW: the gap between social requirements and technical feasibility. Int J Hum-Comput Int 15(2–3):179–203
2. Ackerman MS et al (2013) Sharing knowledge and expertise: the CSCW view of knowledge management. CSCW 22(4–6):531–573
3. Backhouse J (2009) Social media: impacting the enterprise. In: EMCIS, Izmir, pp 1–9
4. Bandini S et al (2007) WWW in the small towards sustainable adaptivity. World Wide Web 10(4):471–501

5. Brzozowski MJ (2009) WaterCooler: exploring an organization through enterprise social media. In: GROUP'09. ACM, New York, pp 219–228
6. Cabitza F, Locoro A (2016) From 'care for design' to 'becoming matters': new perspectives for the development of socio-technical systems. In: Spagnoletti P, De Marco M, Pouloudi N, Te'eni D, Vom Brocke J, Winter R, Baskerville R (eds) Reshaping organizations through digital and social innovation. Springer, New York. ISSN: 2195-4968
7. Cabitza F, Simone C (2012) Affording mechanisms: an integrated view of coordination and knowledge management. Comput Support Coop W (CSCW) 21(2–3):227–260
8. Cabitza F, Simone C (2015) Building socially embedded technologies: implications about design. In: Wulf V, Schmidt K, Randall D (eds) Designing socially embedded technologies in the real-world. Springer, London, pp 217–270
9. Christidis K et al (2012) Using latent topics to enhance search and recommendation in enterprise social software. Expert Syst Appl 39(10):9297–9307
10. Ciborra C (1997) De profundis? Deconstructing the concept of strategic alignment. SJIS 9(1):67
11. Di Micco J et al (2008) Motivations for social networking at work. In: CSCW'08. ACM, New York, pp 711–720
12. Grudin J (1988) Why CSCW applications fail: problems in the design and evaluation of organizational interfaces. In: CSCW'88. ACM, New York, pp 85–93
13. Holtzblatt L et al (2013) Evaluating the uses and benefits of an enterprise social media platform. JSMO 1(1):1
14. Jussila JJ et al (2011) Benefits of social media in business-to-business customer interface in innovation. In: MindTrek 2011. ACM, New York, pp 167–174
15. Kaplan AM, Haenlein M (2010) Users of the world, unite! the challenges and opportunities of social media. Bus Horiz 53(1):59–68
16. Leonardi PM et al (2013) Enterprise social media: definition, history, and prospects for the study of social technologies in organizations. JCMC 19(1):1–19
17. Majchrzak A et al (2009) Harnessing the power of the crowds with corporate social networking tools: how IBM does it. MISQE 8(2):103–108
18. McAfee AP (2006) Enterprise 2.0: the dawn of emergent collaboration. MIT Sloan Manag Rev 47(3):21–28
19. Miller M et al (2011) Social software for business performance the missing link in social software: measurable business performance improvements. Deloitte Center for the Edge, San Francisco
20. Moradi E et al (2012) The relationship between organizational culture and knowledge management. IJII 12(3):30–46
21. Nahapiet J, Ghoshal S (1998) Social capital, intellectual capital, and the organizational advantage. Acad Manag Rev 23(2):242–266
22. Orr JE (1986) Narratives at work: story telling as cooperative diagnostic activity. In: CSCW'86. ACM, New York, pp 62–72
23. Peruta A et al (2014) Organisational approaches to brand identity on social media: comparing brand websites and facebook pages. JDSM 2(1):91–102
24. Piskorski MJ (2011) Social strategies that work. Harv Bus Rev 89(11):116–122
25. Richter A, Riemer K (2009) Corporate social networking sites – modes of use and appropriation through co-evolution. In: ACIS 2009, Daegu
26. Riemer K et al (2012) Eliciting the anatomy of technology appropriation processes: a case study in enterprise social media. In: ECIS 2012, Barcelona
27. Schmidt R, Nurcan S (2009) BPM and social software. In: BPM 2009. Springer, Berlin/New York, pp 649–658
28. Sena J, Sena M (2008) Corporate social networking. IIS 9(2):227–231
29. Smith M et al (2009) Analyzing enterprise social media networks. In: CSE'09. IEEE, Los Alamitos, pp 705–710

30. Steinfield C et al (2009) Bowling online: social networking and social capital within the organization. In: C&T 2009. ACM, New York, pp 245–254
31. Steinfield C et al (2010) Social capital, ICT use and company performance. Technol Forecast Soc 77(7):1156–1166
32. Strauss AL, Corbin JM (1990) Basics of qualitative research, vol 15. SAGE, Newbury Park
33. Tierney ML, Drury J (2013) Continuously improving innovation management through enterprise social media. JSMO 1(1):1

# Chapter 5
# From Eco-feedback to an Organizational Probe, Highlighting Paper Affordances in Administrative Work

**Matthieu Mazzega, Jutta Willamowski, Yves Hoppenot, and Antonietta Grasso**

**Abstract** In this paper we present a pilot study of the Print Awareness Tool (PAT). We initially designed PAT as an eco-feedback tool for paper waste reduction, but in our pilot study, it proved additionally even more valuable as an organizational probe providing the opportunity to question organizational paper-based workflows in general. Our findings illustrate that this is particularly true for administrative work where individuals have little agency, i.e. control over the printing tasks and processes they are involved in. We saw, however, that to capitalize on this effect, and to gather and benefit from the knowledge coming to the surface, the tool has to be enriched and managed accordingly. In addition, our study also showed evidence of paper affordances for administrative work that go beyond those discussed in the literature so far. From our findings we finally derive design requirements to digitally support such affordances and to extend PAT from a paper waste reduction tool into an infrastructure that would support organizations with a paper to digital transition.

## 5.1 Introduction

In this paper we present results of a pilot study of the Print Awareness Tool (PAT). PAT is the productised version of a research prototype that was initially designed as a tool for paper waste reduction, targeting individual employees in a work setting. Its explicit aim was to raise awareness and reflection on individually decided transient printing, i.e. printing constituting either pure waste or being used for the informal organization of work. Indeed, paper waste is not negligible: industry reports [9] have shown that around 15 % (slightly varying in different industries) of the paper printed in an office environment is never collected from the printer. It directly ends

M. Mazzega • J. Willamowski (✉) • Y. Hoppenot • A. Grasso
Xerox Research Centre Europe, 6 chemin de Maupertuis, 38240 Meylan, France
e-mail: jutta.willamowski@xrce.xerox.com

© Springer International Publishing Switzerland 2016
A. De Angeli et al. (eds.), *COOP 2016: Proceedings of the 12th International Conference on the Design of Cooperative Systems, 23–27 May 2016, Trento, Italy,*
DOI 10.1007/978-3-319-33464-6_5

75

up in the waste basket. The same studies report that, while noticing waste, people do not relate it to their own behaviour and are not aware of their personal paper consumption.

To address this issue and to motivate employees to print more consciously, with PAT, we had followed a typical eco-feedback approach [8] providing the users with ambient awareness of their printing habits. With respect to the initial objective, the approach proved indeed effective: in a first experiment, described in [14], PAT made users reflect on their reasons for printing and think twice before hitting the print button. In consequence, they reduced unnecessary printing where they could and started using more digital alternatives, e.g. reading and annotating documents on screen instead of paper. Furthermore they optimized paper-based workflows to reduce printing when empowered to do so. Nevertheless, in a work setting the large majority of printing is not a personal decision, but mostly governed by well-established organizational work processes that are beyond the individual employee's control. Thus, in this first experiment, when questioning the necessity of the various print jobs they issued (or had to issue), PAT users spontaneously started to pinpoint paper intensive organizational work processes they were involved in, that they could not change, and that hindered them from printing less and "doing better". For us, this was a first intuition that, beyond deploying PAT as a personal paper waste reduction tool, i.e. targeting the individual employee, it could furthermore serve as an organizational probe creating the opportunity to discuss, question and reconsider more widely organizational paper-based workflows, especially in the context of organizational paper-reduction and paper to digital transition efforts.

The first experiment was carried out in a very particular setting: a research lab, with participants whom we all knew personally, and with whom we already interacted on a daily basis. It was thus natural for those participants to provide us with immediate and spontaneous feedback on their printing pain points, on the organizational processes forcing them to print, and sometimes even with suggestions for improvements. These reactions already gave us evidence that the tool could be extended and used more widely as a means to elicit printing processes to be optimized or even replaced completely. However, considering the industry reports on printing waste and the customer pull, the commercial units decided that there was already enough customer benefit to transfer the tool as it was, and to commercialize the resulting product (Fig. 5.1) as a paper waste reduction tool. Indeed, in the initial experiment the print consumption had decreased by around 10 % [14].

When the commercial unit engaged their first customer, they asked us to follow a pre-commercialization pilot, focussing on possible usability issues and verifying the tool's adoption among its users and its impact on their printing habits. We decided to accompany and study this pilot, to assist the business groups with the commercial productisation steps, and also, more interestingly for us, to confirm and extend the first analysis to a "real setting" outside a research organization.

In this new study, targeting mainly administrative work, PAT functioned indeed as an organizational probe. Yet, this effect was even stronger than in the initial experiment. As we will see, this difference is mainly due to the work role of the users involved. Indeed, in contrast to the first experiment where the participants

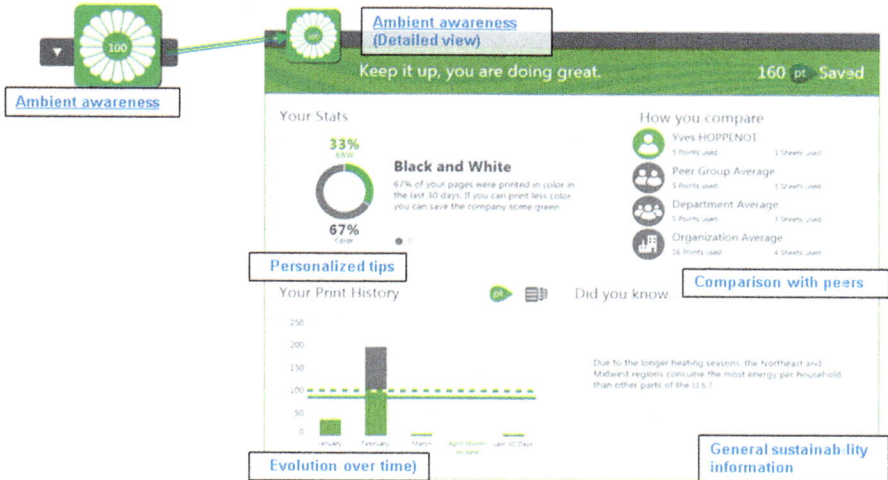

**Fig. 5.1** The print awareness tool providing ambient awareness of the user's personal print consumption and access to more detailed and comparative information

were for a large part researchers, i.e. knowledge workers who themselves control the major part of their printing (scientific papers to read etc.), the new study involved mainly administrative assistants who are more constrained by their workflows and hierarchy and who have essentially very little control over their printing. Indeed, the character of administrative assistants' work creates an antagonism. On one hand, administrative assistants typically have a particularly high print consumption that would be particularly desirable to target and reduce for the organization: this is why they had been chosen by the customer as first pilot users. On the other hand, they are among the most un-empowered employees with respect to taking decisions to reduce their print consumption. The reason is that they mostly print either for others, managers or team members, or in the context of established, even if often organizationally not well understood processes that they do not control.

Our study highlighted this particular character of administrative assistants' work, making it difficult for them to achieve paper (waste) reduction. However, it showed also that particularly for these users PAT creates the opportunity to express their printing pain points and to question the processes they are involved in, creating wider opportunities for print reduction. Beyond these insights, our study also uncovered novel paper affordances of administrative work, involving in particular recognition and expertise. To enable paper reduction and facilitate the transition from paper to digital those affordances have also to be considered. On the basis of these observations we derive design requirements addressing both aspects, the extension of PAT from a waste reduction tool to an enabler for paper to digital solutions, and the digital support for administrative paper affordances.

Our paper is structured as follows: we first describe the customer context and setup of our pilot study. We then discuss in detail the findings from this study. First of all, the study illustrates how PAT acts as an organizational probe, but also that it has to be accompanied by appropriate management actions to fully benefit from this effect. Second, our study highlights novel paper-affordances for administrative work, beyond those already well known and discussed in [11]: on one hand, paper makes the administrative employees' work accountable, visible and tangible, for themselves, but also for their colleagues and hierarchy. On the other hand, paper relates to and materializes those employees' expertise. These affordances have to be taken into account when attempting to smoothly replace paper with digital solutions. In the last section of our paper we reflect on how to embed PAT in a paper to digital transition effort and how to translate these affordances into proper digital metaphors when designing digital solutions.

## 5.2   Pilot Study

Following the positive results observed with the first internal PAT experiment in a research centre [14] and the traction the tool got when demoed at customer visits, it was transferred into a commercial product. Once this product available, the business groups as well as the first early adopting customer were keen to involve us in the pilot deployment. This gave us the opportunity to verify the intuitions and findings gathered from the initial experiment and to extend the analysis to a real setting.

### 5.2.1   Context

The customer is a well-established French retail chain, with proximity stores in many cities. PAT has been deployed in the group headquarters, where they have around 1200 employees managing the global activity of the company and aspects of its retail stores (HR, supply, global communication and legal support). The organizational structure is based on departments and services covering a large spectrum of activities – technical, financial, legal, etc. The same diversity exists in the professional roles ranging from assistants, to managers, controllers and administrators. The commercial purpose of our pilot study was to assess the appropriation of PAT by its users as well as to accompany the customer with the management of the tool on their site.

The first pilot was limited to 30 employees and started in May 2014. As paper (waste) reduction was the advertised objective of the product, considering their typically high paper consumption, the customer selected mainly administrative employees as pilot users: 21 out of 30 pilot users were administrative assistants. The participants worked in 12 different departments, with only 2 departments having more than 3 participants, IT (7 participants) and HR (13 participants). In consequence, the effort of the participating users was in some cases rather isolated, not involving the whole department or work group. This also meant that their managers were usually not involved in the pilot and thus only superficially aware of their assistant's involvement. This did not facilitate discussions about printing issues between assistants and their managers or team mates for whom they were printing documents.

Concerning our research-oriented study, it was mainly qualitative, but included also the analysis of some quantitative material, used to feed the commercial units with numerical results about the print volume reduction achieved. For the qualitative part, during three on-site visits, we conducted three workshops and two series of interviews with 11 users and the customer's local team managing the pilot on the site. For the quantitative part, we have extracted various empirical data from the client's print tracking database and collected complementary data during the pilot period. The analysis of the print volume showed a slight reduction, in the order of 5 %, was much less than in the first experiment, but still satisfying for the customer.

We will not further discuss how the tool helps to reduce paper waste as this was already done in [14]. In the remainder of the paper, we will rather focus on analysing why, in this case, the impact in terms of paper reduction was lower than in the first experiment. We argue that this is due to the little agency that the selected (administrative) pilot users have with respect to their printing tasks.

## 5.2.2 Beyond Paper Waste Reduction

One of the major findings with the PAT pilot was the opportunity it created for its users to discuss, appreciate, and/or criticize the relationship between their work and their printing habits. Whether during collective workshops or individual interviews, users expressed both motivation and confidence to express and share their personal opinions, tricks and pain points with respect to printing.

### 5.2.2.1 From Print Reduction to Workflow Assessment

We observed that the figures provided by the tool (Fig. 5.1) as well as the graphic representations presented during our workshops (Fig. 5.2) facilitated such discussions by offering the users an objectified view of their printing practices. As a first general insight, we were surprised by the considerable knowledge that individual users, and particularly assistants, showed regarding their printing patterns. This observation was reinforced by an experiment inspired from the concept of *ethno-mining* [1, 3] during the second series of interviews: For these sessions we prepared a set of graphics representing the user's print consumption over the last 3 months, addressing different temporal scales and aggregated according to different print job attributes (length, color/black and white, simplex/duplex . . . ). These visualizations showed the consumption either in detail for specific dates or weeks or as an average illustrating typical periodical consumption patterns, e.g. on the different working days (Fig. 5.2). We then asked the users to talk us through these visualizations.

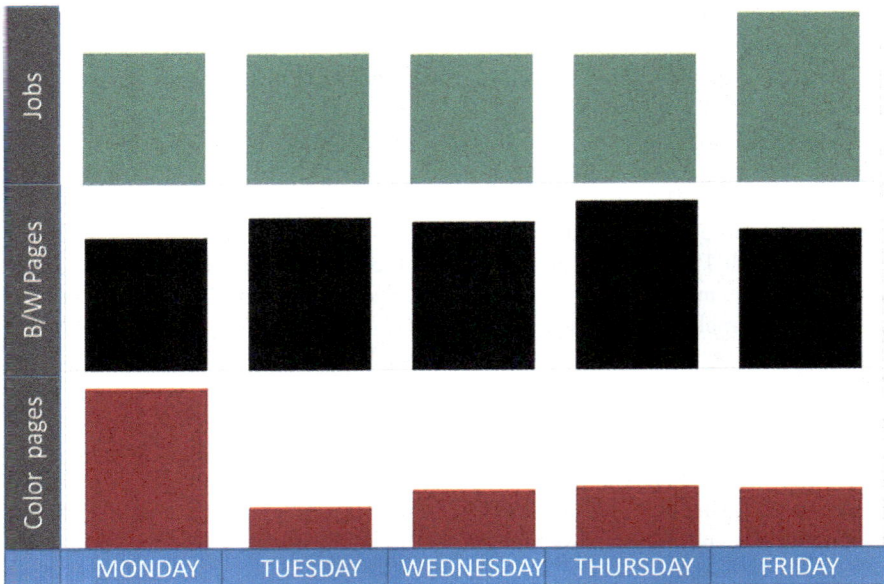

**Fig. 5.2** Visualization of the user's average weekday-specific print consumption (number of print jobs, paper consumption according to the print job characteristics, i.e. color, b/w ... )

We noted that assistants, when confronted with these visualizations, were particularly efficient in interpreting and explaining them. They easily put daily and weekly consumption patterns in relation with their work. One user for example explained her typically high color print consumption on Mondays (see Fig. 5.2) as corresponding to one of her typical workflows: she has to distribute a particular color document every Monday before noon. Another user explained that she is responsible for printing and distributing a specific set of documents to her whole team every third week of the month. Assistants also easily identified and recalled exceptional extra-printings, i.e. print jobs not pertaining to their regular and recurrent workflows. For example, an assistant named a particular voluminous color print job, executed 2 months before, to explain a high amount of color pages on that Tuesday's column. Assistants were able to make these connections in spite of their high daily print consumption and even when those print jobs occurred several months before. After all, this experiment also helped us to grasp and understand the general characteristics of the assistant's actual work in terms of types of tasks and rhythm.

As these examples illustrate, starting from the print consumption, organizational and workflow issues quickly came up during our interviews with admins. Indeed, admin work is often at the center of organizational workflows and admins are usually the ones responsible for executing corresponding printing tasks. In consequence, discussing print patterns often became an occasion to discuss the corresponding workflows in which the printing occurred. Initially designed for paper-waste reduction, PAT has thus rapidly created an opportunity to discuss administrative work in terms of paper-based processes. In that way, as [5] defines probes as "a means of collecting information", in parallel with its eco-feedback/awareness function, we found evidence that the deployment of PAT can be turned into an "organizational probe" generating qualitative data about paper-based processes. In our study this highlighted in particular the difficulties and/or lack of clarity of many organizational workflows admins were involved in. In the following, we discuss and illustrate the relationships between paper use and workflow assessment we observed, and enter in the details of the difficulties that emerged.

### 5.2.2.2   Unfolding Print Activities That Are "taken for granted"

During our on-site visits and our experience with ethno-mining most of the users explained that never before they had had the opportunity, time and space to discuss their daily work and their related printing habits and duties. In particular the graphic representations letting them see and appreciate their paper consumption allowed them to put their own work routines and organization in perspective. More generally, by exploring and assessing their printing patterns, admins objectified the processes they were responsible for in terms of rhythm and content. Interestingly, most of the interviewees explained that "traditionally" all these processes and workflows were taken for granted, that is to say never directly questioned. Conversely, during our interviews, some corresponding process pain points and limits were regularly tackled. One admin working in the training department explained:

> In my role here in this department, I'm responsible for collecting the different candidates' information and then to produce the listing for the next monthly training session. On the 15th, I have to print a paper version of this listing and handle it to the financial department. However, the list of participants often changes even after the deadline. Then I regularly have to reprint and resend updated versions of the listing. This can have an impact on my consumption on certain complicated months.

The issue tackled by this admin is particularly illustrative of how paper usage can point to more general and organizational issues. Here, the discussion about the printing pattern has identified a lack of optimization regarding a specific workflow. In the same way, another assistant, in the juridical department, described another issue:

> I was told to print this document [a sort of memo listing the various pieces contained by a case] at the end of each project and then to store it in this storage. It is "just in case" but I never had to present any of this yet. I don't know if it's really useful to continue to do this but as I was asked to ...

In both cases, those print jobs, and by extension the workflows generating them, as well as the issues they created in terms of paper consumption had never been discussed before. Embedded in the daily working routine, those printing tasks are often taken for granted and thus never questioned nor publicized by the admins. However, as our interviews showed, this indicates that the initial focus on print-reduction and print-awareness can in turn, and in a bottom-up fashion, generate observations and critical assessments of organizational workflows.

### 5.2.2.3   Questioning Paper-Based Workflows

Following our exploration of workflow limits and pain points raised by PAT users, the logical next question concerns the resources provided to the employees for raising and addressing those issues to eventually reduce their paper-consumption. When interviewees described pain points with workflows and tasks, we asked them if they knew how and with whom to tackle them. In the majority of cases, employees were able to identify neither the procedure to follow nor the person to contact. In the case of administrative assistants, while some processes were directly imposed by their manager and could therefore be questioned (at least if the assistant's relationship with her manager allowed for that), many others were more complex and related to the overall organization. Such printing tasks were usually explained and characterized by the admins as "organizational" - or "legal obligation". Even after discussion this categorization and its appropriateness remained ambiguous and unclear, both for the interviewees and for the interviewer. In the case of "organizational obligations", some users explained that they had to print a document so that the organization could keep track of the corresponding activity. These documents were then archived, often in the user's office, "just in case" (e.g. previous quotation). When we asked the users who decides on that process, most of them were unable to determine a process owner or designer but only knew that "it is like that". We made similar observations when users characterized printing as legal duty. When questioning, we often found out that those "legal" print-jobs were not legal per se but rather similar to the previously stated so-called "organizational obligation". For example, one interviewee described:

> Here we "double" everything as we are concerned by different legal obligations from external entities

This quote is particularly interesting as it combines two issues. On one hand, after discussion with this interviewee, only some (not all) of her duties were really concerned by "legal obligations". However, it had become a collective practice in her department to "double" everything, certainly for simplicity and commodity reasons. On the other hand, it is interesting to analyze how the "legal" motive is often presented, and thus understood, as an external and unsurpassable motive of mandatory printing. As a consequence, it is never questioned, neither by the admin nor by the department, even when those obligations and regulations may have changed over time. These observations highlight what would really be required to enable print reduction: first employees should be prompted and encouraged to question the various processes and printing tasks they are involved in instead of taking them for granted; second employees should be provided with concrete means to find out more about processes and tasks, enabling them to understand which of their processes and printing tasks are really mandatory and/or linked to legal obligations. All in all, the way in which this experience about paper-reduction has progressively slipped towards discussing work roles and organizational processes shows the complexity that surrounds paper artefacts and their central role in the workplace, both in a social and in a symbolic dimension.

### 5.2.3 Paper Affordances for Administrative Work

The ways in which paper documents support work has been deeply studied previously, especially in [11], uncovering a number of affordances that have to be taken into account when aiming at replacing paper documents with digital ones. The Myth of paperless office study has mainly addressed the *content* of work, with a focus on paper use in knowledge work, defined as producing and analyzing information. In our settings, we were focusing on administrative work and its relation to printed documents. As illustrated before, one particularity of administrative work, is the inscription of the *contents of the work* in structured and complex workflows. In parallel, we also found that the role of admin is particular in the way that paper supports its *character* and "significance with respect to the whole group" [7]. During our interviews and observations in admin work, we met various affordances of paper already identified in [11], but we also observed specific behaviors and cases where paper affordances support the accountability and *character* of the admin role.

#### 5.2.3.1 Personal Organization and Working Style

When we discussed with users about their printing habits and possible changes, some admins started pointing out their need to use paper for personal organization such as:

> The new recruits are really comfortable with screen reading and general informatics. But me, I need this [memo] on my desk . . .

Whether for memos or to-do lists, whether printed or handwritten, many admins explained that they need such material artefacts in order to organize and plan their various tasks. Some of them expressed fear to become less organized if they change this habit. Moreover, admins often receive urgent requests from their managers or colleagues and therefore have to update and adapt their task list and priorities regularly. Therefore, as shown in [11], pen and papers appears as the *"primary means of organizing the work and writing the plans"* (*p. 53*) echoing particularly with the fact that, for general admin work, organization and reactivity appear to be the main required characteristics. Admins also expressed their attachment to paper and printing for reviewing activities. In their daily work, admins have to read, asses and compile documents for their managers or teammates. Many of them expressed needs for printing in order to properly achieve those tasks, as described in [11]. In general, the ability to read efficiently, annotate and/or highlight information quickly has been raised by various interviewees as one of the essential paper affordances in administrative work. Consequently, for many participants, their print consumption associated to these activities and work duties cannot be reduced.

### 5.2.3.2  Supporting and Facilitating Other People's Work

Besides personal activities, the major part of an administrative assistant's work consists of supporting and facilitating *other people*'s work. For instance, besides having to do reviewing activities themselves, admins are often responsible for distributing documents – e.g. reports, presentations, data sheets – to their managers or team-members for review and validation. We observed that, in such cases, admins often unconsciously projected their own preferences onto their managers (or other third party) and explained that their managers would certainly *also* be more comfortable to do these tasks on a paper-based version of the document. For instance, two different admins explained:

> I know that is it easier to review and annotate on paper so I often give paper version to my manager as he'll be more comfortable to work on it.
> My manager prefers to read and adjust his presentation directly on paper; thus I have to print it for him.

In the first case, the need for a printed version seems projected by the admin onto her manager while in the second case the printing task seems to belong to the admin's duties to satisfy explicit manager requests. Similarly, some admins also justified that they often printed presentation slide decks before a meeting as preferable for their managers: then, even in case of a technical problem, the material would still be directly accessible during the meeting. Interestingly, we noticed that, again, those requirements had not always been clearly expressed by the manager him/herself, but sometimes only projected on him/her by the admin who prepared for all events, feeling somehow responsible for the success of her manager's meeting. These observations show that the role of admin consists also in facilitating and ensuring the success of her manager's work. Paper and printing can literally support this mission. It also highlights the fact that paper and print consumption is to a certain extent dictated by the role a user fulfils in the organizational structure. In the case of the admin, part of her consumption is directly impacted by her manager's duties and real or supposed preferences. Therefore changes and paper-reduction cannot be directly decided and adopted by a user alone, but only in agreement with hierarchy and colleagues, even for documents that are not part of organizational workflows, like paper versions of presentations projected in meetings. This illustrates that, in the context of a paper reduction effort, all concerned collaborators and work roles must be involved to understand and discuss related responsibilities and interdependencies.

### 5.2.3.3   Materializing and Assessing Work

During our interviews, and while we explored how users addressed possible changes in their printing habits, we also identified particular habits and "functions" of printing, related to the *character* of admin work and the way it is assessed. Indeed, when we asked users to explain their everyday work and print jobs, we realized that the amount of pages printed was perceived as related to – and representative of the amount of work achieved. Thus, for an assistant, for whom the majority of work consists in organizing, designing and distributing reports on behalf of the manager, the fact to print the report and to archive it can correspond to a personal need of recognition. For example, when wanting to show us the importance of his work, one admin opened his curtain and pointed to the documents stored behind:

> Look, here are all the reports and files I have produced during my career.

While he justified the printing and archiving through his need of "keeping a personal track" of his work, this shows that the print volume has a symbolic relationship with the importance and amount of work done by the individual. The use, presence and movement of paper are also meaningful in the organization and understanding of work. Its physicality makes things readily visible, tangible and graspable and this is clearly important to people. Thus, the paper on the desk has also a function of showing the actual rhythm of work. One assistant illustrated this point:

> Look at all these documents here; it refers to all urgent work I have to complete for my department. So, yes, my role here implies to be really responsive and organized.

Indeed, many assistants who explained that they are very busy and working 'just-in-time" illustrated this by pointing to the actual amount of paper sitting on their desks. This element also highlights the importance and affordances paper provides for work/performance assessments both personally, – where am I in my work – but also socially – providing others with information about my current workload [2].

### 5.2.3.4   Paper and Document Management as an Expertise

During our observations and visits, we also encountered situations where paper-reduction initiatives can have a negative impact on the work-related expertise of an employee. These are cases where the employee has specific printing related knowledge and expertise and where removing the corresponding printing part of a process would make this knowledge irrelevant. Once again, this printing expertise was particularly visible in the working area of assistants. For instance, one explained a particular process to us, where other assistants from her department have to retrieve specific letterheads from the reprography internal service and then place it carefully in the printer in order to print within a specific area of the sheet. She explained:

This is particularly tricky and you have to produce a proper printing before sending it. But yes as the times goes, it's easier

The assistant then explained that her colleagues regularly ask her for help as she manages to do it properly. Some time ago, new employees had complained about this difficult and time consuming task and proposed to simplify it. Due to legal reason – the head-letter is an official document with a complex template – their request was rejected. The assistant acknowledged this refusal in saying that some processes, especially legal ones, have to be kept as is and have to respect administrative constraints. This example is close to other situations we met. It shows that a specific printing task can represent a perimeter of expertise for an individual, and provide him or her with a "gatekeeper" role on the corresponding process. Such an employee is then recognized as the (only) one competent and expert in that process. Given that such process-specific knowledge is acquired over time, especially long term employees often have this kind of "expertise". For those individuals, changing the associated process can thus be problematic, because, at the same time, they would lose some of their expertise and personal value at the workplace.

## 5.3   Socio-technical Implications

We will now discuss socio-technical implications from our observations and findings. Based on how PAT functioned as an organizational probe in our study – at least to some extent and facilitated by our interviews – we first propose a number of organizational management measures and technical extensions to fully support this functionality. Based on the paper affordances for administrative work that we identified, we will then discuss in more detail how to translate the most prominent of those affordances into an appropriate digital metaphor.

### 5.3.1   Management and Communication

As illustrated above, PAT can serve as an organizational probe, making printing within an organization a collective and participatory issue and raising discussions among the employees. During our study, the participants took our workshops and interviews as the opportunity to bring up issues and questions with respect to paper usage in the organization. This, in turn, allowed us to identify the paper affordances presented in the previous section. Nevertheless, being external to the organization, it was not our role to gather the precise pain points raised with respect to particular organizational workflows, let alone to reconsider and redesign those workflows to palliate these problems. To enable an organization to collect the remarks and to capitalize on the opportunity PAT provides as an organizational probe, we therefore suggest the following management measures to accompany the tool's deployment.

First, we suggest appointing an *organizational print champion*. This responds to the lack of an interaction point we observed in our study: Indeed this print champion should respond to the employees' questions about their workflows and printing tasks. He or she should follow up employees' remarks and arbitrate on printing guidelines. On one hand the print champion should collect, aggregate and analyze employees' remarks in depth, and in consequence question and redesign the pinpointed problematic processes. On the other hand he or she should collect, identify and promote already existing good practices across the organization to document and communicate them to the employees with the same respective roles, across the different departments. In addition, the print champion should also foster abilities for change within the organization, by promoting knowledge and competencies with respect to existing tools providing digital alternatives to particular types of paper usage, e.g. electronic notes, to-do lists etc. This enables and encourages also less techy employees, as the ones we have seen in our study, to try out such digital alternatives.

Second, we suggest *accompanying PAT with vertical and horizontal communication and management measures* to make printing a collective and participatory issue. Facilitating vertical communication responds to the need, observed in our study, to foster larger discussion about complex workflows, among the different roles and individuals involved in these workflows. Such vertical communication allows questioning processes involving different departments or roles within the hierarchy through the corresponding individual employees, be it decision makers, e.g. managers, or people who execute tasks, e.g. assistants. Vertical communication furthermore allows to increase not only the motivation of participants but also to facilitate the adoption of improvements decided with respect to printing processes. Horizontal communication in contrast allows sharing and discussing issues pertaining to a given role among the employees fulfilling that role, e.g. the particular needs and barriers assistants face in their work. This helps to identify and share best practices among employees with the same role but distributed over different departments, something we also observed happening at the workshops in our study.

## 5.3.2 Integrating an Organizational Learning Infrastructure

To technically support the collection and aggregation of feedback, pain points and already existing good practices, we suggest the creation of a learning infrastructure around PAT. Such an infrastructure will enable employees to describe and state their issues with paper usage, and to share and elaborate them with colleagues facing similar ones. Through this infrastructure, the organizational print champion can (1) monitor new and open issues, (2) initiate deeper discussion to clarify them, (3) arbitrate on the corresponding processes, and finally (4) provide feedback to the employees on how adopted changes relate to the initial pain points they raised. Showing the participants that their remarks are taken into account and reacted upon can motivate them to contribute further and keep the flow alive. In this way, change based on employee raised pain points becomes easier to introduce and to accept by the employees carrying out the tasks.

As a first functionality of this learning infrastructure, the system should enable the users to declare and describe their printing pain points (or good ideas and practices). They could do this either spontaneously, i.e. when they run into them, or when prompted by the system. Inspired by our positive experience with ethno-mining during our interviews; we propose to confront participants with visualizations of their typical paper consuming print patterns on one hand, and with detected atypical exceptional print behaviors. The system can indeed extract typical print patterns from the participants' long and short term print history and then, from there, detect also atypical behaviors. For instance, such visualizations may highlight recurring heavy color printing typically in the end-of-the-month period, and therefore identify specific costly paper-based workflow to assess and maybe replace, or the exceptional printing of a large number of long documents in a particular week. The underlying idea is to motivate the participants through these visualizations to explain the observed pattern, to indicate the corresponding processes, print reasons and pain points. At the same time they could also suggest ideas or directions for process improvements. Figure 5.3 illustrates a possible integration of such visualizations with PAT.

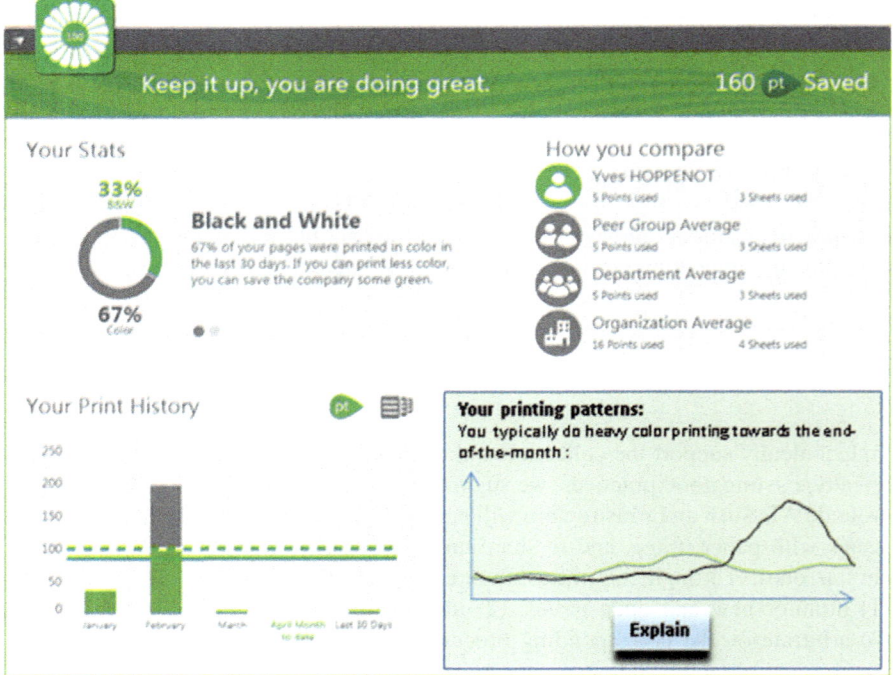

**Fig. 5.3** Visualizing typical print patterns to prompt users for explanations

As a second functionality, the system should support the sharing and elaboration of these notes among relevant colleagues on one hand and with the organizational print champion on the other hand. Colleagues may thus react on and review each other's notes. The print champion may group, aggregate and filter them. He may prompt relevant individuals for comments to get a deeper understanding, either individually and separately or as a group and collaboratively in round table discussions. This allows considering and reconciling different perspectives on the same process, by involving people with complementary roles in the process. It also allows identifying and sharing best practices put in place by individuals. To facilitate this process, the system must enable the print champion to group and filter the notes according to the context in which they were taken (department and role of the user, exceptional or typical printing pattern visualized, attributes of the print job, print settings used, etc.).

### 5.3.3   Materializing Work Through Digital Representations

The propositions discussed in the previous section relates to exploiting PAT as an organizational probe in the context of a paper to digital transition. The other major insight from our study concerns the paper affordances for administrative work we identified and which constitute barriers for replacing paper with digital tools and solutions. Some of these affordances are well known. Others are novel, and among those we want to address the one that seems the most prominent to us: the way paper materializes work and makes it visible to the individual employee himself on one hand, and to his colleagues and hierarchy on the other hand. While document and work technologies have often used the desk metaphor to organize the *content* of work, mimicking the physical desk organization as in [13], and to represent information and possible user actions, this affordance, addressing the *character* of work along the lines also described in [2], has to be translated into another appropriate digital metaphor to enable reducing corresponding paper usage.

There are two aspects in paper materializing work. The first one is the way paper represents the past achievements of the employee. The total amount of paper produced materializes the (total) amount of work the individual has achieved in the past. It shows and demonstrates the individual's overall contribution to his organization, department or work group. The second aspect focusses rather on the employee's actual status of work, how busy he currently is, and how much (urgent) work is actually waiting on his desk. This awaiting work can furthermore appear more or less organized reflecting the type of work of the user and, if appropriate, how well he or she organizes this work, through corresponding piles of paper documents to work through for instance.

To address both of these aspects, we propose to replace the existing physical cupboards and piles of paper in the office and on the employee's desk with virtual, digital ones, represented and displayed on a screen visible to the employee himself on one hand, and to his colleagues and hierarchy on the other hand. Such a display

can be physically located in the corresponding employee's office, visible to the
employee himself and to the colleagues stepping into the office. The same display
or a reduced version can furthermore be made accessible remotely to the colleagues
such that they can appreciate the work load of the individual, even before assigning
novel tasks to him. To replace the physical paper in the office with a display of
virtual digital piles (or similar objects), these virtual objects must be characterized
by their height or color corresponding to the amount of work and/or urgency they
represent. However, the values used to adjust their display, e.g. their heights or
colors must be acquired or computed. As many if not most of the work tasks
are nowadays attributed and communicated via Email, one way to compute these
values is to analyze the worker's Mailbox and categorize the incoming Email into
different tasks. Another option would be to let the employee establish and do this
categorization, for instance via dragging-and-dropping Email into dedicated folders.
Furthermore, as the display reflects the individual's work and contribution, the
employee should always be able to correct and adjust the virtual display of his work
status (just as he can do this currently in the physical world).

## 5.4   Conclusion

In this paper we reported on a pilot study of the Print Awareness Tool. Our
main findings were twofold. On one hand, we observed that the tool, initially
conceived of as "simple" eco-feedback technology, can have a much deeper impact
as an organizational probe questioning established organizational paper workflows.
Eco-feedback can thus play a facilitation role fostering debate on resource usage
as alluded to in [12], moving and enlarging its typically narrow focus [6] from
the individual end-user to the overall work organization. On the other hand, we
highlighted novel paper affordances corresponding to the particular organizational
administrative work we observed in our study. Following these two lines, we
proposed socio-technical guidelines, first for an infrastructure extending PAT to
properly support the paper to digital transition, and, second for translating the most
prominent of the identified paper affordances into corresponding digital metaphors.
We close with a short discussion about the significance of our main findings on
(1) using eco-feedback as an organizational probe and (2) paper affordances for
administrative work.

*Using Eco-Feedback as an Organizational Probe* We have experimented and studied the effect of eco-feedback technology in an organizational setting. The central
function of eco-feedback is to make users aware of their resource consumption
motivating them to reduce it. Other alternative solutions for (waste) reduction
exist, alternative in the sense that they do not involve raising awareness in the
first place. For instance, to reduce paper waste, such a solution may involve
the automatic setting of eco-print options, the facility to release print jobs only
at the last moment (i.e. at the printer), or the possibility to remove undesired

web content before printing [15]. Nevertheless, in an organizational context, these alternative solutions lack the positive side-effects eco-feedback produces through raising awareness, i.e. to make "waste" a public issue and to initiate reflection and discussion on the topic in the organization. As a result eco-feedback technology can have a much stronger impact, in our case questioning, eliciting and improving the organizational workflows consuming paper. We thus argue that using eco-feedback as an organizational probe is a means to understand how the work context conditions resource usage, and, ultimately, how this context may be changed to reduce it. In [10] Pousman et al. propose another approach to foster open ended discussion on sustainability related to printing: displaying community print data in printer areas. However, it seems to us that providing users with personalized feedback will provoke more and stronger reactions, which, in turn, will facilitate organizational learning [4] from those reactions.

*Paper Affordances*  The paper affordances we identified correspond to the particular organizational and administrative types of work we observed in our study: indeed, we observed paper usage in organizational workflows, in the context of administrative work, whereas [11] mainly observed paper usage by knowledge workers. In contrast to knowledge work, organizational workflows are often complex and well-established, and furthermore transmitted over time from one employee to the next. In consequence the reasons for using paper are often lost and/or hidden and not well understood by the users who actually execute them and do the printing. Also the administrative type of work we observed here exhibited particular characteristics where paper is a means to measure and assess the work. While technologies have often taken into account the functions and material characteristics of paper in the design of digital artefacts, we think that the symbolic and social functions supported by paper must also be tackled, as far as possible, in future applications. More than supporting only explicit and concrete information and interactions, the presence and the circulation of paper in space, either personal or organizational, are sustaining multiple shared representations and means that support employees work practices.

# References

1. Aipperspach R, Rattenbuy TL, Woodruff A, Anderson K, Canny JF, Aoki P (2006) Ethno-mining: integrating numbers and words from the ground up. Technical Report, Electrical Engineering and Computer Sciences, University of California at Berkeley
2. Anderson RJ, Sharrock WW (1993) Can organisations afford knowledge? J Comput Supported Coop Work (JCSCW) 1(3):143–161
3. Anderson K, Nafus D, Rattenbury T, Aipperspach R (2009) Numbers have qualities too: experiences with ethno-mining. Ethnographic Prax Ind Conf Proc 2009:123–140
4. Argote L (2013) Organizational learning: creating, retaining and transferring knowledge. Springer, New York
5. Boehner K, Vertesi J, Sengers P, Dourish P (2007) How HCI interprets the probes. In: Proceedings of the SIGCHI conference on human factors in computing systems (San Jose, CA, USA, Apr-28–May-03, 2007). CHI'07, ACM, New York. pp 1077–1086

6. Brynjarsdottir H, Håkansson M, Pierce J, Baumer E, DiSalvo C, Sengers P (2012) Sustainably unpersuaded: how persuasion narrows our vision of sustainability. In: Proceedings of the SIGCHI conference on human factors in computing systems (CHI'12). ACM, New York, pp 947–956

7. Dourish P, Bellotti V (1992) Awareness and coordination in shared workspaces. In: Proceedings of the 1992 ACM conference on computer-supported cooperative work (CSCW'92). ACM, New York, pp 107–114

8. Froehlich J, Findlater L, Landay J (2010) The design of eco-feedback technology. In: Proceedings of the SIGCHI conference on human factors in computing systems (CHI'10). ACM, New York, pp 1999–2008

9. Ipsos Study for Lexmark, http://www.infohightech.com/CPpdf/lexmark3.pdf. Accessed July 2015

10. Pousman Z, Rouzati H, Stasko J (n.d.) Imprint, a community visualization of printer data: designing for open-ended engagement on sustainability. In: Proceedings of the 2008 ACM conference on computer supported cooperative work (CSCW'08). ACM, New York, pp 13–16

11. Sellen AJ, Harper RHR (2003) The myth of the paperless office. MIT Press, Cambridge, MA

12. Strengers YAA (2011) Designing eco-feedback systems for everyday life. In: Proceedings of the SIGCHI conference on human factors in computing systems (CHI'11). ACM, New York, pp 2135–2144

13. Tyson PJ (1992) The desk as a social institution, EuroPARC technical report EPC-92-130, Rank Xerox EuroPARC, Cambridge, UK

14. Willamowski JK, Hoppenot Y, Grasso A (2013) Promoting sustainable print behavior. In: CHI'13 extended abstracts on human factors in computing systems (CHI EA'13). ACM, New York

15. Xiao J, Fan J (2009) PrintMarmoset: redesigning the print button for sustainability. In: Proceedings of the SIGCHI conference on human factors in computing systems (CHI'09). ACM, New York, pp 109–112

# Chapter 6
# The Many Faces of Computational Artifacts

**Lars Rune Christensen and Richard H. R. Harper**

**Abstract** Building on data from fieldwork at a medical department, this paper focuses on the varied nature of computational artifacts in practice. It shows that medical practice relies on multiple heterogeneous computational artifacts that form complex constellations. In the hospital studied the computational artifacts are both coordinative, image-generating, and intended for the control of nuclear-physical and chemical processes. Furthermore, the paper entails a critique of the notion of 'computer support', for not capturing the diverse constitutive powers of computer technology; its types if you will. The paper is a step towards establishing a lexicon of computational artifacts in practice. It is a call for a wider effort to systematically conceptualise the multiple and specifiable ways in which computational artifacts may be part of work activities. This is for the benefit of design and our understanding of work practice.

## 6.1 Introduction

In this paper, an attempt is made to achieve a better understanding of computers and their role in work practice. Previous studies have focused on ecologies of artifacts [2, 8], information infrastructures [5], and computational tools broadly speaking [9]. This paper builds on these studies and explores the nature of computational artifacts for the benefit of design within CSCW and related research fields. What is the role of a computer? How can we understand these roles for our purposes? Can they be taxonomised in useful ways?

According to Wittgenstein [12], it is an error to assume that there is a single essence to a phenomenon just because we use one word for it such as, for example,

L.R. Christensen (✉)
IT-University of Copenhagen, Rued Langaardsvej 7, 2300 Copenhagen S, Denmark
e-mail: Lrc@itu.dk

R.H.R. Harper
Social Shaping Research, 23 Kings Rd, Cambridge Cams cb3 9dy, UK
e-mail: Richard@socialshapingresearch.com

© Springer International Publishing Switzerland 2016
A. De Angeli et al. (eds.), *COOP 2016: Proceedings of the 12th International Conference on the Design of Cooperative Systems, 23–27 May 2016, Trento, Italy*,
DOI 10.1007/978-3-319-33464-6_6

93

'computer"; one needs to look at how a word is used in diverse settings. We might find there are differences in what the word is applied to (or for) and hence subtleties in its meaning. Previous studies of ecologies of artifacts [2] show that artifacts contribute to practice in many different and often complementary ways, where one artifact "creates the environment of the other" [7]. Hence, we cannot expect to achieve just one theoretical understanding or conceptualization of computational artifacts in practice, there are most likely many different relevant understandings and conceptualizations in the sense that "computational artifacts" are not one thing but in fact many that work in significantly different (yet complementary) ways in various contexts and situations. The point is that 'computational artifact' is not one monolithic concept, nor is there one single phenomenon – the 'computer' – that underpins the correct use of that concept in studies of work practice.[1] There are a variety of different kinds of relations pointed to by the abstract term 'computational artifact' and, similarly, a variety of different, though apposite, uses of the term; and these may well vary according to different purposes.

In this study, accordingly, we will take a plural view of computational artifacts and attempt to show the variation of ways in which computational artifacts may be an integral part of medical practice even within the same hospital department. That is, we will work towards a lexicon of computational artifacts as the basis for conceptualisations of computers in work practice and for design. This move builds on previous work on ecologies of artifacts [2], information infrastructures [5], and computational artifacts [9]. Furthermore, despite the multiplicity of ways that computational artifacts may play a part in practice there is a feature shared by all the computational artifacts described in this study of medical practice. The common denominator across the computational artifacts in the practice is related to algorithms. Although this communality only becomes visible on a rather high level of abstraction, and various in significance from instance to instance, we will discuss the implication of this for our understanding of computational artifacts towards the end of our discussions.

The papers empirical material originates from a study of work at a medical department at a large hospital. At the department multiple computational artifacts enter into various constellations by virtue of their diverse nature and contribute to cooperative work practice. By investigating the multiplicity of computational artifacts in practice at the department, we aim to characterise each computational artifact and how they are part of practice. Such a view is important for a discussion of our object of design.

The paper will proceed as follows: first, we will introduce the methods and the fieldwork setting. Second, we will provide a view of the multiplicity of computational artifacts at the medical department. Third, we will discuss the many faces

---

[1]Perhaps on the engineering level 'computer' may be described in more monolithic terms. Turing's concept of the 'Universal Computer' comes to mind. However, we are concerned with the level of work practice, not the generic features of engineered tools.

of computational artifacts in medical practice. Fourth, we will discuss implication for CSCW, specifically implications for our use of the notion of computer support. Finally, a conclusion is provided.

## 6.2  Methods and Setting

The empirical data was generated over a period of 6 months fieldwork at a medical department at a large university hospital in Denmark. The fieldwork included observations of work practice as well as 12 interviews. During data generation and analysis, particular attention was paid to how different computational artifacts where part of medical practice, and how many of these where used in conjunction, rather than in isolation, suggesting that each performed a different role in supporting work practice.

The department studied is part of the diagnostic centre at the hospital. The department mainly performs diagnostics services for other clinical departments such as for example departments of oncology from both inside and outside the hospital. The department is highly specialized within the area of nuclear medicine; it focuses on diagnostic enquiries. Nuclear medicine can be described as centred on medical imaging that uses small amounts of radioactive material to diagnose a variety of diseases, including many types of cancers, heart disease, neurological disorders and other conditions. The practice of nuclear medicine at the department is a complex enterprise, which involves many computational artifacts in for example patient administration, in examinations, in the production of pharmaceuticals, and in lab work (we will return to this below).

The department has no patient ward as all patients come from other departments within the hospital as well as other hospitals, and are only at the department for the duration of their examinations. Positron emission tomography–computed tomography (PET-CT) is central in the diagnostic efforts at the department. It is best described as a medical imaging technique using a machine which combines both a positron emission tomography (PET) scanner and an x-ray computed tomography (CT) scanner (we will return to this below).

An overview of a patient's journey through the department may look something like this: (1) the patient is referred to the department by one of many clinical units from inside or outside of the hospital, (2) the patient referral is handled by the departments secretariat and physicians on call, (3) the secretariat schedules such things as the PET-CT examination of the patient, (4) on the day of the PET-CT examination a bioanalysts interjects a radioactive tracer into the patient's body – following a quality check of the tracer by the departments laboratory, (5) the patient's body is examined in the PET-CT scanner, (6) the images of the patients body produced by the PET-CT scanner is interpreted by the departments physicians, (7) the departments physicians present the PET-CT images along with an interpretation of them to members of the referring clinic, and the future treatment and examination of the patient is discussed in a conference, (8) a precondition for these activities is the production of radioactive tracers at the departments cyclotron unit, where the tracers are produced early in the morning before the start of the day.

There are approximately 60,000 patient investigations per year and the department has a permanent staff of 125 healthcare professionals; it also hosts 25 PhD students ongoingly.[2]

## 6.3   A View of Computational Artifacts at a Medical Department

The computational artifacts at the department are part of an *ecology* (see also e.g. [2, 8]). An ecology or constellation of artifacts may arise as a specific contingent situation occurs such as a patient emergency or because the usual practice is somehow derailed. In this section though, we will focus on a constellation of a quite stable nature (see Fig. 6.1).

We will focus on the constellation of primarily computational artifacts that are internal to the practice of diagnosing cancer patients in nuclear medicine. This is perhaps *the* core practice at the department involving the majority of the department's patients. For the purposes of commencing our analysis, we may note that technology can be said to mean 'the systematic application of techniques' [9], and this is a good way to begin our descriptions. At the department there is a wide range of systematically interconnected computational (and non-computational) technologies, and they are used together in a precise and particular manner. They are organized to stand in a particular relationship to each other, and are connected in particular ways. Being integral to the practice of nuclear medicine and the diagnosis of cancer patients, the constellation partly constitutes the practice; when combined with work practice, the totality comes into shape.

We will now turn to describe this practice while highlighting the role of computational artifacts, and we will see that this entails treating them (i.e. the computational artifacts) as either coordinative, image-generating, or for the control of nuclear-physical and chemical processes themselves.

### 6.3.1   Computational Coordinative Artifacts

In brief, the diagnostic practice at the department involves the examination of patients using various forms of nuclear medicine. A precondition for the examination and diagnosis of the patients is their administration through various coordinative practices. At the department, coordinative activities are widely constituted by computational artifacts in various guises. As the patients are referred to the

---

[2]The department has significant research activity with 125 peer-reviewed publication pr. year.

**Fig. 6.1** A wide range of systematically interconnected computational artifacts at the department (montage). Seen from the *top left* corner: Administrative application, Geiger counter, PET-CT scanner, control software for PET-CT scanner, tablet for e.g. ordering nuclear tracers, control application for cyclotron, part of nuclear cyclotron for the production of radioactivity, Tracer Shop on laptop, control interface for chemical synthesis lab, automated synthesis lab, semi-automated unit for quality check of tracers, mobile phone

department, the department's secretariat, as well as physicians on call, handle the patient referral, including scheduling the PET-CT examinations of the patients. A comprehensive software suite, including several coordinative systems such as a calendaring and a patient record system, enable this task. The patient record holds the patient's demographics (e.g. name, home address, date of birth) and details all patient contact with the hospital and the department, while the calendar system makes it possible to schedule the patients for one of the five PET-CT units at the department. Such coordinative practices and coordinative tools are common to cooperative work in healthcare [6] and elsewhere [11].

The further example of a computational coordinative artifact at the department is *Tracer Shop,* which is a web-based application capable of running in any browser both on desktop computers, on laptops, and on handheld devices. Using Tracer Shop, the bioanalysts can order tracers and monitor when they are ready for pickup (using an app on a tablet), and the physicists making the tracers in the cyclotron unit can see what kind and quantities are needed and when they are needed (on a laptop computer). The tracer must be ordered the day before use in order to allow the physicists time to make them up. However, computational artifacts play another role besides being constitutive of coordinative work. That is, computational artifacts are key in the diagnostic process by virtue of the role in the generation of images in nuclear medicine, to which we now turn.

### 6.3.2   Image-Generating Computational Artifacts

The PET-CT scanners and their control software and hardware play also play a key role in the constellation of artifacts at the department – but a different one. They complement the patient administration system as a designated point for the booking of patient examinations. The capacity of the five PET-CT scanners, as well as the other nuclear medicine equipment such as the three SPECT-CT scanners, largely dictates the capacity of the department to do patient examinations in relation to, as a case in point, cancer patients. The PET-CT nuclear medicine imaging procedures are non-invasive, with the exception the infusion of radioactive tracers in into the patient's body. Depending on the type of nuclear medicine exam, the radiotracer is either injected into the body, swallowed or inhaled as a gas, and eventually accumulates in the organ or area of the body being examined. A PET-CT imaging device then produces pictures and molecular information derived from and calculated by radioactive emissions from the radiotracer (for an example see Fig. 6.2).

At the department, the nuclear medicine images (PET) are superimposed with computed tomography (CT) to produce special views, a practice known as image

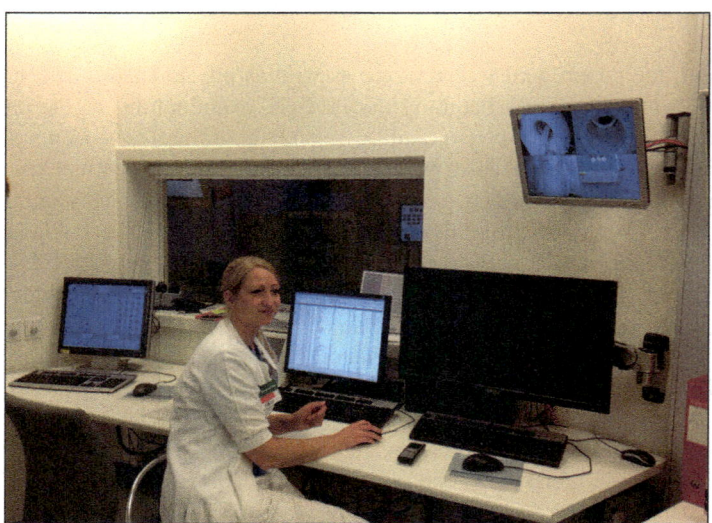

**Fig. 6.2** Computational artifacts and bioanalyst working in the control room of a PET-CT unit

fusion or co-registration. PET shows the molecular activity in the body while the CT images provides images of the hard (bone) structure of the patient. These views are then combined to allow the information from two different exams to be correlated and interpreted on one image. As the two kinds of images are made to overlap, the radioactive emissions detected on the PET images are accurately positioned within the feature of the body provided by the CT images. Having only PET images of the radiation would make it harder to locate exactly where in the patient's body the radioactive emission is coming from.

Because nuclear medicine procedures are able to pinpoint molecular activity within the body, they offer the potential to identify disease in its earliest stages as well as a patient's immediate response to therapeutic interventions. For example, cancer patient's response to chemotherapy treatment is monitored using PET-CT technology. 'Are the chemotherapy drugs destroying the cancer cell? Can we see the tumour shrinking when we are comparing PET-CT scans of the tumour over time?' are the kinds of questions physicians ask with this technology. The objective for the physicians is, for example, to identify when tumours in cancer patients improve ("respond"), stay the same ("stabilise"), or worsen ("progress") during chemotherapy (see also [3]). Most of the patients being diagnosed at the department are cancer sufferers.

The images are ordered, distributed and displayed via a type of software suite referred to by its acronym PACS – Picture Archiving and Communication System. This is an imaging system that enables storage and access to images from the five PET-CT units at the department. The images are transmitted digitally via PACS. Non-image data, such as text, may be incorporated using digital document formats such as PDF. In conjunction with PACS are workstations where the clinicians of the department interpret and review the PET-CT images when doing diagnosis. This process also incorporates a database for the storage and retrieval of the images and associated text.

### 6.3.3 Computational Artifacts for the Control and Manipulation of Nuclear-Physical and Chemical Processes

If PET-CT scanners are intended to let physicians see, other computer technologies are intended to let them manipulate the materials of their trade – their pharmaceuticals. As it happens, the radiopharmaceuticals (radioactive tracers) used for PET imaging are usually extremely short-lived. For example, the half-life of radioactive fluorine used to trace glucose metabolism (synthesized in a lab with glucose into FDG18) is only 2 h. Its creation therefore requires a production line nearby. The department has such a production line that includes a cyclotron unit, a synthesis lab, and a quality test lab.

It is the cyclotron unit that produce the radioactive substances. A cyclotron works by accelerating particles outwards from the centre along a spiral path inside the unit. The particles are held to a spiral trajectory by a static magnetic field and accelerated by a rapidly varying electric field. A one point of operation the accelerated particles are let out of their spiral path, out of the unit, forming a beam that endues radioactivity in whatever material is put in front of the beam. Such beam targets may be, for example, fluoride but can also be water or gasses. But the radiopharmaceuticals (tracers) need not only be radioactive they also need to be somehow able to interact with the human body in order to register in a meaningful way on the PET/CT images. This is why the work in the cyclotron needs to be complemented with work in the chemical synthesis lab.

In the automated synthesis lab the radioactive substance is synthesised with a biologically active agent (see Fig. 6.3). For example, radioactive fluorine-18 is incorporated into deoxyglucose producing the tracer FDG18. It is the glucose that makes the tracer register in the body, it accumulates in the cells where the glucose is metabolised.

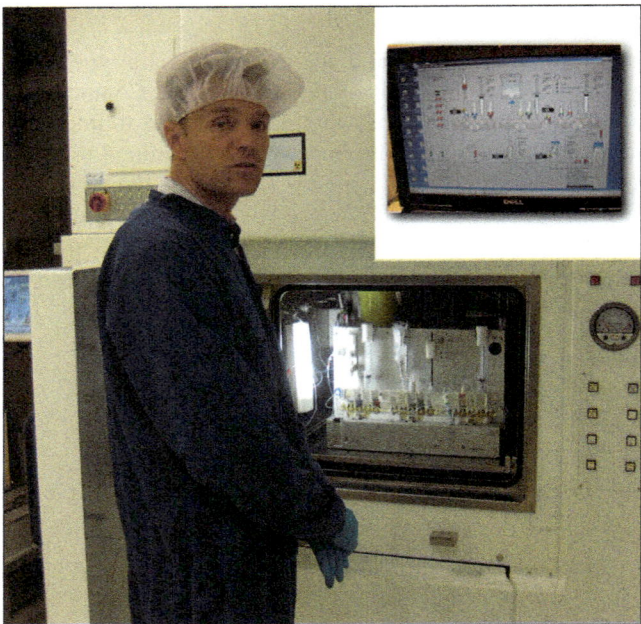

**Fig. 6.3** Inside the synthesis lab. Here are the radioactive substances, coming from the cyclotron, synthesised with biological agents in order to make an effective tracer for PET-CT. The insert in the *top right* corner shows the control software for the process, it is running on a laptop placed on a stool right next to the leaded hot-chamber shown in the main picture

With a half-life of 110 min FDG 18 is rather short lived as a radiopharmaceutical. The automated synthesis process in the tracer lab has the advantage of being rapid, it can produce the agent quickly, and this is clearly important given the relatively short half-life of the substances in question (such as fluoride-18 just mentioned). The automated tracer lab is preconfigured to handle the synthesis process and is composed of several leaded compartments where the fluoride-18 and the deoxyglucose is synthesised and packaged for later use as a radiopharmaceutical in PET/CT. However, before the newly produced radiopharmaceuticals can be administered to the patients as part of their PET/CT scans, the quality of the production batch in question has to be assured. The semi-automated equipment of the quality assurance lab complements the other artifacts in the radiotracer production line by providing measurements of the levels of the various ingredients in the radiotracer compound.

Having considered some of the multiple roles of computational artifacts in the department's medical practice, we will now turn to discuss our findings.

## 6.4   The Many Faces of Computational Artifacts in Medical Practice

What is it we are doing when we design computational artifacts? What is a 'computational artifact' seen from the perspective of practice? What is the job it does? How many jobs are there? Do different designs support different tasks? Of course they do. But we all too often neglect seeing this, and as result too often label computer artifacts in a unitary way. As we began by saying, according to Wittgenstein, it is sometimes an error to assume that there is a single essence to a phenomenon just because we use one word for it. As the pages above indicate, computational artifacts, as a case in point, are many things when measured by the roles they have even within the same organisational unit. We have seen that they take on the role of coordinative artifact in the context of patient administration and coordination in the secretariat (i.e. administrative software suite), and in relation to the production of the radioactive tracers (i.e. Tracer Shop). We see that computational artifacts are part of generating complex images of the human body within the context of nuclear medicine (i.e. PET-CT), allowing physicians new fields of perception; and we have seen how computational artifacts are used for the ordering, distribution, display and interpretation of these images (i.e. PACS), supporting both workflow and ways of seeing. In addition, we have seen how computational artifacts are key in the control and manipulation of physical processes in the context of the production of radioactive substances (i.e. cyclotron control software), and in the control and manipulation of syntheses of the radioactive tracers (i.e. automatic synthesis lab). We could mention other ways that computational artifacts are part of practice at the department, including for example in the guise of Geiger counters and in the guise of mobile phones, just to name two additional pervasive examples.

The upshot of all this is that we must consider computational artifacts a many-faced phenomenon, and we must take care to render the particular ways that computational artifacts are part of practice. Doing so, it seems to us will be much more effective if we are *systematic* about it since this will help provide a repeatable basis for understanding the structured diversity of the role that computers have in work practice; their plurality as we suggested at the outset. Our purpose in this paper is just to point towards the potential or need for such an approach and in the above makes it clear that there is already a subtle lexicon waiting to be developed. The term coordinative is well known, of course, but others come to mind – manipulative, for example, perceptual in another case.

Further distinctions could be added that we have not elaborated here. Whether a computational artifact is part of an administrative coordinative practice or used in the manipulation and control of physical processes in the material field of work makes a difference, for example (see also [4]). At the very least, clarification of what kinds of computational artifacts that we are interested in designing would help in that design process, we believe. Being more precise about the various kinds or various ways that computational artifacts are part of practice may help us in our design efforts in significant ways.

Just as there are differences across the spectrum of computational artifacts there are also perhaps commonalities, but we have to be careful of these. After all, the computational artifacts described above, all shared important features at the 'engineering level', and this may perhaps best be described as surfacing in practice in terms of algorithmic performance. Basic to all the computational artifacts described above, albeit on different levels, is the inclusion of algorithms in their various workings. They are, in this sense, all versions of Turing's Universal Computing Machine but that is not the question we are addressing here. That would be like saying that all metal frames are the same – irrespective of whether it is aircraft, washing machines or tables in which the frames have a role. The important point is what the devices they frame are for, not the existence or need of the frame itself.

This does not deny the importance of algorithms as features of interactive salience in the workplace. The question in CSCW is just at what level are the computational algorithms significant or central for the actors in their practice. For it is all very well to say that computers are best not approached with algorithms in mind but rather with a starting point that has to do with the orientations of work that the 'algorithm machines' support and engage with. The control of the cyclotron unit and the synthesis lab, for example, relies on complex computational algorithms that are partly configured and executed by the human operators working with the control software. Here the algorithms and the automation that follows are central to the human actors in the performance of the work; that they are algorithm machines matters since working the algorithms is part of the task at hand – even though this would not be called software engineering or computer science; this is medicine at work, cancer specialists doing their trade. We may say that the actors are actively relating to what kinds of algorithms to configure and execute.

This is also partly true in terms of how the PET-CT scanners generate images of the human body in the context of nuclear medicine, where the scanners are using various pre-set (yet configurable) image-generating algorithms. It is also user-selected algorithms that influence the toning, shading, and general appearance of the PET-CT generated images as the physicians display them as part of their diagnostic interpretation process (via e.g. PACS). It is harder to see the computational algorithms surfacing as central in the view of the human actors working with for example the administrative suite; here it is coordination that is afoot, and the algorithmic basis of the machines is subordinate to the manifestation of coordinative representations – calendars and such like. One might argue that there is several coordinative protocols at play (indeed there are), but these must not be confused with users directly configuring, manipulation or selecting computational algorithms as a central part of their task. If we turn to the administrative suite we may note that on the practice level the algorithms are mostly silent in these sense that the users are not actively engaging with them per se, the algorithms are doing background work on the operation system and on the 'engineering level" of the computational artifacts.

In sum, computational artifacts are a many-faced phenomenon in work practice, and this has consequences for our understanding of our object of design. It seems clear to us that we are not designing one kind of thing but multiple kinds, which are part of work practice in many different ways. That they all depend upon and are constituted by technology that involves the general application of algorithms, is best treated as a given, not a constraint and certainly not governing how we label our designs. Terms are an important issue but when used grossly can be distracting, leading us to bundle together very distinct tools as one and the same: as computers at work.

## 6.5   Computer Constituted Cooperative Work?

In the seminal writing of Kjeld Schmidt and Liam Bannon [10] we can read that the raison d'être of Computer Supported Cooperative Work (CSCW) is to improve our understanding of cooperative work in order to be able to better computer support it. This idea has been the leading light of the research field for many years. However, is 'computer support' still an adequate short handle for what we are designing? The notion of computer support has long been criticised by for example Marc Berg [1]. Berg argues that the notion of 'computer support' conjures up imagery that overlooks the fundamental ways human capabilities are transformed through their interlocking with computational artifacts. Berg finds that human capabilities such a communication and memory are fundamentally changed into something else through the introduction of new technology [1].

In the same vein, but in relation to the concept of practice, we may for our part say that the notion of computer support can be criticised for having connotations towards reducing the role of computing to something singular, which stands in a meta-relationship or secondary relationship to practice. Arguably technology is constitutive of practice – it is not merely having a 'supportive role'. This is a subtle but important point. Moreover, it is a point that has been confirmed by the analysis in this article, which shows that the diagnostic process of nuclear medicine, from beginning to end, is based on computational artifacts in various guises. To begin we have seen how the computational coordinative artifacts such as electronic calendar systems and electronic patient records are an indispensible part of the specific administration, referral, and general handling of patients. Perhaps even more pronounced, we have seen how the image-generating computational artifacts at the department are indispensible to what one might say is the perceptual field of medical practice in this area. That is, the PET-CT scanners and their control software and hardware are completely indispensible when it comes to creating images of the distribution of radioactive-tracers inside the human body – and this is central to how nuclear medicine entails tractable ways of seeing the problems at hand. Without this technology the whole enterprise of nuclear medicine would arguably be null and void – something that could not be done. The same argument could be made for the computational artifacts used in the nuclear tracer production line but here it is the manipulation of pharmaceuticals that is at issue, the materialities that need to be controllable, manufacturable features of medical practice. If the former is about seeing crudely put, the latter is about grasping and altering, making with hands mediated into the form of computer tools.

The implications are for example that nuclear medicine would not be nuclear medicine, as we know it, without the myriad of computational artifacts that populate this practice. As we have seen, computational artifacts do not merely support practice at the department, *they are part of its very fabric (together with numerous other elements)*. The point here is not that certain technologies in part make certain practices possible (although they do). The point has to do with our choice of words when describing this state of affairs. Computational artifacts shape and structure medical practice to such a diverse and contrasting ways that taking about 'computer support' makes little or no sense. 'Support' is simply not strong enough a word. As a verb it may connote 'giving assistance to' which is not the kind of connotations we want as we wish to express how computer technology is constitutive of practices not 'assisting a practice'. Neither is it strong enough as an adjective (i.e. as supporting) where it connotes 'something of secondary importance'. As a noun it may work a little better as 'a thing that bears the weight of something or keeps it upright' – but here we also see that it is not part of the practice it is merely 'keeping it upright'. The situation, then, is that we have to look beyond the notion of 'computer support' to a bigger lexicon. In fact we may have to abandon the expression 'support' all together as it is creating an unhelpful image of computers technologies role in practice as being merely supportive.

One alternative to 'support' is that of 'constitution' as in computer *constituted* cooperative work. This might work considering our field. Not as a name (that would be unpractical), but as a short handle for what we are ethnographically unearthing and aiming to design. As a verb it may connote 'to be part of a whole' or 'combine to form a whole' which is exactly the kind of connotation we want as we want to be to be able to express that computer technology in many cases give decisive form to practice, rather than merely 'assist it' or 'support it'. We want to express that computational artifact combine with many other elements to create practice as we have seen it happen in the case of nuclear medicine – to give just one example.

We must design for the constitution or making of practice not the support of it.

## 6.6   Conclusion and Perspectives

For the sake of clarity, we will now briefly take stock and provide a conclusion.

This paper set out to address the fundamental CSCW challenge of characterising computational artifacts in practice for the purposes of informing design. This agenda was addressed through the premise that there is not one single essence or nature to computational artifacts – this is true both conceptually and empirically. Based on fieldwork, the article showed that within a medical department, the computational artifacts can be both coordinative artifacts, image-generating artifacts, and artifacts for the control of nuclear-physical and chemical processes. The implications of this kind of analysis is that we must consider computational artifacts to be a many-faced phenomenon, both empirically and conceptually, and we must take care to render the particular ways that computational artifacts are part of practice, and we must do so in a *systematic way*. At the very least we must clarify what kinds of computational artifacts that we are interested in designing. We must make an attempt to systematise computational artifacts into 'kinds' if for no other reason than heuristics. Being more precise about the various kinds or various ways that computational artifacts are part of practice may help us in our design efforts in significant ways. For example, it may contribute to better and more precise foreshadowing of the workings of our proposed design from the point of view of practice (rather than e.g. the point of view of technical realization). This paper represents an indication of the potential and need for such an approach to be further developed.

Concretely, one future step could be to start work towards a categorical framework of computational artifacts that may, as called for, systematise computational artifacts into 'kinds'. One challenge is to find an analytically valuable ordering principle that may sort multiple examples of 'computational artifacts in practice' into telling kinds; a lexicon if you like. This work may ideally be based on data from several domains and cases in order to try the robustness of the taxonomy as it is created. Although no taxonomy is all encompassing the goal must be to create one that is analytically valuable both in ethnographic- and in design terms.

**Acknowledgements** First, a warm thanks to the employees of the nuclear-medical department – without your openness and generosity this research would not be possible. Thank you. Second, note that this work is part of the Computational Artefacts research project (VELUX33295) and is funded by the Velux foundation. Thanks to Velux and everybody within the project.

# References

1. Berg M (1999) Accumulating and coordinating: occasions for information technologies in medical work. Comput Supported Coop Work (CSCW): J Collab Comput 8(4):373–401
2. Bødker S, Nylandsted Klokmose C (2011) The human–artifact model: an activity theoretical approach to artifact ecologies. Hum Comput Interact 26(4):315–371
3. Christensen LR (2016) On intertext in chemotherapy: an ethnography of text in medical practice. Comput Supported Coop Work (CSCW): J Collab Comput. doi:10.1007/s10606-015-9238-1
4. Christensen LR, Bertelsen OW (2015) A view of causation for CSCW: manipulation and control in the material field of work. In: Wulf V, Randall D, Schmidt K (eds) Designing socially embedded technologies in the real-world. Springer, London
5. Ellingsen G, Monteiro E, Røed K (2013) Integration as interdependent workaround. Int J Med Inform 82(5):e161–e169
6. Fitzpatrick G, Ellingsen G (2013) A review of 25 years of CSCW research in healthcare: contributions, challenges and future agendas. Comput Supported Coop Work (CSCW): J Collab Comput 22(4–6):609–665
7. Hutchins E, Klausen T (1996) Distributed cognition in an airline cockpit. Cognition and communication at work, pp. 15–34
8. Jung H, Stolterman E, Ryan W, Thompson T, Siegel M (2008) Toward a framework for ecologies of artifacts: how are digital artifacts interconnected within a personal life?, In Proceedings of the 5th Nordic conference on Human-computer interaction: building bridges. Aarhus, Denmark. pp. 201–210
9. Schmidt K (2011) Cooperative work and coordinative practices: contributions to the conceptual foundations of Computer Supported Cooperative Work (CSCW). In: Harper R (ed) Computer supported cooperative work. Springer, London
10. Schmidt K, Bannon L (1992) Taking CSCW seriously: supporting articulation work. Comput Supported Coop Work (CSCW): Int J 1(1–2):7–40
11. Schmidt K, Bannon L (2013) Constructing CSCW: the first quarter century. Comput Supported Coop Work (CSCW): J Collab Comput 22(4–6):345–372
12. Wittgenstein L (2001) Philosophical investigations. Blackwell Publishing, Oxford

# Chapter 7
# Let's Look Outside the Office: Analytical Lens Unpacking Collaborative Relationships in Global Work

**Stina Matthiesen and Pernille Bjørn**

**Abstract** Global software development (GSD) outsourcing setups are assumed to allow IT developers to work *anywhere* and *anytime*, removing the contextual contingencies of physical location. However, we challenge this assumed flexibility in our ethnographic study on GSD work as we unpack the nature of the collaborative work through the experiences and the concerns of the collaborators in Denmark and in India. We explore the *difficulties* in global work to understand how the everyday work practices in the global collaboration are enacted locally. The study shows how the dissimilarities in the local conditions for work are distinctly tied to the societal infrastructures outside the office, which also shape the work within the office. Reflecting on our analytical approach, we propose three analytical moves to investigate the nature of local contextual contingencies posed by the local infrastructures and impacting global work conditions. We argue that CSCW research on global work should include analytical considerations for how societal infrastructures at the different sites impact how work is accomplished locally in transnational encounters.

## 7.1 Introduction

For many companies, the outsourcing of IT services and software development is an emblem of today's globalization [1], which has led to an increasing interest in exploring global software development (GSD) practices in computer-supported cooperative work (CSCW) research [2–5]. Seeking to bridge temporal and spatial distance among IT workers in distributed teams, the facets of GSD research broadly cover aspects such as routines [5]; cross-cultural issues [6–8]; the use and development of software development tools, methods, and processes [9]; how

S. Matthiesen (✉) • P. Bjørn
Department of Computer Science, University of Copenhagen, Njalsgade 128,
DK-2300 Copenhagen, Denmark
e-mail: matthiesen@di.ku.dk; pernille.bjorn@di.ku.dk

© Springer International Publishing Switzerland 2016
A. De Angeli et al. (eds.), *COOP 2016: Proceedings of the 12th International Conference on the Design of Cooperative Systems, 23–27 May 2016, Trento, Italy,*
DOI 10.1007/978-3-319-33464-6_7

107

software bugs and defects are resolved and handled [10]; and how knowledge, coordination, and communication are managed in GSD projects [see e.g. 3, 6, 11]. The dedication to understanding the complexities of GSD practices is generally driven by an interest in creating new technologies to support communication and coordination. However, the preconditions for communication and coordination, for example, to take place in transnational collaborative environments (such as GSD) have received less attention. In fact, we know little about the contextual contingencies—present at the various locations involved—and if or how they impact collaboration. As it is a core interest for CSCW to explore the basic nature of collaborative work, we join others in paying attention to the underlying structures and local situations [12], the power dynamics at play [13], to unfold whether these structures impact the collaborative work situations or the use and design of technologies. In doing so, we argue that the literature has yet to come up with analytical directions that can help capture and unfold issues in global work when collaborations fail—issues that are otherwise neglected, left unnoticed, or reduced to general terms such as "*culture*" [14].

Through a 6-month ethnographic study of GSD organized around the transnational work between Denmark and India, we investigate the differences in global outsourcing practices by comparing the contextual contingencies that shape the work differently between an Indian IT vendor and its customer, a Danish IT company. One particular interview set us on this course of research, namely an interview with a tester currently working out of India, but who had spent 6 months working onsite in Ballerup, Denmark. She said:

> [ . . . ] its two different cultures and its two different worlds. We have our own set of difficulties here [in India]. [ . . . ] I feel it is very easy living there [in Denmark], while it is difficult living here. (*11/27/13, Interview, Tester, India*)

We found it intriguing that the tester expressed how working out of Bangalore was more difficult than working in Ballerup, thus we asked ourselves: What makes it easier to do *global work* in Ballerup compared to Bangalore? Understanding this experience of *difficulty*, we began to unpack the socio-economic relationship manifested in the outsourcing setup. By the tester's ability to compare her bodily experience of working at each location, she explained how global work is performed in "*two different worlds*". Exploring the nature of the seemingly diverse circumstances for work in Ballerup and Bangalore, our attention was directed at understanding how the location of *your body matters* when engaging in global work. Our analysis took us on a journey from unpacking ethnographically how central language constructs about global work are performed in practice toward moving outside of the office to include considerations on the infrastructural aspects of the particular cities involved in global work.

On the basis of our ethnographic inquiry and the questions above, we then ask: *How do the local contextual contingencies shape the conditions for collaboration across sites within transnational work?* We find that unpacking the nature of the collaborative work through the bodily experiences and concerns of the software developers requires us to explore the physical contextual contingencies as they manifest in everyday work practices. Also we find that even though collaborative dissimilarities across sites emerge when observing the work inside the office, these issues may be grounded in societal circumstances and infrastructures outside the office walls, which, in a recursive relationship, also shapes the work that takes place inside the office. Based on our findings, we propose an analytical lens consisting of three moves to unpack collaborative dissimilarities in transnational work. Stipulating explorations both inside and outside the transnational offices, the first analytical move examines the local work inside the office in the light of common language constructs for describing transnational work. We show how language constructs are important, as they create certain assumptions about the work and thus impact the nature of the work across sites. The second analytical move then encourage us to step outside the office and explore how the underlying assumptions about global work are enacted locally and related to the contextual contingencies emerging from local societal infrastructures. Finally, we move back into the office, bringing with us insights from outside to re-consider the nature of work as it happens within offices.

## 7.2   Related Work

Recent interest in CSCW research explores the role of technology in global work and life—taking into account the challenges of diverse technological cultures, economic disparities, and digital divides. Research has examined the work of Turkers in India and the US, emphasizing the role of power dynamics and local circumstances in global work [15, 16]. Moreover, we have seen investigations on how politics sneaks into the offices of software companies in the West Bank [17], how political activists use social media to organize demonstrations from a Palestinian village [18], or how multi-lifespan information systems seek to support justice after the genocide in Rwanda [19]. All this work is concerned with the ways in which we can understand the relationship between politics and power balances as nuanced measures enacted through several interlinked historic and economic structures related to technology accessibility and infrastructure [17]. Global software outsourcing is clearly a transnational phenomenon, where we witness a large and growing population of Indian global IT developers working in outsourcing setups with IT developers in Europe or the US [20]. Previous research on IT developers working out of India has demonstrated how the identities of the IT developers are framed by located norms and beliefs as they are constructed and situated in particular locations [21]. When exploring the economic, social, or cultural assumptions and the infrastructural differences that arise in global work, we must enact an alternative sensibility on how to explore the reality of culturally located practices [22–24]. Thus, to investigate the differences in work realities shaped by located contingencies in India and in Denmark, we will pay attention to the localized practices of people engaging in the global work.

The collaborative work in GSD can be challenged by the nature of the software development tasks, the information infrastructural constraints in the system under development [25], as well as the underlying structures that lay the groundwork for the day-to-day collaboration through artefacts and technology use [12]. Furthermore, understanding global software outsourcing also requires investigating the infrastructures that locally affect and facilitate the global work at the different locales. In a study of the displaced population in Bangladesh, certain infrastructural experiences were pertinent to understanding how forced mobility impacted the population's access to technology and thus ways of life, pushing them to create workarounds to sustain life [24]. Building upon these insights, we will explore the ways in which infrastructural work shapes the foundation for the collaboration differently in Denmark and in India.

Time and place matter in global work. Previous research has investigated the timely rhythms and patterns in global software development [5, 26] and the collaboration and negotiation of time across time zones [27]. When exploring the collaboration of global software development, we need to take a close look at how time is organized and decided upon—and by whom. Although work time has been argued to be more flexible in the globalized world, time and place are also related to status and power [13]. Poster [28] shows how workers in Indian call centers face a work-time rigidification and standardization, as the work day is shifted from day to night to sync with consumers' daytime in Europe or in countries such as Japan or the US. She refers to the transformed work time as reversal of work time, which is a pertinent part of the work conditions [28]. Although the demand to work at night is different between workers in call centers and our global IT developers, there are important aspects of time and place that deserve further investigation. When understanding transnational collaborative relationships in relation to time, we found Sharma's work on the taxi driver's relationship to time useful for understanding the politics of time and laboring within temporal infrastructures. Sharma introduces the term cab-lag, which "*refers to a condition of labor where people exist in a differential and inequitable temporal relation with another group with whom they are expected to sync up*" ([29], p. 79), which may be an interesting condition in relation to the global IT workers.

## 7.3  Method and Location

Since 2011, we have conducted several ethnographic studies of global software development in different parts of the world as part of a large research project (Next Generation tool and processes for global software development—NextGSD). While each study is uniquely organized with a different purpose and aim, they have all provided us with insights into the practices of GSD in general. Throughout these years, we have spent time in India as well as in the Philippines studying global IT development. In particular, we studied IT developers in India working in outsourcing setups collaborating with European and American clients. In 2013 we initiated

**Table 7.1** Data sources from fieldwork conducted in India (IN) and Denmark (DK)

| Field site | | | |
|---|---|---|---|
| Gathering technique | IN | DK | Online |
| Observation (no./hours) | 17/9.1 | 29/35.6 | 26/14.3 |
| Interviews (no./hours) | 7/5 | 10/8.8 | 4/2.6 |
| Field diary entry (no.) | 9 | 39 | – |
| Time spent in field (hours) | 66 | 137 | – |

a new ethnographic study of an outsourcing setup between an Indian IT vendor (which we call *InData*) and their customer (called *DanTech*). DanTech is a large IT and software company in Denmark, with more than 3200 employees and several branches around Denmark. For more than 40 years, DanTech has developed IT products for both the Danish public and private sector, and since 2005 they have conducted GSD outsourcing projects with InData to offer customers a reduced time to market and to ensure extra resources and growth. In 2013, more than 200 people from five different global suppliers located in Poland and India collaborated with DanTech, where InData is the largest supplier.

The ethnographic study [30] was organized as a workplace study [31] conducted both in Ballerup, Denmark, and in Bangalore, India. The first author spent intensive periods in the field—following the IT workers in their daily work, including observing online and collocated meetings—with frequent reflective breaks at the university. While in the field, activities such as observation, note taking, and shadowing were combined with daily field diary, photographs, and semi-structured interviews. We also conducted formal interviews face-to-face or in online meetings through the company's communication platform, Lync—ranging from 20 min to 1 h (all audio-recorded and verbatim transcribed). Moreover, we retrieved documentary evidence of various company artefacts and internal email correspondence. Our data sources collected in Denmark and India cover 59 h of observations, 21 interviews, and a field diary (cf. Table 7.1), and in total we spent around 200 h in the field.

## 7.4 Results

### 7.4.1 Bodies Inside the Offices

During our ethnographic fieldwork the dissimilarities in the relationship between InData and DanTech became noticeable in various ways, for example, the agency to decide on the course of action, which remains at the client side in Ballerup, as DanTech manages the project. Witnessed through several observations and frequently articulated by the IT developers working out of Bangalore was that they often find themselves in an idle position waiting for a response from Ballerup in order to work.

> Everything is very time consuming here, I feel… over there [in DanTech] everything is fast, it's very quick there. Whatever we do, we get the responses, the answers very quick. Here we have to wait [ … it] is dragging the tasks [ … ] and that is not the only thing, if we are expecting some answers, if we have sent an email, so we wait for further reply. But of course we can take up another task and do but still if it is of importance or if it is blocking [other work]. That's one of the drawbacks. (*11/27/13, Interview, Tester, India*)

The constant waiting and inability to assume control over time create different conditions for global work in Bangalore compared to Ballerup. Even if work was slowed down at InData, this would rarely block the DanTech IT workers from continuing to work on other tasks, but the opposite impact is always present. In addition, we saw how opposed the practices around meetings and schedules were when DanTech tried to control the organization of work with InData:

> Jakob comes to my desk to inform me about the meeting that we were supposed to start now [ … ]. Murali is not there right now, so we will have to wait a little (he tells me with an eloquent smile on his face that refers to our talk earlier about how he had invited Murali to the meeting and he had not yet accepted it). According to Jakob, when the meeting invitation remains unanswered that does not necessarily mean that he [Murali] will not be attending. Instead, Jakob tells me that he often experiences when inviting one of the developers in India to a [online] meeting that they rarely accept the meeting invitation. This does not mean they will not attend. Instead, as Jakob sees it, the Indians do not see the invitations as a negotiation process in the same way as the Danes do: inviting, accepting, rescheduling, etc. in their online calendars. (*07/05/2013, Fieldwork notes, Denmark*)

The situation above with Jakob and Murali was one of many similar situations. Clearly schedules are practiced differently; at DanTech IT workers are expected to be in office when the calendar says so, they are expected to accept or decline meeting invitations, and they are expected to be precisely "on time". We noticed how meticulously the workers at DanTech used their online calendars to register all work activities, leaving colleagues no trouble in detecting whether a person is available or, for example, attending a meeting. The calendar invites are perceived as an opportunity for negotiating time at DanTech, whereas at InData calendar invites come across as commands and not negotiations. You do not negotiate commands, but rather find other workarounds to get out of non-suitable situations:

> At some point during the daily scrum meeting it came up that Ravi is not here today. Martin sounded surprised by this information. Later I hear Martin telling Lisa that it is annoying that on Friday he and Ravi had discussed something that Ravi should be working on, and then today, Monday, they find out that Ravi is not here. [ … ] Ravi was taking a day off. (*07/08/2013, Fieldwork notes, Denmark*)

When Martin and Ravi talked on Friday about getting something done on Monday Ravi knew he would be away that day; however, instead of accepting or declining calendar invites Ravi's strategy avoided participating in the negotiation of time and rather than address the issue directly he simply said nothing and stayed home as planned. From Martin's perspective, taking a day off is legitimate; however, Ravi's failure to tell Martin he would be away that day and the lack of transparency in work time is problematic. What we see here is not simply a lack of transparency in the work; the situation demonstrates the performativity of time in the global work.

There is obviously an asymmetry in the relationship between InData and DanTech, and Ravi's lack of power in scheduling and coordinating his own work demonstrates that agency for negotiation of time plays an important role in global work. Had he initiated a discussion on re-scheduling the meeting, it might have put him in an awkward situation of either not being able to satisfy the 'customer' or causing him to cancel his day off. By ignoring the matter of participation in the scheduled meeting, Ravi can take his day off.

### 7.4.2 Bodies Outside the Offices

The challenge of time was also pertinent outside the office. A tester working out of Bangalore explained: "*We have to drive or come from a long distance, and we have to be here for nine-and-a-half hours.*" The daily commute in Bangalore, combined with the fact that the InData staff work 2 h more every day compared to DanTech, creates different work conditions related to time. Most foreigners would find the Indian road traffic noisy, complicated, frenzied, and slow. Travelling a distance that might be estimated without traffic to take about 20 min might easily last more than 2 h during rush hour. In Bangalore—the Silicon Valley of India—most of the IT companies are located outside the city in industrial parks or campus-like spaces. InData is situated in Electronics City—one of India's largest electronic industrial parks—and due to the complexity of the transport infrastructure, most of the companies in Electronics City offer their employees bus transportation each day for a monthly fee. The bus transportation is organized by picking up employees at certain times and places and driving them to and from work. InData has more than 23 different buses with seats for 40 people in each. Buses run twice in the morning, striving to arrive at the office campus at 9:00 a.m. and 10 a.m. In the evening, buses leave twice, at 6:30 p.m. and again at 7:30 p.m. Because time to commute in Bangalore is highly unpredictable, coming in "on time" or coming home "on time" are variables produced by the local circumstances and less by the individual. Thus, some IT developers choose alternate commuting practices, traveling at less jammed hours:

> [ . . . ] Usually Rati does not go by bus, but because of visits from DanTech today, she will come into the office at 9 a.m. Her normal routine is to take a company car—a car provided by DanTech [ . . . ] the car will leave at 11 a.m. to reach the office around noon, and leave again at 10 p.m. to reach her home at 11 p.m. That way Rati will then skip spending time in the heavy traffic, and it is also very good for her, as a tester, to work at the same time as her colleagues onsite. (*12/04/2013*, *Fieldwork notes*, *India*)

According to Rati, the staggered working hours are preferred, although not required, by DanTech; however, she really appreciated the benefits of skipping the heaviest traffic. She further explained that getting into the office around noon and leaving work late suited her lifestyle for now while she is unmarried.

Commuting in Ballerup appears quite different. While the IT developers at DanTech commute every day, foreigners will be surprised to see the regularity and punctuality by which people arrive each morning between 7:30 a.m. and 9:00 a.m by bike, train, bus, or car. The typical work day is 7–8 h, and most IT developers will leave around 3:00–5:00 p.m. Transportation is articulated by several of the IT developers in DanTech as an opportunity to get exercise and not simply as commuting. Thus, many travel by bike and then shower and dress in the company locker room before walking into the office and booting up their computer. Most roads have dedicated biking lanes, which goes well with the widespread trend of exercising to and from work, wearing full cycling clothes, and riding an exclusive racing bike. The public transportation in Denmark is generally reliable and predictable, and it is possible to plan transportation in detail, including calculating the time it takes to transfer between trains or buses as well as the time it takes to walk to the office. Also, the trains and buses run in routine patterns on a regular schedule, including every ten minutes during rush hour, allowing the IT developers to flexibly plan and organize their travel between home and work.

Besides time, place also emerged as an inevitable object of inquiry in our search to understand the differences in global work at the two locations. In Ballerup we experienced how those with families make sure to plan and customize their time spent physically at the office by taking advantage of flex-time agreements, which means that they can distribute their work hours flexibly over a time period (typically across a month or year) and chose to come into the office later or leave earlier as long as work hours are carefully registered in advance in the online calendar. Thus, the location of the workspace is not necessarily physically bounded; instead, work might take place at different places.

All DanTech workers are provided with a laptop that they can carry around and bring to meetings or the like. When the IT worker returns to her/his sit-to-stand desk, s/he simply places the laptop in the installed docking station and continues working using the desktop screen, keyboard, and mouse. The laptop not only facilitates movement around the office workplace, it also enables the IT workers to, for example, work evenings from home if, in the daytime, they have to accommodate family emergencies or the like. Thus, in many ways, the location of the workspace is not only flexible and non-fixed in time, but also in space. In this way the work for the IT workers at DanTech was *not* characterized by clear demarcation between work and home. Instead, the work caused by the global circumstances in working across time zones increased the lack of work/life boundaries for the individual, who might choose to wake up early to answer emails in bed before breakfast and getting kids to school to accommodate the remote colleagues waiting for answers.

To overcome the infrastructural challenges of transportation in Bangalore, some IT workers choose to move out to live near the workplace. By near we mean significantly shorter time spent on daily commute, for example, from 1–2 h by bus or car twice a day, to 20–30 min spent walking or going by car. However, leaving one's family or immediate community behind to be able to move closer to the workplace may come at a price, and often these rapidly created housing facilities are dull and characterless. People will stay there during workdays and on weekends they will head back to the villages where their families live.

We also became aware of a certain way of living that was particularly popular among the female junior IT developers and testers at InData, namely living at women's paying guest hostels. Several of the young and unmarried women at InData live at these women's hostels, located walking distance from the workplace. Here they do not have to attend to the daily chores of cooking and cleaning. Instead, they can fully focus on work, while living in a safe environment—side-by-side with "travelling companions" that one can walk with when moving on foot to and from the office. Of course, this kind of living situation fits certain types of workers—those who have not yet established a family of their own or those who may live separate from their family during workdays because the family lives in a village far away. In this way, a clear demarcation between home and work is drawn up for the global IT developers in Bangalore. The majority of their time is spent "away" from home and family, and when they are away they engage only with other "away" colleagues, even in their "free" time.

A final and recurrent theme that demonstrates a form of asymmetry in the global collaborative work concerned the rotation plan for the IT workers to travel abroad. For the InData workers, to go "onsite" (i.e., travel to Denmark and work at DanTech for a period of time) is considered a great opportunity:

> [ . . . ] the people working offshore, they always aspire to go and work with the client onsite, and so it's always good to give people an opportunity, even if it is a short one. [ . . . ] to go abroad and work there [onsite at DanTech] we can earn some good money, do some good work, see around, and comeback, so it's a big motivation factor. (*12/3/13, Interview, IT developer, India*)

While it is a motivational factor for the Indian workers—boosting their CV and getting monetary benefits—going abroad to work onsite also challenges the family life. Thus, the length of the stay may be critical depending on the worker's marital status: "[ . . . ] *if he is a bachelor, then no problem moving for six months or nine months*". According to the Delivery Manager at InData, traveling abroad is problem free when the workers are unmarried, as compared to when having a family. However, even when married, some IT workers make sure they can travel abroad when the opportunity arises, like this InData tester: "*I asked my husband and he said if it is for a short term, then its good, so even I can get some opportunity to learn and meet new people. So I took this and went for six months*".

During our fieldwork we noticed tensions related to the rotation plan, as some of the workers felt they were treated unequally:

> When waiting for the elevator going to the 7th floor for lunch, Anjeneya says—out of thin air—that the developers who are getting the opportunity to go onsite and those who are not are very unequally divided. He says that he thinks that the rotation should be more frequent instead of keeping only a few people onsite for two years or more [ . . . ] That way more people would be knowledgeable about the business. (*12/02/13, Fieldwork notes, India*)

When we asked a manager at InData about the rotation plan, his answer somewhat aligned with Anjeneya's view on the current rotation plan:

> [ . . . ] *rotation should happen, but that did not happen—at least Hina traveled there and then came back, but after that nothing happened, so no one traveled. Vernon, Ranjit, Paturi,*

*and Ashish were there for a long time, more than one year. And obviously the team is waiting for some of them ... will be waiting to get that opportunity [to travel onsite] I think that some of the people who already left might have stayed here if they had been offered the opportunity to travel abroad.* (12/3/13, Interview, Delivery manager, India)

Around the fall of 2013 half of the offshore team left InData in search of greener pastures. According to the manager, the unequal divide in the rotation plan had an impact on their decision to leave. Interestingly, the prestige of getting the "opportunity" to travel offshore from DanTech to visit and work with colleagues at InData was hard to find in Denmark. Those who worked closely with the offshore workers had difficulties finding the motivation to go, as there were no great incentives for traveling abroad. The DanTech employees would not cash in any monetary benefits, and without being allowed any days of leave or compensation when returning home, they would have to sacrifice the time spent with family to go offshore. The expectations for continuous development are high at both locations; however, both the willingness and the expectation to spend time abroad are unequally distributed due to the dissimilarities, for example, in career incentives and temporal infrastructures, at the different locations.

## 7.5   Discussion: The Analytical Lens

As we were intrigued by the InData tester's bodily experience of transnational work being more *difficult* depending on which *world* you are located in, we first set out to understand what made it difficult, and then to question how the local embodied experience of dissimilarities and difficulties were shaped by the conditions for collaboration within transnational collaborative work.

First, in understanding the ways in which the collaborative relationships in global work are manifested in the work practices, we *move inside the office*. Here, the first analytical move is to destabilize taken-for-granted assumptions about knowledge and language as they appear in the practices under investigation [32]. The purpose is to unpack supposedly objective and authoritative vocabulary about the work, which creates certain conditions for the people involved [33]. Following this strategy exploring global work, we find that unpacking key vocabulary and rhetoric of global work—such as "anywhere" and "anytime"—demonstrates an interesting starting point for our analysis. The rhetoric that global work transcends geographical boundaries since work can be done anywhere [34] creates certain imaginaries on how work is accomplished.

In our case, we see how the pressured work time is pertinent at both locations; however, the politics of time—the power to control time and aspects of how time is managed—is differently performed. While we experienced the IT developers in Bangalore to often wait passively for tasks to be delivered to them, they would stay in the office for many hours. Although the hours might not be fully productive, they would always be there, ready, as cab-lagged workers *"waiting to be necessary for others' time needs"* ([29], p. 75). This observation points to the type of relationship that is embedded in the economics of outsourcing practices—the client views the remote IT developers as available resources standing by, ready at all times. The IT developers working out of Bangalore are dependent on the work and knowledge located at the client—leaving them with less flexibility and agency in the negotiation of synchronous meetings [27]. In the structural organization of work, it is difficult for the IT developer at InData to take initiative, to perform independent agency, since knowledge and power lie elsewhere. On the contrary, we saw DanTech workers face challenges in the collaboration due to disparate practices around the meeting schedules, which at times led to an InData worker's non-appearance at an online meeting. When looking into the work within the shared practices and commonalities of the global collaborative work, the variety of circumstances, habits, and routines become apparent as helpful direction for where to look when understanding collaborative work.

At DanTech, agency and knowledge are a core and central part of the work that also impact the ways in which work time is organized. Pressure to perform within time is pertinent in Ballerup. However, rather than waiting for others to take initiative, they experience the time pressure in terms of performing efficiently and knowledgeably to not lose work to people elsewhere. Time is money in Denmark, literally speaking, since the most expensive part of software companies is the employees' salaries. Typically IT developers' contracts state the exact amount of hours per week (typically 37 h), which means that all extra work either means extra salary to those involved or that they accumulate additional vacation time, which by law has to be executed within the current year. This means there are certain organizational structures that support efficient working days and discourage working extended hours. Although work time has been argued to be more flexible in the globalized world, clearly workers in Bangalore face a different practice of rigidification and standardization of time at work [28] than in Denmark. Previous research demonstrated how shifting work hours can result in temporal work patterns being out of sync locally to accommodate the challenges of asynchronous work globally [28, 35]. While our data did not demonstrate a completely out-of-sync situation, it was clear that evenings of week days were dedicated for work, reducing time for family and leisure.

At InData, the time dedicated to work on a daily, weekly, monthly, and yearly basis is quite high: a 10-h work day, 5 days a week, and in many cases a 2-h commute both ways. Fourteen hours a day dedicated to work leaves only 10 h a day for sleep, eating, family, and leisure, meaning you work and sleep most of the time. IT workers in Bangalore are encouraged to stagger their daily working hours to align with overseas colleagues by working from noon to late at night. In practice it meant that the global IT workers in Bangalore, rather than becoming "free" and "flexible" in time, often experienced a hyper-management of time, which controls important aspects of their lives. On the contrary, the norm for many global IT workers at DanTech is to have the flexibility to work from home by simply taking their laptop home and having direct access via VPN to all the information required for their work. In this way, the boundaries between work and private life are getting blurred, and previous research has pointed to the challenge of increased attention on work at the expense of leisure time [36]. The hybrid organization of work in Ballerup is of a different kind than in Bangalore, as transnational encounters blend into private life (early morning and late evening), and also into the private space. While we do not see migration in terms of moving into, for example, hostels inside the tech-hub in Ballerup or in regular travels to offshore locations, migration becomes an intertwined relationship between the work place and the home on a daily basis.

Bringing your work laptop out of the office is *not* the norm in Bangalore. Anyone who has visited an IT company in India has experienced the hassle of registering laptops by serial numbers in advance, and how upon arrival computers and other technical equipment are scanned by security. Part of the reason for these routines involves proving to the western clients that the Indian companies are professional and can ensure good security: they demonstrate that data is not leaving the premises. However, it also means that global IT workers at InData are not given laptops so they can work from home on a regular basis.

The reasons *why* some IT workers can work from home, while others obviously cannot, is not what is interesting here. Instead, to unpack global work, it is important to realize the existing and various constraints and limitations placed not only by the local work practices within the collaborating organizations but also by the physical contextual contingencies that emerge upon the infrastructures involved locally. In this case, infrastructural aspects of, for example, the Danish data privacy legislation may contribute to our understanding of the dissimilar collaborative relationship. Moreover, we learnt how the rotation of IT workers was imbalanced in relation to incentives and rewards for those involved in the global work, which may be explained through important infrastructural aspects of, for example, the hierarchical structures within the transnational collaboration, or by the difficulties of acquiring immigration visas for India or Denmark.

Moving out of the office, we consider the infrastructural circumstances in which the global work is embedded. Thus, we travel outside of the spaces where we normally study global work (the offices) and include considerations about how life and the *infrastructures outside the office* create certain conditions for work. We explore the infrastructures of the society, which serve as fundamental for the global work. When we report on the bodily experience of commuting in Bangalore on potholed and polluted roads in worn out busses, we are not trying to neglect that long commutes take place all over the world. Indeed, we are not saying that transportation alone is in fact what challenges globally distributed and collaborative work. Instead, we use it as an example to demonstrate how and why studying GSD work in CSCW needs to include the infrastructural issues that provide the foundation for the global work, including Internet access, transportation, childcare, domestic responsibilities, etc. The point it not to evaluate whether these infrastructures are good or bad, but to make visible the emergent dissimilarities in the collaborative relationships embedded within temporal and infrastructural aspects of the geographical locations, which often fall to the background in our analysis.

So in the same way that the cab-lagged taxi drivers have no ability to control time [29], due to certain temporal inequitable relationships and trafficable infrastructures, the inequitable work relationship as well as the infrastructures in Bangalore take away agency from the InData IT workers to control time and place. Conversely, for the IT workers at DanTech who have some capability to control time due to, for example, the infrastructural circumstances allowing them to work from a laptop, the separation between work and private life is erased. Increased by the many hours of commuting in Bangalore, the move between places for life and places for work becomes separated in both time and space. We saw how the IT developer *migrates* into the tech-work environment in Electronics City in Bangalore, away from family and friends. The migration [28] becomes a fact when the global IT developers leave their homes and families to travel to the workplace and the workplace becomes the dominating activity in their lives. Our case demonstrated, for example, how women choose to leave home and live in women's hostels closer to the workplace to reduce the time spent on transportation. While this *move* reduces time spent commuting to work, it also increases time required for travelling to their home villages on weekends and holidays to visit family. The migration experience between life and work becomes more pertinent.

We found that global work based upon transnational encounters is rather hybrid engagements where at both sites the intensity in attention toward work is increasing based on how time is practiced. Clearly the politics of time take different forms— coarsely outlined as either long (at times in idle) hours or as fragmented hours with a constant pressure for efficiency; all depend upon the infrastructural foundations, some of which make certain aspects of work possible while others do not.

## 7.6  Conclusion

In this paper we set out to unpack the nature of global work through the concerns and the bodily experiences of the IT workers within the collaborative relationship of a GSD setup. In particular, we were intrigued to understand why the difficulties of doing global work—among others—depended on the embodied experience of being at certain physical locations. Triggered by our wonderment and as a first analytical move, we questioned the common language constructs that assume GSD work to allow the flexibility of working anywhere and anytime. When looking into the work practices enacted within the office walls of the global collaboration, it became clear how the flexibility in GSD was merely a matter of how politics of time and place were performed at the various locations. Thus, as a second analytical move, and in order to discover how politics of time and place mattered in the global collaboration, we found it necessary to travel outside the office to investigate the local contextual contingencies and the infrastructural aspects involved. In our third and final analytical move, we returned to the office, now with insights useful for re-considering the transnational collaborative work as it happens within offices.

We found that the place for work is produced differently for the IT workers located in Bangalore and Ballerup, which means that the language construct of "anywhere" is not descriptive for workers in Bangalore. Instead, we saw that the remote client controls the places for work. Moreover, the politics of time were also enacted differently at the two sites, where IT developers at both locations struggled in different ways. In Ballerup, time became "all the time", while in Bangalore it became "here and now". The dissimilarities in the conditions for work emerge since coordination across sites was required and enacted on the premises of the time of the IT workers at DanTech. The existing asymmetry in the collaborative relationship was clear when an IT worker at InData refrained from answering calendar invites to avoid conflict in taking a day's leave of absence. Finally, the underlying infrastructures in terms of Internet access, transportation, and domestic work clearly placed different conditions for work in both locations. Support from grandparents and paid domestic workers was essential for the IT workers at InData to be able to participate in the transnational work under the conditions of how work was organized. At DanTech, governmental daycare infrastructure was an important part of the work for the IT workers. It also meant that the workday might be cut into two (morning and evening), leaving the afternoon for children, shopping, and cooking. To make this possible, the facility for a home office was an essential infrastructure.

Within global collaborative relationships in GSD there are difficulties and dissimilarities in the work emerging from infrastructural aspects such as trafficable infrastructures, housing possibilities, domestic obligations, technology availability, and flexibility in work hours. Together these infrastructural aspects appear as a multiplicity of relations, which we need to include when exploring particular cases of transnational work. It is important to stress that our proposed analytical lens is not intended as a fixed model. Rather, we see the three analytical moves as an inspiration for opening up transnational studies on collaborative work, bringing into consideration the infrastructural multiplicities embedded within global work as they emerge both inside and outside the office walls.

**Acknowledgments** The study is conducted as a part of "Next Generation Technologies and Processes for Global Software Development," #10-092313. Go to www.nexgsd.org for more information. We would like to thank all the anonymous volunteers at InData and DanTech who generously offered their time for this research. Moreover, we would like to thank Marisa Cohn, Irina Shklovski, Nina Boulus-Rødje, Lars Rune Christensen, Nanna Gorm, Naja Holten Møller, and Paul Dourish for their contribution in discussing previous versions of this paper, and finally a great thanks to the anonymous reviewers for insightful comments.

# References

1. Walsham G (2008) ICTs and global working in a non-flat world. In: Barrett M, Davidson E, Middleton C, DeGross JI (eds) Information technology in the service economy: challenges and possibilities for the 21st century. Springer, Boston, pp 13–25
2. Boden A, Nett B, Wulf V (2009) Trust and social capital: revisiting an offshoring failure story of a small German software company. In: Wagner I, Tellioğlu H, Balka E et al (eds) ECSCW 2009. Springer, London, pp 123–142

3. Christensen LR, Bjørn P (2014) Documentscape: intertextuality, sequentiality, & autonomy at work. In: Proceedings of the SIGCHI Conference on Human Factors in Computing Systems (CHI'14). ACM, 2451–2460. DOI = http://dx.doi.org/10.1145/2556288.2557305
4. Herbsleb JD, Mockus A, Finholt TA, Grinter RE (2000) Distance, dependencies, and delay in a global collaboration. ACM, Philadelphia, pp 319–328
5. Esbensen M, Bjørn P (2014) Routine and standardization in global software development. In: GROUP'14. ACM, p 12–23. DOI = http://dx.doi.org/10.1145/2660398.2660413
6. Boden A, Avram G, Bannon L, Wulf V (2009) Knowledge management in distributed software development teams – does culture matter? In: IEEE Computer Society, pp 18–27
7. Krishna S, Sahay S, Walsham G (2004) Managing cross-cultural issues in global software outsourcing. Commun ACM 47:62–66. doi:10.1145/975817.975818
8. Søderberg A-M, Krishna S, Bjørn P (2013) Global software development: commitment, trust and cultural sensitivity in strategic partnerships. J Int Manag 19:347–361
9. Hossain E, Bannerman PL, Jeffery DR (2011) Scrum practices in global software development: a research framework. Springer, Torre Canne, pp 88–102
10. Avram G, Bannon L, Bowers J et al (2009) Bridging, patching and keeping the work flowing: defect resolution in distributed software development. Comput Supported Coop Work 18:477–507. doi:10.1007/s10606-009-9099-6
11. Avram G (2007) Knowledge work practices in global software development. Electron J Knowl Manag 5:347–356
12. Matthiesen S, Bjørn P, Petersen LM (2014) "Figure out how to code with the hands of others": recognizing cultural blind spots in global software development. In: CSCW'14, ACM Press, pp 1107–1119. DOI = http://dx.doi.org/10.1145/2531602.2531612
13. Hinds P, Retelny D, Cramton C (2015) In the flow, being heard, and having opportunities. In: CSCW'15. ACM Press, New York, pp 864–875
14. Jensen RE, Nardi B (2014) The rhetoric of culture as an act of closure in a cross-national software development department. In: ECIS 2014, Tel Aviv, Israel, 9–11 June 2014
15. Martin D, Hanrahan BV, O'Neill J, Gupta N (2014) Being a turker. In: CSCW '14, ACM, New York. p 224–235. DOI = http://dx.doi.org/10.1145/2531602.2531663
16. Irani L (2015) Difference and dependence among digital workers: the case of Amazon Mechanical Turk. South Atl Q. doi:10.1215/00382876-2831665
17. Boulus-Rødje N, Bjørn P, Ghazawneh A (2015) "It's about Business not Politics": software development between Palestinians and Israelis. In: European Conference on Computer Supported Cooperative Work ECSCW
18. Wulf V, Aal K, Kteish IA, et al (2013) Fighting against the wall: social media use by political activists in a Palestinian village. In: CHI '13. ACM, New York, p 1979–1988. DOI = http://dx.doi.org/10.1145/2470654.2466262
19. Yoo D, Lake M, Nilsen T et al (2013) Envisioning across generations: a multi-lifespan information system for international justice in Rwanda. ACM, New York, pp 2527–2536
20. D'Mello M (2006) Gendered selves and identities of information technology professionals in global software organizations in India. Inf Technol Dev 12:131–158. doi:10.1002/itdj.20031
21. D'Mello M, Sahay S (2007) "I am kind of a nomad where I have to go places and places" . . . Understanding mobility, place and identity in global software work from India. Inf Organ 17:162–192. doi:10.1016/j.infoandorg.2007.04.001
22. Irani L, Vertesi J, Dourish P, et al (2010) Postcolonial computing: a lens on design and development. In: CHI'10, ACM, New York, p 1311–1320
23. Philip K, Irani L, Dourish P (2012) Postcolonial computing: a tactical survey. Sci Technol Hum Values 37:3–29
24. Ahmed SI, Mim NJ, Jackson SJ (2015) Residual mobilities: infrastructural displacement and post-colonial computing in Bangladesh. In: Proceedings of CHI 2015, ACM Press (2015). doi:10.1145/2702123.2702573
25. Matthiesen S, Bjørn P (2015) Why replacing legacy systems is so hard in global software development: an information infrastructure perspective. In: CSCW'15, ACM, New York, New York, USA, pp 876–890

26. Massey AP, Montoya-Weiss MM, Hung Y-T (2003) Because time matters: temporal coordination in global virtual project teams. J Manag Inf Syst 19:129–155

27. Tang JC, Zhao C, Cao X, Inkpen K (2011) Your time zone or mine?: a study of globally time zone-shifted collaboration. ACM, Hangzhou, pp 235–244

28. Poster WR (2007) Saying "good morning" in the night: the reversal of work time in global ICT service work. Res Sociol Work. doi:10.1016/S0277-2833(07)17003-5

29. Sharma S (2014) In the meantime. Duke University Press, Durham

30. Randall D, Harper R, Rouncefield M (2007) Fieldwork for design. Springer, London

31. Luff P, Hindmarsh J, Heath C (2000) Workplace studies. Cambridge University Press, Cambridge

32. Anderson W, Adams V (2008) Pramoedya's chickens: postcolonial studies of technoscience. The Handbook of Science and Technology Studies, Cambridge, MA, pp 181–204

33. Mainsah H, Morrison A (2014) Participatory design through a cultural lens: insights from postcolonial theory. doi:10.1145/2662155.2662195

34. Perry M, O'hara K, Sellen A et al (2001) Dealing with mobility: understanding access anytime, anywhere. ACM Trans Comput-Hum Interact 8:323–347. doi:10.1145/504704.504707

35. Shome R (2006) Thinking through the diaspora: call centers, India, and a new politics of hybridity. Int J Cult Stud 9:105–124. doi:10.1177/1367877906061167

36. Gregg M (2011) Work's intimacy. Polity Press, Cambridge, UK

# Chapter 8
# Design of Digital Environments for Operations on Vessels

**Yushan Pan**

**Abstract** This paper reports on observations and interviews conducted through fieldwork at an offshore supply vessel to investigate offshore operational systems in use. The intention with the fieldwork was to get a better understanding of the knowledge and relationship that operators living in workspaces to use modern digital technologies. The findings are presented and analyzed through the lens of actor-network theory (ANT). The analysis shows that systems are involved in three main networks during different operations which I call host actor-network, parallel actor network and reconfigured host actor network. It also shows that these relationships contribute to dynamically changing safety issues on board, such as risky operations during tasks between the offshore support vessel and the oil platform. This paper addresses the critical issues of how different social, digital technologies and workspaces connected as networks affect the character of safety operations and the implications for the design of marine technology in workspaces and systems in a digital environment on a ship's bridge.

## 8.1 Introduction

There is increasing interest in the development and use of operational systems to meet hi-tech maritime products in offshore fields, specifically in the west of Norway, which is one of the most important maritime hubs in the world. The Norwegian Petroleum and Maritime Company calls to focus on research that expands interdisciplinary perspectives and can adequately integrate the many factors influencing ship design. These include factors rooted in digital devices, intelligent machines, advancing IT technologies and in the interface between technology, safety, social and physical environments [1]. This paper is a response to the call

Y. Pan (✉)
Norwegian University of Science and Technology, Trondheim, Norway
e-mail: yushan.pan@ntnu.no

© Springer International Publishing Switzerland 2016
A. De Angeli et al. (eds.), *COOP 2016: Proceedings of the 12th International Conference on the Design of Cooperative Systems, 23–27 May 2016, Trento, Italy,*
DOI 10.1007/978-3-319-33464-6_8

and provides a possible solution from an interaction design perspective to propel an understanding of future digital environments on a ship's bridge.

This paper reports on some initial exploratory fieldwork with the operators on the bridge of an offshore supply vessel and the use of modern digital technologies in their situated environment, e.g. computers, email, dynamic positioning (DP) systems, integrated automatic systems (IAS), printers, chairs, paper-based checklists and other workspaces and operational systems. Overall 5 months (not continuously, 7–12 days per time, six times in total) fieldwork at an oilfield at sea was conducted to learn more about operators' experiences with digital technologies and workspaces currently available to them. This provides opportunities to observe operators using, or attempting to use, existing digital technologies and workspaces in a digital environment and to interview them about their understanding and perspective on the use of operational systems. The fieldwork is in nature and informs further research to develop a methodology for evaluating complex working environments, such as a ship's bridge. The paper addresses some of the experiences gained through the fieldwork and uses actor-network theory (ANT) as an analytical lens for investigating how workspaces associated with offshore operational systems on a ship's bridge increase unsafe activities. In turn, this will show how operational systems that result in unsafe actions have the power to reshape workspaces.

ANT is a social theory that provides a range of different concepts and perspectives that are suitable for the analysis of socio-technical relationships [2]. It is a powerful tool for those who want to explore the interplay between human society, technology and design [3]. ANT perspectives are used to explore the capacity of nonhumans to act in operational systems and participate in networks with humans [3]. It is argued that the design of artefacts, through multiple socio-technical entanglements, becomes an act of defining and reconfiguring individual and collective agencies. Interaction design is not only the work to create an individual product, it is about enabling the hidden potential in everything – in you, your organization and the world around us [4]. For example, Aanestad [5] uses ANT to show that the introduction of telemedicine technology into surgery became a process of alignment and negotiation of diverse and conflicting interests. She argues that the camera becomes an actor that, through its socio-technical presence, affects and reconfigures the existing work practices. Moser and Law [6] use ANT to show how the specificities of the different networks of materials with which actors engage in their everyday lives contribute to dynamically assisting them in a variety of ways.

In marine design, workspaces and system designers work separately. Researchers focus mostly on the usability of a workspace, such as whether a tool is easy to use. However, a ship's bridge is complex and involves cooperative work among operators and must factor in other organizational contexts [7]. I have argued elsewhere that it is insufficient to use traditional design methods in this domain [8, 9]. It is important to investigate the relationships between workspaces and operational systems because all of them are part of a digital environment. It is difficult to articulate where workspaces end and systems begin in operations. Hence, this paper draws on these concerns to explore how ANT can contribute to presenting operators, despite the fact that they are still fully capable of working on a ship's bridge as they have always done. It concludes with some discussions and critical reflections on how we can offer design ideas to designers.

## 8.2   System Design

Currently, designing systems is understood as a process of defining and developing systems to satisfy the specified requirements [10] of the user, such as offshore control environments on vessels and platforms, onshore coordination centers and so on. Operational system design is treated as a process of decomposition of requirements. Engineers use this to design a system by breaking it into a collection of interacting pieces [10]. For example, a whole operational system on a ship's bridge [11] is divided into heating systems, freshwater systems, electrical charging, navigation gear, offshore operations and so on.

The pieces of each system are designed solutions and activities from one or more engineers. Through mechanical and industrial engineering, engineers combine those solutions and endeavor to make the pieces fit together [10, 12]. This system design is a way to deconstruct the functionality of a system; however, it does not need to think of how these digital technologies are used. Both industrial and mechanical philosophies discount an understanding of how to effectively design a system, especially when we finally reconstruct the systems' pieces [12, 13]. Designers in the information technology (IT) field also play roles as evaluators in digital environments, such as healthcare information systems, to improve the user experience. Researchers describe problems within systems and advise operators on how to use IT solutions and work cooperatively with colleagues [14]. These cases approach design in a different way. The designer observes and interviews operators during real-time operations. For example, in designing cooperative segments in healthcare systems [15–18], researchers explore the dynamic of cooperative work practices in hospital systems and suggest how to design computer systems for humans. Another study in the maritime domain addresses the design problems of systems [19]. Researchers in the field of designing a cooperative system analyze the interactive relationship within systems and workspaces [9, 18, 19]. However, such interests in marine design are rarely without reasons. It requires an interactive relationship [7, 10, 20] between all participants: operators, operational systems and workspaces in the working context. Are these elements working together successfully and conforming? This leads to the research question for this paper: How do operators work properly in a real-time environment with workspaces and operational systems during operations?

## 8.3   Empirical Setting and Methods

The study area is the operational part of a ship's bridge on an offshore supply vessel. Unlike navigation systems, this part of the system is only used for offshore operations on oil and gas platforms. Two teams of two people each work in 6 h shifts on a ship's bridge. The operational systems have several subsystems, such as DP systems, IAS, radar systems and so on. DP is a computer-controlled system that automatically maintains a vessel's position and heading by using its own propellers and thrusters [20]. IAS refers to a system that controls the subjective (flesh water, mud or types of liquids that are requested by different offshore missions) in 12 containers under the deck. IAS also offers capabilities for operators to control containers manually to support platforms. Both DP and IAS are distributed in 18 displays in operation areas (ahead and in front of chairs) associated with radar, monitors and alarm systems (ahead) (see Fig. 8.1). Two operators face these displays to manipulate different systems from time to time and from task to task. Additionally, communication devices are also used in operations. There are four communication devices for internal communication in vessels. Communication devices can be used for multiple purposes. These communication devices are placed on a shared table between two operators (see Fig. 8.1).

On board, I was allowed to take notes and photos. I also conducted formal and informal interviews with operators on the bridge at the sea during offshore oilfield trips. Permission was obtained to observe maritime operators' knowledge and use of technology. This was clarified and approved by the national authority on privacy and

**Fig. 8.1** Offshore operational systems (Operational part of ship bridge on an offshore supply vessel)

data protection in research involving human subjects: Norsk Samfunnsvitenskapelig Datatjeneste [NSD]. An informal consent form was also obtained during the field studies.

Operators working on the ship's bridge were observed while using, or attempting to use, different technologies, devices and workspaces. They were interviewed in order to understand the problems or challenges they experience and to find appropriate solutions. In many cases, I was invited into the living areas on board during lunch and dinner time in order to address their concerns about current technologies-in-use on the bridge. This leads to many informal conversations about their use of technology and workspaces and other experiences and practices in everyday life during operations. These activities helped me understand current technologies-in-use on board and acquire a deeper knowledge and understanding of behavior on the bridge during operations.

## 8.4  Theoretical Lens

Work on the ship's bridge is not a simple interaction between an operator and a computer system [7, 19], nor is it simply operators' doing their own work. It involves a large social environment integrated with systems, workspaces and other devices in cooperative processes among operators [19]. In order to deal with the relationship between workspaces and systems where a group of operators interact with the digital environment, ANT is appropriate. It is helps to establish a theoretical discourse around the working environment under study. When an operator uses systems on the bridge, the operator is influenced by operation regulations, his colleague's responses to specific tasks, his own experience using it, the functionality of the systems and workspaces' capabilities to support systems. All these issues are connected to how the operator works. An operator does not work in a vacuum but under the influence of a wide range of factors [21]. Hence, when I understand an operation in a digital environment, I consider all these influencing factors together, since the actions of operators are linked with influencing factors to produce the network.

Unlike other theories, ANT does not distinguish technology from non-technology [3]. Instead, an actor-network consists of and links together both technical and non-technical components, and priority is not given to human or nonhuman in the network. The actor-network is heterogeneity involving every element equally [22]. ANT offers a way to term how, where and to what extent technology influences human behavior [21]. ANT does not purely dig into technical components or distinguish a priori between social and technical elements of a network [23], rather, it emphasizes [24] that the focusing points should be the dynamic relationships between non-technology and technology. When dealing with the design of technology and examining the technologies-in-use, ANT gives us the power to unpack the potential problematics of an integrated digital environment by following participating humans and nonhumans in actions in different network relationships [25].

In particular, I have flexibility to analyze any research interests in the project by zooming in and out on the interested work routines from a 'work-net' in an network environment [21, 26]. By visualizing ANT, designers are able to provide a readable and designable for engineering world [27]. Hence, it is helpful to use ANT as a theoretical lens because I am more concerned with how operators use technology in reality, when they are immersed in a digital environment rather than the technology itself, such as the definitions of two concepts I have developed – Host Actor-Network and Parallel Actor-Network. Since offshore operations are dynamic, the operation networks are shaped and reshaped from task to task because ANT analysis represents interests in the place where what designs and what is designed mutually shape one another [4]. However, in some tasks a network can generate to different small networks. For example, one is maintaining the original purposes of an operation which I call Host Actor-Network. Another one is running with purposes to bring new interests into the Host Actor-Network in order to reconfigure the original network. I call this network as Parallel Actor-Network, and the new Host Actor-Network is called reconfigured Host Actor-Network.

## 8.5   A Vignette

This section describes situations where offshore operators on the ship's bridge are observed in the use of different digital technologies associated with physical structures in a digital environment. This digital environment consists of operational systems and workspaces around offshore operators, such as paper-based checklists, chairs, tables and a gap between workspaces. This vignette comes from operations on an offshore supply vessel at sea. I selected this vignette because I believe that this case presents the relationships between workspaces and systems on the ship's bridge. This is important for improving potential risky operations from a technology point of view and includes users' performance and perceptions in technology-in-use in reality. In addition, all names in this paper are anonymous treated.

Tom is an operator on the bridge of a vessel called 'Alterfjorden'. He is 29 years old. His main job is to perform DP operations and control the IAS during operations. Andrea is 55 years old. He is the captain. His main job is to make final decisions and to assist Tom during tasks, such as printing checklists and checking and marking the amount and weight of cargo that is loaded from platforms during operations.

It was a sunny day. Waves and wind were within a reasonable fluctuation range. Tom piloted the vessel near a platform called 'Sjona'. Tom stopped the vessel and walked to the operation systems area where Andrea was ready for the day's mission (Fig. 8.1). The following dialog is from the field notes and audio recordings.

> **Tom**: Andrea, did you check and approve the checklists (paper based forms)?
> **Andrea**: Yes, here you are. But remember, we have an old version of the cargo and mission lists.
> **Tom**: Well, let's hope they (crew on the platform) will not change the scheduled work during our operations.

**Andrea**: Ah, ha-ha-ha ... it is possible.
**Tom**: Ok, let me check whether the engine is ready.

Tom picked up a communication device and called the engine room. This is required of any operator working on the bridge before performing DP operations.

**Tom**: Good day! Are you guys ready?
**Engineers**: Yes, (we) can't wait for it ...
**Tom**: Thank you!

This time, Andrea signed and approved the checklist. After this communication between the ship's bridge and the engine room, Tom and Andrea were ready for their main DP task: giving and retrieving water and mud (a special liquid) from the platform and recording cargo given to and retrieved from Alterfjorden. Tom positioned the vessel near Alterfjorden, and Andrea helped him to position the vessel directly below the Alterfjorden's crane (DP operation).

**Tom**: Andrea, now you can monitor and record the cargo from Sjona.
**Andrea**: Yeah, I have it (a paper-based form). Pay attention to the IAS.

As mentioned before, IAS refers to an integrated system that controls the containers under the vessel's deck. Tom and Andrea were working on different tasks, such as maintaining the balance of the vessel, water, mud and cargo tasks. Tom paid attention to the IAS system. He needed to know how much water or mud he needed to provide Sjona from the vessel's containers. Andrea needed to work on recording the amount of cargo, since these numbers can help him to estimate the weight of each unit of cargo. For these operations, the decision power is not on the hands of the people who work on the ship's bridge. Sjona decided how much water and mud its needs, including what types of mud. Tom and Andrea had to help Sjona finish operations. Usually, cargo, water and mud are handled at the same time. Crews on Sjona also decided how much waste water needed to be returned to Alterfjorden. This information is not available beforehand for bridge operators and the shipping company because it is immediate and dynamic. Based on dynamic information about water, mud and cargo, Tom and Andrea could balance Alterfjorden during their offshore work and keep the vessel in a safe situation by avoiding imbalance. This is important since an unbalanced vessel can easily rollover due to waves.

After 43 min of providing mud to Sjona, the communication device rang.

**Sjona**: Alterfjorden, Alterfjorden, Alterfjorden.
**Tom**: Yes, bridge crew, Alterfjorden.
**Sjona**: We don't need type II mud now. We have enough. We want to change to type IV. We will send you an email about the how much type IV mud we need.
**Tom**: Ok. No problem.
**Tom**: Andrea, could you please check the email?

Tom asked Andrea to check email because he was in charge of DP operations to maintain the vessel in a proper position. At the same time, he was also working on receiving waste water from the platform. Before he was asked to check the email, Andrea was recording the cargo loaded from Sjona. Tom needed cargo information

**Fig. 8.2** Office area on the bridge

associated with the IAS system to make sure the vessel was in a safe situation, i.e. balance and distance to the platform due to sea waves. If Andrea left immediately to check email in the office (Fig. 8.2), Tom would have to factor in possible risks because he would not be able to get information about the cargo. Hence, it was a dilemma for both Andrea and Tom. Unfortunately, there is no good solution because neither Tom nor Andrea could wait until their task at hand is finished. They had to respond as quickly as possible. There are many uncertainties during operations, such as wind, wave, changing muds, water, exchanging cargo and so on. If the weather conditions do not permit these operations, they have to wait. However, work time is limited, and operators have to get back to the quay on schedule, otherwise the company will incur unnecessary expenses on the booked quay. Waiting time at sea also incurs costs, such as fuel. Hence, operators normally react when the work has to change even though there may be some risks.

Andrea ran to the office area immediately as Tom requested (Fig. 8.2). He ran along a narrow channel on the bridge (Fig. 8.3) rather than using the moveable chair (Fig. 8.1). He used the computer and checked the email from the platform. Then, the email was printed out and Andrea picked up the new checklist.

**Andrea**: Tom, type IV right?
**Tom**: Yup. How much do they (the platform) need?
**Andrea**: Wait, I need to check the work list and confirm with the company first.

Andrea then picked up the satellite phone and asked the company for permission to change the mud type. This kind of change is related to the economic interest of the oil and shipping companies. As a captain, Andrea had to report this information before undertaking any action. When he got permission, he had to sign the form and return it to the oil platform. After signing, he spoke to Tom about how much mud the

**Fig. 8.3** A narrow channel on the bridge

vessel could provide to the platform. Simultaneously, Tom pressed the emergency stop because the platform told him that some cargo was put down wrong. Tom could not execute operation himself, so he chose to shut down all operations because the ship was already significantly unbalanced. This information was reported by the cook who complained via a communications channel that his cooking utensils were falling everywhere. Andrea quickly ran back to his seat from the office area via the narrow channel to help Tom. He picked up the communication device to coordinate with Sjona to take back the cargo.

**Andrea**: Sjona, which cargo you mean?

## 8.6   Relationships Between Workspaces and Systems

### 8.6.1   A Network Is Established

From this vignette, I find several components are connected in a network during operation procedures. If I look at the vignette closer, I find that the network is connected when Tom and Andrea check the paper-based checklist. Tom, Andrea and the paper-based checklist are actors in the network. All actors share an interest in this task. Tom wanted Andrea to check and prove the checklist. Andrea had to look at the checklist and give final approval. The checklist needed to present all the information the operators' needed. The checklist connected both Tom and Andrea. However, in this process, the network was still in an operational area.

The network grew when Tom picked up a communication device. It was easy to see where the communication device participated. Tom was interested in getting information from the engine room because it was important to know the status of the vessel. Zooming out again, the Engine room engineers became connected to the existing network via the communication channel. Engine room engineers had to share their knowledge with the bridge operators. This is required by the work procedure; however, they also want to share this information with other people even though that is not required.

> **Engineer**: We want to let others know the engine status of the vessel. It is important for everyone to know, since we do not want to put others at risk during offshore operations.

All members in this network share interests and translated these interests into a common understanding: safety. In this network, members come and go until the network becomes stable.

### 8.6.2   Host Actor-Network

When the vessel is positioned, the network is reshaped. Engine engineers leave the network, since their task for the rest main operation is finished. At the same time, the platform people join this network. The actors this time are Tom, Andrea, Sjona's crew, the IAS systems in the systems and the cargo on Sjona and Alterfjorden. This network call the 'host actor-network'; since the network now is stable for operation until other actors bring in new interests. These interests do now have a common focus but upset the balance of this network. The host actor-network refers to the main offshore operation. This is a different definition from other research that allows silent or passive actors to participate in the network, such as an airport study [22]. In this paper, every actor in the host actor-network has to speak their interests in order to have a common interest for the entire offshore operation. It is a process-based organizing [28] where each participant in the network have to speak out their interests and agree upon a common understanding for operations – safely finish the mission. When the network is unbalanced, an actor has to make an indispensable identification of problematics in order to find an appropriate way to express interests and lock other actors when enrolling a new balanced network [29]. All participants in this process are seeking to stabilize network from negotiation of enrolment of interests to ensure the adhesion of the collectives to the network [28] until a common voice is establish in dynamic process of operation.

Tom had to balance the vessel during the operation, i.e. monitor the status of containers under the deck via IAS and get information from Andrea about the cargo's weight. Information from the IAS and cargo was important so Tom could judge how to properly operate the offshore operational systems, such as manually changing information in the IAS systems, running DP operations and communicating with Sjona during the operations to coordinate the position of the cargo on the deck. This network seemed stable; however, once any actors bring new interests into this straightforward operation process, the network has to be reconfigured and interests have to be reassessed. When Sjona asked Tom to change the mud, this interest broke the host actor-network.

The interest Sjona introduced forced Andrea to consider several interests from the company's side, particularly expenses for the quay and cost of everyday expenses at sea. When he decided to check the email and ask for company permission to change mud, his interests could not be translated into the host-actor-network. For example, Sjona requests changing mud, and Tom had to change it. However, Andrea had a different interest because he needed final approval before changing. If Andrea had gone back to call the company, the host-actor-network would have broken down because of Andrea's new interests: email, new checklist, the company on land and the narrow channel. These bring new interests to expand the host actor network. It was a difficult process, since Sjona did not want to stop the work with Tom. Tom had to stay in the host actor network until he pressed the emergency stop button due the Sjona error. In this case, the host network dynamically shrank to allow Andrea to leave for the office.

### 8.6.3   A Parallel Actor-Network and Reconfiguring Host Actor-Network

When Andrea undertook other tasks, i.e. running via the narrow channel on ship's bridge, checking email, making a new checklist and calling company on land, a parallel actor-network was established. It is called 'parallel actor-network' because the advent of this network does not prevent the operation of the host actor-network. However, this network weakened the host actor-network and compelled the operations to take more risks. When Andrea joined in the parallel actor-network, Tom in the host actor-network faced difficulties and could not handle the rapidly increasing work, i.e. he could not operate the vessel, pump water or mud from and to Sjona and record cargo. I can see that the problem is that systems are currently closed systems. Systems have no ability to receive and process any information from the outside, e.g. request to change the mud from Sjona is an example. Andrea had to respond to this request in order to finish the offshore operation. When he finished his work and went back to his seat to help Tom, he brought a new interest into the host actor-network. When Andrea got permission from the company and let Tom know how much mud the vessel could provide Sjona, the parallel actor-network ended.

However, Andrea came back to the host actor-network with new interests: different information about the type of mud. Tom had to reconfigure the mud process to keep the vessel balanced. Sjona had to reconfigure because the mud was changed. Hence, every actor in the old host actor-network had to reconfigure their interests when performing new operations. Before this reconfiguration, there was a break between the parallel actor-network and the reconfigured host actor-network that resulted in the emergency stop due to the loading of the wrong cargo. In order to fix this problem, actors had to work together to return the wrong cargo and keep the vessel's balance. IAS, Tom, Andrea, the paper-based checklist, mud, cargo and Sjona reformulated their interests to a common value due to safety considerations.

As uncertainties happen all the time in oilfields, jumping from the host actor-network to the parallel actor network is frequent. It results in a high workload on the bridge and increases safety issues. The actor network is dynamic [30] and unavoidable [31]. When actors reconfigured the host actor-network, this network's original actions changed. Every interest was new and had to be retranslated. When the old host actor-network was broken and reconfigured, Andrea has to stop his original work to bring other interests into the process – the computer, the printer, the narrow channel and so on. When I zoom out to analyze the parallel actor-network and the reconfigured host actor-network, it is not difficult to see two problems. First, for the operators on the bridge face different challenges to reach the needed workspaces around them, e.g. the office area. Current systems could not help them with changing requests. Extra tools from daily work and life have to be brought in [19] to assist them. The moveable chair is observed as useless during the offshore operations. The narrow channel (Fig. 8.3) is his path. As Andrea and Tom state, this narrow channel is more useable than the moveable chairs.

> **Andrea**: If any changes have to be made, like changing water or mud type, I just quickly run to the computer, check email, print and talk to the company. I do so because we have limited time to work each day. We have to [be concerned with] the waves and wind, and I also need to make sure Tom can use this time to handle everything. So we have to save time, otherwise, we will waste thousands krone per day without doing anything.
>
> I never use the moveable chair because it is too slow. Tom cannot wait that long for me. Actually, I want to have a small digital device that can help me to check and print without moving, but [unfortunately] there is no such technology, like something on my mobile phone.
>
> **Tom**: Sometimes we have to leave the operational area together because I have to observe cargo from the platform when Andrea cannot help me. It is the most dangerous moment because I need to balance the vessel by shifting water or mud from each side, right or left, to ensure the vessel is ready to take cargo. I cannot work on that many tasks at the same time.

Second, when the network becomes a reconfigured host actor-network, workspaces and operational systems are not able to support safe operation procedures. Current operational systems cannot support operators' needs to check email and print out checklists in the operational systems area; the operator has to leave the host actor-network to join a parallel actor-network to finish this task. It is not possible to avoid reconfiguring the host actor-network because new interests are introduced into the operation. Hence, in this vignette the designed chair should be a participant in the parallel actor-network, but it is not. Instead, the narrow channel joins. Workspace designers may learn that operational systems can cause the operators to abandon some workspaces. It opens a room for researchers to investigate more about how to better redesign ship's bridge in the near future, such as designing for individuals' disruption of a piece of workspaces while they may remain connected to one another or to the whole workspace.

**Andrea and Tom**: We would prefer to only have displays in front of us without the chair. Because the chairs are a hindrance in our work, we have to use that narrow channel most times. When we are trained onshore, we never think this is a problem. But now as you can see, we are struggling with this [in the] work environment.

## 8.7  Reflections on Digital Environment Design

In current design, workspace designer and software designers work separately without a common purpose when designing a digital environment. However, different thinking is needed in the maritime domain [32]. An approach proposes that both workspaces and systems designers should engage in the field to understand the working context. I think this approach should be investigated further. In order to design a coherent digital environment for offshore operations, the relationship of 'space to place' [33] and information spaces [34] should be considered. When people, workspaces and systems meet in different operational situations, reconsideration of the guidance for design should consider two aspects: interaction in workspaces and interaction in systems.

Most of the time, operators on a ship's bridge only use systems. Interaction problems in systems arise when a change request comes from Sjona. In this case, operators have to interact in workspaces to accomplish this request in order to make the whole offshore operation coherent. Since the printer and computer are far away, if operators could move the chair quickly, they wouldn't end up in a risky situation to finish their work. Current ship bridge design needs a holistic understanding of the bridge as a digital environment with the simple assemblage of software, hardware and physical tools [32]. Designers may overlook the fact that human operators are integrated with workspaces and operational systems. Every human action is constrained by the organizational context, which consists of workspaces, operational systems and social meaning in offshore operations.

Some control room designs, such as anthropometrics and the biometrics of the operator population [35], can help to create a digital environment. These designs may separate the relationships between workspaces and operational systems. I argue that marine design should assimilate operational systems' design processes, such as seat height, seat depth, leg room, desk height, the character on the screen, the brightness of the character on the screen, free reflective glare of the screen and number of screens, so they are valuable parts of the operational systems. This can be understood as a reconfiguration of segments in interactions [36]. The workspace should be placed in different spatial areas that can support different tasks, and each area should have its particular social meaning. The social meaning should be defined by the operators based on their everyday life on board. For example, operators know better than the designer that the printer and email systems are also used in their offshore operations and not just for printing out logbooks. My findings draw attention to the need to support the actions of the operator so he can easily reach the email system and check the requested information from the oil platform. This forces us to rethink the interaction patterns in the operational area on the ship's bridge.

Some may argue that training operators can conquer these problems by restricting operator behavior, i.e. they must wait until they finish the work at hand. I argue that the training and supervision of operators only helps the work in a simulated environment; it does not help in reality [8]. Operational mistakes happen for a reason; when an error occurs, researchers should think about technical issues and why some technologies-in-use do not match the original design purposes [37] in different social settings. In additional, economic considerations restrict the operators' behavior and the company's decision. When an operator decides to check email and respond to the oil platform quickly, he not only determines the function of the systems but also need to accommodate specific workspaces, i.e. the narrow channel.

Workspaces and digital technologies have the relationship 'you support me; I support you'. Hence, it is important to understand the social, technical and organization factors that shape how operators, workspaces and systems are configured [18]. Such configurations directly point to the breakdown of offshore operations, which must be addressed by an interaction of both workspaces and systems. Operators know they cannot finish the offshore operation only in operational areas. They know the degree of risk they need to run to reach the office area. They also know what kind of support they need from outside of the operational area. Hence, our design shall support their interactions with workspaces across distributed information sites [38]. This is fundamental for designing systems on a ship's bridge. We need to redesign to help when operational system designers, operators and workspaces meet to set common goals.

## 8.8  Conclusions

This paper reports on fieldwork related to a technology support service for offshore operators. The motivation for the fieldwork was to investigate how operators relate to and use operational systems. It also aimed to inform further research into designs for offshore operations on vessels. The vignette is used to illustrate some of the observations and experiences gained through this fieldwork. The vignette is analyzed through the lens of ANT, and the analysis explicates how technology use is immersed in web of workspaces and operational system relationships that dynamically affect the actors involved.

The operational systems used by operators do not provide a theoretical-based experience or support safety operations. These systems are largely used in the current domain. Nevertheless, the vignette illustrates two important lessons that are relevant for the design of operational systems: first, the power of technology-in-use lies in its appropriate introduction into an existing network of workspaces and operational systems. The determining factor for successful introduction of technology lies in how to enable operators to do what they need to do. Second, operators are relatively uncomfortable with the current design of operational systems, and they have to put themselves in risky situations in order to find the operational systems that are useful to them. They also need to adapt to use different workspaces and to know what to do when they break down. It is crucial that in our quest to develop new technologies for operators, we do not forget to provide the support and safety products needed to ensure that the work is conducted successfully.

**Acknowledgments**  Thanks to reviewers and to Sisse Finken for their constrictive feedback. This research is found by the Research Council of Norway.

# References

1. Forskningsrådet (2012) Work programme MAROFF, The Research Council of Norway
2. Latour B (1999) On recalling ANT. Sociol Rev 47(S1):15–25
3. Hanseth O, Aanestad M, Berg M (2004) Guest editors' introduction: actor-network theory and information systems. What's so special? Inform Technol People 17(2):116–123
4. Storni C (2010) Unpacking design practices: the notion of thing in the making of artifacts. Sci Tech Hum Values 37:88
5. Aanestad M (2003) The camera as an actor design-in-use of telemedicine infrastructure in surgery. Comput Supported Coop Work 12(1):1–20
6. Moser I, Law J (1999) Good passages, bad passages. Sociol Rev 47(S1):196–219
7. Pan Y (2015) Evaluating the interactive relations of complex systems: offshore operations as research resources. In: 18th annual dilemmas international research conference, Marcus Wallenberg. In press
8. Pan Y (2016) Cooperative systems for marine operations using actor-network design: a discussion. In: 20th international conference on computer supported cooperative work and design, IEEE. Accepted
9. Pan Y, Finken S, Kom S (2015) Are current usability methods viable for maritime operation systems? In: The eighth international conference on advances in computer-human interactions, IARIA. pp 161–167
10. Waldo J (2006) On system design. In: Technical report 2006-062006, Sun Microsystems Laboratories
11. Leonard BA, Starzinger E (2006) Simple but sophisticated: an alternative approach to boat systems design. http://www.bethandevans.com/pdf/SimpleBoatsystem.pdf
12. Peiwei M, Scacchi W (1991) Modeling articulation work in software engineering processes in software process. pp 188–201
13. Woodhouse E, Patton JW (2004) Design by society: science and technology studies and the social shaping of design. Design Issues 20(3):1–12
14. McFarlane P, Hills M (2013) Developing immunity to flight security risk: prospective benefits from considering aviation security as a socio-technical eco-system. J Transp Secur 6(3):221–234
15. Bardram J (1998) Designing for the dynamics of cooperative work activities. In: ACM conference on computer supported cooperative work. pp 89–98
16. Bossen C (2002) the heterogeneity of cooperative work at a hospital ward. In: ACM conference on computer supported cooperative work. pp 176–185
17. Reddy M, Dourish C, Pratt W (2001) Inating geterogeneous work: information and representation in medical care. In: ECSCW 2001: Proceedings of the Seventh European Conference on Computer Supported Cooperative Work. pp 239–258

18. Li J, Robertson T (2011) Physical space and information space: studies of collaboration in distributed multi-disciplinary medical team meetings. Behav Inform Technol 30(4):443–454
19. Pan Y, Komandur K, Finken S (2015) Complex systems, cooperative work, and usability. J Usability Stud 10(3):100–112
20. IMO (2004) A guide to DP-related documentation for DP vessels. International Maritime Organization, Sweden
21. Monteiro E (2004) Actor-network theory and information infrastructure. In: From control to drift: the dynamics of corporate information infastructures. Oxford University Press, London, pp 71–83
22. Mähring M et al (2004) Trojan actor-networks and swift translation: bringing actor-network theory to IT project escalation studies. Inform Technol People 17:210–238
23. Latour B (1990) On actor-network theory. A few clarifications plus more than a few complications. Finn Olsen Om Aktor-Netvaerksteroi Nogle Fa Afklaringer Og Mere End Nogle Fa Forviklinger – Philos 25(3):47–64
24. Latour (1987) Science in action: how to follow scientists and engineers through society. Harvard UP, Cambridge, MA
25. Cordella A (2010) Information infrastructure: an actor-network perspective. Int J Actor-Netw Theory Technol Innov 2(1):1–27
26. Latour B (2007) Reassembling the social an introduction to actor-network-theory. Oxford University Press, Oxford
27. Akama Y (2015) Being awake to Ma: designing in between-ness as a way of becoming with. CoDesign 11(3–4):262–274
28. Hernes T (2010) Actor-network theory, Callon's scallops, and process-based organization studies. In: Process, sensemaking, and orgainzing. Oxford University Press, Oxford
29. Callon M (1984) Some elements of a sociology of translation: domestication of the scallops and the fishermen of St Brieuc Bay. Sociol Rev 32:196–233
30. Callon M (1986) The sociology of an actor-network: the case of the electric vehicle. In: Callon M, Law J, Rip A (eds) Mapping the dynamics of science and technology: sociology of science in the real world. Macmillan, London, pp 19–34
31. Hanseth O, Monteiro E (1998) Changing irreversible networks: institutionalisation and infrastructure. In: European conference on information systems. pp 1–8
32. Lurås S, Nordby K (2014) Field studies informing ship's bridge at the ocean industries concept lab. In: Human factors in ship design and operation. pp 1–10
33. Ciolfi L, Fitzpatrick G, Bannon L (2008) Setting for collaboration: the role of place. Comput Supported Coop Work 17(2–3):91–96
34. Schmidt K, Bannon J (1992) Taking CSCW seriously. Comput Supported Coop Work 1(1):7–40
35. Stanton NA et al (2010) Control room layout, human factors in the design and evaluation of central control room operations. CRC, London, pp 249–271
36. Suchman L (2007) Human-machine reconfigurations plans and situated actions. Cambridge University Press, Cambridge, UK
37. IDF (2013) User error: who is to blame? [cited 2016 050216]
38. Groth K (2008) The role of technology in video-mediated consensus meeting. Telemed Telecare 14:349–353

# Chapter 9
# Shifting Patterns in Home Care Work: Supporting Collaboration Among Self-Employed Care Actors

**Khuloud Abou Amsha and Myriam Lewkowicz**

**Abstract** In this paper, we describe and analyze the work practices of an association of self-employed health and care professionals promoting a collaborative approach to home care in France. Our study shows (1) that coordinative artifacts (e.g. a liaison notebook) are central for sharing information and coordinating the work, (2) that focusing on patients' quality of life leads care actors to address issues beyond the medical scope, and (3) that team members experience different rhythms of collaboration depending on the patient's situation. We use the concept of knotworking proposed by Engeström [16] to better understand the challenges faced by people involved in this innovative way of organizing work, and suggest some guidelines when designing a system to support this type of work.

## 9.1 Introduction

The interest in home healthcare is increasing due to the social and economic challenges faced by the majority of health care systems in the developed world. Many studies show the potential of home care to enhance the well-being of patients and simultaneously reduce the expenses of health delivery via decreasing patient hospitalizations, particularly hospitalizations for handling emergencies [20].

In this context, collaboration between care actors becomes essential for providing a good quality of care. However, collaborative care raises challenges related to including a broad set of evolving care actors (health professionals –physicians and nurses –, professional caregivers, home helpers, social workers and informal caregivers) that do not always belong to the same organization and in many cases do not belong to any organization. This is particularly true in France, where independent health and care professionals provide the majority of home care work.

K. Abou Amsha (✉) • M. Lewkowicz
Troyes University of Technology, ICD, Tech-CICO, UMR 6281, CNRS, Troyes, France
e-mail: khuloud.abou_amsha@utt.fr; myriam.lewkowicz@utt.fr

© Springer International Publishing Switzerland 2016
A. De Angeli et al. (eds.), *COOP 2016: Proceedings of the 12th International Conference on the Design of Cooperative Systems, 23–27 May 2016, Trento, Italy,*
DOI 10.1007/978-3-319-33464-6_9

139

We are interested in understanding the collaborative practices of care actors involved in caring for the patients at home in order to inform the design of technologies that support collaboration in such context.

To do so, we conducted a qualitative study of a French group of self-employed health and care professionals organized as an association that promotes a collaborative approach to home care. The main objective of this association is to preserve the quality of life of the patients and their relatives. This association is successful in the sense that it allows patients with complex conditions to stay at home with their family. However, its members express frustration related to their inability to share and extend their model, and to convince more care actors to join them. We (along with the founders of this association) hypothesize that a computer-based system could help them manage their collaborative work in a more sustainable way. To do so, this system must be aligned with their current collaborative practices. Thus, we use the knotworking concept introduced by Engeström [16] to understand the complexity and the challenges raised by the collective care that we observed, and to identify the challenges hampering sustaining this collective care. This understanding and identification of challenges give us insights for designing technologies supporting collaboration in such context.

In the following sections, we start by reviewing the literature on home care and related technologies. We then describe our study and report our findings. Finally, we discuss these findings, suggest implications for design, and conclude with future research perspectives.

## 9.2   Related Work

Many studies have explored home care from multiple perspectives, putting emphasis on places, actors, roles, technologies for monitoring or sharing information, and coordinative practices.

The studies that focused on the specificity of home as a place for caring investigated issues such as: the role of spatial arrangements in collaboration with the healthcare workers visiting home [26]; how domestic practices of health management are inseparable from other personal or family activities [29]; and the fact that formal and informal caregivers adopt different attitudes toward the caring tasks [10].

Besides, home care provision depends on care networks that include a variety of care actors including informal caregivers (family members, friends, or neighbors), home helpers, professional caregivers (nurses, physiotherapists, dieticians), and even pharmacists and technicians [11]. Patients themselves can also play a role in their care plan [13], and some work has focused on how to increase patients' awareness of their health status using monitoring technologies [5, 23], and how to assist patients to manage their daily life while being sick [12, 21, 26, 31, 33].

In addition to people involved on an individual basis, we can see institutions involved in providing home care, like community care centers, call centers, and providers of social and technical services [8]. Studies investigating technologies to support collaboration in these broad care networks focused either on the use of monitoring technologies or the use of shared information systems. Many researchers have focused on monitoring systems that couple sensors and web-based data management to monitor the progress of patients with chronic conditions like diabetes and heart diseases [1, 5, 6, 23, 32], and some studies suggest that these monitoring technologies enhance the awareness among 'care network' members [3, 11], and provide rich context information about the home of the patient [25]. Shared information systems can take the form of electronic patient records (EPR) that enhance coordination in the secondary sector (i.e. hospitals) [18], shared patient record among different care professionals, relatives of the patients and patients themselves [19], or personal health records (PHR) used by patients to organize their health-related information, and to share it easily within their care network [29].

Thus, home care work requires coordination, and more specifically, articulation work among the various care actors [7, 10]. Pinell and Gutwin [28] have shown in particular that care professionals switch between synchronous and asynchronous collaboration to avoid hindering their work. Moreover, the use of temporal rhythms to support caregivers collaborative activities in tightly regulated and mobile work settings was studied by Nilsson and Hertzum [24]. Finally, some studies investigate artifacts such as the shared binders used to support collaboration at home [2, 27].

Our work addresses collaborative practices of people involved in home care in order to design supporting technologies for this kind of collaboration. To explore the challenges related to collaboration in this context, we conducted a case study investigating the collaboration practices of a group of French self-employed care professionals organized as an association named "E-maison médicale", in the city of Troyes.

## 9.3  The Study

As previously mentioned, home care services in France are primarily provided by self-employed health professionals [9]. Although this situation fosters the personalization of care (patients are being treated by "their own" health professionals), the patients and their families must nonetheless transmit information from one health professional to another. To enhance the quality of care at home and to make it more sustainable, the reforms of the French healthcare system encourage innovative initiatives that aim to organize self-employed care professionals' efforts around the patient at home. In the following, we focus on one of the first successful initiatives in France.

### 9.3.1  The E-Maison Médicale Case

The E-maison médicale association is a group of self-employed health profession-als, caregivers and home helpers who are mostly located in several cities around Troyes (N-E France). They aim to promote a collaborative approach to home care delivery because they consider the quality of life of the patient to be a common goal that requires the collaboration of all the care actors.

The Champagne Ardenne region was chosen for the fieldwork because it is confronted by an increasing demand for care due to a growing aging population, and suffers from a lack of doctors [22]. This gave us the opportunity to witness how health professionals innovate in their work practices.

The E-maison médicale association promotes the concept of working together. All care actors – including patients and their families – participate in creating the care plan (usually defined first by the physician), which examines patients' medical and social needs, outlines the type of support the patient should get, describes why and when they should receive that support, and provides details regarding who is meant to provide it.

### 9.3.2  Data Collection and Analysis

We conducted a study over a period of 15 months. During this time, we used ethnographic methods [30] and we collected a variety of empirical materials. In line with the precepts of "combinatory ethnography" [14], we combined interviews and observations, and we organized discussion sessions. The aim was to reveal different forms of activity that are original or at least noteworthy. This offered us a broad picture of the home care actors' collaborative practices and the artifacts used. Inspired by the grounded theory approach to qualitative analysis (Corbin and Strauss 1990), we used open coding and analyzed the data collected from our different sources (interviews, observation, and discussion sessions). We iteratively coded the data over three rounds of coding. These rounds where conducted by the first author, but the resulted codes were discussed with the second author. In the first round, we were looking at the collaborative practices, we were coding information like the kind of collaboration strategies, and we defined codes like "acting together" or "asynchronous coordination". We also coded the different kinds of information the people were sharing; so used codes like "medical instructions", "clinical finding" or "logistic needs". In the second round, we identified a relationship between the collaboration practices adopted by the care actors and the kind of information they are sharing, thus we coded different situations where we had a pattern of practice-information structure: e.g. "treating an emergency", "modifying care plan", or "solving a problem". In the third and final round of coding, we recognized a second level of classification related to different dimensions of the management

**Table 9.1** The sample of collected liaison notebooks

| Patient | Number of notebooks | Number of pages | Period of time covered |
|---|---|---|---|
| SS | 1 | 50 | 11/2011–06/2014 |
| MD | 1 | 84 | 08/2011–06/2014 |
| LD | 1 | 100 | 11/2011–05/2014 |
| SG | 8 | 340 | 2007–2014 |

of the patient's conditions: "medical", "logistic" and "social"). This classification highlighted how care issues emerge, and how these issues that might span multiple dimensions are treated collectively.

We started the field work with a discussion session involving five members of the association. Participants included a physician, a registered nurse (both are founders of the E-maison médicale), a physiotherapist, and two home helpers. We recorded the discussion and noted the remarks. This discussion session lasted 3 h and was the starting point of an observation to see how actors coordinate their work in situ.

Hence, we followed the registered nurse for 3 days (15 h total). We visited 20 patients' homes per day. We took photos and recorded information; our main focus was the work of the nurse, and before taking photos, we obtained the permission of the patients or their family members. During and after each visit, we posed questions to the various care actors (primarily home helpers and family caregivers).

The observation gave us a useful insight into the care practices of E-maison médicale members and highlighted the potential and the centrality of the "liaison notebook", as we reported in [2]. Care actors read and write messages to coordinate their work in this notebook, which provides an asynchronous way of sharing information and communicating.

Based on this first result, we decided to deepen our understanding of the use of liaison notebooks. Thus, we organized a 3 h discussion session with the founders of the network, focusing on how the notebooks support the collaboration between the care actors. We recorded the meeting, took notes and photos of the different liaison notebooks. Additionally, we studied a sample of 11 liaison notebooks (Table 9.1).

### 9.3.3 Findings

#### 9.3.3.1 The Central Role of the Liaison Notebook

The liaison notebook first provides information about patients' care actors; usually, the first page contains a list of their names and contact information. This helps new care actors, or one-time care actors, to contact the current care actors to reveal more about the patient's situation.

Some notebooks also contain a page describing the patient's conditions. This information is not always present because of privacy issues: not all care actors have officially the right to read patients' medical information.

**Fig. 9.1** A diary for a diabetic patient (Mr. SG) – The nurse writes a message for the physician, who responds to him

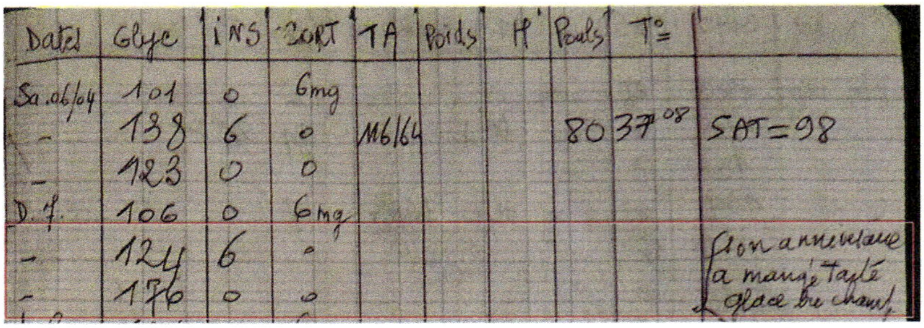

| Date | Glyc | iNS | 2oRT | TA | Poids | H | Pouls | T° | |
|------|------|-----|------|------|-------|---|-------|------|---|
| Sa.06/04 | 101 | 0 | 6mg | | | | | | |
| | 138 | 6 | 0 | 146/64 | | | 80 | 37°08 | SAT=98 |
| | 123 | 0 | 0 | | | | | | |
| D.4. | 106 | 0 | 6mg | | | | | | |
| | 124 | 6 | 0 | | | | | | on anniversaire |
| | 176 | 0 | 0 | | | | | | a mangé taçte glace bu chaud |

**Fig. 9.2** A diary for a diabetic patient – The family caregiver comments on the relatively high blood sugar level, explaining that the patient was attending a party and that he ate dessert

We observed different types of liaison notebooks. The information documented about patients varies according to patients' conditions. For some patients, the notebooks are not structured, and the kinds of physical values that are registered change according to the patient's situation. The notebook is, in this case, a chronological record of the physical values and related care actions. Other patients, such as those suffering from diabetes, require more precise monitoring, and specific notebooks are designed for this reporting (Fig. 9.1). Structured documentation helps care actors prescribe and modify medications. Care actors might comment the numeric values (Fig. 9.2). Additionally, care actors might use messages in the notebook to discuss certain numbers (Fig. 9.1).

Finally, for some patients, physiological constants are mixed with the clinical findings and with the remarks of different care actors regarding the patient's status. In this case, the documentation constitutes an ongoing, asynchronous conversation between the care actors about the patient's situation. Despite the limitations of using the liaison notebook (e.g., accessibility and readability), this tool provides a flexible way to support the variety of information that is necessary for the collective management of the patients' conditions at home, as we will show.

### 9.3.3.2  Different Dimensions of Home Care

Facing the complexity of care at home, and to create a more sustainable model of home care, the members of E-maison médicale extend their objectives beyond medical care to include maintaining the quality of life of patients and their families.

**Medical Issues** To keep the patient safe at home, care actors are challenged every day by medical issues. Care actors collaborate to anticipate emergencies and to address problems properly. Medical challenges include keeping a patient stable, handling the secondary effects of medications, and accidents that could worsen the patient's condition.

To manage the day-to-day medical decisions, care actors rely on the vigilance of each other. In caring for patients with chronic diseases, for example, monitoring plays a significant role. The nurse explains here how he, the home helper and the physician work to keep an aged diabetic patient at home:

> JSS (nurse): *I have to look at what he ate or else I will give him an inadequate insulin dose, and he risks having hypoglycemia* [decreased blood sugar concentration] ... *In his case, he* [the patient] *has memory problems, so I can count on the home helper who keeps a record of meals. In my turn, I write in the notebook the insulin doses and the blood glucose measures. The physician then can decide to maintain or modify the treatment based on this documentation.*

The different care actors meet rarely, and the absence of a shared history of the patient might affect the patient's safety. The nurse (JSS) explained the necessity of a written record.

> JSS (nurse): *I think that we are largely disrupted by a lack of written follow-up. When you have nothing to read, one is bothered, especially in monitoring like this* [referring to the case of patient Mr. LD, mentioned later]. *We are monitoring the risk of effects related to the administration of a corticosteroid and observing the couple that is aging.*

Unlike in a hospital, home care actors lack available logistic resources such as medical equipment and available human resources. Anticipating medical problems often helps fill the logistics gap. The physician (DS) explains what they mean by anticipating:

> DS (physician): *The anticipation is to listen to all care actors, analyzing the patient case and to create a collective responsibility to avoid maximum urgent cases. It is better to spend time anticipating and to forecast, rather than spending time on managing emergencies. Exchanging feelings of health professionals around the patient, is a key to anticipation.*

Care actors handle current medical issues and anticipate possible future problems based on their experience and acquaintance with the patient. They share their impressions in the notebook. For example, the nurse remarks that the patient has signs of lack of oxygen; he writes a note alerting the physician and proposing having oxygen concentrator at the home of the patient.

However, if the care actors see signs of potential risk for the patient, they call each other and try to fix the problem and avoid an emergency. For example, the nurse signals a problem with the patient: 'He is suffocating and has a stomach ache'. The nurse calls the physician; they discuss the solution, and the doctor visits the patient the next day.

Sometimes, the problem requires changes in the care plan. In this case, all care actor's work together to stabilize the patient's situation. Changes in the care plan might come after an emergency that requires temporary changes; for example, the patient has an injury or a broken leg. The case of Mr. WD illustrates the situation of a more permanent degradation of the patient's condition.

Mr. WD started having severe diabetes episodes; the physician asked the nurse to start diabetic surveillance and insulin treatment.

The nurse and the patient cooperated to implement the diabetic monitoring. The nurse taught the patient how to take the necessary measurements and how to document them. The patient recorded the results of his blood glucose tests and the meals he ate. The nurse came twice a day (morning and evening), and he measured the patient's tension and blood glucose. The physician communicated with the nurse and followed the status of the patient. Three months later, care actors decided to reduce the nurse visits to once a day.

**Social Issues** Keeping the patient at home safely depends, in many cases, on the involvement of informal caregivers (usually the spouse or the children, but it also might include friends or neighbors). Indeed, when patients are fragile (cognitively, physically, or both), the informal caregiver role becomes vital to assure the safety of the patient. Thus, care actors watch out for the deterioration of the informal caregiver's moral or physical state as a part of patient care.

For example, Mr. LD is a patient with Alzheimer disease who suffers from heart problems. He lives with his wife, Mrs. LD, who is his main informal caregiver. Mrs. LD injured her wrist while gardening. The home helper called the physician who suggested sending her to his clinic instead of the local hospital. Once Mrs. LD arrived, the physician managed to see her between two patients. He diagnosed a fracture and contacted the x-ray clinic to make sure she will have the x-ray as fast as possible.

After the x-ray was performed, and according to the request of the physician, the radiologist contacted the hand surgeon so the wife had her hand plastered and could come back home later in the afternoon.

The intervention of the physician and the involvement of all the care actors allowed a fast management of the situation (Mrs. LD broken wrist). If not, she might have waited for hours at the emergency room for her radio image. Shortening this process was vital for her role as caregiver:

> DC (physician): *Mr. LD is unable to stand alone, to wash, or to feed himself. Most importantly, he would panic without his wife. If his wife goes to the grocery shop and does not come back in two hours, he will panic.*

The care actors are also reactive to the modification happening in patients' social environment, and they reorganize the patients' care to ease the charge on the informal caregiver.

The case of Mr. AK illustrates how the members of E-maison médicale take into account the burden on the informal caregivers. This patient is epileptic and paralyzed; he depends on the care of his wife. Normally, the couple goes on vacation in the summer for 2 weeks to visit family. However, this year, they had a complication: the airline company refused to have the patient on board, and the wife then decided to cancel the trip. To enable her to go on the trip, the members of E-maison médicale proposed changing the organization around the patient so she could take some time off. The nurse explains the situation:

> JSS (nurse): *She loves her husband* [referring AK couple], *and she looks after him all year, but she needed a break. We discussed the situation with her, and we put a team in place, the physician, me, and a home helper who comes three times per day to feed him, and his son sleeps at home.*

**Logistic Issues** Caring for patients at home include handling administrative formalities (e.g., asking for prescriptions or medical appointments, hiring care actors), handling the medical equipment (functioning, maintenance) and dealing with environmental safety hazards (such as tripping obstacles, stairs without handrails).

Care actors discuss these logistic issues when starting or modifying a care plan. They ask questions such as, do we need special equipment? Can we have the necessary medical equipment at home? Do we need additional care actors? Can we afford it? Can we have financial help?

As the patient's social and medical conditions change, the logistic issues develop, such as in the case of Mrs. LD. After her wrist injury, she had her hand in a cast, which hindered her ability to look after her husband (the patient). Care actors proposed increasing the number of hours spent by the home helper, to help the wife and to avoid admitting the patient to a care setting. Care actors took into account the patient's situation:

> JSS (nurse): *"This is a case that will have consequences for the management of her husband because the lady will be more or less disabled, so, we have set up the needed help* [ . . . ]. *As for the husband, he is very attached, as a patient with Alzheimer's, to his routine. You change the routine of this gentleman; he will be like an atomic bomb."*

This decision has a cost, and again, the care actors discussed whether the couple could afford it. The couple did not get any financial support, and they paid the home helper with their own money:

> DS (physician): *We have realized that the couple paid the home helper, and they did not get any financial help. They did not benefit from the APA* [the Elderly Financial Help granted by the general council]. *We just told her* [the wife] *to contact the social worker of the General Council. We know it is going to be a month or two before aid is launched. Even for emergency situations, the General Council procedures are always very long. So we asked her to call at the same time her insurance company because they may pay for the extra hours done by the home helper, as the need for these hours was caused by an injury.*

Usually, care actors use the liaison notebook to document logistic issues such as administrative needs (e.g. asking the physician to renew the prescription), equipment problems, and organizational issues (e.g. documenting a medical appointment and asking to call a medical taxi before).

Care actors also address logistic issues concerning modifying environmental safety hazards, like installing a grab bar in a shower, replacing a gas stove by an electric one, or even moving in another flat:

> JSS (nurse): *We are almost predicting the future [ . . . ] for a couple of psychiatric patients [ . . . ] the physician and I are thinking about finding them another, more suitable apartment. You see, it goes that far; we will try to find another place.*

### 9.3.3.3   Articulating Different Collaboration Rhythms

Patients' evolving situation affects the way care actors coordinate their activities around patients. We have identified two interchanging phases for the rhythm of the care actors' work: a "standard" and an "intense" coordination rhythm.

In the "standard" phase, the patient's situation is relatively stable, and care actors handle emerging problems individually according to their roles; they coordinate their work conforming to the care plan. They collaborate sometimes tightly to handle urgent problems, and collaborate loosely for less urgent ones. If the problem is urgent, care actors call each other and might meet in the patient's home:

> JSS (nurse) *The phone, DC* [the physician] *and I, we use it a lot. When there are complications, I use the phone, and DC always answers me, so oral communication is working.*

When the problem does not affect patient safety, care actors use the patient's notebook to exchange questions, answers or suggestions. For example, the nurse remarks that the patient has a high blood pressure, and thus gives the patient the necessary medication but also leaves a note for the home helper. In his note, the nurse asks the home helper who cooks the meals to cut down on salt in the patient's diet.

The "intense" phase starts when unexpected (medical or not) events arise and lead to a crisis challenging the current care plan. All care actors then collaborate in modifying the care plan to stabilize the patient. The care actors organize a "care meeting" at the patient's home to characterize the problem:

> DC (physician): *"This meeting can be initiated when a care actor signals a problem (e.g., a deterioration in the patient's condition), or when the patient is saying something is wrong with the care plan. This meeting allows us to see what is going wrong.*

This meeting consists of a discussion of the problem and the different possible solutions. All care actors, including the patient, might participate in the discussion depending on the treated issues:

> DC (physician): *The number of participants varies according to the reasons why the meeting was organized. For example, we might discuss a change in the overall care plan or make decisions such as placing the patient in a nursing home, all of that in front of the patient.*

The care meeting ends with changes in the management of the patients' conditions. Care actors may decide to include a new care actor, ask for one-time interventions or change how the current care actors provide care.

The case of Mr. MD illustrates how care actors work together to adapt the care plan and keep the patient safe at home. Mr. MD, 80 years old, suffers from an inflammatory rheumatic disease that evolves in spurts, and the pain justifies a cortisone-based treatment. The patient is treated at home, where he lives with his wife (main informal caregiver). A home helper comes twice a week to help the wife with caring activities. A registered nurse visits the patient when needed, particularly when he needs cortisone. The physician also visits home when needed. All care actors (wife, home helper, nurse, and physician) write their observations in the liaison notebook.

The patient started having severe diabetes episodes caused by the cortisone treatment; this triggered a care meeting where all the care actors (including the wife) reorganized the care plan of the patient. The physician asked the nurse to start diabetic surveillance and insulin treatment; the nurse and the wife cooperated to implement the diabetic monitoring; the nurse taught the wife how to take the necessary measurements and how to document them. All care actors adapted their practices, including the documentation ones because the patient needed a record of blood glucose.

## 9.4　Discussion and Implications for Design

As we have seen, providing collective care at home is a complex issue. Care actors must adjust their practices and negotiate with patients and their families to successfully perform their work [8]. Previous studies in the domain of Computer-supported cooperative work (CSCW) have explored challenges related to the complexity of implementing home care networks and care teams.

However, whereas previous work has focused on the collaboration among members of interprofessional care teams working within the same organization [28] or across organizations [4, 27], our work focuses on what we see as a new form of organizing the work and the collaboration of care actors who cooperate on a voluntary basis though they do not share common protocols or routines to coordinate their work, and they cannot rely on any sustainable information system.

In contrast with the shared binder studied by Petrakou [27], the liaison notebook that we have presented above does not have any predetermined structure because each patient offers a different case and is managed by different care actors. Collaboration in the context we are observing is based on the motivation of care actors to organize their work, and they do not share any infrastructure contrary to the context covered in the work of Bossen et al. [7].

As we mentioned in the introduction, the collective management of patients that we have observed shows similarities with what Engeström defines as "knotworking" [16]:

a boundary crossing, collective way of organizing work, in which intensive collaborative periods vary according to the changing requirements of the current situation" [17] (p.2). This concept describes an innovative model of organizing work in which professionals and their client form 'knots' in order to work on a shared object [17]. In this model, collaboration happens inside improvised constructions of people and artifacts that are called knots; "the knot symbolizes a rapidly pulsating, distributed and partially improvised collaboration between loosely connected actors and activity systems [15] (p. 972).

Knotworking also describes "a longitudinal process in which knots are formed, dissolved, and re-formed as the object is co-configured time and time again, typically with no clear deadline or fixed end point" [15] (p. 973). In other words, knotworking addresses relatively fixed objectives (e.g. curing a disease) with evolving members (e.g. health professionals), contrary to teamwork, which involves a relatively stable group of participants that deals with evolving objectives [17].

We argue that the knotworking concept is useful to analyze the collaboration and identify the challenges of the care actors who organize themselves around patients in the form of knots.

Hence, an emerging issue for a patient represents a pulse that triggers the formation of a knot. This knot represents the "intense" phase of the collaboration where care actors try to understand the problem, discuss options and find compromises to re-configure the care plan. Finally, care actors adopt the new care plan, going back to the standard collaboration phase and dissolving the knot. In this context, the care plan is central but is not objectified in any document. It is the subject of the discussions around a patient that allow all the care actors to be aware of each other's activity around the patient.

The reactive organization of care reassures the patients because they can count on the collaboration of the care actors when there is a problem. However, we identify challenges regarding the sustainability of knotworking in collective care:

1. **Integrating new care actors**. New professionals constantly participate in providing care for the patient, like for instance when specialist doctors intervene occasionally to handle a specific situation. These new care actors can profit from a brief review on the situation of the patient. However, current care actors have a very busy schedule and cannot meet them to give this information. Therefore, to give this picture, they refer to the liaison notebook. But, for new care actors, being able to identify the most important information or to get a global vision of the situation of the patient takes a considerable amount of time.

2. **Nurturing the ongoing role negotiation**. The success of the home care depends on the collective adjustment of care actors. However, some care actors (e.g., informal caregivers and home helpers) take a lot of time before they find their place in such organization. Thus, many care actors focus on their individual tasks and do not invest in the collaborative dimension of care because they do not understand what their role is in such collaboration. In fact, the collective management of care represents a shift from the traditional hierarchical organization to a more horizontal and dynamic organization in which all care actors play a role in defining and modifying the care plan.

3. **Ensuring the constant motivation of all care actors**. It is difficult to keep care actors involved and motivated particularly during relatively long "standard" collaboration phases. Many care actors consider coordination as extra work and they do not always realize the benefit of this work.

Acknowledging these challenges, and based on our analysis of the collaborative practices of the care actors, we suggest that to support the sustainability of this kind of collaborative work the system need to:

**Foster discussions around the situation of the patient**. To support care at home in the way we have observed (constant negotiation and adjustment through ongoing conversations about the patient's situation), technology has to offer the possibility to discuss the case of a patient. We suggest a system in which care actors can post a message, comment others messages, and by then participate in the asynchronous conversations around a patient. This discussion-based documentation would enable the different care actors to participate in identifying issues (before they become critical) and to provide answers. In this way, the system would provide a way to support care actors coping with the unpredictable issues.

**Identify major steps in the trajectory of the patient**. We suggest that the system should provide a timeline in which all care actors can add major changes in the patient's situation from different perspectives (medical, social and logistic). This timeline will provide new care actors a brief review of the situation of the patient, and will offer a shared place for care actors where they can visualize the evolution of the situation of the patient and thus, support their decisions when they address emerging issues.

**Provide an open indexation**. In order to implement the previous suggestions, we propose to enable the care actors to tag the information they post and identify as important for the collective management of the care plan (a physiological measure, a comment, a specific demand . . . ). These tags will enable the care actors to group different conversations about the same theme (represented by a tag) whereas at the same time preserving the conversational context in which the information was collected. In order to reflect the specificity of each patient's situation, the wording of the tag will be chosen from a list or created by the care actor.

## 9.5   Conclusion and Future Work

In this paper, we have presented our observation of an original approach to home care provision in France. We showed the centrality of the liaison notebook in sharing information and coordinating the work among the different and evolving care actors. We also explored how focusing on patients' quality of life drives the care actors to address issues spanning medical, social and logistic dimensions. Finally, we showed how collaboration in home care teams is not a steady process; care actors experience episodic rhythms of collaboration depending on the patient's situation.

These findings led us to identify challenges encountered by the care actors willing to move towards knotworking: (1) integrating new care actors, (2) nurturing the ongoing role negotiation, and (3) ensuring the constant motivation of all care actors. We finally suggest a potential way to support this knotworking: by both fostering discussions around patient's care plan and identifying major steps in a patient's trajectory. We offer to use tags to index the information gathered by the care actors during the discussions or when filling the timeline. In this way, the care actors are able to flag the information that they consider important with their own words, this important information is then easily accessible, and can be sorted according to different points of view.

We are currently designing and developing a prototype of this system in collaboration with core members of the association. We hope that it could contribute to a better understanding of the ways to support this particular form of collaborative health care work.

**Acknowledgments** This work is supported by a grant from the Regional Council of Champagne Ardenne (convention n° E201207353).

We would like to thank the members of "e-maison medicale" association for their incredible support and cooperation.

# References

1. Aarhus R, Ballegaard SA, Hansen TR (2009) The eDiary: bridging home and hospital through healthcare technology. In: Wagner I et al (eds) ECSCW 2009. Springer, London, pp 63–83
2. Abou Amsha K, Lewkowicz M (2014) Observing the work practices of an inter-professional home care team: supporting a dynamic approach for quality home care delivery. COOP 2014-Proceedings of the 11th international conference on the design of cooperative systems, 27–30 May 2014, Nice (France). Springer International Publishing, 2014
3. Abowd GD, Hayes GR, Kientz JA, Mamykina L, Mynatt ED (2006) Challenges and opportunities for collaboration technologies for chronic care management. The Human-Computer Interaction Consortium (HCIC 2006)
4. Amir O, Grosz BJ, Gajos KZ, Swenson SM, Sanders LM (2015) From care plans to care coordination: opportunities for computer support of teamwork in complex healthcare. In: Proceedings of the 33rd Annual ACM Conference on Human Factors in Computing Systems. pp 1419–1428 ACM, New York, NY, USA
5. Andersen T, Bjørn P, Kensing F, Moll J (2011) Designing for collaborative interpretation in telemonitoring: re-introducing patients as diagnostic agents. Int J Med Inf 80(8):e112–e126
6. Bardram JE, Bossen C, Thomsen A (2005) Designing for transformations in collaboration: a study of the deployment of homecare technology. In: Proceedings of the 2005 international ACM SIGGROUP conference on Supporting group work. pp 294–303 ACM, New York
7. Bossen C, Christensen LR, Grönvall E, Vestergaard LS (2013) CareCoor: augmenting the coordination of cooperative home care work. Int J Med Inf 82(5):e189–e199
8. Bratteteig T, Wagner I (2013) Moving healthcare to the home: the work to make homecare work. In: Bertelsen OW et al (eds) ECSCW 2013: proceedings of the 13th European conference on computer supported cooperative work. Springer, London, pp 143–162, Paphos, Cyprus
9. Chevreul K, Durand-Zaleski I, Bahrami SB, Hernández-Quevedo C, Mladovsky P (2010) France: health system review. Health Syst Transit 12(6):1–291, xxi – xxii

10. Christensen LR, Grönvall E (2011) Challenges and opportunities for collaborative technologies for home care work. In: Bødker S et al (eds) ECSCW 2011: proceedings of the 12th European conference on computer supported cooperative work. Springer, London, pp 61–80, 24 – 28 September 2011, Aarhus Denmark
11. Consolvo S, Roessler P, Shelton BE, LaMarca A, Schilit B, Bly S (2004) Technology for care networks of elders. IEEE Pervasive Comput 3(2):22–29
12. Dalgaard LG, Grönvall E, Verdezoto N (2013) Accounting for medication particularities: designing for everyday medication management. In: Proceedings of the 7th International Conference on Pervasive Computing Technologies for Healthcare. pp. 137–144 ICST (Institute for Computer Sciences, Social-Informatics and Telecommunications Engineering), ICST, Brussels
13. Demiris G (2009) Independence and shared decision making: the role of smart home technology in empowering older adults. In: Annual International Conference of the IEEE Engineering in Medicine and Biology Society, 2009. EMBC 2009. pp. 6432–6436
14. Dodier N, Baszanger I (1997) Totalisation et altérité dans l'enquête ethnographique. Rev Fr Sociol 38(1):37–66
15. Engeström Y (2000) Activity theory as a framework for analyzing and redesigning work. Ergonomics 43(7):960–974
16. Engeström Y, Engeström R, Vähääho T (1999) When the center does not hold: the importance of knotworking. In: Chaiklin S et al (eds) Activity theory and social practice. Aarhus University Press, Aarhus, pp 345–374
17. Engeström Y, Kaatrakoski H, Kaiponen P, Lahikainen J, Laitinen A, Myllys H, Rantavuori J, Sinikara K (2012) Knotworking in academic libraries: two case studies from the University of Helsinki
18. Granlien MS, Hertzum M (2009) Implementing new ways of working: interventions and their effect on the use of an electronic medication record. In: Proceedings of the ACM 2009 International Conference on Supporting Group Work. pp 321–330 ACM, New York
19. Hägglund M, Scandurra I, Moström D, Koch S (2007) Bridging the gap: a virtual health record for integrated home care. Int J Integr Care 7:2
20. Hillcoat-Nalletamby S, Ogg J, Renaut S, Bonvalet C (2010) Ageing populations and housing needs: comparing strategic policy discourses in France and England: ageing populations and housing needs: comparing strategic policy discourses in France and England. Soc Policy Adm 44(7):808–826
21. Lee ML, Dey AK (2011) Reflecting on pills and phone use: supporting awareness of functional abilities for older adults. In: Proceedings of the SIGCHI Conference on Human Factors in Computing Systems. pp 2095–2104 ACM, New York
22. Magniez C, Tonnellier F, Oswalt N, Lucas V, Tallet M-AC (2008) Quelles zones «fragiles» pour l'accès aux soins en Champagne-Ardenne? Rev DÉpidémiologie Santé Publique 56(6):S358
23. Mamykina L, Mynatt E, Davidson P, Greenblatt D (2008) MAHI: investigation of social scaffolding for reflective thinking in diabetes management. In: Proceedings of the SIGCHI Conference on Human Factors in Computing Systems. pp 477–486 ACM, New York
24. Nilsson M, Hertzum M (2005) Negotiated rhythms of mobile work: time, place, and work schedules. In: Proceedings of the 2005 International ACM SIGGROUP Conference on Supporting Group Work. pp 148–157 ACM, New York
25. Paganelli F, Giuli D (2007) A context-aware service platform to support continuous care networks for home-based assistance. In: Stephanidis C (ed) Universal access in human-computer interaction. Ambient interaction. Springer, Berlin, pp 168–177
26. Palen L, Aaløkke S (2006) Of pill boxes and piano benches: "home-made" methods for managing medication. In: Proceedings of the 2006 20th anniversary conference on Computer supported cooperative work. pp. 79–88 ACM, New York
27. Petrakou A (2007) Exploring cooperation through a binder: a context for IT tools in elderly care at home. In: Bannon LJ (ed) ECSCW 2007. Springer, London, pp 271–290
28. Pinelle D, Gutwin C (2003) Designing for loose coupling in mobile groups. In: International Conference on Supporting Group Work. pp 75–84

29. Piras EM, Zanutto A (2010) Prescriptions X-rays and grocery lists. Designing a personal health record to support (the invisible work of) health information management in the household. Comput Support Coop Work CSCW 19(6):585–613
30. Randall D, Harper R, Rouncefield M (2007) Fieldwork for design: theory and practice. Springer, London
31. Verdezoto NX, Wolff Olsen J (2012) Personalized medication management: towards a design of individualized support for elderly citizens at home. In: Proceedings of the 2Nd ACM SIGHIT International Health Informatics Symposium. pp 813–818 ACM, New York
32. Villalba E, Peinado I, Arredondo MT (2009) Self care system to assess cardiovascular diseases at home. In: Stephanidis C (ed) Universal access in human-computer interaction. Intelligent and ubiquitous interaction environments. Springer, Berlin, pp 248–257
33. Williamson JR, McGee-Lennon M, Brewster S (2012) Designing multimodal reminders for the home: pairing content with presentation. In: Proceedings of the 14th ACM International Conference on Multimodal Interaction. pp 445–448 ACM, New York

# Chapter 10
# Supporting Informal Carers' Independency Through Coordinated Care

**Aparecido Fabiano Pinatti de Carvalho, Hilda Tellioğlu, Susanne Hensely-Schinkinger, and Michael Habiger**

**Abstract** Dependency research in informal care has a long history. Studies within this area usually focus on the dependencies that care receivers have in relation to those providing the care: the informal carers. They usually take for granted the dependencies that informal care brings upon the carers. This paper draws attention to these important (unpaid) workers of our current society and discusses how engaging in caring can constrain one of their most valued personal attribute: their independency. Not only that, the paper discusses how coordinated care can come to the rescue of some of this independency, introducing a few simple but yet effective ICT solutions that can create opportunities for it. The findings presented in this paper come from rich ethnographic data collected within TOPIC, a European AAL joint project conducted across Austria, France and Germany. Finally, we show our research framework in the setting of informal care with the complexity and dimensions in human and non-human supported caring activities.

## 10.1 Introduction

Care is undoubtedly a very complex endeavour. Informal carers, independent of their age, health condition or job situation, are often under high psychological pressure for they have to: know how to take care of their care receivers; properly organise the care and the necessary treatments; be responsible for the care receivers' everyday activities; manage financial and legal issues concerning the care; and especially be 100 % available and poised for care around the clock [1, 2]. This situation requires their active involvement in seeking and organising information and, at the same time, makes them strongly dependent on the care situation they are handling. The data presented in this paper shows that this dependency worsens

A.F.P. de Carvalho (✉) • H. Tellioğlu • S. Hensely-Schinkinger • M. Habiger
Institute of Design and Assessment of Technology, Multidisciplinary Design Group, Vienna University of Technology, Favoritenstraße 9-11/187, 1040 Vienna, Austria
e-mail: Fabiano.Pinatti@tuwien.ac.at; Hilda.Tellioglu@tuwien.ac.at; Susanne.Hensely-Schinkinger@tuwien.ac.at; Michael.Habiger@tuwien.ac.at

© Springer International Publishing Switzerland 2016
A. De Angeli et al. (eds.), *COOP 2016: Proceedings of the 12th International Conference on the Design of Cooperative Systems, 23–27 May 2016, Trento, Italy*,
DOI 10.1007/978-3-319-33464-6_10

155

the burden stemming from the care work, making informal carers' lives even more difficult. The findings herein presented urge that special attention should be paid to the matter and solutions should be devised to mitigate such a burden.

Dependency in the context of care has been widely discussed in the literature as can be seen in the works of Wilkin [3], Fraser and Gordon [4], and Kittay [5]. These discussions usually turn to deep philosophical debates and usually address power relations and issues of (in)equality [6, 7]. Although such debates are definitely valuable and relevant, this paper does not delve into them. Instead we turn our attention to what we term *practical issues* of dependency in informal care – i.e., those related to the things that prevent informal carers to decide or act freely. Furthermore, we discuss how coordinated care – i.e., care organised and negotiated between the different actors involved in it, e.g., carers, care receivers, health professionals, etc. – is associated to what Tellioğlu et al. [8] term as *modes of independency.*

Another differential of the paper refers to the subject of analysis. Whilst the dependency-in-care literature focuses on what issues care receivers experience and how informal carers become dependency workers, this paper approaches the dependency matters experienced by the carers. We discuss how coordinated care can support independency and which types of technologies could be effectively used for it. We argue that supporting informal carers' independency is important to reduce their burden and to give them condition to continue providing care effectively. Although dependency can have positive connotations, as for example when it is seen as "a normal, indeed necessary, social condition" that "ties people together" ([7], p. 605), it is widely accepted that most of the times "dependency is a negative state that should be alleviated wherever possible by public policy measures, treatments or other interventions" ([7], p. 607). The data presented in this paper supports the latter view and suggests that carers are in need of mechanisms that support their independency.

In terms of informal carers' independency Tellioğlu et al. [8] discuss four different aspects related to it, namely *action, emotion, decision* and *finance.* This paper builds upon these four modes of independency within the context of informal care whilst it discusses how coordinated care can impact upon each of them and how ICTs (Information and Communication Technologies) can potentially strengthen the positive impacts of coordinated care whilst lessening the negative ones. As Bossen et al. [9] put it, the "network of care [ ... ] can be augmented with new technology that allows all member of the network to follow, influence and be a part of the cooperative care . . . " (p. 189). We contextualise our discussion with empirical findings and illustrate our arguments with technological solutions on which we have been working. We finally summarise our research framework in the setting of informal care with the complexity and dimensions in human and non-human supported caring activities.

The remainder of this paper is organised as follows: Sect. 10.2 presents the context of this research by introducing the research project in which the data herein analysed has been collected and the methodology that led to our findings; Sect. 10.3 goes through related work that is relevant for the understanding of our arguments and propositions; Sect. 10.4 presents our findings and discussions concerning the central aspect of the paper, i.e., the relationship between coordinated care and informal carers' modes of independency and the design of technological solutions for improve ding it; finally, Sect. 10.5 summarises our research framework before concluding the paper.


## 10.2  Identifying Informal Carers' Needs

This paper is based on the results of the data analysis conducted on the rich ethnographic data collected in Austria during the first phase of the TOPIC project[1] – the *pre-study* – which has been conducted to deeply understand the users' contexts and identify the users' needs. In addition to that, it refers to the technological solutions proposed as a response to the emerging needs from such results.

TOPIC is a European research project funded by the AAL Joint Program that aims to advance the understanding of elderly informal carers' needs and design ICT solutions to support their daily lives [10, 11]. It addresses the lack of an integrated social support platform and the lack of accessible ICT applications for elderly people involved within informal care. The project congregates nine partners located in Austria, Germany and France.

One of the TOPIC main strengths is the *user-centred participatory design* approach that it employs. The evolutionary development strategy used in the project facilitates the intermediary artefacts in design and development to be evaluated by the same users (and many others), so that the artefacts in question can be improved and adapted for future use.

Based on the premises of user-centred participatory design approaches, which entail the involvement of end-user representatives throughout the design, development and evaluation processes, we planned our effort to cover all four phases traditionally associated with them [12]: (1) understand the users and establish the requirements, (2) design and redesign, (3) prototype, and (4) evaluate the outcome.

Since the project is an AAL initiative, its target group includes informal carers who are over 55 years of age. The profile of the care receivers (age, gender, health condition, etc.), the working condition of the informal carers (e.g., employed full/part time or retired) and criteria like gender, marital status and so forth have not limited the selection and inclusion of participants in the project. It is worth pointing out that within the project *informal carers* are defined as any person who provides care without any employment ties. That is to say that informal carers do not receive for the service they provide – i.e., informal care is a type of unpaid work[2]. On the

---

[1]For more information visit the TOPIC project (AAL-2012-5-169) website available at http://topic-aal.eu

[2]Research in informal care has argued that, although it is not properly paid, it should be seen as work, because of its high economic value [13, 14]. In so doing, informal care has previously been

other hand, *professional carers* are paid for the services they provide – i.e., their jobs are to care for somebody and they usually receive appropriate training on care procedures. It is not uncommon as well that professional carers are bond to a care association.

In the pre-study phase considered for this paper, it was possible to gather data on the real situation of our participants by combining different ethnographic methods, like in-depth interviews, shadowing and data inquiry methods such as diaries and cultural probes. The material collected during the pre-study have been submitted to a *thematic analysis* [15], which led to the identification of relevant themes to describe the distinct care situations observed and the needs of the fieldwork participants. Emerging themes have undergone a careful *triangulation* process [16], so to assure the reliability of the findings. In so doing, before deciding to keep a theme as part of the components of the thick description of the care contexts explored, we always checked whether the emerging theme would manifest across the different data artefacts collected from the same informant – e.g., the interview transcripts, the shadowing field notes, the diary entries provided, etc. – as well as in the data inquired from at least another participant.

In total the pre-study included around 10 participants in each of the three countries involved in the project (9 in Austria, 8 in France, 13 in Germany: $n_1 = 30$). Following the pre-study, we engaged in elaborating design ideas to support our informal carers in their daily lives; discussed and refined these ideas through a series of focus groups; elaborated medium fidelity prototype of our refined design solutions; went on to evaluate our prototypes in usability tests performed in controlled settings; further refined our design solutions based on the results of the aforementioned usability tests; implemented a platform to be developed for informal carers; and, finally, deployed this platform to the participants' homes, so to test how the platform would be used and appropriated across the time. Currently we are in the middle of the longitudinal study in which our platform is being tested.

In regard to participatory design, the three first focus groups conducted during the *pre-study* were combined with design workshops, in which the participants commented on the mock-ups elaborated for the system and suggested changes in the organisation of the interface as well as in the naming of the different functionalities. Furthermore, participants have also provided suggestions regarding the look and feel of the system, which have been considered for the elaboration of the medium fidelity and consequently the functional prototypes of the system. The user inputs in the design of our platform have extended throughout the usability test phase and the longitudinal study currently happening.

---

defined as: "A quasi-market composite commodity consisting of heterogeneous parts produced (paid or unpaid) by one or more members of the social environment of the care recipient as a result of the care demands of the care recipient" [van den Berg et al. 2004 cited in 14, 169–170]. Arno et al. [13], for instance, estimated that the economic value associated with informal care in the USA in 1997 was around $196 billion. The authors conclude that informal care should be considered the bedrock for USA chronic care system and that proper support should be provided to informal carers.

It is worth pointing out that additional 5 users have been recruited in Austria, 7 in France and 6 in Germany ($n_2 = 18$) for the *usability test* phase of the project and other 11 users ($n_3 = 11$) for the *longitudinal study* (7 in Austria and 4 in France). We found extremely relevant to bring some new users in each phase of the project, so that we could not only get feedback from those involved in the previous phases of the project, but also from totally fresh eyes. In the end the project will have involved 59 participants ($n = n_1 + n_2 + n_3 = 59$) across the three countries.

As mentioned above, this particular paper focuses on the ethnographic data collected in Austria during the pre-study, specifically the data concerning the subject *independency*, which emerged during the first round of data analysis that we have performed. In the next section, we will present some related work, in which our findings and discussions will be contextualised.

## 10.3  Issues of (In)Dependency and Coordinated Care

*Independency* can be defined as the person's ability of self-governing, self-management, self-direction, self-sufficiency, self-reliance, and self-subsistence. It is somehow close in meaning to the concept of *autonomy*, which comes from the Greek word *autonomous*, whose meaning implies living by one's own laws. On the other side of this coin lays the concept *dependency*.

Dependency has been defined in several different manners in the healthcare literature. Fine and Glendinning [7] argue that the term do not have "simple, uncontested meanings" and "should not be regarded as having a fixed or rigid meaning" (p. 618). Nevertheless, it is worth pointing out that potentially all definitions found in the literature share the essence of a condition that prevents people to act or decide by themselves.

### 10.3.1  Dependency and Independency in the Healthcare Literature

In terms of the healthcare literature, the main focus of dependency research lays on the care receivers [9, 17–21]. However, for the past number of years a few research studies have been stressing the need to pay attention to (in)dependency issues concerning informal carers, especially in terms of financial, social and emotional assistance [11, 17, 19].

When it comes to the context of elderly care, *dependency* is used in contrast to the term *care* – the former assuming a negative meaning in comparison to the latter. Even if "dependency ties people together" in private life ([22], p. 11), it has been found shameful in public. Fraser and Gordon [3] define four *registers of meaning* for dependency: economic, socio-legal, political dependency and moral or psychological. In old age, other forms of dependency can be manifested, for instance [23], life-cycle dependency, physical and psychological dependency, political dependency, economic and financial dependency, and structural dependency. While dependency is "an individual attribute rather than a social relationship in which the behaviour and perceptions of all the actors contribute to the construction of the situation" [3, p. 872], it can be said that dependency is social in the context of care giving.

In regard to *independency*, it has been interpreted in the literature as a structural notion suggesting the absence of practical, social or economic ties with others. It is *relational autonomy* [24]. Recognising human interdependency leads to the replacement of the term *care* by *help* emphasising alternative forms of social support and informal practices [20, 25]. As Fine and Glendinning [7] put it, "... independency can be seen as the result of reciprocity between partners, exchanges between dependent actors over time, and the networking of these relations of dependency" [7, p. 612]. Kittay [18] calls it *nested-dependencies* by extending the reciprocity to an exchange-based form. For Kittay, dependency is a normal and natural social condition that occurs in human life course.

## 10.3.2   Modes of Independency

Considering the different approaches to dependency and independency, Tellioğlu et al. [8] introduced a model of independency by mainly focusing on the context of care giving (see Fig. 10.1). In a caregiving context, *independency* is described as an interrelation among four factors: action, decision, emotion and finance. These four factors are related to each other. Each factor has impact on the other one. For instance, if someone is financially independent then s/he is also autonomous in most of his/her actions (interrelation between finance and action independency). If there is no one who will be affected by one's decision then this person makes better decisions and can act based on his/her decisions regardless of others (interrelation between decision and action independency). To achieve the best possible level of independency for a person these four factors must be balanced.

**Action dimension**. The action dimension of the independency model above is about being able to act without waiting for support or permission of someone else. It

**Fig. 10.1** Model of independency in the context of informal caregiving [8]

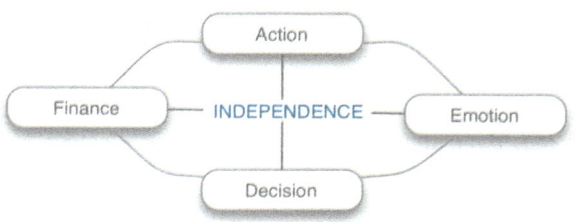

includes temporal and locational aspects. It means being independent in relation to the time of action and in relation to the place where the action is performed.

**Decision dimension**. This dimension refers to situations when one can make choices for oneself without being shy to go through challenges in life. If a person is independent than s/he can easily make a new decision, because s/he is not scared to make choices in fear of upsetting others. This relates to the dimension of dependency as being an individual attribute and a product of social relations at the same time.

**Emotion dimension**. This facet concerns the capacity people have to be emotionally comfortable to engage in activities other than caring. Less emotional dependency means that a person has reduced stress and his/her happiness is promoted. The person is not easily emotionally influenced by the care giving situation or the health or mental condition of the care receiver. At the same time, emotionally independent people are rather prepared and free to meet new people and try new things. So, they are open to other people and new opportunities.

**Finance dimension**. This dimension corresponds to controlling one's income and expenditure without answering to anybody. This enables gaining freedom and satisfaction and makes one independent, also in terms of decisions and actions.

## 10.3.3 Coordination in Healthcare

Domestic healthcare cannot be carried out without *coordination* of care work among carers, both professional and informal. From CSCW systems point of view, coordination is a function of the collaborative application that contains encodings and representations of the content it is dealing with [26]. CSCW systems combine the support for content work and the support for coordination in a collaborative application. Tellioğlu [27] shows different aspects building up the context of (work associated) coordination by differentiating between factors related to work processes, to mechanisms and to the impact of coordination work (see Fig. 10.2). *Artefact-based coordination* [28], as one of the coordination mechanisms in this typology, implements coordination support implicitly in work practices by using different types of artefacts, like notes, documents, tangible objects, etc. These artefacts can be atomic or composed, accessed simultaneously or asynchronously, owned by one or many, visual or textual, material or virtual, common or private. Besides enabling implicit communication these artefacts mediate the status of work-in-progress and make participants aware of others' activities. They help create common understanding of tasks and situations to deal with. They also facilitate talking about tasks, by reminding principles, approaches and methods connected to a task, by keeping track of activities and materials, by hosting work plans, etc.

Artefacts help reduce coordination effort. For instance, they make additional communication or articulation obsolete. On the other hand, artefact-based coordination makes the background information explicit [29]. It is static, formal, indirect, implicit, coupled, predefined and individual. In the context of informal care, a few

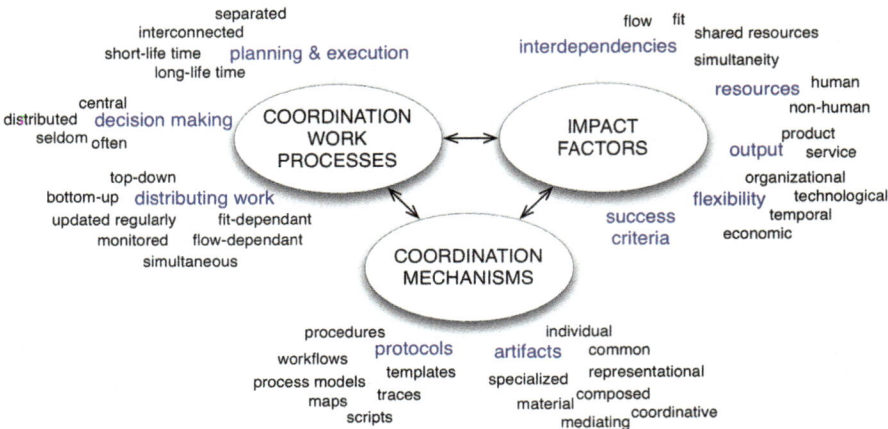

**Fig. 10.2** Different aspects showing the context of (work related) coordination [27]

technological solutions have been proposed to augment the coordination between the actors of the care network, such as the ones presented by Christensen and Grönvall [21] and Bossen et al. [9]. In the next sections we discuss informal carers' emerging needs for systems supporting coordinated care, so that they could get a hold of their independency.

## 10.4    Coordinated Care Support to Foster Informal Carers' Independency

The fieldwork performed for the pre-study of our project yielded rich data on the dependencies that carers develop over the time as they engage in different facets of care giving. For instance, we could observe time dependencies being established as the care work were distributed across different actors, e.g., more than an informal carer, health care professionals that visit their homes from time to time, etc., and place dependencies being formed due to the limited mobility of the care receivers. These dependencies make it difficult, sometimes even impossible, for informal carers to act or decide by themselves on matters concerning the care they provide, e.g., when they have to wait for somebody before starting a care procedure with the care receiver, or personal matters that have nothing to do with care, e.g., going out with friends or engage in some activity that they like. We discuss such dependencies in the following subsections, illustrating them with empirical data collected during our fieldwork. So, the next sections are meant not only for presenting results of our investigations, they are also integrating the analytical discussion of different issues addressed in this paper. In addition to that, we introduce the solutions that we have been developing within the TOPIC project to address such issues. These solutions should trigger thinking about choosing the right combination of existing technologies to support informal carers, nevertheless by taking additional configurations described below that have emerged during our investigations seriously.

## 10.4.1 Needs and Support Regarding the Action Mode of Independency

As we proceeded with our fieldwork, the burden experienced by our participants started emerging strongly from the collected data. In terms of action mode of independency, informal carers frequently referred to things that they can no longer do because of the dependencies created by the care work. For instance, Mrs. Liebe[3], a 60-year-old, married, part-time employed carer, who looks after her 39-year-old daughter goes on to say:

> ... I perceive it as a problem that we [her husband and her] never can do anything alone. We can't go for a drink or so. He doesn't need it. I would like to do so from time to time. Eating breakfast or walking while holding hands. This isn't possible since the wheelchair [of her daughter] needs to be pushed. You can't link arms with each other. I miss that. (Mrs. Liebe, *Interview 3*)[4]

The quote above illustrates how the informal carers' everyday lives are mainly arranged around care receivers and restricted by care activities. This situation is the same for all carers in our study. At some point, this becomes a real burden for the carer. Coordinating some breaks with the care receivers, when possible, has emerged as a relevant strategy, as stressed by Mrs. Liebe in the following quote:

> ... And in the afternoon there is always one-hour break, mostly between three or four o'clock my husband puts her into bed or also me. Where there is silence and we also get a bit of rest for us. So that we can drink some coffee together and just say: 'exhausting exhausting'. [ ... ] During this time she gives us a break. She knows that her dad and mum need this time and this works quite well. And then there is her afternoon coffee after getting up. (Mrs. Liebe, *Interview 1*)

In addition to the coordination with care receivers, there is also another type of coordination involving other actors sharing or influencing the care. That is because at some moment the care work will have to be distributed, so that the main carers – i.e., those in charge of the care for most of the time – do not collapse. As Kittay [5] argues, distribution of care is a "question of justice and interactions between carers, cared for, and the larger community" (p. 443).

When it comes to *shared care*, it is common that carers plan their activities around the arrival and presence of other people who are helping them with their

---

[3] All participants' names used for the paper are pseudonyms, used to assure our participants' confidentiality.

[4] All quotes presented in this paper have been freely translated from German.

responsibilities. Without these people, the carer cannot do what needs to be done, as evident in the quote from Mrs. Pünktlich, a 79-year-old, married, retired carer, who takes care of her 84-year-old husband, tetraplegic since an accident in the garden 7 years ago:

> ... as a last resource [when the homecare professional does not come] I can of course call my son. But he also needs his rest in the evenings. He isn't at home all the time or he is away on business. What should I do then? (Mrs. Pünktlich, *Interview 2*)

Moreover, if these people are not on time – and that means either arriving earlier or later – it might happen that other appointments have to be postponed or even cancelled, as illustrated in the quote below from Mrs. Wandern, a 72-year-old, married, retired carer, who looks after her 74-year-old husband, suffering from Alzheimer's disease for the past 2 years:

> ... The home care, which should look after him, arrived earlier than planned. I was still in the middle of the preparations. She was there already, I had to care for him and for her. [ ... ] I was stressed a bit and could leave about 30 minutes later than planned. [ ... ] I arrived four minutes late. This is stupid – if you are responsible and arrive late. But I could impossibly leave. (Mrs. Wandern, *Interview 2*)

Furthermore, there are still cases in which the informal carer does not live in the same household as the care receiver [e.g., the case reported by 30]. In such cases, it might be necessary, but not possible, to inform the person sharing the care responsibility about certain care activities or changes in the care situation.

One of the solutions that we have been working on to enhance informal carers' modes of independency is a notes-board-like solution to facilitate exchange of information between the persons involved. The *NotesBoard* feature implemented and integrated to TOPIC platform allows the carers to write a message wherever they are, so this message is displayed in any device where the *NotesBoard* is being shared (see Fig. 10.3). This means they can leave a tablet at the entrance of the

**Fig. 10.3** TOPIC *Notes Board*

care receivers' place, so that people coming to the house can easily notice it – a strategy similar to the one used for the *PressToTalk* device presented by Christensen and Grönvall [21]. That means that anyone who has access to this device could read the notes they write and take the appropriate measures, independent of having an account in the TOPIC platform. Moreover, *NotesBoard* is being prepared to allow private message exchange with the people involved with the care situation. This is important when the carers want to share some information only with particular members of the care network in question. Another relevant feature of the *NotesBoard* is that as soon as a note is entered to it, carers are notified about it.

**Some Analytical Aspects . . .**

Both of the above-mentioned solutions refer to the concept of *temporal coordination* [31, 32] to understand some of dependencies in shared care and how these dependencies can be overcome. For instance, in the case where the carer does not leave in the same household as the care receiver, temporal coordination might be necessary due to the fact that the carer is not at the care receivers' at the time when the homecare professional arrives. Since the professional might need to know the changes in the care receivers' condition, so to adjust the care procedures accordingly, this communication channel is very relevant.

One would argue that a telephone call would solve this situation. Apparently in Austria it is not possible to contact the homecare professionals directly for several good reasons like to protect them from being called regularly, mostly for issues, which are not relevant for the health care processes. Because of company policies in place to protect the homecare health professionals, carers would not be able to reach the person coming to the care receivers' home.

Another argument – this one regarding the private exchange between the actors of the care network – could be that any traditional groupware system accessed through secured connection by both ends of the communication channel could do what *NotesBoard* does. However, considering that the health professionals will not be registered users of the TOPIC platform, as this is a system for informal carers, it would be important for the system to allow the access to people not enrolled in the platform to read private messages. Thus the need for guest accounts and private messages unlocked through a security code (or any other artefact that would afford the same coordination mechanism) emerges.

Now focusing on another issue of temporal coordination addressed by Palen [31] related to supporting carers' independency – that of *tracking*, i.e., recording events as they happen in the present – once carers are notified, they can read it immediately and if something that demands further clarification is part of the note, they can take the appropriate action as soon as possible.

The fieldwork data also revealed the relevance of tracking for what Palen [29] terms as *temporal orientation*. This became noticeable in situations which informal carers wished to track upcoming visits of people providing external help, especially to learn about delays – see Mrs. Pünktlich and Mrs. Wandern cases in the description above. Not being able to know if the person is coming or not, how long it will take for them to arrive and so forth were acknowledged as disruptive.

As a response to this requirement, we have been working on the conceptual design of a feature for notifying delays and changes in the appointment schedule that would allow service providers to keep informal carers better informed at the same time that they can protect the privacy of their employees. This would enhance carers' independency, for they would be able to re-plan their daily activities according to the changes in the schedules.

## 10.4.2  Technology for the Decision Mode of Independency

An interesting observation from our data is that most of our participants were once decision makers, sometimes even not only for themselves but also for the whole family. The situation changed at the moment they start taking care of their beloved ones. Their decisions started then being influenced by the circumstances and restrictions brought by the care situation they engaged in. Mrs. Pünktlich, for instance, recounts how the care situation impacted upon her and her husband's lives:

> ... We had many friends back then, we used to travel and meet other people very often but this became a bit less frequent. Yes... Well... First, it is difficult, [because] my husband cannot leave home easily anymore. We can't invite [people]; I mean, sure, we could invite but it must always be for dinner. Too inconvenient, you know? Well, that is because the homecare health professional visits either at 6, 7 or 8 o'clock. Planning is difficult. Well planning is very difficult. ... Well, maybe not everyone can cope with that. That is the problem I guess... (Mrs. Pünktlich, *Interview 1*)

The previous quote shows the dependencies on the care situation impacting upon the decision dimension of Mrs. Pünktlich, which to some extent overlaps with action dimension previously discussed. For instance, her husband and she can no longer decide to go on a trip, due to his mobile impairment. He cannot also plan and invite friends over in times that would fit them, because it usually clashes with care appointments with health professionals. In fact, there is little room for her to decide on anything. Everything should fall within the daily routine established due to the care situation, as illustrated in the following quote:

> ... The morning routine is always the same till half past nine. Sometimes it takes till 10 o'clock, like today. One hour shopping, then cooking. Lunch and later on therapy. A small chat during coffee. Various chores until 5 o'clock, later on dinner. Between half past 6 and 7 o'clock the home help comes over and puts the patient to bed. Finally free time with watching TV or reading. (Mrs. Pünktlich, *Diary*)

As can be seen, Mrs. Pünktlich has to juggle different aspects of care and everyday life. For her, being absent for long periods of time is not a possibility:

> ... Usually I'm at home in two hours. It has to be an unfortunate coincidence that something happens to him during this time. I don't go away, if I see that he doesn't feel good in the morning. Or I just go away for only half an hour. (Mrs. Pünktlich, *Interview 2*)

There is no room for her to take on casual opportunities as, for example, if she finds a friend in the shopping centre she usually does her shopping. She is always concerned whether something is happening to her husband, whilst she is away. There are also situations in which care receivers are really demanding:

> ... For instance, when I do the shopping I tell her [daughter]: look at the clock – I'll be back in one hour. Well, if I come back 10 minutes late she already wet her pants as a form of punishment . . . so I have to change her clothes. (Mrs. Liebe, *Interview 2*)

The quotes above show how heteronomous the lives of informal carers can be. This heteronomy hinders their decision power and they become captive from the care situation, for they knowing that their decisions will affect the care receiver. As observable in Mrs. Liebe's quote, sometimes carers are even scared to make choices because they think that they upset their care receiver or any other family member.

**Some Analytical Aspects ...**

Most carers are shy and very careful in their decisions, especially when it comes to decide things for themselves, like going on a vacation or meeting a friend somewhere outside the home. In so doing, their mobility becomes limited due to their care work.

Taking account of the importance of supporting carers in taking decisions – especially the ones related to engage in activities for themselves, as withdrawing from the care responsibilities from time to time can be most salutary – we are investigating how we can create a safe space in our platform where carers can decide to do certain things what they want to do. As addressed before, distributing the care work with other carers is a plausible alternative and once again coordinating the care surfaces.

This happens by providing information on our online platform, by connecting them with other peers, by offering them a community that has similar life situation, and by enabling exchange of information with others. We are offering in the platform a calendar-based tool where carers can plan events – both online and face-to-face – or inform other carers about events they would like to attend. Providing this information is a way to start negotiations for a coordinated care initiative where carers can be absent for a period of time without feeling guilty or concerned.

Another solution being implemented in the platform corresponds to the possibility to check upon the care receiver even when they are not co-located. This is possible through our *CareCamera* module, which allows carers to have a look on what is going on at their places whilst absent. Technological solutions presented in this paper are only a few examples of simple solutions that can make a difference in the informal carers' lives. Preliminary findings from the longitudinal study that we are currently carrying out demonstrate the relevance and appropriateness of such solutions. However this requires a deeper discussion in a different paper.

### 10.4.3  Coordinated Care and the Emotion Mode of Independency

As observed by Christensen and Grönvall [21], family members tend to be more emotionally attached to the care of their care receivers than professionals. Our data resonates with their findings and demonstrates that this is very strong if parents are taking care of their needy child like in case of Mrs. Liebe:

> ... you know how it is, if you have this tube directly connected with your stomach, the food never goes into your mouth [ ... ] then, when [my husband and I] want to eat [ ... ]she sits next to us and watches us [ ... ] or [we have to eat] secretly in the kitchen. But she knows when we are eating in the kitchen. Even though she cannot see us, she is able to hear us from the other room [ ... ] we know that she is currently suffering and this makes it impossible for us to eat. (Mrs. Liebe, *Interview 1*)

Anything that looks like a progress in the health condition of the care receiver or anything new in the treatment as an unexpected hope for improvement of the health or care situation are reasons for moments of pleasant frames of the parents' mind. Sometimes it is enough to feel emotionally relieved when the carers only know that their care receiver feels good.

> ... We try not to be too sad that things are as they are. It is that way, isn't it? If she feels good, we feel good and that's simple as that. If the children feel good, then the parents feel good. (Mrs. Liebe, *Interview 1*)

In order to cope with the emotional load of care, informal carers try to coordinate the care with people close to them. For instance, Mrs. Liebe coordinates the care work with her husband, who is not her daughter's father – she married him a few years after her daughter's father passed away. Mrs. Liebe and her husband take turn in actively being responsible for the daughter, mainly to enable the other to rest or recreate. They also need each other to overcome the emotional and physical burden they have since the injury.

> ... When my daughter is with me and her wheelchair is in the kitchen and she wants to help me – and she then realises that this doesn't work anymore – and therefore despairs, then I really become aware of her impairment. Her small, swift hands, she used to help me gladly – much I can stand, the caring already has become routine and I think that my husband and me are doing good – but if my daughter cries or is sad – then my heart breaks as well. Comforting her – although I would need comfort myself – is beyond my strength. (Mrs. Liebe, *Diary*)

Although supported by external professional care services, carers are constantly under pressure of delivering the highest quality of care possible and their full attention to their care receiver. They feel the same if care activities are carried out by other people like care workers. In this regard uncertainty – whether care workers carry out specific tasks correctly – may leave family members in a state of uneasy confusion. Furthermore carers may become frustrated if their views on specific caring tasks conflict with the care carried out by the care workers. Christensen and Grönvall [21] report that there are informal carers who withdraw from caring emotionally as well as physically.

In TOPIC we are attempting to foster the establishment of local communities of informal carers, whose members could support each other. One of the possibilities that have been discussed in the series of focus groups that we have conducted is a type of service exchange offered through the platform. This way, members of the platform could offer to take over the care responsibilities of one of their peers, depending on their availability, when one needs to withdraw from the care situation for a short while. However, our informants have stressed that in order for that to happen, first of all a trust relationship needs to be constructed. Having that in mind, we are offering in the platform mechanisms for carers to find peers in a similar situation as theirs, living close to them, sharing the same interests, etc., as a first step for rapport to be established. These mechanisms are based on groups, forums and social network technologies.

## 10.5   Conclusion

The facets and nuances of informal care are many and those involved with it are subject to some unfortunate and detrimental experiences, being the partial (or total) loss of independency. In this paper we presented and discussed findings from a deep ethnographic study focusing on informal carers' daily life concerning the dependencies that the care work brought upon them. We defend that technology-supported coordinated care is an important instrument for informal carers to recover part of the independency taken from them.

In this context, ICT solutions can be a relevant aid, for they can create opportunities for carers to decide upon a few situations and engage in activities other than the ones regarding the care work that they provide without worrying (too much) about the care receivers' well-being. We presented a series of solutions devised within the TOPIC project and discussed how these solutions can support coordinated care for enhancing informal carers' independency in three different dimensions: action, decision and emotional. As future work we set ourselves to investigate further to what extent these solutions can in fact support informal carers' mode of independency. For that we are currently conducting a longitudinal study in which our solutions have been deployed to our participants' home and are being used in an everyday basis.

Figure 10.4 helps relate our research concerns and conceptual framework. Our target group – the informal carers – and their independency are central in our framework, which is integrating qualitative research with user-centred participatory design approach, to informal care setting by showing the complexity of this research context. Around the carer there are persons demanding or helping care, care activities to carry out, coordination issues related to caring, and finally some examples of possible technology support based on experiences in our current research project TOPIC.

We are aware that technologies not always work or are used in the way they have been thought. But we are also aware that it is not possible to achieve useful

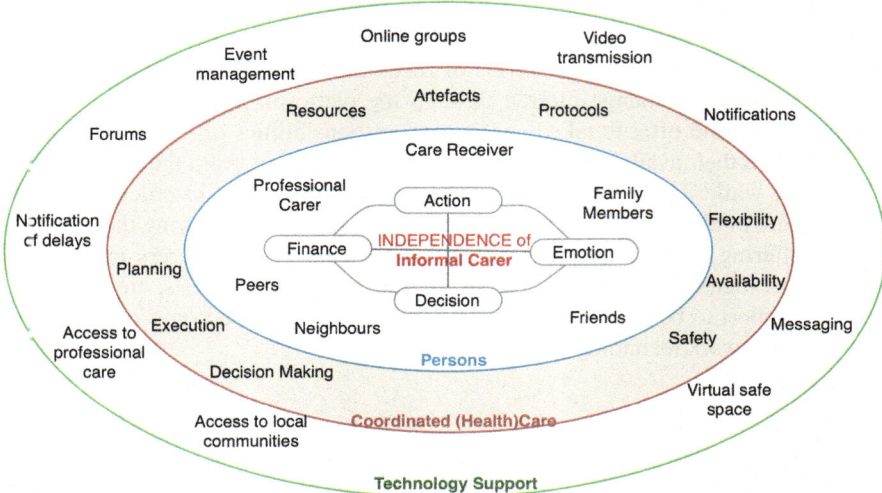

**Fig. 10.4** Our research framework in the setting of informal care shows the complexity and dimensions in human or nonhuman supported caring activities

and usable solutions without working closely with representatives of the target group to deeply understand their needs and how experimental solutions respond to them. We are very committed to this process and confident that our findings are advancing the current state of the art. Above all, we urge that informal carers must be supported with their duties, so to mitigate the burdens stemming from informal care, in response to the demands from an ever-growing aging society, where they provide more than 80 % of the care.

**Acknowledgements** We would like to thank the Ambient Assisted Living Joint Programme for financial support, the members of the TOPIC consortium for the insights and input in the project development, and all the informal carers participating in the project without whom this research would not be possible.

# References

1. Brouwer WBF, van Exel NJA, van de Berg B, Dinant HJ, Koopmanschap MA, van den Bos GAM (2004) Burden of caregiving: evidence of objective burden, subjective burden, and quality of life impacts on informal caregivers of patients with rheumatoid arthritis. Arthritis Care Res 51(4):570–577
2. Cranswick K, Dosman D (2008) Eldercare: what we know today. Can Soc Trends 86:10
3. Wilkin D (1987) Conceptual problems in dependency research. Soc Sci Med 24(10):867–873
4. Fraser N, Gordon LCFW (1994) A genealogy of dependency: tracing a keyword of the U.S. welfare state. Signs 19(2):309–336

5. Kittay EF (2005) Dependency, difference and the global ethic of longterm care. J Polit Philos 13(4):443–469
6. Saraceno C (2010) Social inequalities in facing old-age dependency: a bi-gerational perspective. J Eur Soc Policy 20(32):32–44
7. Fine M, Glendinning C (2005) Dependence, independence or inter-dependence? Revisiting the concepts of 'Care' and 'Dependency'. Aging Soc 25(2005):601–621
8. Tellioğlu H, Hensely-Schinkinger S, de Carvalho AFP (2015) Modes of independece while informal caregiving. In: Proceedings of the 13th AAATE conference, Budapest, 9–12 Sept
9. Bossen C, Christensen LR, Grönvall E, Vestergaard LS (2013) CareCoor: augmenting the coordination of cooperative home care work. Int J Med Inform 82(5):e189–e199
10. Breskovic I, de Carvalho AFP, Schinkinger S, Tellioğlu H (2013) Social awareness support for meeting informal carers' needs: early development in TOPIC. In: Adjunct proceedings of the 13th European conference on computer supported cooperative work (ECSCW 2013), Paphos. Department of Computer Science Aarhus University, Aarhus, 3–8
11. Hensely-Schinkinger S, de Carvalho AFP, Glanzinig M, Tellioğlu H (2015) The definition and use of personas in the design of technologies for informal caregivers. In: HCI International, Los Angeles, 2–7 Aug
12. Sharp H, Rogers Y, Preece J (2006) Interaction design: beyond human-computer interaction, 2nd edn. Wiley, West Sussex
13. Arno PS, Levine C, Memmott MM (1999) The economic value of informal caregiving. Health Aff 18(2):182–188
14. van den Berg B, Brouwer W, Exel J, Koopmanschap M (2005) Economic valuation of informal care: the contingent valuation method applied to informal caregiving. Health Econ 14(2):169–183
15. Gibson WJ, Brown A (2009) Working with qualitative data. Sage, Los Angeles, 222 p
16. Bryman A (2008) Social research methods, 3rd edn. Oxford University Press, New York, 800 p
17. Brownsell S, Blackburn S, Hawley M (2012) User requirements for an ICT-based system to provide care. Support and information access for older people in the community. J Assist Technol 6(1):5–23
18. Kittay EF (1999) Love's labor: essays on women, equality, and dependency. Routledge, New York, 257 p
19. Manthorpe J (2001) Caring at a distance: learning and practice issues. Soc Work Educ 20(5):593–602
20. Shakespeare T (2000) The social relations of care. In: Lewis G, Gewirtz S, Clarke J (eds) Rethinking social policy. Sage, London, pp 52–65
21. Christensen L, Grönvall E (2011) Challenges and opportunities for collaborative technologies for home care work. In: Bødker S, et al (eds) ECSCW 2011: proceedings of the 12th European conference on computer supported cooperative work, 24–28 Sept 2011. Aarhus Denmark. Springer, London. p 61–80
22. Nies H (2004) A European research agenda or integrated care for older people. 24 p
23. Torp S, Bing-Jonsson PC, Hanson E (2013) Experiences with using information and communication technology to build a multi-municipal support network for informal carers. Inform Health Soc Care 38(3):265–279. doi:10.3109/17538157.2012.735733
24. Kraner M, Emery D, Cvetkovic SR, Procter P, Smythe CS (1999) Information and communication systems for the assistance of carers based on ACTION. Inform Health Soc Care 24(4):233–248
25. Schulz R, Beach SR (1999) Caregiving as a risk factor for mortality: the carer health effects study. J Am Med Assoc 282:2215–2219
26. Tellioğlu H (2010) Coordination 2.0. Using web-based technologies for coordination support. In: Proceedings of the international workshop on web intelligence and virtual enterprises 2 (WIVE 2010), Saint-Etienne, 11–13 Oct

27  Tellioğlu H (2010) Coordination of work: towards a typology. In: Proceedings of the 11th international conference on computer systems and technologies, (CompSysTech'10), Sofia, 17–18 Jun, 311–316

28  Cadiz JJ, Gupta A, Grudin J (2000) Using web annotations for asynchronous collaboration around documents. In: Proceedings of CSCW'00. Philadelphia, 2–6 Dec, pp 309–318

29  Carstensen PH, Nielsen M (2001) Characterizing modes of coordination. In: Proceedings of GROUP'01. Boulder, 30 Sep–3 Oct, pp 81–90

30  Schinkinger S, de Carvalho AFP, Breskovic I, Tellioğlu H (2014) Exploring social support needs of informal caregivers. In: CSCW 2014 workshop on collaboration and coordination in the context of informal care (CCCiC 2014), Baltimore, 15 Feb 2014. TU-Wien. pp 29–37

31  Palen L (1999) Social, individual and technological issues for groupware calendar systems. In: Proceedings of the SIGCHI conference on human factors in computing systems, Pittsburgh. ACM, pp 17–24

32  Bardram JE (2000) Temporal coordination – on time and coordination of collaborative activities at a surgical department. Comput Supported Coop Work 9(2):157–187

# Chapter 11
# Tinkering Around Healthcare Infrastructures: Nursing Practices and Junction Work

Enrico Maria Piras and Alberto Zanutto

**Abstract** Introduction of healthcare infrastructures is often accompanied by workarounds, persistence of paper-based documents and of technologies that the innovation was intended to replace, raising the question as to whether they are by-products or intrinsic to infrastructure innovation processes. This work, through a longitudinal case study of a hospital information system long in use, investigates their origin, their role in enabling the system's affirmation, and the difficulty of eliminating them. Through a qualitative methodology, semi-structured interviews and ethnography, we reconstruct the history of the system and the information management practices around it. Our analysis reveals that the effectiveness of the tool implemented derived largely from 'junction work' performed by the nurses, which ensured the flow of data among different electronic and paper-based information systems. Moreover, in carrying out their junction work the nurses intervened to modify, enrich and complete the information contained in the different systems.

## 11.1 Introduction

Healthcare systems have been massively characterized by investments in ICTs since such systems promised to confer effectiveness and efficiency on healthcare structures and that the automated data management would have substantially simplified service activities for both doctors and patients [1]. The adoption of infrastructures was supposed to increase information exchange among diverse

E.M. Piras (✉)
Fondazione Bruno Kessler, Trento, Italy
e-mail: piras@fbk.eu

A. Zanutto
Dipartimento di Sociologia e Ricerca Sociale, Università di Trento, Via Verdi 26,
38122 Trento, Italy
e-mail: alberto.zanutto@unitn.it

© Springer International Publishing Switzerland 2016
A. De Angeli et al. (eds.), *COOP 2016: Proceedings of the 12th International Conference on the Design of Cooperative Systems, 23–27 May 2016, Trento, Italy*,
DOI 10.1007/978-3-319-33464-6_11

173

healthcare professionals which would improve inter and intra organizational coordination [2]. By now, however, that promise has been largely unfulfilled [3, 4]. Any simple activity intended to gauge the quantity and quality of the information systems operating in healthcare shows that a great deal of work needs to be done before these infrastructures fully respond to the needs of complex systems like those of healthcare [2, 5] mostly because medical technologies, even within a single operational unit, are unable to exchange information [6], which often require workarounds, and in which paper persistence is observed [7, 8]. Several studies have shown that this integration is problematic due to a superficial analysis of complexities at organizational level [6, 9, 10]. Expectations in regard to the introduction of health infrastructures has clashed with the organizational structures, professional practice, and often caught in a web of information systems devoid of connectivity and interoperability [11–13]. These experiences have emphasised the obstacles to work caused by these innovations and the gap between design and the reality of the clinical settings where such systems are implemented and used [14, 15]. The excessive trust in the standardization of procedures and the scant attention paid to workflows of individuals has been considered a key factor in determining these issues [10]. Post-implementation analyses show that the full success of innovation processes is infrequent, and that when healthcare information infrastructures are indeed successfully introduced, this comes about in ways and for reasons different from those hypothesised in the development and implementation phase. Elements such as workarounds and persistence of paper-based information systems and of the communication technologies that the innovation was intended to replace are often presented as by-products and indicators of incomplete realization of the project design [16]. The recurrence of these elements in different analyses, however, raises the question as to whether they can actually be considered by-products, or whether they should instead be interpreted as intrinsic to infrastructure innovation processes.

This paper concentrates on these phenomena investigating their origin, their meaning in the overall operation of the system, their role in enabling the system's affirmation, the difficulty of eliminating them, and, not least, their undesired effects on certain organizational processes. Through the analysis of the transformation of a teleconsultancy system into an Electronic Patient Record (EPR) we focus in the junction points among diverse infrastructures and the invisible work needed to manage the flow of information among them.

The paper is structured as follows. The next section introduces the concept of infrastructural inversion as proposed in Science and Technology Studies. The following section presents the research design and methods. The findings are set out in two sub-sections. The first outlines the history of the infrastructure, from its ideation as a platform for synchronous teleconsultancy to its redefinition as an EPR. The second sub-section describes the information management practices in that department, focusing on the activities by which the nurses made communication possible among non-interoperable systems. Finally, the discussion section considers the implications of the research, and particularly how activities, which enable communication among non-interoperable systems. These activities are 'junction work' [17], not always eliminable, nor replaceable by infrastructures, precisely because of their intrinsic complexity and their organizational value.

## 11.2  Studying Infrastructures and Local Practices

Successful infrastructures rapidly become part of the taken-for-granted of those who use them [5]. They merge into individual actions and organizational practices, of which they become constitutive parts; and only when malfunctions or breakdowns occur do they re-acquire their visibility [18]. The strategy adopted here to restore visibility to our object of analysis goes by the name of 'infrastructural inversion'. This consists in shifting the attention from the 'tubes and wires' of the technical system to, on the one hand, the process of installing the infrastructure from design to implementation, and on the other, the work on and around the infrastructure necessary to keep it working [19, 20]. Retrospective analysis of infrastructure-in-the-making directs attention to the ethical, political and social issues, the conflicts, the negotiations, the compromises, and in general all the choices that have made the infrastructure into what it is. Reconstructing how an infrastructure has been created makes it possible to identify the key and peripheral actors, and to determine whether and how asymmetries of position have been incorporated into the technical object. The first paragraph of the findings will be devoted to this retrospective analysis.

Attention to the work necessary for the infrastructure to function is tied to the idea that infrastructure are such only in relation to organized practices, and that only in relation to these practices does it possess the characteristics of invisibility and taken-for-grantedness [21]. Shifting the focus from the users envisaged by the designers to those who work to keep the infrastructure functioning makes it possible to observe the competences, complexities, and the workarounds necessary to maintain the infrastructure within a broader infrastructural system. This will be discussed in the second paragraph of the findings section.

Our approach consists in shifting the attention from the infrastructure as a mere technical device (tubes and wires) to the activity meaningful to the organizational actors involved. In both the sections, our units of analysis will be the organizational practices defined as "the ways, relatively stable in time and socially recognized, in which heterogeneous items are ordered into a coherent set" ([22], p. 34).

Organizational practices have two characteristics.

- **A practice must be 'named' as a specific object of study, knowable from the outside, known to the researcher and to the actor as well**. It consists of regularities or schemes that guide the linkage with other practices. Finally, it is imbued with meanings socially accepted by the organization, which allow its reproduction with a certain stability over time.

- **Performing a practice involves 'knowing in practice' rather than an abstract knowledge**. A practice is a process, a negotiated symbolic order that emerges from its function in the organization. Through practice, connections and constraints among the resources available are learned, together with a practical knowledge that allows the management of practice's unpredictable trajectories and the linkage of several practices into a broader set.

We shall concentrate on two types of practices. The first are the 'medical practices of the future' imagined by the designers and by the doctors involved in design of the system and engaged in constructing a new technical system and redefining the roles of the users as mediated by the system itself. This will enable us to observe the different degrees of involvement of the actors concerned, the decision by some of them to withdraw from the project, and the substantial redefinition of the infrastructure's overall purposes. The second set of practices analysed are those of the nursing staff, which were not expressly foreseen in the design phase and emerged during the infrastructure's implementation and everyday use. These practices will enable us to observe how the introduction of the infrastructure produced effects in areas different from those expected. We shall focus in particular on the nursing activities that enable the transfer of data among non-interoperable systems (junction work).

## 11.3   Research Context, Research Design and Methods

The research in what follows is the preliminary phase of an evaluation of communication practices in the oncology Day Hospital (DH) of a regional hospital with 10 doctors (full-time), 11 nurses (7 full-time, 4 part-time) and 2 secretaries. The DH treats around 60–70 patients a day plus those who arrive via Accidents and Emergency. The oncology department is the only one of its type in the region, and it handles patients from a mountainous catchment area of around 6200 km$^2$. The doctors at the outlying hospitals consult with the specialists in the department observed by our research, and refer the most complex cases to them. For more than 10 years, the department has used SYS (fictitious name), an EPR developed as a pilot project whose history will be detailed in the findings section.

We started with an exploratory study (2 weeks) intended to gain an overview of the kinds of information management in place since 2010, understanding the tasks associated with document management, the tools (electronic and otherwise) used, and critical areas. Preliminary observations showed that the doctors managed both clinical and administrative information almost entirely by means of the EPR, whilst the nurses used numerous other information systems, both paper-based and digital, spending most of their time on duplicating information present in diverse systems to ensure the flow of information within the department, among different departments, with the hospital administration, with other hospitals, with the clinical analysis laboratories.

Following this exploratory phase, two research questions were formulated: (i) what are the obstacles against the deployment of a infrastructure, and what adjustments does the organization make to overcome them? (ii) from an analytical point of view, in what does junction work among the various systems consist? These questions were addressed with two research actions:

- Retrospective reconstruction of the ideation, development, and implementation of SYS. This objective was pursued through semi-structured interviews with members of the IT research team (managers, computer scientist and developers of the IT centre which managed the design) and accounts furnished by the department's doctors and collected during the observation period (see below).
- Analysis of the information management practices of the department's nurses. This was carried out in 8 weeks of observation of the day hospital nurses across 6 months, seeking to cover the department's life cycle as far as possible. Observed each week was a nurse engaged in a specific practice (taking blood samples; paper-based clinical records retrieval; chemotherapy infusion; reception; assisting the doctors during examinations; coordination). Two of these settings, reception and coordination, required 2 weeks of observation each.

The ethnographic technique selected for the fieldwork was shadowing consisting in flanking an organizational actor to track and reconstruct his/her activities, paths, and intersections with other actors and processes throughout the working day [10, 13]. Shadowing of personnel with greater seniority, like those to whom priority was given in our research, allows to reconstruct the evolution of activities insofar as the shadowees are willing to describe how tasks were performed in the past, the relative changes made to procedures and rules, as well as their perceptions of change in their roles during the process. The shadowees described the changes in information management following the introduction of SYS in the department in relation to the hospital's information systems subsequently introduced. It was thus possible to integrate the information collected on the history of the project with the interviews conducted with the researchers and developers of the SYS system. The materials collected and transcribed were analysed first through historical and retrospective reconstruction that used turning-points in the project as its units of analysis, and then through reconstruction of the everyday work performed by the nurses to ensure that the systems produced the effects for which they had been designed. All research activities have been carried out from fall 2009 to spring 2010. These activities included collecting documents related to the first phases of the project.

## 11.4   Infrastructures, Local Practices and Junction Work

The historical reconstruction of the process that had led to SYS enabled identification of two significant turning-points: the withdrawal from the project by all the hospital departments involved except the oncology centre and the decision to re-orient the project on the oncology department by transforming an infrastructure enabling inter-department communication into a tool for intra-department information management.

## 11.4.1  Birth and Abandonment of the Territorial Infrastructure

SYS is the result of a process started in 1997 to create a synchronous teleconsultancy tool for the shared management of cancer patients between the medicine, gynaecology and dermatology departments of five outlying hospitals in a region of northern Italy and the oncology unit of the region's central hospital. The purpose was to make the competences of the region's sole expert centre in oncology available to all the outlying hospitals through a telecommunication system that would allow the simultaneous navigation of electronic pages and discussion of the patient's data supported by an audio channel on IP, a chat tool, and a shared board for the visualization and annotation of diagnostic images. The envisaged advantages of the project were the possibility to take more accurate decisions and to avoid travel by oncologists from the central unit to the outlying ones to furnish consultancy.

However, from the design phase onwards, the doctors at all the centres involved expressed doubts as to whether it would be possible to hold regular sessions of synchronous teleconsultancy given the often unpredictable flow of the department's activities. This led to the integration into SYS of an asynchronous teleconsultancy tool based on text messages. After this first design phase, the heads of the peripheral departments lost all interest in the original project claiming that the asynchronous teleconsultancy was all they needed.

## 11.4.2  Implementation of the Information Management Practices and the Interconnected Infrastructure

The lack of commitment of the majority of hospitals and doctors jeopardized the whole project. The existence of SYS is due to the continuing interest in it of the oncology unit of the central hospital. A crucial role was performed by the newly-appointed chief consultant, who re-oriented the entire synchronous teleconsultancy project to the production of a oncological EPR tailored to the management of the department. The chief consultant's determination to develop this infrastructure was substantially due to two factors. Firstly, he wanted to introduce the processes of information automation that he had experienced at his previous hospital. Secondly, his desired to reorganize the work practices setting up a model whereby every oncologist would be able to treat every patient, thus superseding the current organization of work whereby each patient was treated by a single doctor. The SYS, he believed, was the instrument best suited to the sharing of information about patients among the various doctors [23].

To this end, SYS was designed so that it compelled the doctors to standardize information as far as possible (i.e. by reducing the text boxes and increasing the structured information). When planning the system, the designers worked in close contact with the oncology medical staff as regards both the information to enter and the procedure for doing so. In particular, SYS was structured by files, each of which contained information on one step in the treatment process, so that the oncologist could be followed/guided as he or she entered information during examination of the patient. The design of SYS thus proceeded *pari passu* with reorganization of information-management practices jointly with the oncologists. In 2000 the EPR was officially adopted in the department, first by the medical personnel.

In this first phase, the SYS application allowed the management of strictly clinical information. However, the first trials showed that clinical practice required the doctors to manage information of other kinds as well. This led to requests for further functionalities, such as management of administrative information, compilation of the department diary, the booking of clinical tests, specialist examinations, and so on. In short, the doctors requested the IT research team to develop tools for the management of information present in other systems (paper-based) and mainly managed in the department by the nursing staff.

The nurses, despite the system was supposed to be used by them as well, were not involved in the design process. This was partly due to the clinical record's symbolisation as an artefact of direct pertinence to the doctors. The main reason for their exclusion, though, was the close bond that had formed between doctors and designers. After the loss of interest by doctors of the outlying hospitals, nor the designers nor the doctors wanted to put the project at risk. Including the nursing perspective in SYS was regarded a possible source of destabilization of a project which, after a traumatic start, was becoming to have promising outcomes. Whilst doctors could speak for themselves when discussing with the designers, the nursing staff could not make their voice heard and was obliged to adjust to the changes. As a result, some nursing activities were inscribed in the SYS. The most significant of these was the requirement that SYS data should be entered manually through data entry templates. Some information entering and exiting the system requires work by the nursing staff to transfer/copy the information contained in SYS, or to transmit it to other paper-based and electronic information systems through an activity we call here junction work.

Over time, the number and the type of data entry templates have undergone changes because of modifications in the SYS's capacity to interface with other information systems. For example, the need to enter the results of blood tests manually has decreased since SYS was made interoperable with the inter-hospital system, so that the operation is necessary only for results from private laboratories. The opposite case is represented by the birth of new services, (e.g. CT or PET scans), for which it has been necessary to create templates for recording appointments.

We shall now discuss the implications of this for the nursing staff.

## 11.4.3   Junction Work and Nursing Practices

The introduction of SYS into the practices of doctors and nurses had different effects. For the doctors, the use of SYS was an integral part of fluid working practices almost entirely paperless. For the nurses, instead, SYS was sometimes an element that disrupted the orderly flow of work activities as they were delegate the task of feeding the SYS with the information that the system cannot receive automatically from other information infrastructures.

Paper-based documentation reappeared on the admissions counter, in the department's corridors, in the secretaries' offices, in the infusions rooms, and more generally, everywhere that nursing practices took place. And alongside the documentation were staplers, fax machines, telephones, photocopiers, paper clips, post-its, all the physical and 'analogical' equipment required to manage documentation.

Preliminary observation revealed the complex interplay between the paper documentation and SYS, and the role performed by nursing staff so that the doctors could work (almost) exclusively with the latter. Research thus shifted from the infrastructure to the activities going on around it. In this section, we concentrate on these activities, and in particular on junction work, by which is meant actions intended to "facilitate the exchange of data among different information systems (both electronic and paper-based) involving direct and explicit action to overcome barriers impeding data exchange among two or more of them. These activities may take the form of the transcription or digitization of dates, their transfer from one system to another with memory devices (e.g. USB keys, hard drives) or manual uploads, changes of format, and so on" [20].

Our ethnographic observation showed that such activities assumed very different forms in the department according to the information and the information systems to be linked. Only rarely did they consist solely of the simple transcription of data from one system to another. More frequently, the transfer of information between information systems required multiple operations, the use of different tools, the collaboration of several nurses over an extended period of time, as shown by the procedure for booking Positron Emission Tomography (PET) in Box 11.1.

---

**Box 11.1. PET Request Management**

*The doctor compiles the request for PET on a paper-based form and hands it to the nurse, along with the patient's clinical record, when s/he is accompanied out of the surgery after the examination. The nurse faxes the request to the nuclear medicine department (where the PETs are performed), clips the fax receipt to the original, puts the sheets in the folder and takes it to the admissions counter. The admissions nurse, as soon as she finds the time to do so, puts the folder in a cupboard on a specific shelf marked 'PETs without appointments'. After some days (three approx.), the secretariat sends*

(continued)

**Box 11.1.** (continued)
*the reply from the nuclear medicine department to the admissions counter. This reply is the same fax sent by the first nurse with the date and time of the appointment hand-written in one of its corners. The arrival of the fax means that the nuclear medicine nurses have registered the appointment in the Hospital System (HS). The oncology nurse takes the folder from the shelf and attaches the fax to its front with a paper clip. She then searches the SYS register for the patient's telephone number, and the department's diary for a new appointment date which falls some days after the PET appointment so that she can be sure that the doctor can carry out the examination when the PET results have arrived. She transcribes this information (telephone and new appointment) on the booking fax in order to have all the information to give the patient on a single sheet of paper. The folder will remain on a corner of her desk until the patient has been informed (if s/he cannot be contacted, the folder may remain on the desk for hours/days). Only then is the appointment entered into the SYS diary. The nurse then writes on the fax that the patient has been informed about the appointment. She puts the fax sheet in the folder, which she places on the shelf of the cupboard marked 'PETs with appointments'. On the day of the PET, an auxiliary will take the folder and accompany the patient to the examination room. Although the folder is an almost exact duplicate of the SYS, doctors in other departments, for which SYS does not have legal value, require it.*

This is a particularly complex case of junction work among those observed, and it has been described here because of its exemplary value. In other cases, presented below, the activities connected with the transfer of information among unconnected systems are less intricate, with a smaller number of operations, technologies, and actors involved. Analysis of the example, however, makes it possible to grasp some distinctive features of junction work.

Firstly, in a complex organizational context, the transfer of an item of information between systems not directly interconnected requires a series of activities that involve diverse actors in a variable period of time, which depends on numerous factors. In this case, complexity derived from a mix of factors among which the differing procedures followed by the departments, the cooperation of the nuclear medicine department, the telephone contactability of patients, as well as the decisions of the department's nurses to perform other activities deemed more urgent.

Secondly, the action of the nurses in the management of information is never directed to the simple transfer of a datum from one system to another. At each step, the nurses work to facilitate intra-/extra-department coordination through the matching of information to create data sets useful for performance of a particular duty. For example, the information relative to an appointment is always linked with other data and documents (fax receipt, clinical record, the patient's telephone number) useful for managing a task more complex than the simple transfer of information from one system to another. The entry of the examination date into the SYS is only one segment of more general junction work among colleagues, with the doctors, with other departments, as well as with the patient. These tasks are accomplished through junction work among documents: clipping the fax receipt and the appointment request together so as to register the handover between departments, putting these documents into a folder so as to keep everything necessary for the PET together, annotating the patient's telephone number and the date of the new appointment on the fax in order to facilitate communication with the patient by colleagues, and so on.

Thirdly, the junction work is supported by a shared topography of organizational environments that assigns a space to each stage of the information processing. The secretariat, the 'PETs with/without appointments' shelves, part of the admission nurse's desk, are all spaces dedicated to information (in its paper-based materiality) in transit between the two computer systems. This mode of work enables the nurses to understand with a glance both the stage reached by the process and the composition and weight of the activities still to perform.

Finally, the junction work is the outcome of a series of micro-actions situated within other, broader working practices undertaken in different ways. In the case in question, for instance, the notification of the appointment by fax, coupling with the receipt, and delivery to the admissions counter, are actions that interrupt the activities in which the coordination nurse is engaged. Vice versa, the information search in SYS, the booking of the appointment, the telephone call to the patient, and placement of the folder in a special space, are actions that the admissions nurse performs in sequence.

This last point requires closer examination. During the research it was observed that there are three types of relation between junction work and nursing practice:

- Junction work disrupts a practice;
- Junction work is an integral part of a practice;
- Junction work marks out boundaries among distinct professional practices.

Some examples will illustrate these distinctions.

## 11.4.4   Junction Work Interrupts (or Interferes with) a Nursing Practice

In some cases, the lack of interconnection among systems required the nurses to interrupt the normal flow of their practices. These were the most frequent cases of junction work identified. We now describe the exemplary case of orchestration of the flow of patients through the department performed by the 'coordination nurse', a role that requires a perfect knowledge about the department's overall functioning and the timing of its activities. She supervised the flow of patients from the reception counter, their transit to the infusions rooms, and the dispatch of requests to the pharmacy for medicines. More generally, she had to ensure that patients, medicines, or information arrived on time where they were supposed to arrive. This practice required constant monitoring by computer or telephone, or by going in person to verify what was happening.

Besides these activities, one of the tasks required of the coordination nurse was keeping account of the flows of patients and medicines in the department. Although this was an activity that did not figure among coordination tasks, it was useful for statistical/administrative purposes. It consisted in compiling forms with information contained in the printouts of pharmacological therapies and in the hospital's electronic information system and SYS. This junction work served to replicate in a new document information present in other information systems (both paper-based and electronic) and required the nurse to put coordination on stand-by.

Specifically, whenever a therapy was administered, the doctor placed the prescription on the nurse's desk (around 40 times in a morning). This prescription had to be sent to the hospital pharmacy for preparation of the drugs. First, however, the nurse had to transcribe the information on the paper-based form. The coordination nurse gave different priorities to this activity according to flows in the department. But it was usually a task attended to before others, because failure to perform it blocked a series of connected activities (preparation of the drugs, the patient's dispatch to the chemotherapy unit, beginning of the drugs infusion). In this case, the junction work between the SYS (where the prescription has been compiled) and the paper-based accounting system interfered with the nurse's other activities and increased the risk of errors. The nurses admitted, in fact, the forms had only indicative value because during the hours of heaviest workload, they were compiled in a chaotic environment.

## 11.4.5  Junction Work as an Integral Part of a Practice

In other cases, the transcription of information from one system to another does not have disruptive effects on a practice but is an essential part of it, as happens in the case of the booking of blood tests. The procedure is that the doctor prescribes the test by entering the information in SYS. Given that SYS and the analysis laboratory's system are not interoperable, the nurse must do the junction work of transferring the prescriptions to the latter (so that the doctor can work only with SYS, without using the hospital system). This work is performed every morning by a nurse who devotes the first hours of her shift to blood sampling, a work practice that consists in the complete management of both the sample and the information connected with it (e.g. printing the adhesive labels and affixing them to the test-tubes containing the blood). The junction work here consists in entering the tests requested by the doctor via SYS into the hospital system. To perform this operation, the nurses usually print the pages of SYS because their computer has only one screen.

While performing this practice, however, the nurse checked the tests requested by the doctor and intervened in two ways: informing the doctor about some missing tests, or even directly adding them to the list. This typically happened when the doctor had not included among the tests requested those that enabled the anaesthetist to evaluate the patient before inserting a portacath. This instrument serves to ensure that the chemotherapy treatment is administered causing least possible damage to the patient's veins. The nurses were very sensitive to this aspect because, as one of them said, "it's awful to see a patient attached to the infuser for hours and hours with burning veins". Moreover, as said by another nurse in another circumstance, patients who suffer during the therapy require greater care and attention. In these cases, it was routine in the department for nurses (especially those with greater length of service) to intervene directly by introducing new tests and subsequently reporting them to the doctor.

In this case, unlike those described previously, the junction work between the systems is not a mechanical operation but rather an activity in which the professional skills and the experience of the nursing staff play a significant role in verifying and integrating the information so as to facilitate other work practices (e.g. improving the patient's comfort and his/her ability to tolerate the infusion).

## 11.4.6   Junction Work as a Boundary Among Different Practices

Finally, in several cases interconnection between SYS and other systems, although technically feasible, was not considered desirable. The lack of connection between systems was functional to showing the differences between professional roles and competences by distinguishing between medical practices and administrative ones.

The most representative case was management of access to the car park reserved for oncology patients. For the latter, the hospital had reserved an internal car park, access to which was regulated by a bar that the patient raised by swiping his/her health card managed by a specific information system. The regulations on access imposed a maximum number of accesses for a limited period of time. The decision on times and accesses was taken by doctors according to the type and duration of the therapy administered to the individual patient. The procedure was that the doctor wrote this information (e.g. ten accesses authorized for the next 60 days) in a text box of the SYS. The printout was given to the patient, who took it to the department office. Here the secretaries entered the information into the software dedicated to management of the car park, thus activating the permit. The limits of time and access to the car park, however, could be redefined according to the progress of the patient's disease. A period of weakness or the toxicity of a drug, for example, might lead to suspension of the therapy, and to a request for the period of parking permission to be extended. Likewise, patients could go to the department without an appointment if their condition had deteriorated and required an increased number of accesses to the car park. In these cases, changes and extensions were directly managed by the secretaries.

In this case, the lack of connection between systems and the junction work that this required was functional to marking out different professional practices, as emphasized by the secretaries. Although an information system could automatically establish the times and number of accesses and send them to the system managing the car park lot, it would not be able to handle exceptions. The delegation to the secretaries seemed intended to make the patients understand that all the procedures concerning management of access to the car park were to be performed without consulting the doctors, thereby marking out a professional boundary between competences.

## 11.5 Discussion

Before we proceed any further we need to answer a simple but fundamental question: can we consider the SYS just a case of bad design? Should we answer positively junction work could be regarded as a mere by-product of a poorly designed information system. Much of the observed junction work, after all, could have been avoided had the nursing staff being involved in the making of the SYS. Their exclusion is a breach of the key principle of participatory design: actively involve all relevant stakeholders. The historical analysis, however, offers a more complex explanation. It suggests that after the outlying hospitals backed off the project the main concern of designers and doctors of the oncological department was strengthen the collaboration ties to keep the project alive. The inclusion of nursing staff would have helped to have a comprehensive picture of the requirements but it was regarded as a source of uncertainty in a process that had already been close to a failure.

The infrastructural inversion invites to reflect on a different question: bad design for whom? Doctor and nurses have different representation of the infrastructure and for the former the SYS has improved their work practices eliminating most of the clerical tasks now delegated to the latter.

In more general terms, directing our attention at the points of juncture between the infrastructure and other systems and the work practices necessary to connect the former to the latter made it possible to observe how the fluid integration of the infrastructure into the medical practices partially relied on the ability of the surrounding socio-technical system, and in particular on the junction work of the nurse and secretaries, rather than being an intrinsic property of the infrastructure itself. The infrastructural inversion [5] confirms the process of co-construction between organizational practices and the infrastructure, demonstrating the impossibility of separating technology and organisation [24]. Nevertheless, although implementation processes lead to changes not foreseeable at the outset [2], some actors can exert closer control over the final outcomes. The greater capacity of some actors (doctors) to reshape their practices as they preferred enabled them to render the system into a taken-for-granted infrastructure by delegating, through that system, work to other organizational actors (nurses and secretaries) obliged to change their work activities in order to accommodate the new technology. Moreover, a trade-off was observed between the possibility of the doctors to make SYS their main tool of information management and the professional content of the work of the nursing staff. In the opinion of the nurses with longer service in the department, over the past decade nursing work had been characterized by an increase in information and document management, with the effect of substantially modifying job profiles (for specific treatment see [17]. Observation of nursing work in the day hospital showed, in fact, that it comprised a large amount of information management, and to a lesser extent, actions directly concerning the care and assistance of patients. With the exception of the chemotherapy unit (where patients were constantly monitored and assisted), most of the work time in all the nursing tasks observed was devoted to retrieving, filing, and transferring information about patients.

A second consideration concerns the genesis and persistence of forms of paper-based information management. In the case described, one cause of this phenomenon was the distinctive history of the infrastructuration project and the change made to its purpose. The decision to create a system enabling the doctors to manage almost all information using a single system required integration with the other sources of information present in the department and in the hospital, many of which were paper-based. However, this only partly explains this persistence. As we have seen, in fact, forms of junction work also persisted where the systems to be integrated were electronic and their elimination did not seem always easy to achieve. Although the junction work always consisted in the transfer of information from one system to another, it assumed different dimensions according to the content of the work, the skills required for its execution, its timing, and the actions necessary for its automated performance (Table 11.1).

Observing junction work on these four dimensions reveals its relations with work practices, being at times an obstacle to work practices, an integral part of them, or in yet others it is an organizational practice in itself which comprises different skills.

In the first case (e.g. tracking the consumption of medicines), interoperability between different systems appears both feasible and desirable for the actors

**Table 11.1** Dimensions of junction work (rows) and their relation to organizational practices (columns)

|  | Interference with practices | Part of a practice | Organizational practice per se |
|---|---|---|---|
| Content of the work | Data management | Data management + professional knowledge | Data management |
| Skill required | Mechanical | Expert | Expert |
| Timing | On call | Predictable | Adaptable to the workflow |
| Eliminability | Enhancing interoperability | Not possible (or extremely complicated) | Not desirable |

involved. The nurses would welcome integration between systems, which relieved them of a mechanical work they are required to perform on call and they considered tiresome, at constant risk of error, and consisting in mere mechanical transcription.

The second case is different (e.g. transfer of prescriptions for blood tests). Here the junction work is not immediately eliminable except at the price of an overall decrease in the quality of performance. In the example given, the junction work appears to be a moment exploited by the nurses to deploy their expert knowledge (checking the completeness of the medical prescription) and to connect the practice of blood sampling with that of chemotherapy infusion, ensuring that the patient has been prescribed the insertion of a portacath. Moreover, the junction work needs to be performed at a given moment of the blood sampling practice and its predictability allows for a smooth accommodation in the workflow. In this case, the skills and knowledge of the nursing staff would be bypassed if seamless communication existed between the systems. In this case, elimination of the junction work, the amount of care given remaining equal, would substitute the work currently performed by the nurses by including in the infrastructure expert systems able to alert doctors or nurses of wrong or incomplete prescriptions. At present, however, the substitution of a human actor's expertise with that of a computer system does not seem feasible.

The third case illustrated (e.g. car park access) instead demonstrates that there are situations in which integration between systems, although technically feasible, is not organizationally desirable because the junction work serves to mark out distinct professional practices and competences, specifically to avoid that doctors perform strictly administrative tasks. In the example given, the lack of integration between SYS and the system managing the car park barrier was the occasion for handover between the medical personnel and the office staff, which demarcated their different professional domains and made explicit to patients who they should ask for extensions of their car park access. In this case junction work is an organizational practice in itself, performed by expert personnel and integrated in their daily routine.

On this basis, it can be argued that a lack of interoperability is not in itself a negative factor in all circumstances. Consequently, its elimination need not always be a priority when installing systems. It is instead more significant to consider the relation between junction work and organizational practices. From the analytical perspective outlined in the second section, following Gherardi [22, 25] we have defined organizational practices as socially recognized ways in which heterogeneous items are ordered into a coherent set. In this framework, support for clinical activity must consider practices ('coherent sets') rather than their individual elements, the purpose being to make practices more flexible. Hence, the work support furnished by new infrastructures should enable actors to construct courses of action meaningful to them. The elimination of a task (for instance, by means of a new infrastructure), therefore, cannot be evaluated in and of itself, but only in light of its positive or negative contribution to the overall coherence of working practice. Consequently, the apparently mechanical operation of transferring information from one system to another that we have called 'junction work' – and which it is widely believed could be eliminated by increasing interoperability between systems – may be a 'heterogeneous item' part of a 'coherent set' as an extraneous and disruptive element whose elimination should be evaluated case by case.

## 11.6 Conclusions

This study has sought to answer the question of why forms of paper-based document management still persist following the introduction of electronic infrastructures. Such persistence is often observed and it is usually interpreted as indicative of only partial success in the design and implementation of systems. The study has shown the relations among the introduction of an infrastructure, the work practices that it was intended to support, and the work practices of other organizational actors not considered at the design stage. Infrastructures can achieve the results expected of them in ways very different from those envisaged by the rhetoric of technological innovation. They do so by redistributing tasks rather than solving problems. Every new connection both lessens work for some and creates extra work for others. Junction work – the human and material activity of connecting systems together – signals the difficulty of creating a seamless web in a context like that of healthcare characterized by a plethora of different systems. The elimination of such work, however, cannot be considered only as an interoperability problem because, in some circumstances, its execution appears functional to the correct or desirable performance of organizational practices.

By reconstructing the process of infrastructure installation, it has been possible to observe the differing capacities of organizational actors to maintain or reinforce the homogeneity and fluidity of their work practices by delegating, via the system, service tasks to other actors. The latter, the nurses in our case, may see their work significantly modified in terms of both the skills required and their composition. This has a paradoxical implication for infrastructuring processes in the healthcare sector: intended to reduce and facilitate information management tasks, such processes end up by increasing the time devoted to them by organizational actors who in principle should not have be affected by them.

A limitation of this study is the risk of generalizing results obtained from research on the effects of the introduction of an ICT system in a single healthcare organization characterized by a distinctive history of infrastructuration. In the future, therefore, it will be important to verify these results by studying other healthcare contexts.

## References

1. Haux R (2005) Health information systems – past, present, future. Int J Med Inform 75:268–281
2. Vikkelsø S (2005) Subtle reorganization of work. Attention and risks: electronic patient records and organizational consequences. Scand J Inf Syst 17:3–30

3. Black A, Car J, Pagliari C, Anandan C, Cresswell K, Bokun T, McKinstry B, Procter R, Majeed A, Sheikh A (2011) The impact of eHealth on the quality and safety of health care: a systematic overview. PLoS 8:e1000387
4. Zanutto A (2008) Innovazione Tecnologica e Apprendimento Organizzativo: la Telemedicina e il Sapere Medico. Franco Angeli, Milano
5. Bowker GC, Star SL (1999) Sorting things out: classification and its consequences. MIT Press, Cambridge, MA
6. Østerlund CS (2008) Documents in place: demarcating places for collaboration in healthcare settings. Comput Supported Coop Work 17:195–225
7. Saleem JJ, Russa AL, Neddo A, Blades PT, Doebbeling BN, Foresman BH (2011) Paper persistence, workarounds, and communication breakdowns in computerized consultation management. Int J Med Inform 80:466–479
8. Vezyridis P, Timmons S, Wharrad H (2011) Going paperless at the emergency department: a socio-technical study of an information system for patient tracking. Int J Med Inform 80:455–465
9. Winthereik BR, Vikkelsø S (2005) ICT and integrated care: some dilemmas of standardising inter-organisational communication. Comput Supported Coop Work 14:43–67
10. Hartswood M, Procter R, Rouncefield M, Slack R (2003) Making a case in medical work: implications for the electronic medical record. Comput Supported Coop Work 12:241–266
11. Heeks R (2005) Health information systems: failure. Success and improvisation. Int J Med Inform 75:125–137
12. Roine R, Ohinmaa A, Hailey D (2001) Assessing telemedicine: a systematic review of the literature. Can Med Assoc J 165:765–771
13. Bowns IR, Rotherham G, Paisley S (1999) Factors associated with success in the implementation of information management and technology in the NHS. Health Informatics J 5:136–145
14. Berg M, Aarts J, van der Lei J (2003) ICT in health care: sociotechnical approaches. Methods Inf Med 42:297–301
15. Hyysalo S (2010) Health technology development and use. From practice-bound imagination to evolving impacts. Routledge, New York
16. Feufel MA, Robinson FE, Shalin VL (2011) The impact of medical record technologies on collaboration in emergency medicine. Int J Med Inform 80:e85–e95
17. Piras EM (2011) This is not something I should be doing. Junction work and professional identity of nurses grappling with health information systems. In: Svanæs D, Faxvaag A (eds) Proc. 5th human factors engineering in health informatics symposium. Tapir University Press, pp 115–120
18. Star SL (1999) The ethnography of infrastructure. Am Behav Sci 43:377–391
19. Bowker GC (1994) Science on the run: information management and industrial geophysics at schlumberger, 1920–1940. MIT Press, Cambridge
20. Bowker GC, Baker K, Millerand F, Ribes D (2010) Toward information infrastructure studies: ways of knowing in a networked environment. In: Hunsinger J, Allen M, Klasrup L (eds) International handbook of internet research. pp 97–117. Springer, Netherlands
21. Star SL, Ruhleder K (1996) Steps toward an ecology of infrastructure: design and access for large information spaces. Inf Syst Res 7:111–134
22. Gherardi S (2006) Organizational knowledge: the texture of workplace learning. Blackwell Publishing, Oxford
23. Piras E, Zanutto A (2014) Le Infermiere sanno Quello che i Medici Vogliono": il Lavoro di Congiunzione nei TDE. Studi Organizzativi.pp 29–49
24. Berg M (2001) Implementing information systems in health care organizations: myths and challenges. Int J Med Inform 64:143–156
25. Corradi G, Gherardi S, Verzelloni L (2010) Through the practice lens: where is the bandwagon of practice-based studies heading? Manag Learn 41:265–283

# Chapter 12
# In Due Time: Decision-Making in Architectural Design of Hospitals

Naja L. Holten Møller and Pernille Bjørn

**Abstract** We analyze the cooperative work involved in creating the architectural design of a hospital based upon digital technologies of the future, before we know whether future digital technologies will be mature and reliable enough for use. The entire process, from initial architectural design until opening of the hospital for patients, takes approximately 10 years, which is a significant amount of time considering the hitherto pace of digital technology development. Therefore, due time decision-making is essential. We conceptualize *due time* in cooperative design work as a quality measurement of whether "the right path" is followed when alternative future paths are available, without reducing the space for design maneuverability prematurely. But how do we determine the "right path" in due time? By exploring the ways in which artefacts are used to achieve due time decision-making on future digital technologies in hospital design, we find that artefacts are used to assess the relationship between dependencies and sequences of activities with the aim of pushing all irreversible decisions for design as far as possible. Thus, we argue that the practices of handling due time decision-making in complex cooperative activities are characterized as the practices of handling the relationships between dependencies, sequentiality, and irreversibility of the material matter (in our case the future hospital) shaping the course of action.

## 12.1 Introduction

Timely coordination refers to the role of time in handling articulation work [1] when following due processes [2] in cooperative work [3]. CSCW studies have demonstrated how temporal coordination is organized by applying certain configurations of artefacts, categories, and gesticulations in the cooperative work [4–8]. Expanding this work, we in this paper use a Danish case of architectural work to explore the basic nature of *due time* as part of critical decision-making in complex cooperative work situations.

N.L.H. Møller (✉) • P. Bjørn
Department of Computer Science, University of Copenhagen, Copenhagen, Denmark
e-mail: naja@di.ku.dk; pernille.bjorn@di.ku.dk

© Springer International Publishing Switzerland 2016                                  191
A. De Angeli et al. (eds.), *COOP 2016: Proceedings of the 12th International Conference on the Design of Cooperative Systems, 23–27 May 2016, Trento, Italy*,
DOI 10.1007/978-3-319-33464-6_12

"In due time" refers to the practices by which a certain activity is finished or completed at "the right time", in such a way that the following courses of action are shaped in certain anticipated ways. This is different from "clock-time" and "on time", as in a certain activity (e.g. surgery [4]) is done according to a schedule at a particular time of day. In contrast, due time in decision-making is a quality measurement where "the right path" is followed when alternative future paths are available. In due time is a notion evoked by practice. In Danish, the word 'rettidig', literally translated as "right time", connotes both senses used here: It refers to the *quality* of decisions that are made in due time or timeliness according to due process. The question then becomes what is the "right path"? In critical decision-making, due-time decisions concern how to create accurate forecasts for a field of action based upon assumptions about the work [9]. Cooperative work is open-ended and situated, thus the right path cannot be determined as a casual relationship [10, 11]. Architectural decisions have practical effects on the material matter, as in what gets constructed and built in materials such as concrete, steel, or wood; thus, closing down the open-ended decisions reduces the maneuverability for how the architectural design can develop over time. Therefore, the keywords in architectural work when designing for the future are also *robustness* and *flexibility*.

This also means that in the architectural proposal it is essential to predict "the right path" early on without prematurely reducing the space to maneuver. Certain questions cannot be postponed for decision-makers of the future. The number of elevator shafts necessary in a hospital depends upon the choice of logistic technologies, e.g. which logistic technologies might be reliable alternatives, and how to take these into account in the design? We see this challenge of decision-making as the *challenge of handling due time in cooperative work*.

Handling due-time decisions in architectural cooperative design concerns ensuring that irreversible decisions are not made prematurely nor too late. Due time is a quality measurement of decisions in the same way as a decision can be timely. Due time is the point in work where the closing of ends shapes the course of action irreversibly and limits the options for further action. Due time is the point of no return. In architectural design, a due-time decision emerges when the foundational structure of the building (e.g. ceiling heights or elevator shafts) is set, thus all future courses of action will be based upon this foundation. Premature decisions on, for example, ceiling height, will consequentially determine whether, for example, drone technologies will be able to operate inside the hospital or not, regardless of whether future drone technologies will be stable enough for in-door use in 10 years. We explore the basic nature of how uncertainty in due time decision-making is handled in architectural design, and thus add to the CSCW conceptual understanding of cooperative work in general, while joining specific CSCW research on architectural practices in particular [12–14].

The paper is structured as follows. First, we develop a theoretical conceptualization of due time based upon prior work, followed by an introduction to our empirical case and method. In the analysis we zoom in on the use of artefacts in architectural practices for handling uncertainties in due time decision-making in four sub-sections. Finally, we characterize due time decision-making as an after-the-fact quality measurement of work organized as a relationship between sequentiality, dependencies, and irreversibility.

## 12.2   Related Work: Sequentiality, Dependencies, and Irreversibility

Certain activities follow others, and *sequential ordering creates an important structure of due time in cooperative work*, since due time is about discovering a path to somewhere. Sequentiality in work does *not* imply that work is *not* situated. Clearly, due time is a situated concept; however, what is important is to figure out the role of sequentiality in the domain at hand. Sequentiality in work has been explored in prior work on architecture [13], flight strips [15], software development [16], and surgical operations [17]. Sequentiality does not mean that iterations cannot occur, or that work is organized in a straight line. Instead, it only points to how specific courses of action will lead the work down certain paths that impact the material matter of the work—whether it be the path in the software program or the path of landing flights at the airport. When we investigate the accomplishment of due time, we need to pay attention to the sequential nature of the work by examining the use of artefacts in critical decision-making.

*Due time is related to temporal dependencies* emerging from the activity and involved in the work. Dependencies in collaborative work are immediately important for CSCW studies, since it is part of the very definition of collaboration [10]. Collaborative partners "engage in cooperative work when they are mutually dependent in their work and therefore are required to cooperate in order to get the work done" [ibid p. 13]. Several studies have investigated dependencies in collaborative work, particularly in software design [18, 19], and pointed to the work required in meshing, linking, and relating individual yet dependent activities when accomplishing larger collaborative activities. Exploring dependencies in our case, we are able to identify the multiple different individual activities that together create the common field of work. This suggests that when we explore due time empirically, we must pay attention to the interlinked multiple individual activities and how interdependencies are organized and executed as part of critical decision-making in the collaborative work.

*Due time has an irreversible nature.* When exploring due-time incidents it is important to state that "wrong time" and "wrong future paths" are always available in the critical decisions. When we explore due time in architectural work, our purpose is to figure out exactly how to support actors in their work before the chosen path shapes the course of action in irreversibly constraining ways. Irreversibility has in previous work been explored in scientific translations ([20], p. 149). Based upon this work, we will explore irreversibility of due time in architectural work by exploring the degree of irreversibility in concrete situations of artifact use depending upon: (a) the extent to which the chosen action makes it subsequently impossible to go back to a point where the chosen path was only one amongst others and (b) the extent to which the chosen course of action shapes and determines subsequent actions.

Irreversibility in architecture is essential, and it is normal practice to postpone critical decisions of, for example, logistic technologies once the winning project of an architectural competition has been found. But in the competition brief the architecture firms competing to win the tender have to make these decisions and argue their choice. Exploring irreversibility in due time in architectural work in the architectural competition includes investigating the multiple interrelationships that serve as the infrastructure of alternative courses of action, and the situation when these become foundational and material and thus not possible to transform in future activities. Due time is the point of no return. Exploring the accomplishment of due time in architectural work, we will explore the role of sequentiality, dependencies, and irreversibility as they are performed in *design of future hospitals*.

## 12.3   Research Method

We explore the ways in which practitioners involved in the architectural work of future hospital design handled due time applying cooperative artefacts. The first author has been involved with and done research on the policies, digital technologies, and practice related to healthcare in Denmark over the last decade. On this basis, she became involved in the design of future large hospitals in Denmark working as a consultant in an architectural firm.

In 2013 the Danish government decided to invest more than €5,6 billion in building 16 new hospitals over the next 10 years [21]. The first author's role in the architectural firm was to participate in projects on hospital design, taking into account the cooperative work practices and future technological opportunities that should be designed into the architectural foundations of the hospitals. One key concern emerged, namely the challenge of making critical decisions in due time without prematurely reducing the opportunities for including future digital technologies. We made this challenge the center of attention, and in this way take advantage of *"firsthand experiences of the events under study" through active participation* ([22] p. 131).

The data collection was focused in the period between April 2013 and October 2013 in Denmark. During these 8 months the first author's participation in the field focused on designing future hospital and digital strategies, including close participation in creating proposals for architectural competitions. The design work involved evaluative discussions about workflows in hospitals and imagined flows of work and, in particular, how digital technology would best support the hospital work of the future. Over the period, observation notes were transcribed. We relied on thick descriptions in the analysis: Themes were identified in the material and the concept of due time was tested against various scenarios from the empirical material. In the end we decided to zoom in on the decision-making concerning storerooms. In particular, we found that analyzing the role of artefacts (i.e. spreadsheets, sketches, 2D and 3D models) made it possible for us to identify particular critical points in time where altering a decision had direct material consequences for the hospital design, and thus taking the "right path" was critical.

The work on the architectural competition was organized in collaboration between six companies, including 28 participants such as architects, healthcare specialists, construction specialists, hospital technologies specialists, etc. The architectural competition was initiated in February 2013 by a competition brief that described proposal requirements (i.e. number of patient beds). The future hospital should be an "acute hospital" in a Danish region and covering a total gross area of 128.000 m$^2$. The hospital is expected to be ready for use in 2020 [23]. The final winning project was appointed in April 2014.

The purpose of our data analysis is not to unpack all complexities involved in hospital design; instead, we use the empirical insights to explore the use of artefacts when practitioners try to identify due time during critical decision-making situations. In particular, we focused on empirical situations where the closing of ends affects all future decision-making. Another important point for our analysis was the uncertainty involved in critical decision-making for not limiting the space for design maneuverability prematurely—or what is referred to in the competition brief as the *flexibility* and *robustness* of the project [23]. Unpacking the characteristics of due time, we examined how sequentiality and dependencies were handled in practice, pushing the irreversible decisions for design as far as possible.

## 12.4   Analysis: Due Time in Hospital Design

How do practitioners decide what is due time in the architectural practices of hospital design? We begin by entering the architectural firm and locating the team involved in the architectural competition; we find an interdisciplinary team consisting of architects and various types of specialists. One key discussion concerns the nature of the logistic technologies of the hospital, which are to ensure that medicine, equipment, and other physical devices can be transported within the hospital from the storerooms to where they are needed. Here a key topic was requested by the competition brief: to consider the opportunities for introducing automation technologies into the hospital design. Let's take a closer look.

The early architectural phase involves analyzing and creating a coherent design proposal that stipulates the vision of the hospital. This was a period of 3 months with a strict deadline, May 6th, 2013, for submitting the proposal (competition entry). The competition brief that describes the requirements of the tender specifically requested that at least two standard wards in a hospital department be prototyped in the proposal, each ward with 32 patient beds [23]. Where to locate storerooms (divided into clean and dirty spaces) in the hospital and how to organize the transportation of equipment between storerooms and the patient beds are critical design decisions. Currently, storerooms are typically designed as local storerooms in close proximity to patient wards in Danish hospitals. Such a building structure entails that local departmental storerooms form the central infrastructure of the complete hospital. However, storeroom design could also be based upon one central storeroom for the whole hospital.

Hence, decisions on the design of storerooms shape the communication and coordination and the role of logistic technologies in practice in important ways. Decisions will have a huge impact on how healthcare professionals will carry out work and collaborate; therefore, these decisions cannot be taken lightly. So the question becomes, what happens when the foundational structure of storerooms (including clean and dirty spaces) is on the design table, and how does the interdisciplinary design team decide on how best to support the just-in-time services and central stock without compromising important measures for a hospital, such as hygiene practices embedded in local clean and dirty spaces in the design? What would it mean if local stocks were replaced with one central stock and the building needed to be able to support technologically supported just-in-time services as we know them from different types of industries? How and when do you make such a decision, and when do you know these crucial decisions are made in due time, without premature closure?

## 12.4.1   Sequentiality in Hospital Design

The design of storerooms in the future hospital architecture entailed many important decisions. The tender competition in this case requested "greenfield" hospital projects designed and constructed from anew—including future visions for the use of digital technology. However, the scale of the entire Danish hospital project (16 new hospitals) means that there has been considerable interest in modernizing the Danish hospital sector and healthcare services. The government describes the modernizing strategy as a process which *"enables dissemination of the newest knowledge, technology, and best practice throughout the country. Increasing digitalization ensures efficient operation of core services in hospitals, with the new equipment and new technologies, and organizations"* ([21] p. 18).

Analyzing the requirement for the design to save space for patients rather than equipment, existing local storerooms gained specific attention. According to the competition brief, for a standard hospital department the storeroom would have to be a shared resource of, at minimum, each ward (32 beds). In this way, it was already a requirement that the existing workflow around local storerooms would have to be reconsidered. In addition, the competition brief also required that the infrastructure in the future hospitals should be able to handle storeroom delivery using automated technology if possible. The competition brief states: *"the right product should be delivered when it is to be used. If implemented, this principle would mean that there would be no surplus products in storerooms and that fewer products would be scrapped. As a consequence, less storage space would be needed in the individual units"* (Ibid p. 114).

Local storerooms are essential for hospital work, since nurses and nursing assistants have immediate access to the storerooms with different medical remedies that they use in their daily work when they tend to patients. Thus, being local means easy access. Different types of storerooms exist in hospitals, and are critical for the execution of healthcare work. We have clean storerooms, where all stored items must be clean and sterile to ensure that infectious diseases are not spread. Medication rooms are sometimes separate and sometimes they are collocated with the clean storerooms. Dirty storerooms are used for all the dirty equipment and leftovers from, for example, fluid examinations, such as blood and urine samples.

The division of storerooms into "clean" and "dirty" spaces avoids the spreading of contaminating microorganisms, which constantly jeopardize the hygiene in hospitals. As the interdisciplinary team began to explore the potential automation of exchange between storerooms and hospital wards it became clear that every decision would have to be based upon other decisions about the foundation for the hospital infrastructure. At this point the hospital architecture had evolved to the stage of diverse sketches depicting the basic principles of the future hospital. A decision was already made in the competition brief to have a remote central storeroom in addition to a number of shared local storerooms. This meant that the process of delivery from the remote storeroom to the local storerooms was important to figure out by the team.

The question became how to design the requirements of fast and timely automated deliveries between storage and department. Given that the hospital would first be opened in 10 years' time, it meant that the vision of digital technologies for automated delivery had to be based upon the future vision of digital technology in 10 years' time. This is a very difficult decision since it is practically impossible to predict exactly how digital technologies might change in this long-term perspective, and yet the decision would have huge consequences for the rest of the design process. The *sequentiality* in the work activities, as in which order the different decisions have to be made, is thus an important feature of handling due time in hospital design.

## 12.4.2   Dependencies in Hospital Design

Hygiene issues in hospitals are critical and thus are highly prioritized in the design requirements for the new hospitals to avoid adverse events that are not directly related to a patient's diagnoses. The infrastructure of clean and dirty storerooms guides nurses and nursing assistants in hygiene issues by ensuring that new medicines are only mixed in spaces with strict hygiene rules, whereas used containers of medicine or used medical remedies, such as catheters, are disposed of in the area referred to as a dirty space or the dirty storeroom. Recycled catheters or other relevant equipment will typically enter the washing machine in the dirty space to be recollected in the clean space on the other side of a wall dividing the local storeroom into two separate spaces.

Nurses and nursing assistants in hospital departments are tending to multiple different patients simultaneously, and their activities often involve moving between the storerooms and the patients. Nurses and nursing assistants have recurrent activities, which they perform many times in a day (i.e. giving patients their medicines), while other activities are only performed once in a while (i.e. changing the catheters of a patient), depending on the specialty of the particular hospital department and the patient population at the department.

One important issue with the decisions on local storeroom design is that they take up space in hospital departments. Lack of space for patients is a recurring issue for existing hospitals, and sometimes patients are placed in beds located in the corridors rather than in rooms. This space problem is an ongoing challenge in all Danish hospitals, which regularly face the problem of too few beds for the incoming patients. In fact, it is part of the head nurse's daily routine to negotiate the transfer of responsibility for patients to other hospital departments with available beds. The space problem is not a unique Danish phenomenon, and it has been reported in other studies [e.g. 24]. The head nurses from the diverse departments meet at 12 pm (midday) to coordinate possible transfers and reorganization of patients.

To accommodate this challenge of bed-booking and bed assignments, architectural designs of future hospitals are based upon the principle of *robust* and *flexible* space, which means that space can be "transformed" accordingly with use, rather than being fixed and dedicated space. Still, to create architectural designs based upon robustness and flexibility in relation to patient beds, the challenge of storerooms (local versus central and clean versus dirty) is an open question.

The space dedicated to local storerooms in existing hospital architecture is up for consideration as a way to rethink the future visions of hospital design, infrastructure, and digital technologies. There are clear *dependencies* in terms of how decisions of infrastructure will be based upon decisions on storerooms, and the routine patterns of healthcare professionals, which impact the ways in which the interdisciplinary team in the architectural firm is able to push foundational decisions about the design until later, while not holding up the design process.

### 12.4.3  Irreversibility in Hospital Design

Remote central storerooms make design considerations on infrastructures supporting transportation within the hospital essential. The available logistic technologies to support remote central storerooms had three different strategies for automation of transportation infrastructure: Mini loads (moves in the hospital walls based upon infrastructures integrated into the very construction of the building); AGVs (automated guided vehicles, which are designed to move on the hospital floors, and thus as robots driving around the hospital, able to transport themselves in

**Fig. 12.1** Example of mini loads and automated guided vehicles (AGVs) [25]

the available elevators together with hospital personnel and patients), and drones (move in the air, and thus require high ceilings and space to travel from the remote storeroom to the department with required equipment). Lets look at each in turn. Deciding which logistic technologies would be the most appropriate in the future is difficult, and the decision has consequences for many parts of the hospital design. To be able to place certain building blocks (e.g. drones), the dimensions of the space must be able to accommodate certain standards (e.g. high ceiling). Lets look more closely at the accommodating standards for each technology.

Mini loads are basically built-in automated robots that are able to move equipment within walls (see Fig. 12.1). The mini load technology requires that all elevator shafts in the hospital design are constructed and built into the walls. Exploring this option involves many estimations and possible forecasts for the future hospital, for example, what is the expected minimum number of mini loads required in a standard hospital department to avoid bottlenecks in deliveries from the remote storage. The risk involved in miscalculating the number of mini loads is bottlenecks for getting deliveries in due time, and mistakes in calculations that support decision-making may have severe consequences for the work of nurses and nursing assistants in their future daily work. Designing the hospital to accommodate mini loads is the same as designing the basic infrastructure for the hospital, since the built-in frames in the walls would have to be vertical, but also horizontal. Using mini loads, nurses and nursing assistants will be relieved from the activity of keeping track of local storerooms, which is not considered to be key in their work and is thus viewed as taking time away from their core work, namely tending to patients. The potential of designing for mini loads technologies is thus fundamentally changing hospital design. This potential is particularly viewed in relation to the reduction of waste by the remote storage, since medicines and medical remedies would not exceed their date of expiration when distributed in relation to the specific needs of the different hospital departments.

AGVs are robot vehicles that drive around the hallways in the hospital. They are able to take the elevators and thus can travel all over the hospital without being dependent upon new built-in wall structures. Despite not requiring a total re-design of the concept of walls in the hospital, the AGVs still require certain accommodation from the design of the building construction. AGV technology requires certain design for the elevators or lifts, which will be their main form of transportation. In addition, they take up space in the hallways and thus the size of hallway to accommodate both AGVs and people must be taken into account. The advantage of AGV technology compared with other logistic technologies is the ability to transport large amounts of goods, particularly at night. Transportation during nighttime reduces the risk of creating bottlenecks in the hallways, since fewer people move around at night. However, much of the transportation in the hospital imagined to be organized by AGV technology is delivering meals to patients, which cannot be accomplished in the middle of the night. The AGV technology is operated through computer simulations that allow the hospital to plan in advance what, where, and when individual AGVs will deliver various goods to relevant places in the hospital. Sensor technology ensures that the individual AGVs do not collide with people walking in the corridors. However, it is reasonable to expect that AGVs in practice will require a space or path of some form on the floor to ensure that people do not get in their way.

The drone technology as the basic infrastructure for the hospital design was actually never considered as a realistic solution to the automation of deliveries, since drones represented a new technology that was yet to be tested in a complex work setting. Neither were the predecessor of drones, *mono-rail systems*, which can also move along the ceiling and have been explored in hospitals but are still only in use in Denmark in one hospital; in other cases the mono-rail systems have been abandoned as the hospitals were being extended with new building structures or transportation needs changed [25]. Thus, it is not hard to imagine a hospital design where transporting medicines and medical remedies by flying drones would be ideal, since drones do not take up floor or wall space. However, the drones, like the two other logistic technologies, require certain infrastructures to accommodate their movement, for example, ceiling height. What emerges here is the paradox of designing [26, 27], in this case, a future hospital to be ready for use in 2020. The extended time span makes the basic assumptions about logistic technologies to some extent imaginative, rather than predictive.

There is no clear evidence that new technologies (e.g. drones) will be reliable when the future hospital is ready for use. In the end, the choice of technology for the automation of substantial deliveries was a decision between mini loads and AGV technology. As the submission date for the architectural proposal came closer, the architects began to work towards a solution including both mini loads and AGV technology. Discussions went on about an estimation of how many mini loads would be required to support a standard hospital department of 64 patient beds with a structure of one central remote storeroom—while keeping a focus on hygiene issues.

### 12.4.4 Artefacts Supporting Due-Time Decisions

Discussing logistic technologies while ensuring important divisions such as "clean" and "dirty" spaces are kept following hygiene standards, different artefacts were used to "prototype" the hospital design. The standard hospital departments with 64

**Fig. 12.2**  Example of 2D-model [28]

| Primary functions | | | | | |
|---|---|---|---|---|---|
| Room type | Function | Number | m2 | m2 in total | Comments |
| Patient room | | | | | |
| Patient restroom /bath | | | | | |
| Work stations | | | | | |
| **Secondary functions** | | | | | |
| Storage of food etc. | | | | | |
| Clean space | | | | | |
| Dirty space | | | | | |
| Patient common room | | | | | |
| Staff restroom | | | | | |
| Staff common room | | | | | |
| Staff offices | | | | | |
| | | | | | |
| Total m2 | | | | | |
| Net to Gross Ratio | | | | 1,7 | |

**Fig. 12.3**  Example of spreadsheet (room list)

patient beds was prototyped using artefacts such as 2D floor plans, 3D modelling (foam and CAD), and produced as numbers in an Excel spreadsheet (room lists). These artefacts were vital for fundamental due-time decisions about future logistic technologies. The team contrasted and compared the different prototypes, for example, 2D-model prototype (see Fig. 12.2) and the spreadsheet prototype (see Fig. 12.3), to test and challenge the different alternative solutions. The spreadsheet, in particular, turned out to be a sophisticated computational artefact, although it appears less rich in detail compared with the 2D-models.

The spreadsheet (also known as a room list) was structured in such a way that design changes were calculated immediately and related to Gross/Net Ratio. This was an important function that enabled the team to see in real time how the total Net and Gross areas of the particular hospital department evolved in relation to Danish recommendations for hospital design [29]—and how it was aligned with the total Gross area of the hospital, including technical areas. The Net area refers to the different rooms that reflect the main functions in a hospital department; the Gross area refers to the sum of the Net area, "traffic areas", and more technical areas. The Gross/Net Ratio is calculated by dividing the Gross area of the particular hospital department by the Net area. The desired Gross/Net Ratio is 1.7, which provides a buffer to ensure future changes to the technical areas can be made; thus, it is recommended [29] to add extra 30 % of a net area as a buffer for potential changes in the technical areas in the future hospital while these are the areas that are the most difficult to adjust once a hospital is built.

The spreadsheet also functioned as a cost estimator, ensuring that regulations are followed, e.g. a minimum of square meters (m$^2$) must be dedicated to bathrooms to ensure appropriate workspace for the hospital professionals when patients need assistance. The Net area of a standard hospital department is expected to meet a Gross/Net Ratio of 1.7. When the interdisciplinary team explored the different options for automated logistic technologies, Gross/Net Ratios were explored to assess changes in m2 of clean and dirty storage spaces in both the 2D-model and the spreadsheet.

What is interesting in these discussions and decisions about technologies in the future hospital is the eminent element of irreversibility and the link between the Gross/Net Ratio produced by comparing artefacts. When the Gross/Net Ratio was calculated as 1.7 it included the buffer for future changes in relation to technical areas. Thus, to ensure flexibility and robustness in the future hospital, the Gross/Net Ratio became a timely aspect representing the buffered technical area sizing of the flexibly designed space for future yet-to-be determined logistic technologies.

Other aspects cannot be accounted for in the Gross/Net Ratio, for example, the ceiling height. Regulations of a minimum ceiling height are of course followed and detected by the Ratio, but it cannot be used to determine how the ceiling height shapes the design path in all the sequential steps in the architectural procedure. New sketches produce ripple effects for all other designs and prototypes sequentially. Decisions on the ceiling height produce certain ripple effects that make it possible or impossible for, for example, installation of drone technology, while decisions on the size of hallways produce certain ripple effects that make it possible or impossible to implement AGV technology. In this way, decisions shaping the design at a certain time become irreversible in a material way, not because the building is erected, but because of the impossibilities of sorting our large number of nested un-dos, which makes it impossible to identify the complete effect of re-doing past fundamental changes.

Once the mini loads are built into the walls of the hospital they become part of the installed base and infrastructure of the hospital, and cannot be changed. The AGVs rely on elevator shafts or lifts that are also integrated into the very base of high buildings. At the point in time when this decision is made, all following decisions will be based upon this fundamental decision and thus are materially irreversible. There is no point of return. Here the 2D-model was extremely important for exploring the practical consequences for how work is carried out in the future hospital based on how the numbers in the spreadsheet changed. The competition brief stated that each section of 32 patient beds must share a clean space, dirty space, and storage, and two sections totalling 64 beds must share a medication room [23].

To explore the alternative logistic technologies, unpacking the reality of time in the future practice is important. Exploring the logistic technologies in relation to time was understood in terms of the frequency in entering storerooms and medication rooms in a day (the mini load technology combines the two)—but also the time it would take nurses to get to a critically ill patient, particularly during the night shift with fewer staff. Time in work was largely imported from medical practice, and measured in terms of alarm colours (code red, yellow, or green).

To make *due-time decisions* on logistic technologies thus included assessing whether, for example, mini loads—and the distance to patients' beds—would support the daily work in hospital departments efficiently, by assessing and keeping track of relationships between material matter represented by 2D-models and spreadsheets and, on the other hand, the notions of time in medical practice. The alternative technological solutions were tested in relation to whether they could meet the target number of square meters in the spreadsheet model as well as whether the solution could function in the 2D-model of the standard hospital department of 64 beds.

Hesitation to design hospitals with highly complex technological infrastructures, which might or might not be applicable in 10 years' time, reflects professional experience with the irreversibility of major construction infrastructures that might turn out to be false.

## 12.5  Final Remarks

The case demonstrates how decisions on logistic technologies are entangled with the hospital design practice in closely coupled ways. There are times during architectural design work where former alternative paths are excluded, since the inertia of the installed base or foundation [30] is robust and persistent. This is the time when all new architectural and digital strategic decisions have to be backwards-compatible with former decisions, even though future experiences tell otherwise. We might learn that drone technology is suitable for support of remote storage and coordination in hospitals in 10 years, but the ceiling of the hospital does not take extra space for flying objects into account; thus, the ceiling height will possibly be experienced as a constraint in the future, but not in the present.

Assessing when architectural decisions have been made in due time can only be fully established after the fact, and thus it is difficult to predict. Collaborative decisions in architectural design work scrutinize the dependencies between sub-parts in relation to the sequential decision-making organized across the whole design project. Due-time decisions on, for example, storage design emerge as a bundle of interrelationships tightly coupled within the design project [20], where any attempt to modify a sub-part leads to much larger impact on the common designbreak project.

In architecture, modifying the installed infrastructure for, for example, storeroom design creates ripple effects in the larger hospital design requiring re-design of other parts of the construction. We might say that the former decision upon alternatives in design no longer holds, since the fundamentally designed infrastructure has in fact become normalized, without any competing future visions for the hospital. The irreversibility of due-time decisions in architecture work is therefore the impossibility to return to competing visions, and thus is synonymous with normalization [Ibid p. 151]. Before this point of no return, the dependencies within the infrastructures for work (e.g. storerooms) are to some extent malleable and reconfigurable.

This paper explores how due-time decisions shape the course of action in collaborative work. Due time is not about rhythms [32], clock-time [4], or calendar time [6]. Instead, due time is a quality measurement for fundamental decisions shaping the future directions in complex work. Due time can thus been seen as an adverb linked to critical decision-making and timeliness, where the quality of the decision is done in accordance with the nature of dependencies in the work activity taking into account the sequentiality of the collaborative setup, pushing irreversibility embedded within major decisions.

Accordingly, the purpose of pushing fundamental decisions about technologies in the design of hospitals—thus enacting due-time decision-making—is an essential principle in architectural work of not reducing design space prematurely. Reducing design space prematurely would jeopardize and seriously damage the opportunities for using the most recent and robust logistic technologies, since the time between architectural design and the erection of the hospital is approximately 10 years.

*In due time* is a notion evoked by practice. This paper expands the research domain on time in CSCW research by not focusing on temporal coordination and rhythms in work [4, 5, 31, 32] and instead by offering a way to think about the *quality* of timely decisions. Due-time decisions are important in cooperative work when the material matter of the work activity switches from reversible to irreversible. By unpacking how practitioners involved in hospital design enact what they refer to as "due time", we are not claiming that we can easily determine which is "the right path" or "the wrong path". Instead, we argue that "the practices by which due-time decisions are made" is an area for technology design, where decision-making is supported by representations of diverse sets of sequentiality, interdependence, and irreversibility in complex architectural constructions.

**Acknowledgements** We would like to thank colleagues that provided comments during the process of writing this paper, and in particular we would like to thank Jørgen Bansler, Kjeld Schmidt, Marisa Cohn, Mary Amasia, and Geraldine Fitzpatrick. Also, we would like to direct a special thanks to Susanne Dam Hoffmann, Head of Health Service Planning, who initiated discussions on how critical decisions are made based on her expertise and long experience with hospital design. Susanne was instrumental in pushing discussions, particularly in the initial part of the study. We would also like to direct a special thanks to the architecture firm. This work was in part funded by the Velux Foundations and is part of the Computational Artifact research project.

# References

1. Boden A et al (2014) Articulation spaces: bridging the gab between formal and informal coordination. In: Proceedings of the 17th ACM conference on computer supported cooperative work (CSCW). Baltimore, pp 1120–1130
2. Gerson EM, Star SL (1986) Analyzing due process in the workplace. Trans Off Inf Syst 4(3):257–270
3. Egger E, Wagner I (1993) Negotiating temporal orders: the case of collaborative time management in a surgery clinic. Comput Supported Coop Work (CSCW): Int J 1(4):255–275
4. Bardram JE (2000) Temporal coordination. Comput Supported Coop Work (CSCW): Int J 9:157–187
5. Reddy MC, Dourish P, Pratt W (2006) Temporality in medical work: time also matters. Comput Supported Coop Work (CSCW): Int J 15:29–53
6. Nilsson M, Hertzum M (2005) Negotiated rhythms of mobile work: time, place, and work schedules. In: Proceedings of the 2005 international ACM conference on supporting group work (GROUP), Sanibel Island, pp 148–157
7. Esbensen M, Bjørn P (2014) Routine and standardization in global software development. In: Proceedings of the international ACM conference on supporting group work (GROUP), Sanibel Island, pp 12–23
8. Palen L, Vieweg S, Anderson KM (2011) Supporting everyday analysts in safety and time critical situations. Inf Soc 27:52–62
9. Tsai C et al (2010) The impact of different decision behavior models in emergency physician on the performance of emergency departments. Emerging M&S Applications in Industry and Academia Symposium Proceedings, Orlando
10. Schmidt K, Bannon L (1992) Taking CSCW seriously: supporting articulation work. Comput Supported Coop Work (CSCW): Int J 1(1–2):7–40
11. Suchman L (1987) Plans and situated actions. The problem of human machine communication. Cambridge University Press, New York
12. Christensen LR (2014) Practices of stigmergy in the building process. Comput Supported Coop Work (CSCW): Int J 23:1–19
13. Schmidt K, Wagner I (2004) Ordering systems: coordinative practices and artifacts in architectural design and planning. Comput Supported Coop Work (CSCW): Int J 13:349–408
14. Schmidt K, Wagner I (2002) Coordinative artifacts in architectural practice. In: Blay-Fornarino M et al (eds) Cooperative systems design: a challenge of the mobility age. [Proceedings of the fifth international conference on the sesign of cooperative systems (COOP 2002), Saint Raphaël, 4–7 June 2002], IOS Press, Amsterdam etc. pp 257–274
15. Berndtsson J, Normark M (1999) The coordinative functions of flight strips: air traffic control work revisited. In: Proceedings of the international ACM conference on supporting group work (GROUP), Phoenix Arizona, pp 101–110
16. Christensen LR, Bjørn P (2014) Documentscape: intertextuallity, sequentiality and autonomy at work. In: Proceedings of the annual ACM conference on human factors in computing systems (CHI), Toronto, pp 2451–2460
17. Svensson MS, Heath C, Luff P (2007) Instrumental action: the timely exchange of implements during surgical operation. In: Proceedings of the European conference on computer-supported cooperative work (ECSCW). Limerick
18. Grinter R (2003) Recomposition: coordinating a web of software dependencies. Comput Supported Coop Work (CSCW): Int J 12:297–327
19. Herbsled J et al (2000) Distance, dependencies, and delay in a global collaboration. Comput Supported Coop Work (CSCW): Int J 319–328 http://dl.acm.org/citation.cfm?id=359003
20. Callon M (1990) Techno-economic networks and irreversibility. Sociol Rev 38(S1):132–161
21. Healthcare Denmark (2015) Innovating better life. 2nd edn. February 2014. Downloaded 16th Nov 2015 http://healthcaredenmark.dk/media/1140741/healthcaredenmark-magazine-winter-2014.pdf

22. Blomberg J, Giacomi J, Mosher A, Swenton-Wall P (1993). Ethnographic field methods and their relationto design. In: Schuler D, Namioka A (eds) Participatory design: perspectives on system design. Lawrence Erlbaum Associates, Inc., Hillsdale, pp 123–154
23. Capital Region of Denmark (2013) Competition brief. Vision and fundamental principles. pp 1–205
24. Clarke K et al (2006) When a bed is not a bed: calculation and calculability in complex organisational settings. In: Clark K et al (eds) Trust in technology: a socio-technical perspective. Springer, pp 21–38
25. Danish Regions (2013) Afrapportering om Transportteknologier [Report on Delivery Technologies]. pp 1–25
26. Theureau J (2003) Course of action analysis & course of action centered design. In: Hollnagel E (ed) Handbook of cognitive task design. Lawrence Erlbaum Associates, Mahwah, pp 55–81
27. Bratteteig T, Wagner I (2012) Disentangling power and decision-making in participatory design. In: Proceedings of participatory design conference 12.–14 Aug, Roskilde, pp 41–50
28. Capital Region of Denmark (2013) Dommerbetænkning [Jury report]
29. Capital Region of Denmark (2008) Region Hovedstadens Arealstandarder for Hospitalsbyggeri [The Capital Region of Denmark's area standards for hospital architecture]. Downloaded Nov. 19th 2015 https://www.regionh.dk/nythospitalnordsjaelland/derfor-bygger-vi/inspiration/PublishingImages/Sider/Regionens-retningslinjer-for-nybyggeri/Arealstandardermarts11.pdf
30. Bowker GC, Star SL (2002) Sorting things out. Classification and its consequences. The MIT Press, Cambridge, MA
31. Jackson SJ, Ribes D, Buyuktur AG, Bowker GC (2011) Collaborative rhythm: temporal dissonance and alignment in collaborative scientific work. In: Proceedings of the 2011 ACM conference on computer-supported cooperative work. Hangzhou, pp 245–254
32. Zerubavel E (1981) Hidden rhythms. Schedules and calendars in social life. University of California Press, Berkeley

# Chapter 13
# Coordinating, Contributing, Contesting, Representing: HCI Specialists Surviving Distributed Design

Netta Iivari

**Abstract** This paper examines distributed design that involved educational science, information and communication technology (ICT) and human–computer interaction (HCI) specialists collaboratively designing a learning application. The design process is characterized by coordinating, contributing, contesting and representing. The HCI specialists "represented the user", but users remained silent during the design process. The design work was dominated by 'coordinating' activity, but also 'proposing' and 'evaluating' activities were prominent. The educational science specialists were the most active ones in the design discussions, heavily involved in 'proposing' and 'coordinating' activities. The HCI specialists were involved in those as well, but distinctly contributed through 'evaluating' activity. Interestingly, also 'challenging' and 'ignoring' activities characterized the distributed design process among the educational science specialists and HCI specialists: design emerged as a political, conflictual process. The very limited ICT support for distributed design became also accentuated. This study opens up interesting avenues for future research in this respect.

## 13.1 Introduction

Information and communication technology (ICT) design is a collaborative process involving multiple stakeholders and a variety of interests [6]. Traditionally, such stakeholders were users and their organizations and developers and their organizations. More recently, however, the situation has changed and the number and variety of stakeholders increased. ICT design is nowadays often taking place in global setting, where people around the world are to collaborate. These people may be representing various nationalities, organizations, disciplines and

N. Iivari (✉)
INTERACT Research Unit, Faculty of Information Technology and Electrical Engineering,
University of Oulu, Oulu, Finland
e-mail: netta.iivari@oulu.fi

© Springer International Publishing Switzerland 2016          207
A. De Angeli et al. (eds.), *COOP 2016: Proceedings of the 12th International
Conference on the Design of Cooperative Systems, 23–27 May 2016, Trento, Italy*,
DOI 10.1007/978-3-319-33464-6_13

professions and their collaboration is highly reliant on different kinds of computer support. Such kind of distributed ICT design has also become discussed within the research literature during recent years. The disciplines of Information Systems (IS) (see e.g. [18,26,31,38]), Computer-Supported Cooperative Work (CSCW) (see e.g. [1,12,28,37]), Human Computer Interaction (HCI) (see e.g. [2,4]) and Software Engineering (SE) (see e.g. [8,16]) have all considered the implications and challenges of distributed development. These studies have also revealed that collaboration in distributed design setting may be very challenging. Overall, these studies indicate that 'Making Together' may not be an unproblematic endeavor in today's global setting.

This study examines collaborative ICT design taking place in a distributed setting. The study concentrates specifically on the work of Human Computer Interaction (HCI) specialists in such a setting. HCI specialists are people expected to 'know the user' and 'to represent the user' in ICT design (e.g. [10,15,20]). There is a long-lasting research interest in the work of HCI specialists and during 2000s there has even been an increase in interest (e.g. [7,15,19–21,27]). However, even though the importance of HCI specialists in ICT design has been extensively discussed, there are still pertinent problems relating to their work in practice. One of those has been that HCI specialists may not have any power of decision or actual impact on the solution under development (e.g. [5,19,20,27]). HCI specialists, if not totally ignored, may be only in informative or consultative roles, i.e. only permitted to provide information or to comment on predefined design solutions, without any power of decision or ability to directly impact the design solution, albeit it has been argued that they should be allowed a participative role, i.e. to actively take part in the design process and have decision-making power as regards the design solution [9,20]. In distributed setting, one could assume that HCI work is not without problems: such setting unlikely has alleviated the problems mentioned above, and the HCI literature has not offered any guidance on how HCI specialists are to survive such a computer-mediated setting. The distributed nature may have made it even more difficult for HCI specialists to have a say and influence on the solution. So far, there is very limited research addressing HCI specialists' work in distributed setting (see [4,22,41]). This paper aims to fill in this gap.

Hence, this paper empirically examines the work of HCI specialists, 'representing the user', in a distributed multiparty project developing a learning application, the project partners coming from four countries and eight organizations, ranging from research institutions to ICT companies, having expertise in ICT, HCI or educational sciences. This paper asks: "How can one characterize distributed collaborative design?" and "How can one characterize HCI specialists' contribution in such a design?" The paper contributes by making sense of collaborative design in distributed setting, specifically inquiring how HCI work survives such a setting.

The paper is structured as follows. The next section reviews related research. The third section discusses the research setting, method and procedure. The fourth section outlines the results of the empirical study, and the fifth section summarizes them and discusses their implications for research and practice.

## 13.2   Related Research

Table 13.1 summarizes the findings of the various literature sources reviewed. The findings are discussed afterwards.

Concerning the participants in ICT design, in IS and HCI research a lot of attention has been devoted to user participation, as users represent different disciplinary and professional background to designers and are thus seen as important participants in design teams (e.g. [6,14,32]). In addition to users and designers, the literature has brought up the importance of different kinds of intermediaries who are to support and enable user participation (see e.g. [23]): e.g. HCI specialists [20], ethnographers [24] or IS change agents [32] have been recommended to do the job. On the other hand, nowadays it has been recognized that the design process tends to involve even a larger number of stakeholders that may represent multiple nationalities, organizations, areas of expertise and disciplines [8,17,30,35,39,41]. In these types of design teams, communicating, collaborating, and arriving at shared understandings may be very challenging [28–31]. Studies [30] have argued that such kind of design work involves political negotiations and shaping and influencing each other's, and conceptualized such design work to consists not only of 'adding on' activities, but also of 'challenging' and 'ignoring' activities.

The nature and the challenges of distributed development have been extensively discussed in the research literature during the 2000s. The development might be distributed physically, organizationally, temporally or among stakeholders: participants may be in different physical locations around the world, they may represent different organizations and the development may be distributed among diverse expert groups [16]. Especially physical distribution is argued to hamper the development work

**Table 13.1**   Characterizing distributed, participatory and collaborative design

|  | Design |
|---|---|
| Participatory | Decades old topic. Need for users and designers to collaborate, while also intermediaries (e.g. HCI specialists) useful for catering for users' interests |
| Collaborative | More recent topic. People representing various disciplines, professions, nationalities, or organizations need to collaborate. This involves political negotiations, formation of power relations and shaping and influencing each other; i.e. 'adding on' but also 'challenging' and 'ignoring' others' activities |
| Distributed and participatory | Recent topic. In distributed design setting, users and designers need to collaborate and various kinds of technologies, practices and intermediaries have been recommended for catering for users' interests. Lack of research on HCI specialists as intermediaries in distributed participatory design |
| Distributed and collaborative | Recent topic. Nowadays people representing various disciplines, professions, nationalities or organizations need to collaborate and in distributed design setting, computer support is needed. Collaboration may take place in discussion, implementation and documentation spaces, consisting of proposing, evaluating, clarifying, coordinating, synthesizing, and deciding activities. Lack of research on HCI specialists as intermediaries in distributed collaborative design |

[8,16]. The main problems associated with distributed development relate to communication, coordination and control [8]. Distributed development is heavily reliant on the use of electronic tools for communication and coordination, such as version control and bug tracking systems, email, videoconferencing, chat, discussion forums, and shared data repositories [1–3,12,28,31,37].

The importance of supporting user participation in distributed design setting has received attention during recent years. These studies outline solutions for inviting users into the design process in a situation in which users and designers are not co-located. In some studies mailing lists are extensively used to enable collaboration [2,3], in others inter-contextual user workshops and inter-contextual commented case studies have been experimented with [35]. Also mediated user feedback through email and bug trackers, and user support through documentation and email are recommended as solutions [17] as well as usability design by blogs [34] and remote user data gathering tools to be used by users [33]. Meta-design and complex socio-technical environments have also been recommended for enabling user participation [13,41] and for fostering cultures of participation more generally [13].

Studies have also identified a variety of intermediaries that are needed to support or enable distributed participatory design. Those are called local implementers [39], active users speaking on behalf of other users [17], communities of interest formed by representatives of different user groups [35], or developer-users taking part in both user and developer communities, mediating between them [3]. However, noteworthy is that there is very limited research addressing the work of the HCI specialists in distributed design setting (i.e. [4,22,41]), while HCI specialists' work has otherwise been under empirical scrutiny for decades. One could assume that studies on HCI specialists work are still needed, as there remain numerous problems as regards it in practice. One of the still relevant problems is the HCI specialists' lack of authority to impact design solutions (e.g. [5,7,15,19,20,27]). One could assume that distributed design setting has not in itself removed this problems.

Collaborative design work has also been studied in distributed setting. These studies have examined situations, e.g., in which there has been marketing, strategy, and graphic design specialists in addition to technical experts and business stakeholders involved, the participants also coming from different organizations [31] or there has been computer scientists and meteorologists representing different institutions involved in various kinds of research and development activities [28]. These studies have discussed the importance of computer support for design work. The design activity can be either synchronous or asynchronous, different tools aiding in them. In a study on distributed engineering design, in synchronous mode whiteboard and shared CAD applications were used, while asynchronous design, in addition to CAD applications, relied on email and common data repositories [12]. In distributed design setting communicating and document sharing have been found as challenging [28]. Studies have also revealed a multitude of different tools in use (e.g. bug tracking and version control systems, email lists, instant messaging, data repositories) and researchers have argued that the most appropriate computer support for distributed collaborative design may be "*a heterogeneous 'assembly' of variably coupled systems*" that help "*keep the work flowing in an orderly fashion*" [2: 477].

Studies on collaborative, distributed design in open source software development projects have argued that design takes place in three different online spaces, i.e. discussion, implementation and documentation spaces, within which associated activities are accomplished and artefacts produced and modified [2,37]. The discussion space is composed of mailing lists and discussion forums, the documentation space consists of the project related documentation and the implementation space contains the code of the project, usually accessible through a concurrent versioning system. Design activity is found predominantly to take place in the discussion space [2,37] and to contain activities relating to solving design problems and group management. Design activities have here been further categorized as proposing, evaluating, clarifying, coordinating, synthesizing and deciding activities [2].

## 13.3  Research Setting and Approach

This study is an interpretive case study on the work practices of the HCI specialists in distributed ICT design with a number of disciplines and areas of expertise involved. In interpretive research, the analyst assumes "*that our knowledge of reality is gained only through social constructions such a language, consciousness, shared meanings, documents, tools, and other artifacts*" and focuses on human sense making and on understanding meanings people assign to phenomena [25: 69]. In this case, the author acted as an "*involved researcher*", having a direct personal stake in the outcomes and interpretations, at the same time being able to get a direct sense of the field from the inside [40]. Hence, she was one participant in the examined project, representing the HCI specialists. The project participants include around ten people having strong background and skills in educational sciences, HCI or ICT development as well as numerous more inexperienced participants building their competence in these areas. The application under development is a mobile learning application with basic and advanced versions serving a variety of learners, to be used both in educational settings with teachers and at home by the learners themselves.

The research material has been collaboratively produced by the project participants during 1.5 years, and it contains some preparatory work before the start of the project, as well as 1 year and 1 month of actual project work. The material consists of documents produced during the timeframe: official project documents (project plan, agreements, etc.), project deliverables (requirements specification and design deliverables), different kinds of memos and unofficial documentation (e.g., sketches, scenarios, and drawings) and email correspondence among the project participants.

The data analysis was a highly inductive process; nonetheless, using the existing research as a sensitizing device (cf. [25]). The steps and influential analytical lenses will be presented next. Overall, the data analysis was focused on distributed design and the variety of spaces (discussion, documentation, and implementation [2,37], within which it took place. The data revealed in this case that distributed design mainly took place in the discussion space (email, voice chat, and videoconferencing), but utilized the documentation space (a shared data repository) as well. The data characterizing distributed design was examined in more detail. It was first categorized into different foci of design (inspired by [9,11][1]): whether the focus of work was on early conceptual design (figuring out what is valuable for users), behavioral design (figuring out how the system behaves) or interface design (figuring out what it looks like). Clearly, all these foci were evident in the design process. Then, the analysis turned to the participants in distributed design: whose voices were present, who was heard and had a say [20,21]? The data showed that the most prominent voices were those of the educational science specialists, ICT developers and HCI specialists, with clear differences among them. Thereafter, distributed design that took place within the discussion and documentation space and among these experts was characterized through the activities identified as characterizing distributed and collaborative design [2,20,21,30,37]. The selection of the activities was guided by the research data – i.e., those that fitted the data were utilized. The activities of synthesizing and deciding [2] were not used, as those totally overlapped with proposing and adding on activities. Each document included in the analysis was classified to represent one or several of the activities. Thereafter, design within each focus was characterized from the perspective of the actors and activities involved. This phase also involved crafting the storyline describing how the 'Making Together' was accomplished in this case, focusing on the foci of design, activities involved, tools used and roles adopted. After the initial data analysis, the technique of member checking was utilized: a case study write-up was delivered to the participants for comments, and corrections were made based on their feedback. Next the empirical findings are described.

## 13.4    Characterizing Distributed Design

### 13.4.1    Conceptual Design: Proposing, Evaluating and Adding on

Conceptual design began when the project was initiated. This phase was dominated by the proposing activity and the educational science specialists were in a very significant position during this phase: they settled the (educational) requirements for the application, i.e. what users were to be able to do with the application with associated educational goals. They communicated their ideas to other partners

---

[1]This categorization of design foci is from a very practical textbook on interaction design, while it provided a highly useful tool for making sense of the design work in this particular case.

through email, including sending a multitude of documents as attachments. The work continued by the educational science specialists drawing scenarios of the future use, concretizing their ideas and requirements. Those were also delivered to other parties for comments through email and stored in the shared data repository. In addition to imposing the requirements, the educational science specialists also collaboratively negotiated them through email.

The work continued with the production of more formal project deliverables. Multiple partners representing educational sciences contributed to the content of the 'Educational Requirements' deliverable that contained data on educational technology solutions, content of the application, context of use, and learning. Interesting from the viewpoint of conceptual design are the descriptions related to the theoretical background of the application and its requirements, and the application's main user groups and their characteristics, and the main purposes of the application and its major components. The educational science specialists collaboratively produced the documents as well as on commented on each other's work.

The HCI specialists contributed to conceptual design especially through their empirical work with users. They started user studies relatively early and asked for other parties' wishes before starting those. The educational science specialists wished for comments for their scenarios and other ideas, and those were collected. In addition, additional feedback provided by users was delivered, as well as users' ideas and designs for the application. Hence, through their user studies, the HCI specialists offered feedback to the other parties' design ideas but also proposed new ones based on their user data. The empirical work with users included user testing, paper prototyping, interviews, observation, and participatory design sessions. Email was the main medium for distributing the results; some documents also were stored in the data repository. The results of the inquiries were debated through email thorough the analyzed time period and also used as arguments for certain design decisions later. A formal 'Usability Requirements' deliverable was created and iterated among the HCI specialists. It included general HCI literature and guidelines, and the results of all the design and evaluation studies carried out with users, offering feedback to the educational science specialists' ideas and suggesting new ones derived from users.

The developers also began to contribute relatively early by proposing technological possibilities and by pointing out technological restrictions to other partners. They communicated their ideas and feedback through email.

Figure 13.1 characterizes distributed design with conceptual design focus. It shows, according to the stakeholder group and activity, the number of documents that could be associated with conceptual design focus. Overall, the most common activity during conceptual design was proposing new ideas; this applies to all project participants. Evaluation also was carried out, particularly by the HCI specialists through their empirical inquiries and the feedback they delivered. In addition, the activity of 'adding on' became important during this phase, even though the participants initially presented their ideas independently of each other's. The evaluations carried out by the HCI specialists also contributed to the 'adding

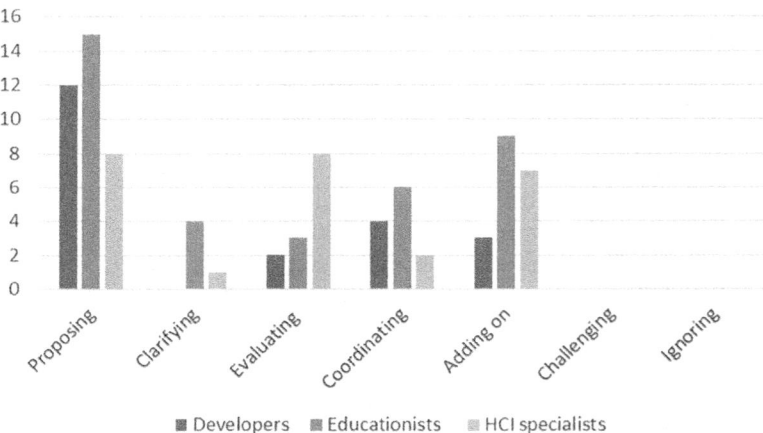

**Fig. 13.1** Characterizing distributed design with conceptual design focus

on' activity. Through this process, users also entered into the design discussions, but the HCI specialists acted as intermediaries between the users and the project partners. Therefore, the users did not take part as actual participants in the design discussions, but instead they were represented by the HCI specialists. The users' voice was brought to the design arena in the textual descriptions produced by the HCI specialists; however, they did not include very lively descriptions, but summaries made by these specialists.

## 13.4.2 Behavioral Design: Coordinating, Challenging and Ignoring

Behavioral design was the most intense activity in the project and took the longest time to undertake. The educational science specialists were again a significant participant group, but now the HCI specialists also adopted a more active role. Influential from the perspective of behavioral design is, to begin with, the Educational Requirements document created by the educational science specialists. The document outlined how the user is assumed to use the application and how it should behave, including portrayals of the main screens of the application, possible user actions in each screen, and system responses. This deliverable was followed by the Educational Design deliverable, which outlined the design of the application from the viewpoint of user interface and user interaction. These were presented both as pictures of the main screens and as text, the design aiming to enable and support the realization of the educational goals outlined earlier. The educational science specialists again collaboratively produced and refined the documentation and communicated through email and sending and storing their documentation in the shared data repository.

Another important participant group in behavioral design was the HCI specialists. Nevertheless, their collaboration with the educational science specialists was not as easy as within conceptual design, within which the HCI specialists mainly provided feedback to the educational science specialists' ideas. As regards behavioral design the HCI specialists more actively started proposing designs themselves. Actually, here it became apparent that it was unclear how the design responsibility was actually shared between the educational science specialists and HCI specialists: the educational science specialists were expected to produce Educational Requirements and Educational Design deliverables, while the HCI specialists were also expected to create Usability Requirements and Usability Design deliverables.

Here, the activities of 'challenging' and 'ignoring' started to feature in the design discussions. During the requirements specification, the HCI specialists already criticized that the educational science specialists were creating design instead of specifying requirements. The same criticism arose when the partners collaboratively produced a Software Requirements deliverable, for which the educational science specialists wrote the major parts. The deliverable was criticized by a HCI specialist as encompassing too much design, instead of pure requirements. Moreover, the educational science specialists were later accused of designing things that already had been designed by the HCI specialists. The HCI specialists had based their work on the educational science specialists' scenarios and evaluated and refined those together with users, based on which they had produced their Usability Design document. The educational science specialists, however, had later on improved their scenarios and thus the HCI specialists had evaluated not the most up-to-date ones. The educational science specialists had then based their designs on the refined scenarios which ignored some of the results of the HCI specialists' work. While producing their documents, the HCI specialists or the educational science specialists did not study the other party's documentation. Instead, both parties, when distributing their documents, brought up that there could be some overlap between their and the other party's documents that they asked others to check Thus, the project ended up in having conflicting designs for the application. Those were extensively discussed, negotiated, and even challenged through email. The HCI specialists emphasized their empirical user data when convincing the other project participants of the suitability of their designs, whereas the educational science specialists highlighted the defined project goals and their expertise to define the content and the educational and pedagogical design of the application – central in the project to begin with.

The developers, on the other hand, created more technical deliverables. Relevant from the viewpoint of behavioral design are textual descriptions of how the user will use the application as well as user characteristics descriptions, product descriptions, needed functions, and numerous kinds of use case descriptions. The developers distributed the results of their work in the form of documents sent through email and stored in the data repository. Later on, the developers also created functional prototypes of the application, accompanied by videos demonstrating the realized functionality or features for other partners. Links to the prototypes were sent through email and project partners were invited to offer comments.

Significant observation is that the coordinating activity dominated the design with behavioral design focus. Intense collaboration among the project partners was expected to occur especially during the production of the Software Requirements deliverable as well as during the production of the design documents, to which nearly all partners were expected to contribute. One of the research institutions with expertise on educational sciences was expected to lead design work as well as the creation of the Software Requirements deliverable, and hence the educational science specialists were heavily involved in the coordinating activity, but actually for all the participant groups, the coordinating activity was the most common activity within behavioral design. Moreover, collaboration was very difficult to achieve in this case: activating partners to define the software requirements or to produce the design documents was difficult, and the end result was not satisfactory in the case of software requirements that had to be iterated numerous times to become satisfactory. As mentioned, the educational science specialists defined the software requirements, following some documents produced by the HCI specialists and their own Educational Requirements document. After delivering the document, a HCI specialist brought up that the end result was not acceptable: there was too much design and many unclear issues and controversies. The project participants exchanged quite a few emails discussing the problem. A HCI specialist offered to go through the deliverable and to develop it further. The refined document was again commented by the educational science specialists, developers and HCI specialists.

Figure 13.2 characterizes distributed design with behavioral design focus. Altogether, the educational science specialists were very active also in behavioral design, but the role of the HCI specialists was more prominent now. The activity of proposing ideas or designs was again important as well as the activity of

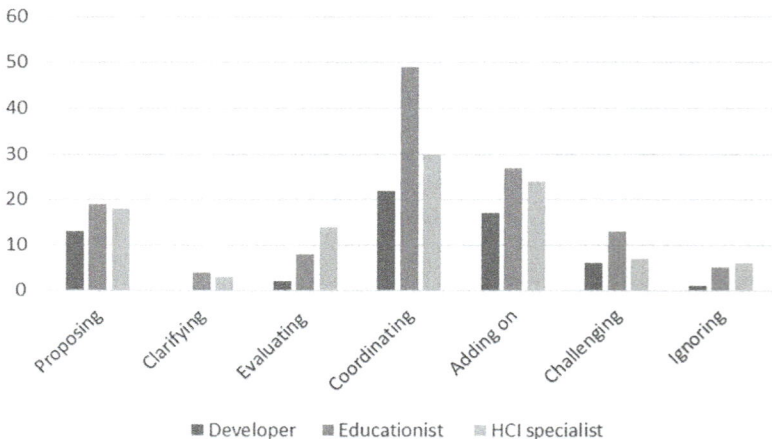

**Fig. 13.2** Characterizing distributed design with behavioral design focus

evaluating, but this time the activity of coordinating clearly dominated. This is because within behavioral design numerous groups of people or individuals distributed to different locations had to collaboratively create deliverables. As mentioned, this was challenging in the project. The 'adding on' activity was also again evident while creating and refining the deliverables, but interestingly, the activities of 'challenging' and 'ignoring' also emerged within behavioral design. The 'challenging' activity emerged in connection with the HCI specialists criticizing the "too designy stuff" created by the educational science specialists, in connection with overlapping design work carried out by the educational science specialists and the HCI specialists, while both supporting their own designs and criticizing the designs of the other party, as well as in connection with the different parties criticizing the Software Requirements documentation and its production process. Furthermore, the 'ignoring' activity could be observed related to the educational science specialists and HCI specialists both producing their own design documents without examining those of the other party. The ignoring activity was identified through the participants criticizing that other parties had ignored their work. The users again entered the design discussions only as representations created by the HCI specialists.

### 13.4.3    Interface Design: Coordinating, Challenging and Ignoring

Interface design started around the same time as behavioral design. Here, however, the HCI specialists were the most active group, while the educational science specialists remained also active. The requirements and design documentation produced by the HCI specialists included quite detailed interface issues. As for the users' contribution, the HCI specialists – after their empirical work with users – had carefully identified users' ideas and designs that could be utilized in the actual application user interface design. They had incorporated those into their usability design. As for the educational science specialists, interface design can be connected with the Educational Requirements deliverable, which included the description of the main screens of the application, possible user actions in each screen, and system responses. More detailed descriptions were presented in the Educational Design deliverable that included user interaction and user interface descriptions.

   The same coordination challenges characterize interface design than behavioral design. Moreover, challenging and ignoring activities can again be connected with the Software Requirements and Educational Requirements documents that were criticized by the HCI specialists as encompassing too much design, including user interface design. Another problem was related to the HCI specialists' Usability Design deliverable that mismatched with the educational science specialists' educational design. The developers remained relatively silent as regards this design phase.

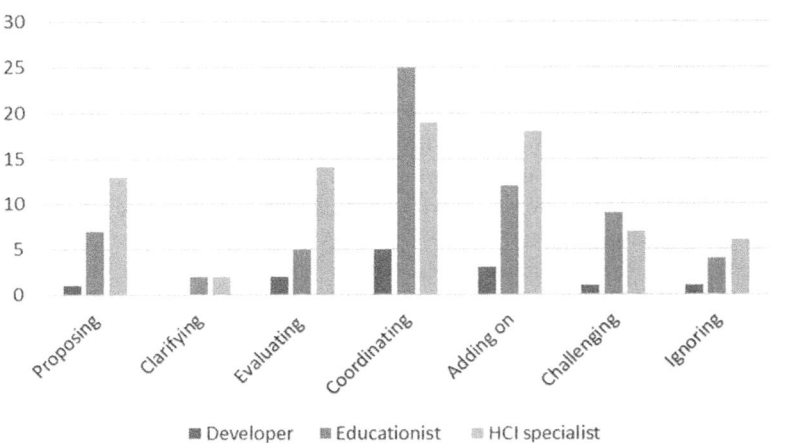

■ Developer  ■ Educationist  ▨ HCI specialist

**Fig. 13.3** Characterizing distributed design with interface design focus

Figure 13.3 characterizes distributed design with interface design focus. All in all, the HCI specialists were now the most active group, while the role of the educational science specialists was also significant. The developers were in a less visible role. Again, the activity of coordinating dominated the discussion space, due to the problems related to the Software Requirements deliverable as well as due to negotiating the application design with the educational science specialists. Proposing and evaluating activities were also evident within interface design, with both relating to the 'adding on' activity. Connected with this, the users' voices were again brought to the arena by the HCI specialists, who presented users' ideas and feedback. The activity of 'challenging' was even more evident in interface design than in behavioral design, connected again with the design dispute between the educational science specialists and the HCI specialists as well as with the difficulty of producing the software requirements in a satisfactory format – interface related issues were quite dominant in these design discussions. In addition, the 'ignoring' activity could again be observed as regards collaboration between the educational science specialists and the HCI specialists, both parties criticizing that their input had been ignored.

## 13.5  Concluding Discussion

The paper examined distributed design with a specific interest in HCI specialists' work and their ability to contribute. The examined project involved distributed educational science, ICT and HCI specialists collaboratively designing a learning application within the project's discussion and documentation spaces. Next, the empirical results are summarized and their implications are discussed.

## 13.5.1  Summary of the Results

The empirical analysis implies that distributed design can be characterized by coordinating, contributing, contesting and representing. HCI specialists' work involved representing the user in the development. Otherwise, the design was dominated by coordinating activity, albeit also proposing, adding on and evaluating activities were prominent. Interestingly, also the activities of challenging and ignoring could be identified from the design discussions. The educational science specialists were the most active ones in the design discussions, heavily involved in proposing, adding on and coordinating activities, dominating especially the last one. The HCI specialists were involved in all these activities as well, but they were the most active ones as regards the evaluating and adding on activities. The developers contributed through proposing, adding on and coordinating activities, but they were the most silent participant group in all these design activities, if not counting the users. The HCI specialists and educational science specialists were the most dominant ones also as regards the challenging and ignoring activities, the educational science specialists being most actively involved in the former while the HCI specialists in the latter.

Considering the different design foci, conceptual design was dominated by the educational science specialists and the proposing and adding on activities. Behavioral design included the most active and intense discussions in this case. It was dominated by the educational science specialists and the coordinating activity, but interestingly, the HCI specialists took here more active role and the challenging and ignoring activities emerged, too. Interface design, finally, involved the most intense disagreements between the educational science specialists and the HCI specialists, who had by now acquired the most active position in the design discussions.

All this indicates that the HCI specialists did succeed in adopting the participative role in the development, in addition to those of consultative and informative (cf. [20,21]). Furthermore, the challenging and ignoring activities reveal that in this case distributed design was also a political, conflictual process with numerous agendas to be attended to and interests to be served. These findings have implications for research as well as for design practice.

## 13.5.2  Implications

The study provided a characterization of distributed design in practice involving a number of experts. Interestingly, these findings are in part in conflict with the existing findings on distributed design [2]: earlier, evaluating and clarifying activities have been found as the most common ones, while here the coordinating activity clearly occupied that position followed by adding on and proposing activities. In face-to-face design meetings, on the other hand, it has been found that coordinating has taken around 20 % of time, while the rest of the time has been spent on developing and evaluating design, which, on the other hand, can be considered as including a lot of coordination, too [36]. In this case one explanation for the dominance of coordinating activity is of course that this was a distributed development endeavor; however, studies in OSS communities that predominantly are distributed in nature show that coordinating activity does not necessarily dominate distributed design discussions [2]. Here, one might speculate that the community aspect may in part explain the difference: in this case specialists from numerous countries and organizations were expected to collaborate without shared history and experiences, probably lacking common ground, the importance of which has been emphasized a lot in design work, [2,36]. An overall implication of the finding of the dominance of coordinating activity in distributed design is that in this kind of projects, it may be wise to allow plenty of resources for the coordinating activity. Better tool support for such could be considered. Here, the tools used were mundane if not even dated (i.e. mainly email and a shared data repository). No more advanced tools were even considered in the case, while definitely tools for coordination would have been available. It is interesting to find out that distributed projects are still trying to manage only with such mundane tools. This is a topic that could be inquired in more depth in the future to understand why this is the case.

This analysis looked at distributed design among experienced HCI, ICT and educational science specialists, and the design process still ended up being chaotic, scrappy, ambiguous, and quarrelsome at times. A prominent finding was that challenging and ignoring activities clearly featured in the design work. In this study the educational science specialists and HCI specialists explicitly disagreed and criticized others' designs and blamed the other party of ignoring own work. Those findings truly reveal that design was a political process that involved rivalry and multiple agendas and interests among the design participants (cf. [6,30]). Arriving at shared understandings among the various experts was of importance, but difficult to achieve (cf. e.g. [29,31]). While there is a lack of studies on the work of HCI specialists in distributed settings, studies on HCI work in co-located settings (e.g. [5,7,15,19,20,27]) and studies on collaborative design work in distributed setting imply that there indeed may be many challenges [8,17,18,26,30,35,38,39], and this study corroborates this.

As regards the existing research on HCI specialists' work practices, this study provides findings that are in line with the current understanding: the HCI specialists' lack of authority was evident also in this study (cf. [5,7,15,19,20,27]). The HCI literature suggests that HCI specialists should be allowed to act as the ultimate owners of product quality and be in participative role that gives them power of decision regarding the design solution (e.g. [9,11,15,20]). In this case, however, the HCI specialists had to collaborate with ICT and educational science specialists and this collaboration was not always easy to accomplish. On the other hand, the HCI specialists gained more prominence within the behavioral and interface design and actively started to contribute through proposing activity. In addition, in the overall design process they were the most active ones regarding the evaluation activity and significant participant group as regards the adding on activity. Hence, one can conclude that HCI specialists definitely succeeded to contribute during the design process, which has not always been the case in ICT development (e.g. [5,19,20,27]). They were in the beginning placed into relatively traditional consultative and informative roles [20,21], but later they started more actively creating design, too.

As regards ICT support for distributed design work, in this case the design work relied extensively on email and a shared data repository (in line with [12,28]). Email was by far the most significant tool. The project, however, might have benefitted from the adoption of communication tools widely in use in distributed open source software development projects, such as mailing lists and discussion forums (e.g. [2,37]). Even though there were lively discussions going on through email also in this case, those discussions could have been planned and initiated earlier and carried out and managed more systematically. Mailing lists or discussion forums would have preserved the communication without individual effort, and discussion forums would have helped to organize the discussions better. Both tools also would have ensured that all relevant parties receive the needed information, as in this case some relevant people might have been left out of discussions as no mailing lists were in use. Overall, one can argue that these kinds of tools could have been useful, although, by themselves, they probably would not have solved the difficulties encountered. The use of these kinds of tools to alleviate the problems encountered in this project should be explored further to be able to make conclusions on the matter.

The distributed, computer-mediated nature might have contributed to the exclusion of users from the design discussions. This study indicates that users entered the design discussions only as represented participants, not being present themselves. Only intermediaries representing the users (in line with [2,3,17,35,39]) were used in this project of all the suggested means for distributed participatory design, and the users' input was delivered only through emails, memos, and more formal deliverables sent through email and stored in the shared data repository. Furthermore, the information was presented as summarizing text that can be criticized as very abstract, dry, and detached from the viewpoint of more advanced participatory design methods and artifacts [23,24], providing very limited glimpses into the life and culture of users. Nonetheless, one can still recommend HCI specialists' participation in the design process, them acting as intermediaries representing the users, even though their representation work was less than perfect. Without them, probably nobody would have considered the perspective of the users and usage in the design process. However, better support for the HCI specialists' work in the distributed design setting could be offered. One could consider, e.g. how to offer more lively glimpses into the life and culture of users. Then again, a variety of tools for communicating user data would have been available for the HCI specialists to use, but they preferred not to utilize those. Interesting would be to inquire in the future why this was the case.

There are several limitations in the study that need to be taken into account. The results are based on only one case. More data should be gathered regarding this case and more cases included. In particular, there is a need to examine different kinds of distributed design cases to achieve comparable results and to deepen our understanding of this relatively recent and challenging development setting that very likely is to stay. On the other hand, this specific case could be examined in more detail. Other researchers could also attempt to identify or develop appropriate technologies and methods for supporting distributed design work, even though this study reminds us that very mundane technologies and tools are currently in use.

**Acknowledgements** I wish to thank the project partners for participating in this study as well as the Academy of Finland and EU for providing funding for this study.

# References

1. Avram G, Bannon L, Bowers J, Sheehan A, Sullivan D (2009) Bridging, patching, and keeping the work flowing: defect resolution in distributed software development. Comput Support Coop Work 18:477–507
2. Barcellini F, Détienne F, Burkhardt J, Sack W (2008) A socio-cognitive analysis of online design discussions in an Open Source Software community. Interact Comput 20(1):141–165
3. Barcellini F, Detienne F, Burkhardt J (2009) Participation in online interaction spaces: design-use mediation in an Open Source Software community. Int J Ind Ergon 39:533–540
4. Blomkvist J, Persson J, Åberg J (2015) Communication through boundary objects in distributed agile teams. In: Proceedings of CHI '15, pp 1875–1884
5. Bødker S, Buur J (2002) The design collaboratorium – a place for usability design. ACM Trans Comput-Hum Interact 9(2):152–169
6. Bødker S, Ehn P, Knudsen J, Kyng M, Madsen K (1988) Computer support for cooperative design. In: Proceedings of CSCW 1988, pp 377–394
7. Boivie I, Åborg C, Persson J, Löfberg M (2003) Why usability gets lost or usability in in-house software development. Interact Comput 15(4):623–639
8. Carmel E, Agarwal R (2001) Tactical approaches for alleviating distance in global software development. IEEE Softw 18(2):22–29
9. Cooper A (1999) The inmates are running the asylum: why high-tech products drive us crazy and how to restore the sanity. Sams, Indianapolis
10. Cooper C, Bowers J (1995) Representing the users: notes on the disciplinary rhetoric of human-computer interaction. In: Thomas P (ed) The social and interactional dimensions of human-computer interfaces. Cambridge University Press, Cambridge, pp 48–66
11. Cooper A, Reimann R (2003) About face 2.0: the essentials of interaction design. Wiley, Indianapolis
12. Detienne F, Boujut J, Hohman B (2004) Characterization of collaborative design and interaction management activities in a distant engineering design situation. In: Proceedings of COOP 2004, pp 83–98
13. Fischer G (2011) Understanding, fostering, and supporting cultures of participation. Interactions 18(3):42–53
14. Greenbaum J, Kyng M (eds) (1991) Design at work. Cooperative design of computer systems. Lawrence Erlbaum Associates, Hillsdale
15. Gulliksen J, Boivie I, Göransson B (2006) Usability professionals—current practices and future development. Interact Comput 18(4):568–600
16. Gumm D (2006) Distributed software development – a taxonomy. IEEE Softw 23(5):45–51
17. Gumm D, Janneck M, Finck M (2006) Distributed participatory design – a case study. In: Proceedings of NordiCHI 2004 Workshop on Distributed Participatory Design. 5 p
18. Hanisch J, Corbitt B (2007) Impediments to requirements engineering during global software development. Eur J Inf Syst 16(6):793–805
19. Høegh RT, Nielsen C, Overgaard M, Pedersen M, Stage J (2006) The impact of usability reports and user test observations on developers' understanding of usability data: an exploratory study. Int J Hum-Comput Interact 21(2):173–196

20. Iivari N (2006) Understanding the work of an HCI practitioner. In: Proceedings of NordiCHI 2006, pp 185–194
21. Iivari N (2011) Participatory design in OSS development: interpretive case studies in company and community OSS development contexts. Behav Inform Technol 30(3):309–323
22. Iivari N (2013) Usability specialists as boundary spanners – an appraisal of usability specialists' work in multiparty distributed open source software development effort. In: Proceedings of INTERACT 2013, pp 571–588
23. Iivari N, Karasti H, Molin-Juustila T, Salmela S, Syrjänen A, Halkola E (2009) Mediation between design and use – revisiting five empirical studies. Hum IT J Inf Technol Stud Hum Sci 10(2):81–126
24. Karasti H (2001) Increasing sensitivity towards everyday work practice in system design. Acta Universitatis Ouluensis, Scientiae Rerum Naturalium, A 362. Oulu University Press, Oulu
25. Klein H, Myers M (1999) A set of principles for conducting and evaluating interpretive field studies in information systems. MIS Q 23(1):67–94
26. Kotlarsky J, Oshri I (2005) Social ties, knowledge sharing and successful collaboration in globally distributed system development projects. Eur J Inf Syst 14(1):37–48
27. Law E (2006) Evaluating the downstream utility of user tests and examining the developer effect: a case study. Int J Hum-Comput Interact 21(2):147–172
28. Lawrence K (2006) Walking the tightrope: the balancing acts of a large e-research project. Comput Supported Coop Work 15(4):385–411
29. Lee C (2007) Boundary negotiating artifacts: unbinding the routine of boundary objects and embracing chaos in collaborative work. Comput Supported Coop Work 16(3):307–339
30. Levina N (2006) Collaborating on multiparty information systems development projects: a collective reflection-in-action view. Inf Syst Res 16(2):109–130
31. Levina N, Vaast E (2005) The emergence of boundary spanning competence in practice: implications for implementation and use of information systems. MIS Q 29(2):335–363
32. Markus M, Mao Y (2004) User participation in development and implementation: updating an old tired concept for today's IS contexts. J Assoc Inf Syst 5(11–12):514–544
33. Nichols D, McKay D, Twidale M (2003) Participatory usability: supporting proactive users. In: Proceedings of ACM Special Interest Group on Computer Human Interaction – New Zealand Chapter, pp 63–68
34. Nichols D, Twidale M (2006) Usability processes in open source projects. Softw Process Improv Pract 11:149–162
35. Obendorf H, Janneck M, Finck M (2009) Inter-contextual distributed participatory design. Scand J Inf Syst 21(1):51–76
36. Olson GM, Olson JS, Carter MR, Storrosten M (1992) Small group design meetings: an analysis of collaboration. Hum-Comput Interact 7(4):347–374
37. Sack W, Détienne F, Ducheneaut N, Burkhardt J, Mahendran D, Barcellini F (2006) A methodological framework for socio-cognitive analyses of collaborative design of open source software. Comput Supported Coop Work 15(2):229–250
38. Sarker S, Sahay S (2004) Implications of space and time for distributed work: an interpretive study of US-Norwegian systems development teams. Eur J Inf Syst 13(1):3–20
39. Titlestad O, Staring K, Braa J (2009) Distributed development to enable user participation. Scand J Inf Syst 21(1):27–50
40. Walsham G (1995) Interpretive case studies in IS research: nature and method. Eur J Inf Syst 4:74–81
41. Zhu L, Mussio P, Barricelli BR (2010) Hive-mind space model for creative, collaborative design. In: Proceedings of DESIRE 2010, pp 121–130

# Chapter 14
# Facilitating Participation of Stakeholders During Process Analysis and Design

**Alexander Nolte and Thomas Herrmann**

**Abstract** Collaboration of stakeholders to contribute to process analysis and design is a common practice in organizations to achieve better results. However, while it has been acknowledged that for stakeholders being able to directly influence design not only makes for better results but also increases their motivation, stakeholders are mostly limited to providing information and leave the design for process analysts or consultants. Furthermore, stakeholders are only involved when process analysts ask them to contribute. Consequently, stakeholders are cut off from many activities that shape the resulting process analysis and design. To overcome this problem, we propose a twofold approach: Firstly, we provide a socio-technical concept that increases – in comparison to existing approaches –opportunities for stakeholders to participate in process analysis and design. Secondly, we propose a mix of methods to evaluate the quality of participatory modeling that allows for evaluating stakeholders' inclusion and support deriving suggestions for cyclic improvement of the concept.

## 14.1 Introduction

The analysis and design[1] of business processes is a complex task and requires contribution from several perspectives. Therefore it is reasonable to involve several roles into analyzing and designing processes using artefacts such as process models as shared material [9, 16]. We mainly differentiate between two types of roles:

- **Stakeholders**: They are domain experts including managers and operative forces who are familiar with a process (or the requirements for a new process). Domain

---

[1]"Design" in this context refers to newly designing a business process as well as re-designing an existing one.

A. Nolte (✉) • T. Herrmann
Department Information and Technology Management, Institute for Applied Work Science,
University of Bochum, Bochum, Germany
e-mail: nolte@iaw.rub.de; herrmann@iaw.rub.de

© Springer International Publishing Switzerland 2016                                     225
A. De Angeli et al. (eds.), *COOP 2016: Proceedings of the 12th International
Conference on the Design of Cooperative Systems, 23–27 May 2016, Trento, Italy*,
DOI 10.1007/978-3-319-33464-6_14

experts know the context of the process that is to be analyzed and designed. Stakeholders also include people who have a certain interest in a process and can contribute additional insights to its analysis and design. Most stakeholders are not familiar with modeling notations or methods and have to be considered as **lay modelers**.

- **Process analysts**: They know how to gather information about a process, ways of analyzing and visualizing it, proposing measures for improvement and design. Process analysts can be considered **expert modelers**. They have a lot of general knowledge about process design but are not familiar with concrete processes and their context.

Both types of roles can overlap but generally there is a knowledge gap between them, especially as process analysts oftentimes do not share the same background with other participants (i.e. they are not part of the same company). Stakeholders are generally not capable of analyzing processes and visualizing them using a modeling notation on their own [28]. They can however contribute their individual domain knowledge [20, 31], but they need support by process analysts to systematically transform this knowledge into graphical processes diagrams based on modeling notation.

To provide this support, process analysts have to gather the relevant information and to be prepared to understand the context of a domain, For this purpose they have a number of different approaches on their disposal such as document analysis, interviews, observations or other ethnographical approaches and workshops (c.f. Dumas et al. [9] for a detailed overview). There are however several problems that are not addressed when only document analysis, interviews or observations take place: Existing processes or the needs for designing new processes are not appropriately understood without an intensive discourse between stakeholders and between them and process analysts. This is especially critical when the process analysts' conclusions about the process are not complemented by the stakeholders' feedback. Furthermore, if knowledge about the context of a process is not systematically taken into account, it will be hard to bring the process into reality. The staff potentially will not comply with the process or at least not be motivated to work in accordance with it [11].

If the aforementioned methods of information elicitation are complemented with discursive workshops, a suitable solution for the knowledge gap problem can be achieved, as workshops allow for perspectives sharing between stakeholders and promote a deeper understanding of the process. However, workshops alone do not provide sufficient opportunities for the exchange of the stakeholders' and process analysts' perspectives because of time constraints and aspects of group dynamics (c.f. Sect. 14.2).

In order to overcome these limitations and subsequently increase the means of stakeholders to participate in process analysis, we propose an approach that intertwines workshops with phases of asynchronous collaboration where stakeholders can access and work on process models. Since stakeholders usually are lay modelers, we suggest that we will not allow for them to modify a model with respect to a modeling notations. We will rather apply an approach has previously been employed in the domain of computer supported collaborative learning: Allow for participants of courses to asynchronously collaborate on course material using annotations [1, 5, 18, 26]. Applying an approach like this for process analysis and design leads us to the following research question:

**RQ 1**: To what extent does the possibility of inspecting and annotating process models between workshops increase the experienced influence of stakeholders on process design?

In order for stakeholders to inspect models and create annotations, they at least have to be capable to understand processes and process models on their own. There is some evidence supporting the assumption that they are capable of understanding models of processes they are familiar with [19, 30, 32]. While this seems probable it remains unclear whether or not allowing stakeholder to use process models and annotate them without support by process analysts actually affects participation. This results in the following research question:

**RQ 2**: To what extend does the concept improve the influence of lay modelers on the outcome of process modeling?

To answer these questions we developed a socio-technical concept that intertwines workshops with phases of asynchronous collaboration using annotations (Sect. 14.3). In order to come up with such a concept, we reviewed relevant approaches from the fields of participatory design and collaborative work (Sect. 14.2). To evaluate the subsequent concept we had to develop a novel approach that combines an evaluation of participants perceptions with document analysis methods, interviews and video analysis which will be presented in Sect. 14.4. This mixed method evaluation allowed us to evaluate the socio-technical approach described in Sect. 14.3 on a deeper level, thus providing better results (Sect. 14.4.2). In Sect. 14.5, we will discuss findings of the study before concluding with a summary of the results and suggestions for future research (Sect. 14.6).

## 14.2   Related Work: Collaborative Participation and Process Analysis

In the context of software development it has been found that participation of future users in the design of new systems results in better (i.e. more fitting) products [3] and motivates people to adopt new systems [11]. Similar experiences have been reported in workflow projects [17] especially when it comes to people taking part in process design [13]. However, in order for stakeholders to become co-designers, process analysts and stakeholders have to collaborate during process analysis and design [23]. This means that process analysts not only have to gather information about a process – as in traditional process modeling approaches [9]. Stakeholders in turn also have to learn about using process models since these models are usually the kind of documentation that process analysts use for process analysis and design. Models in this context can serve as a boundary object [34] which supports both sides – stakeholders and process analysts – to collaborate in process analysis and design. In more general terms it means that there is a knowledge gap between process analysts and stakeholders that has to be closed. In order to intensify interaction about and on process models between stakeholders and process analysts, a number of workshop concept have emerged during which stakeholders are supported by facilitators and process analysts to analyze and design processes using process models (e.g. STWT [16] or COMA [32]).

The presented approach (c.f. Sect. 14.3) extends and improves a participatory workshop concept which was developed to support collaborative process analysis – the socio-technical walkthrough (STWT). The STWT is well grounded in the context of Participatory Design (PD) (cf. [14, 15, 25]) and takes into account the principles of PD as described in the MUST-Method [21] which are relevant for process design. The MUST-Method is also the basis of recent publications about guidelines and principles in the PD-context (e.g. [4]). However, the STWT is focused on co-located meetings in workshops and does not take cultures of participation [10] into account, which would allow for more participation of a broader audience by employing the principles of Web2.0 technologies. Furthermore, the collaboration mode of workshops leads to the problem of production blocking [8]. Production blocking occurs when participants have to listen while others speak and therefore are hindered to develop their own flow of ideas or might forget parts of them while waiting for their turn. Another problem in small groups interaction is evaluation apprehension [8]: The fear of negative evaluations from other participants might prevent people from sharing negative experiences or unconventional ideas. Additionally, workshops are not a lightweight format of collecting information. Workshops cannot be organized spontaneously (especially when information refinement is necessary) but have to be scheduled in advance, participants have to be selected, topics to be announced etc. In order to address these problems, we have developed a socio-technical approach that allows for intertwining phases of synchronous and asynchronous collaboration (c.f. Sect. 14.3). It is essential for such an approach to ensure that decisions are taken collaboratively in order to ensure participation thus arriving at the co-creation level [24].

## 14.3   WASCoMo: An Approach for Facilitating the Participation of Stakeholders in Process Analysis and Design

The aim of WASCoMo (Webbased Annotation System for Collaborative Modeling) is to offer the possibility of bridging phases of synchronous collaboration by intertwining them with an asynchronous mode. The process models serve as shared

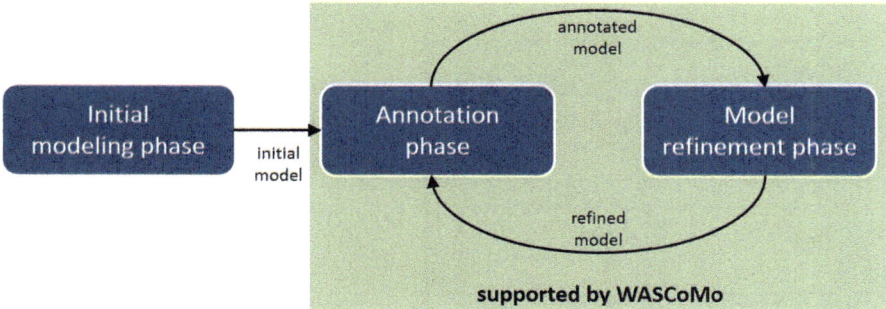

**Fig. 14.1** Phases of the WASCoMo approach

material during synchronous as well as asynchronous phases. WASCoMo is divided into the following three phases (c.f. Fig. 14.1):

- An **initial modeling phase** during which a first draft of a process model is jointly developed or discussed with stakeholders and process analysts. This usually happens within a facilitated workshop where stakeholders are supported by process analysts to visualize a process within a process model. During this workshop it is also possible to start with a model that was developed based on e.g. interviews conducted in advance. After the workshop, the resulting process model has to be graphically restructured to increase its comprehensibility, especially for stakeholders. It is also necessary to decide on guiding questions in order for annotations to focus on certain aspects, such as requirements for software-based support or organizational process improvements. Furthermore, we have to provide means of access control and we also have to enable participants to contribute anonymously in order to prevent evaluation apprehension [8] (c.f. Sect. 14.2).
- An **annotation phase** during which stakeholders may access the respective process model via a web interface (c.f. Fig. 14.2). This interface allows the participants to create annotations on elements by simply clicking on a green plus sign that appears once an element is selected. Afterwards, they can type the intended text into an input field (c.f. Fig. 14.2 top right) and submit it. Participants may also comment on existing annotations by selecting the respective annotation and clicking on the green plus sign that appears next to it. This allows for participants to discuss about e.g. suggestions that others made (c.f. Fig. 14.2 bottom). The color of the annotations alternates for better visibility and – given the annotation was not marked as anonymous – the login name of the person that created an annotation is added next to it in order for others to know to whom they are replying. Before the next phase the facilitator of the next workshop has to look through the annotations as a means to prepare it.
- A **model refinement phase** during which annotations are discussed and the result of those discussions are integrated into the process model. This will

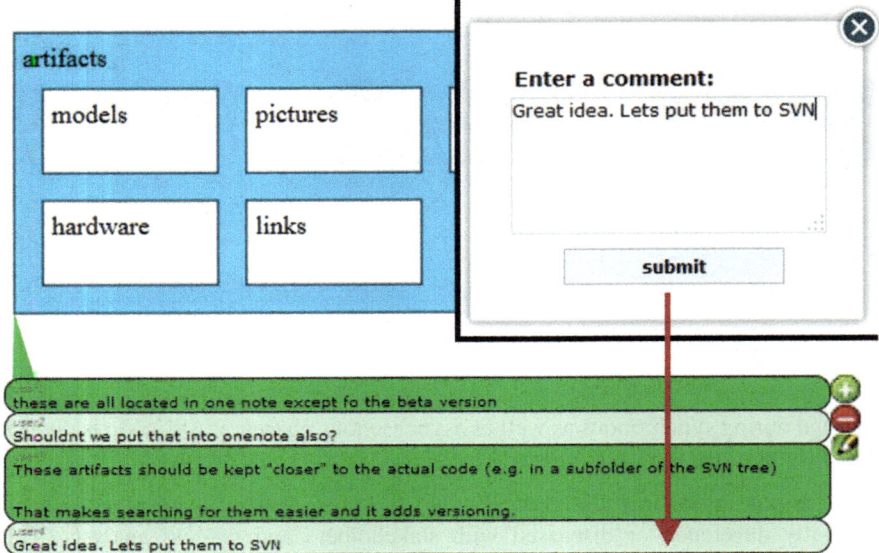

**Fig. 14.2** Annotations on an element (*green bubbles*) with corresponding input dialog (*top right*)

usually happen during facilitated modeling workshops in which stakeholders are supported by process analysts. During this phase stakeholders and process analysts might jointly decide to add another annotation phase or to end the cycle and process the model in a different way. However, if they decide to do another annotation phase they will have to restructure the model again, in order to make it easier to perceive and decide on guiding questions as well. The annotation and refinement phases may be repeated iteratively until a state is reached that both suffices the goal that was originally stated when process modeling started and the needs of the participating stakeholders have been taken into account.

We deliberately decided not to offer the possibility for modification on the level of the modeling notation during the annotation phase but only allow participants to add annotations since:

1. The required understanding of the notation and threshold to make modifications is much higher than just starting with annotations.
2. Creating annotations can happen additively and is more communication oriented, since domain experts can make proposals or criticize aspects of models without providing a solution directly.
3. It has been observed in other contexts that annotations on shared material has a positive effect on future workshops [7], initiates and focusses discussions [5] and simulates reflection [1].

4. Decisions about changes on models have to be agreed upon by all participants (i.e. during workshops) thus ensuring participation throughout the whole course of process analysis and design.

## 14.4 Analyzing Participation in Collaborative Modeling

In order to evaluate the WASCoMo concept with respect to the research questions described in Sect. 14.1 we refer to an approach proposed by Mendling et al. [27] which aims at assessing whether a participant can be considered a lay modeler or not (c.f. RQ 2). With respect to **RQ 1** we had to develop a concept that not only covers process model quality but also collaboration quality and the impact of annotations on both the process models as well as the collaboration itself. While there are approaches available to measure the quality of models [2, 12, 22] as well as the quality of collaborative modeling [33] none is entirely suitable for this context.

Approaches to measure model quality either focus on syntactic quality [12] or on process analysts' evaluations [22]. Syntactic quality is not focal in our setting as we mainly aim at using models to systematically analyze and design processes (c.f. Sect. 14.1). Evaluations by process analysts do assess whether WASCoMo increases the quality and domain-related appropriateness of process models. We are rather looking for measures of the impact of the opportunities to collaborate on models not only in workshops but also in between them using annotations.

We identified the framework by Ssebuggwawo et al. [33] as a potential starting point as they focus on the perception of the participants and differentiate collaboration modeling success with respect to four categories: **Quality of the end-product (model)**, **quality of the modeling procedure**, quality of the usage of the modeling language and **ease of use of the medium**. For the latter we backed the items proposed by Ssebuggwawo et al. up with a usability evaluation using discount usability heuristics proposed by Nielsen [29]. Furthermore, we left out the quality of the modeling language aspect as we are mainly interested in the understandability and domain-related appropriateness of process representations.

However, in order to evaluate the quality of WASCoMo with respect to the research questions we did not want to solely rely on participants' perceptions. We rather developed a mixed-method approach [6] thus adding objective data to the aforementioned categories if available. This data is mainly based on **comparisons of different versions of the process model** while it went through the different phases of WASCoMo (c.f. Fig. 14.1). We put special emphasis on how the models evolved with respect to their content and we also evaluated the **complexity** of each version. The reason for this is that WASCoMo especially aims at supporting lay modelers thus requiring them to understand what the models represent. As Mendling et al. [28] found model complexity being a major factor in process model comprehension, we used the **connectivity** of a model [28] as a means of evaluating the complexity of the models. Furthermore we also developed measures in order to evaluate the impact of annotations on process models thus aiming at finding evidence with respect to RQ 1:

1. **Number of modifications**: Analyzing video footage of the workshops we counted the number of modifications that were conducted based on each annotation. Modifications were considered as adding elements or relations, modifying (i.e. changing their label) or deleting them.
2. **Granularity**: We rated each annotation with respect to the area of a model it referred to. These ratings reach from "single element or relation" via "part of a model" and "whole model" to annotations that are related to the overall approach that is taken when talking about the model.
3. **Number of replies**: As WASCoMo is meant to support collaboration on models it seems adequate to also measure the impact of an annotation with respect to collaboration. We expect annotations to have more impact on collaboration if there are more replies.
4. **Position**: Due to the question whether lay users as well as modeling experts are equally capable of contributing we also analyzed whether an annotation was placed at the right position within the model.

Although this list is not complete with respect to the range of possible measures, it yet provides a good overview of how annotations affected the model (1–3) and the collaboration on it (4). We also developed a **classification scheme for annotations** with respect to whether they aimed at the process depicted in the model, the way the modeling notation was used, the way the model was used and whether or not they were used for communication (i.e. being direct replies to other annotations).

We backed all the aforementioned measures up by conducting **interviews** with selected participants covering aspects such as whether they found it reasonable to be able to create annotations on process models during different workshops, whether WASCoMo affected their sense of ownership and how they used the web interface in order to get a more complete picture. Backing up the aforementioned measurement by Mendling et al. [27] in order to assess whether or not a person can be considered a lay modeler or not, we also asked them about their confidence in understanding the model.

### 14.4.1 Study

In order to evaluate the quality of the WASCoMo concept and thereby answering the research questions described in Sect. 14.1 we studied the concept in several cases. Here we describe the typical procedure of such a study with respect to one case. We deliberately chose a real life context for all studies as we perceived this to affect the motivation of stakeholders to participate actively.

We started each study by conducting an initial workshop during which a first draft of a model was developed (c.f. workshop 1 in Fig. 14.3). Afterwards the model was distributed among the participants of the workshop. The participants then had 2 weeks to work on the models with respect to a guiding question that was agreed upon during the previous workshop. In order to work on the model, the participants

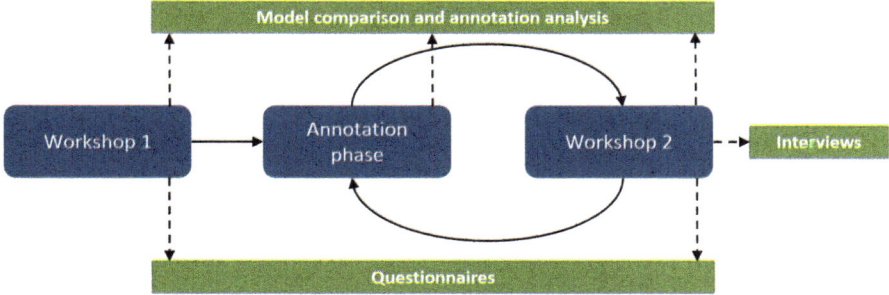

**Fig. 14.3** Concept to analyze WASCoMo

used the web interface described before (c.f. Fig. 14.2 in Sect. 14.3) and created annotations on the model (c.f. annotation phase in Fig. 14.3). After these 2 weeks another workshop was conducted during which the annotations were included into the model (c.f. workshop 2 in Fig. 14.3).

We applied the different instruments mentioned in the beginning of this section on different occasions during the study (c.f. Fig. 14.3 for an overview). We compared three different versions of each process model that emerged during the study (c.f. Fig. 14.3 top). We also analyzed the annotations that were created on the process model with respect to the aforementioned classification scheme as well as to the impact they had by applying the quality measurements described at the beginning of this section. Furthermore we applied the modified questionnaires suggested by Ssebuggwawo et al. [33] after each workshop and compared the respective results in order to find a trend in the respective scales. The first of those questionnaires also contained the questions proposed by Mendling et al. [27] that referred to modeling expertise. Following the final workshop, we also conducted semi-structured interviews with selected participants.

## 14.4.2   Results

We conducted 10 workshops with 18 participant analyzing 5 processes (c.f. Table 14.1 for more information). Participation ranged from two to seven participants in the respective workshops. The models were annotated 95 times in total which results in an average of 19 annotations per model and a maximum of 48 annotations for one model. The majority of the annotations (58) focused on the process depicted in the model while 21 were used for communication, 14 focused on the way the modeling notation was used and 2 focused on the way the model itself was used during the course of the study. Among the participants were 14 people that we consider lay modelers and four participants that were experienced in process modeling. With 7 participants being inactive the remaining 11 participants created

**Table 14.1** Descriptive statistics about the study conducted. In what follows we will describe some of the most relevant findings we derived from the analysis. We will focus on how the participants perceived the approach as well as how it affected the resulting models thus leading to answering the research questions stated in Sect. 14.1

| Participants | N = 18 (11 active) |
| --- | --- |
| | 14 lay modelers, 4 experienced modelers |
| | 8,6 annotations per participant (31 maximum) |
| Models | N = 5 (3 versions per model) |
| | 19 annotations per model (48 maximum) |
| Annotations | N = 95 |
| | 58 focused on the process depicted |
| | 21 were used for communication |
| | 14 focused on the way the modeling notation was used |
| | 2 focused on the way the model was used |

an average of roughly 8,6 annotations per participant and a maximum of 31 for one participant. In the annotation phase, participation overall has thus been considerably lower than expected which leads to proposing a number of potential improvements for WASCoMo in Sect. 14.5.

### 14.4.2.1 Quality of the Annotations

Analyzing the annotations with respect to their quality we found that each annotation on average led to about 1,8 **modifications** with all but 36 annotations leaving a trace. While 36 annotations not leaving a trace might sound to be a lot one has to note that 11 annotations remained unchanged in the models as they e.g. contained examples for process steps. One example for such an annotation is a participant stating: "*Hint: Reports on malfunctions are only accepted via telephone in case of an emergency.*"[2] Furthermore, it can be noted that **models that received more annotations also were changed to a larger extent** during the following workshops (c.f. a model with 48 annotations received 68 modifications while another model with 5 annotations only received 1 modification). It can also be noted that most annotations focused on a future to-be process (31) rather than on the appropriateness of the current as-is process (27) leading to the assumption that the participants were more concerned about altering the process rather than arriving at a complete description of its current state.

We also found that with respect to granularity most annotations (60 out of 95) **focused on specific aspects** of the process. One example for that is depicted in Fig. 14.2: "*Shouldn't we put that into one note also?*".

---

[2]It should be noted that the statements by the participants were translated as the study was conducted in Germany and the participant subsequently communicated in German.

With respect to the **number of replies** we found 21 total replies to 74 annotations which results in an average of 0,28 replies per annotation. While this again seems to be not much, analyzing the interviews showed that communication not only happened on models but also in face-to-face situations between process stakeholders. While this can be expected we found indications in interview statements such as *"I have talked with [participant] and [participant] about the model [ ... ] I integrated the result of our communication in the model afterwards"*. This provides evidence that models were used even during face-to-face communication thus leading us to the assumption that the models were part of communication at work.

We also found different usage strategies with respect to:

- **Time**: Some participants stated that they deliberately chose not to use models at work but rather in the evening (*"I did not think about the models during work"*) while others used the models every time *"something crossed my mind"*.
- **Frequency**: Some participants only used the models once or twice while others used it regularly (mostly between five and ten times).
- **Collaboration**: As stated before, some participants looked at the models together and integrated the result of their communication afterwards while others communicated directly on the models as can be seen in Fig. 14.2.

### 14.4.2.2   Aspects of Model Quality

Looking at the complexity of the models after each workshop it can be noted that it almost stayed identical as it increased from 1,4 to 1,43 on average per model. One aspect of this is that modifications to models were **mostly about details** like the ones depicted in Fig. 14.2 where the elements that represent artifacts just had to be assigned to other process elements by e.g. moving them to a different position. While working on details in general can be perceived to be positive it also led to some people perceiving it as adding too much details to the model. This trend is depicted in Fig. 14.4 which shows a downward trend from workshop 1 to workshop 2 (median down from 3 to 2).

Furthermore, we found a decrease in participants' perceived understandability of the model between workshop 1 and workshop 2 (after workshop 1 the scores were between 3 and 5 while after workshop 2 they were between 2 and 5). However, not a single annotation was placed at the wrong position in the model. This leads us to the assumption that the participants realized the complexity of the process models when working on them alone during the asynchronous phase subsequently leading them to question their ability to understand them. Nonetheless, we did not find any supporting evidence that underpins the assumption that the ability of the participants to understand the models was negatively influenced by the WASCoMo concept.

**Fig. 14.4** Development of
perceived quality from
workshop 1 to workshop 2

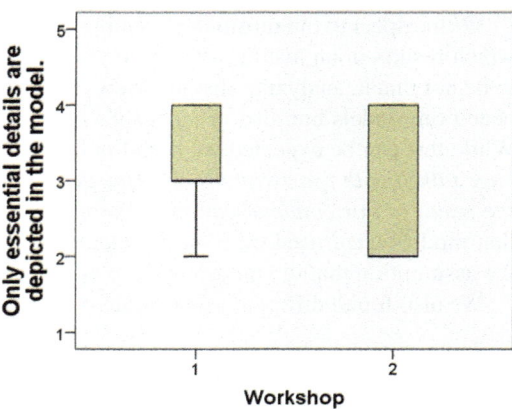

### 14.4.2.3 Aspects of Perceived Quality of the Approach

Annotations were mainly used to **remember to mention certain aspects during workshops**, as the following statement indicates: *"you do not forget what you wanted to say"*, *" . . . would have been gone if not for the comments"*. Furthermore, the possibility of accessing and annotating models also had a **positive impact on the communication during the second workshop** as the respective item (median up from 4 to 4,5) as well as interview statements indicate *"comments led to us discussing about it more"*. Participants even were satisfied with decisions during the second workshop **when their proposals were not accepted**, as the questionnaires indicate. We also found indications that participants **perceived that they had more control of the modeling process** when workshops are complemented with an asynchronous phase. These stem from the fact that all items which cover the influence of a participant of the modeling process either increased (*"My contribution led to us discussing different perspectives on a process"*, scores ranged between 2 and 5 after the first workshop and from 3 to 5 after the second one) or stayed identical (*"I actively participated in achieving the goal of modeling"* and *"I contributed to reaching an agreement"*) or increased between the two workshops. Furthermore, the participants stated that **decision making during workshops became faster** due to the annotations serving as a means to exchange arguments before thus leading to faster decisions during workshops. This assumption is underpinned by the respective item in the questionnaires (median up from 4 to 4,5) as well as by statements of participants during interviews (*" . . . agreement was then achieved during the workshop"*).

### 14.4.2.4 Lay Modelers Compared to Experienced Modelers

Comparing the results for the aforementioned categories with respect to annotations contributed by lay modelers to those stemming from experienced modelers it can be stated that the overall quality of annotations that were created by **experienced modelers** was **slightly better** (median 2,75 for experienced modelers and 2 for lay modelers). This is mainly due to **lay modelers focusing more on details** of the process i.e. specific elements rather than process parts or the process as a whole. Furthermore, it has to be noted that experienced modelers on average contributed more annotations (7) than lay modelers ($\approx$4,79). This effect however is mainly due to all inactive participants being lay modelers. Ruling these out of the calculation even puts lay modelers ahead of experienced modelers ($\approx$9,57 annotations). When it comes to evaluating the **perceived quality of the approach there is no difference** between lay modelers and experienced modelers as they both rate the respective items in the questionnaire equally (c.f. the median on the item "*I actively participated in achieving the goal of modeling*" was four for both lay and experienced modelers). It can thus be stated that lay modelers and experienced modelers participated equally when active with annotations from experienced modelers being perceived as slightly better with respect to the quality dimensions described in the beginning of Sect. 14.4.

## 14.5   Discussion

The evaluation of WASCoMo reveals that – despite participation being lower than expected – the possibility of inspecting and annotating process models between workshops was used by the stakeholders as a substantial opportunity for influencing process analysis and design (c.f. RQ 1) on multiple levels. Firstly, WASCoMo positively affected the quality of the process models especially with respect to the achieved level of details and to prioritizing a future to-be process instead of the current as-is situation. We also found that the more the models were annotated the more they were changed during the following workshops. Apparently, the possibility to inspect models and create annotations between workshops had an impact on their evolution. Secondly, the way people participated was positively influenced by WASCoMo: The participants perceived to have more influence on the modeling process after the annotation phase. Annotations also helped participants to remember aspects they wanted to mention during workshops and allowed for discussions on proposals thus accelerating negotiations and decision making at the second workshop. Furthermore, the web-based availability of process models encouraged people to gather around it and to discuss the model face-to-face while adding results of those communications as annotations. Consequently, we suggest that WASCoMo positively influences the resulting artifacts as well as the way participants perceived their influence on process design.

   Adding onto that, there are also indications that WASCoMo particularly improved the influence of lay modelers on the outcome of process modeling (c.f. RQ 2). Despite annotations stemming from experienced modelers being perceived as slightly better with respect to the quality dimensions described in the beginning Sect. 14.4, it can be noted that both lay modelers and experienced modelers were equally capable of influencing the outcome of process modeling by annotations. We have to mention though that the perceived understanding of the models slightly decreased after the second workshop on the part of the lay modelers. However, there were no other indications that would back up the assumption that understanding actually decreased after the annotation phase. Thus, this might indicate that the perception changed due to the participants realizing the complexity of the model while working on it without expert support during the annotation phase. Compared to other approaches, which focus on the modification of models, the usage of annotations reduces the dependency of lay modelers on experts, and therefore relatively increases their influence. This argument is backed by other findings such as both, lay modelers and experienced modelers, equally perceiving WASCoMo to allow them for actively participating in process modeling and consequently in designing the processes.

Apart from answering the research questions stated in Sect. 14.1 we also aimed at identifying **potentials for improving the concept** with respect to the web interface (the technical support) as well as the overall organizational approach (c.f. Fig. 14.1). Compared with the goals of a workshop's facilitator, who tries to get multiple feedbacks by every participant, the number of annotations and annotators was relatively low. The need for encouraging more intense participation especially with respect to motivating stakeholders to participate at all thus became obvious. To meet this requirement, we identified two approaches: **Increasing the awareness** about ongoing annotating in the models, and **providing external prompts** to activate the participants. Those prompts could e.g. be provided by facilitators or fellow co-workers asking questions or giving hints that an annotation has been commented by another participant. These measures require the socio-technical combination of technical support (such as sending messages to participants) with organizational conventions, such as asking participants to directly address their co-workers when phrasing their annotations, or asking facilitators to prompt comments through provocative statements. Furthermore, participants should be encouraged to ask questions about parts of a model or process they feel that they do not fully understand especially during and after the annotation phase. This in turn could lead to increased participation especially by lay modelers.

There are however also some methodological **limitations** with respect to the evaluation and the findings. It is not possible to confirm hypotheses about the appropriateness of the WASCoMo approach for two reasons: (A) Since we conducted evaluations in practical fields it was not possible to establish control groups which were involved in the same process design under the same conditions but just without an annotation phase. Consequently, we cannot be sure whether the same effects could have been achieved by only running a second workshop after the first one. This shortcoming is due to testing the concept in real practical contexts where the influencing factors cannot be controlled as it is the requirements for repeated experiments. It can also be assumed that it would be extremely difficult if not impossible to control all influencing variables such as differing goals or group composition in an experimental setup. However the practical context not only allowed us to gather a lot of explorative data that includes objective and subjective measures thus covering different perspectives (c.f. Sect. 14.4), it also can be assumed that the real life context affected the motivation of stakeholders to participate as the resulting process affected their everyday work. There is a strong plausibility that the annotation phase had an effect but the possibility of the second workshop interfering with those effects cannot be ruled out. (B) The relatively low number of participants as well as the different contexts in which WASCoMo was used, limits the statistical evaluation with respect to the significance of the observed effects. We tried to mitigate these effects by considering additional data such as annotations, models, server logs and interviews but this cannot compensate the limited evidence of the descriptive statistics.

## 14.6  Conclusions and Outlook

The socio-technical approach of WASCoMo was designed to intertwine phases of synchronous collaboration (e.g. in workshops) with phases of asynchronous inspection and annotation of process models. In the current state, WASCoMo has to be continuously improved or adapted to the requirements of a practical context and is therefore presented in combination with a formative evaluation method. The method includes different measures such as questionnaires (aiming at the quality of collaborative modeling as it is perceived by the participants), interviews and content analysis. It is thus suitable for providing an in-depth perspective on multiple aspects of collaborative modeling considering the quality of the resulting models as well as the perceived quality of the outcome and the impact of annotations on process models. The innovation which is implied with the presented approach is twofold: On the one hand a fine tuned level of involving lay modelers into using graphical representations of processes is provided; on the other hand, a rich methodological basis for formative evaluation and succeeding improvement of the lay modelers' involvement is proposed and has been tested in several cases.

On an exploratory level there is empirical evidence that lay modelers are able and willing to participate in the annotation phase and by doing so have subsequently increased their influence on process analysis and design. We also found evidence suggesting that WASCoMo positively influenced the perception of stakeholders about being in control of the modeling process. Furthermore, we found that the concept gave equal weight to the influence of lay modelers and of expert modelers. Therefore, the concept can serve as an additional method of collaborative process analysis and design as it allows for domain experts and stakeholders to improve the information basis for analyzing and designing processes.

One of the critical aspects is the low degree of participation during the annotation phase. This observation points into two directions. On the one hand it might mirror the need for socio-technical improvement of the WASCoMo concept. On the other hand, the low participation can be an indicator for interest conflicts or insufficient motivation for supporting organizational change with respect to business processes in that particular context where we conducted the study.

Further research should bring insights about how we can reliably differentiate between these two reasons for low participation. It will be interesting to observe how the effects of WASCoMo evolve over longer time periods when the combination of annotation phases with succeeding workshops is repeated several times while working on the same process or when participating in the design of several different processes. A further challenge is the involvement of participants who did not participate in a workshop and are only involved during the annotation phase. This type of involving stakeholders can help to increase the number of potential participants but implies more effort and measures to encourage and motivate people's willingness to take part.

# References

1. Armitt G et al (2002) The development of deep learning during a synchronous collaborative on-line course. In: Proceedings of the conference on computer support for collaborative learning: foundations for a CSCL community. International Society of the Learning Sciences, pp 151–159
2. Bandara W (2007) Process modelling success factors and measures. Queensland University of Technology, Brisbane, Australia
3. Baroudi JJ et al (1986) An empirical study of the impact of user involvement on system usage and information satisfaction. Commun ACM 29(3):232–238
4. Bratteteig T et al (2012) Organising principles and general guidelines for Participatory Design Projects. In: Routledge international handbook of participatory design. Routledge, New York, p 117
5. Brush A et al (2002) Supporting interaction outside of class: anchored discussions vs. discussion boards. In: Proceedings of the conference on computer support for collaborative learning: foundations for a CSCL community. International Society of the Learning Sciences, pp 425–434
6. Creswell JW (2013) Research design: qualitative, quantitative, and mixed methods approaches. Sage, Los Angeles
7. Davis JR, Huttenlocher DP (1995) Shared annotation for cooperative learning. In: The first international conference on Computer support for collaborative learning. Erlbaum Associates, pp 84–88
8. Diehl M, Stroebe W (1987) Productivity loss in brainstorming groups: toward the solution of a riddle. J Pers Soc Psychol 53(3):497–509
9. Dumas M et al (2013) Fundamentals of business process management. Springer/Berlin, Germany
10. Fischer G, Herrmann T (2011) Socio-technical systems: a meta-design perspective. Int J Sociotechnol Knowl Dev (IJSKD) 3(1):1–33
11. Greenbaum J, Kyng M (1992) Introduction: situated design. In: Greenbaum J, Kyng M (eds) Design at work. Erlbaum Associates Inc., Hillsdale, pp 1–24.
12. Gruhn V, Laue R (2006) Complexity metrics for business process models. In: 9th international conference on business information systems (BIS 2006). Springer, pp 1–12
13. den Hengst M, de Vreede GJD (2004) Collaborative business engineering: a decade of lessons from the field. J Manag Inf Syst 20(4):85–114

14. Herrmann T et al (2000) Intertwining training and participatory design for the development of groupware applications. In: PDC, pp 106–115
15. Herrmann T et al (2004) Socio-technical walkthrough: designing technology along work processes. In: Proceedings of the eighth conference on participatory design. ACM, pp 132–141
16. Herrmann T (2009) Systems design with the socio-technical walkthrough. In: Whitworth B, de Moore A (eds) Handbook of research on socio-technical design and social networking systems. Idea Group Publishing, Hershey, pp 336–351
17. Herrmann T, Hoffmann M (2005) The metamorphoses of workflow projects in their early stages. Comput Supported Coop Work 14(5):399–432
18. Herrmann T, Kienle A (2008) Context-oriented communication and the design of computer supported discursive learning. Int J Comput Supported Collab Learn 3(3):273–299
19. Hoppenbrouwers S et al (2010) Towards games for knowledge acquisition and modeling. Int J Gaming Comput Mediated Simul, Spec Issue AI Games 2(4):48–66
20. Hoppenbrouwers SJBA, van Stokkum W (2011) Towards combining thinkLets and dialogue games in collaborative modeling: an explorative case. In: Nolte A et al (eds) Proceedings of the 1st international workshop on collaborative usage and development of models and visualizations at the ECSCW 2011 (CollabViz 2011). CEUR-WS, pp 11–18
21. Kensing F et al (1998) MUST: a method for participatory design. Hum Comput Interact 13(2):167–198
22. Krogstie J et al (2006) Process models representing knowledge for action: a revised quality framework. Eur J Inf Syst 15(1):91–102
23. Lee Y (2006) Design participation tactics: redefining user participation design. In: Design research society international conference
24. Lindsay C (2003) Involving people as co-creators. In: Aarts E, Marzano S (eds) The new everyday: views on ambient intelligence. 010 Publishers, pp 38–41
25. Loser K-U, Herrmann T (2002) Enabling factors for participatory design of socio-technical systems with diagrams. In: PDC, pp 114–123
26. Marshall CC (1997) Annotation: from paper books to the digital library. In: Proceedings of the second ACM international conference on digital libraries. ACM, pp 131–140
27. Mendling J et al (2012) Factors of process model comprehension—findings from a series of experiments. Decis Support Syst 53(1):195–206
28. Mendling J et al (2007) What makes process models understandable? In: Proceedings of the 5th international conference on Business process management. Springer, pp 48–63
29. Nielsen J (1994) Enhancing the explanatory power of usability heuristics. In: CHI'94: proceedings of the SIGCHI conference on Human factors in computing systems. ACM, pp 152–158
30. Nolte A, Prilla M (2013) Anyone can use models: potentials, requirements and support for non-expert model interaction. Int J E-Collaboration. Special issue on Collaborative usage and development of models. 9:45–60
31. Prilla M, Nolte A (2012) Integrating ordinary users into process management: towards implementing bottom-up, people-centric BPM. In: Enterprise, business-process and information systems modeling, LNBIP 113. Springer, pp 182–194
32. Rittgen P (2008) COMA: a tool for collaborative modeling. In: CAiSE'08 forum. CEUR-WS, pp 61–64
33. Ssebuggwawo D et al (2010) Assessing collaborative modeling quality through modeling artifacts. In: Proceedings of the third IFIP WG 8.1 working conference on the practice of enterprise modeling (PoEM 2010). Springer
34. Star SL (1989) The structure of ill-structured solutions: boundary objects and heterogeneous distributed problem solving. In: Gasser L, Huhns MH (eds) Distributed artificial intelligence. Morgan Kaufmann Publishers, San Francisco, pp 37–54

# Chapter 15
# Local Decision Making as a Design Opportunity

Olav W. Bertelsen

**Abstract** In this paper we present the history and declining participation in Danish residents' democracy, and we discuss the possibilities for ICT based solutions exemplified in three design interventions in a housing organization. In particular we discuss the relation between computerized democracy, ICT supported access to democratic processes, and ITC support for community building and inclusion.

## 15.1 Introduction

In Denmark, residents in public housing have the legal power to make decisions about budget and development in the estate they live in; this is called *residents' democracy*. However, many residents do not participate in the democratic processes of their housing organization. In this paper we look into the Danish public housing sector and the challenged participation in residents' democracy, and how ICT could contribute to a solution. We explore a couple of recent technical experiments as a basis for an analysis of ICT based mediation in the intersection between local democracy, in the narrow sense of joint decision making, and community in a broader sense. The empirical cases all come from Boligkontoret Århus (BKÅ), one of the three largest (5500 apartments) housing organizations in Aarhus, the second largest city of Denmark. The reported research has been carried out as a combination of the author's reflections on his own participation in volunteer work in the public housing sector and three project conducted by post graduate students for their Master's theses.

O.W. Bertelsen (✉)
Department of Computer Science, Center for Participatory-IT, Aarhus University,
Aarhus, Denmark
e-mail: olavb@cs.au.dk

© Springer International Publishing Switzerland 2016                                  243
A. De Angeli et al. (eds.), *COOP 2016: Proceedings of the 12th International
Conference on the Design of Cooperative Systems, 23–27 May 2016, Trento, Italy,*
DOI 10.1007/978-3-319-33464-6_15

## 15.2    The Danish Public Housing Model

Historically, public housing in Denmark has been established and organized in a myriad of ways, including social philanthropy and trade-based associations. In the late 1990s a good handful of organizational forms still existed [8].

Life in public housing has changed over time and ideally it cannot be understood as separated from societal norms and conditions in general; mechanisms of social control, social stratification etc. Historically, parts of public housing were thought of as the last resort for the very poor (then often called social housing). However, in our own experience of the sector, locally as well as nationally, over the last 20 years it is quite clear that the proud skilled worker has been the consistent idealized resident. Until the late 1960s good basic and orderly conditions were highest priority. When good healthy conditions had become the basis, people began to question rules. They wanted to use the lawns for play, they wanted a say about renovations etc.

The development of local democracy in public housing is reflected in a number of changes and innovations in the national legislation [8].

• In 1958, resident representatives from housing estates were granted the right to be consulted in a number of cases, like substantial renovations, elevated rent etc.
• In 1967, tenants' associations acquired rights to send representatives to the supervisory boards of housing organizations.
• In 1970, formal estate residents' meetings and elected estate boards were introduced in the legislation. Residents' meetings were to decide over e.g. rules for orderly conduct, whereas the estate board got the role of approving the estate budget.
• In 1982, adjustments to the laws introduced extensive possibilities for democracy in the housing organizations.
• In 1984, residents were giving the majority of the seats in the central boards of Danish housing organizations.
• From 1997, residents were given the majority of seats in the housing organizations' supervisory board. Also, most of the decision powers were formally moved from the estate boards to the estate residents' meetings.
• From 2010 all public housing in Denmark has been regulated by one set of rules enforcing the same basic organizational structure on all organizations.

The Danish model for public housing democracy sets residents in the double position of both being tenants and landlords. This can be seen in contrast to the situation in Sweden, where the tenants have a strong position through their association's hearing rights [10].

In short a housing organization consists of relatively autonomous housing estates. The residents in each estate make decisions over budget, renovations, house rules, etc. at the annual residents meeting. Each dwelling is represented by two votes. The estates are part of the housing organization and send a number, relative to their size, of delegates to the organizations assembly of representatives. The assembly of representatives elects a central board, and decides on matters regarding the organization as a whole (See Fig. 15.1).

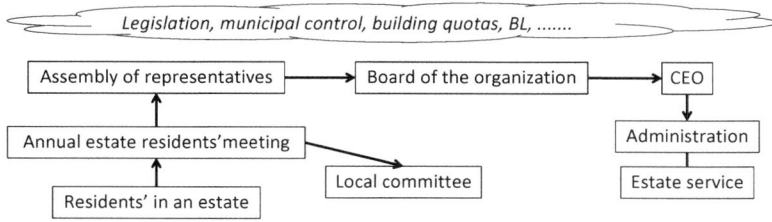

**Fig. 15.1**  Structure of Danish public housing democracy

The Public housing sector is highly regulated by law and monitored by the municipal control unit for public housing with the purpose of securing the soundness and sustainability of the housing estates. New housing estates are established by the housing organizations and supported financially through an intricate municipally controlled quota system.

### 15.2.1  The Residents' Meeting

The fulcrum of residents' democratic engagement is the annual meeting for all residents in the estate. The meeting takes almost all decisions and elects the local committee to implement these decisions. The standard agenda for the ordinary annual estate residents' meeting comprises the following items:

* Election of chairman of the meeting.
* Report of the period since the previous meeting. Including debate.
* Approval of the estate budget for the coming year.
* Negotiation of proposals set to the meeting (if any)
* Elections of members of the local committee including chairperson.
* Election of representatives for the organizations assembly of representatives.
* Any Other Business.

Two items in this standard agenda provide openings where ideas can be sparked, and new wishes be formulated. There is open discussion following the report of the year, as well as an obligatory "Any Other Business" item where concerns and ideas can be voiced but no decision taken.

## 15.3  Issues for Democratic Engagement

Residents' democracy is challenged by the fact that that many residents do not participate. Thus, BL (the Association of Public Housing Organizations) identified the development of new forms of participation in residents' democracy as one of six strategic goals for the period 2010–2014 [3]. The effort seems to be endless

Some may not know the possibilities, or they do not believe they are welcome or that they will get to have a say if they participate. Some experience that a clique of very experienced "residents' democrats" runs the residents' meetings in a closed manner, and others just do not want to spend the necessary time [9, 15].

Very often the preparation process leading to a proposal at the annual residents meeting in a housing estate is closed, involving only staff and the local committee up to the point of taking a formal decision. The ideas and opinions that many residents have are most often not taken into account in forming proposals. Creative co-construction of new visions for the housing estate seems to be relatively rare at meetings. The purpose is to make decisions and often participants focus on avoiding specific decisions or having other specific decisions approved for the sake of very narrow interests. There is an obvious need for exploring new forms of participation that can engage more residents at an earlier stage, and thereby ensure anchoring and decision quality. There is a need for fora where discussions can be made freely without the pressure of the formal decision-making – fora where apparent conflicts can be resolved. Additionally, during the implementation, e.g. of a renovation, control most often is with administrators, technical staff and the local board, and ordinary residents are rarely involved in revision and re-planning beyond mere information. New forms of participation would also be welcome in that context.

Based on investigations into the lack of participation in residents' democracy, primarily among immigrant groups [9, 15], Heath [7] summarized a number of barriers to participation in public housing democracy. On that basis, he developed a prototype system that could help residents who usually did not participate to join and enable more residents to contribute to the development of ideas. The identified barriers seem to be general.

### 15.3.1 Lack of Time to Participate

It seems that it is not only time in general, but more the specific time that is a limit to participation. Residents have a lot of other activities going on in their lives, and prioritizing the annual residents' meeting competes with sports, hobbies, family, or other activities that seem more relevant than participating in a meeting that you are not so familiar with.

### 15.3.2 Lack of Language Competencies

Language may be a particular problem for residents whose first language is not Danish. If it is hard to understand official letters and if it is hard to understand the fast paced dialogue at the meeting, it may not make sense to attend the meeting.

There is a broader literacy problem. The "language of housing democracy" may not always be very understandable, budgets are hard to read etc. On top of that many residents do not write very well and that introduces an asymmetry in written communication.

### 15.3.3   Shyness, Strangeness, and Laziness

Lund-Andersen [15] reports that some of the interviewed immigrants find the concept of local democracy strange, and that many are just too shy to participate. Some of the respondents believed that others did not participate because they were too lazy. All in all, this points to barriers both at the personal level that it is hard to address directly, and with respect to a basic understanding of what democracy is.

Jensen et al. [9 p51] report that 40 % of the respondents did not like to speak at large meetings, and that 41 % would almost never speak at the annual estate meeting. These numbers point to basic limitations of the annual residents meeting, and the need for additional fora and forms of participation.

### 15.3.4   The Old Clique

Lund-Andersen [16] reports stories about local committees who precluded tenants' proposals, as well as statements indicating that the local committee acts as a closed group that is impossible to approach or be a part of.

The old clique problem is paradoxical because the seasoned residence democrats complain about the lack of interest from other residents. However, the same people quite often treat newcomers, e.g. when they are sending in a proposal for the annual meeting, in ways that effectively discourage them from future participation. Part of this problem occurs because the older generations are brought up in a tradition and mindset where engagement in institutions such as trade unions and housing organizations were lifetime and qua social class and interest, whereas younger generations seem to be more oriented to case-by-case engagement. This historical change [14] is an important aspect of the current challenge for residents' democracy.

### 15.3.5   Opportunity Apathy

Another issue not discussed by Heath [7] is opportunity apathy. I.e. the tendency to only engage in processes of decision making when issues such as a substantial rise of the rent in the estate.

As discussed above, some residents are unaware of the possibilities, some feel they are un-welcome or unable to have a say if they participate. Some have experienced the annual residents meeting to be dominated by "the old clique", and others just don't feel they can spend the necessary time.

To a large extent opportunity apathy can be attributed to the above-mentioned barriers to participation. Meetings seem to be centered around an agenda with points to be voted on etc. Ideas and opinions from residents are most often only in an obscure way finding their way to decisions made at the annual meetings. Collaborative creativity in defining the future for a housing estate is rarely organized and transparent. The broad debate is often taken at formalized meetings where focus is on avoiding chaos and non-implementable decisions. This proposal centered meeting logic, which is the very basis of residents' democracy, seems to be a problem. There is a need for new spaces for creative debate to supplement the formalized decision making over budgets and planning taking place at the annual residents' meetings.

It is not enough, however, to change and supplement the meeting forms and the decision focused agendas and reduce the mechanisms of exclusions.

Most people today are much more likely to activate themselves in relation to threats, issues and problems, and less likely to engage in filling out opportunity spaces. In the historical transformation of public engagement from being based in class and social belonging to become single case based [14] opportunity apathy becomes more likely. When you are engaged in a specific issue, you will focus on that and be unaware of the possibilities that are not related to that issue. The issue becomes your perspective. Without an issue people do not engage to realize the space of opportunity. Thus, residents may not see the unused lawn as an opportunity for establishing small gardens, or the vacant activity room as an opportunity for organizing a jam making workshop.

## 15.4    Three Experiments with BKÅ

In this section, we introduce three experiments done by Master's thesis students at Aarhus university in collaboration with BKÅ. In different ways they address issues in residents' democracy, applying a variety of methods. The experiments were carried out and tested in actual estates concerning actual, relevant issues, but were limited by quite limited interaction by residents. The two first experiments demonstrate how an ICT based concept can be realized to solve well-known issues. The concept of the last experiment came out of interaction with a group of young boys over more than a month.

### 15.4.1    Breaking the Meeting Logic, Keeping the Meeting

The Beboermødeportal (Residents' Meeting Portal) [7] was a web-based prototype based on the 1-year cycle of events in residents' democracy as the basic structuring principle for ICT-support for new forms of engagement. The annual estate meeting was acknowledged as the central point of reference in the democratic life of the estate. Decisions were taken at the meeting, but the local board prepares the meetings and undertakes the implementation of decisions and makes that work visible through the portal. The prototype aimed to make transparent the work done by the local board before and after the annual meeting, and to open a space for broad democratic debate. The prototype gave an opportunity to participate asynchronously when it was convenient for the individual resident, eliminating the feeling of not having time to attend the meeting and giving residents a chance to learn if and how participating in the meeting could be relevant. This also provided an opportunity to participate for people who are not confident with talking at meetings. Maybe most prominently, the portal provided an opportunity for all residents to follow the work done by the local board.

The Beboermødeportal was tested in two housing estates in conjunction with the annual estate meetings. Penetration was quite low, and the data are not conclusive. Thus, the main outcome of the project was the proof of concept.

The logic, and some times inhibiting forms of interaction at large meetings was broken down through the introduction of possibilities for asynchronous debate, and broader involvement of residents in the preparation of the annual meeting.

In terms of the barriers for participation discussed above, the Beboermødeportal prototype points to directions for further work.

The "lack of time" barrier, that seems to be amalgamated with lack of perceived relevance, was addressed by making openings for the "too busy" residents to asynchronously look into what happens in the meetings – when it suits them.

The text-based format could, potentially, solve part of the "lack of language" barrier. Not least by not enforcing a specific pace on the individual resident. But as discussed above many residents, as well as the general citizen, do not relate to written text as active creators.

With respect to the "personality oriented barriers" the textual format gives an opportunity to raise views without feeling insecure in the big crowd. But if residents don't see themselves as part of a living democracy the mere access to a process through a web site may not be attractive.

Whether or not the Beboermødeportal could solve the "old clique barrier" highly depends on the willingness among the estate committee and administrators to make accessible the planning and follow up processes through the portal. And it depends on how much they want to exercise control. That being said, it would not be as easy for the local committee to just ignore a proposal from other residents. A future approach could be to develop a Beboermødeportal as a neutral space, controlled by a third party, to avoid unhealthy control.

### 15.4.2  Breaking the Space

Kjeldsen [11], explored technologies for geographically localized debate based on [12]. This concept emerged from the observation that it is often very hard for the participants in the annual residents' meeting to relate the discussion of an issue to their practical life in the estate. The system enabled local committees to make posters presenting an issue in the estate with a QR code based access to a web page where residents could enter thoughts on the issue with their smart phones. The local committee could access the debate and use it as basis for decisions to be made at the estate meeting. The hope was that this would make residents engage with issues and opportunities while being in the relevant location carrying out relevant activities. Thus, the system would tie democratic debate closer to actual life in the estate. With localized debate the opinions raised will be based in actual practice, and residents may get a more nuanced perspective on their need for a certain piece of machinery in the laundry room, and it may be easier to find alternatives to expensive investments that residents at a meeting would feel were needed due to tradition [1].

The localized debate prototypes discussed here [11, 12] do not involve structuring of debate and ideation. A platform, that in a more structured way incorporates elements of future workshops and similar structuring, could be useful, but would require a thorough experimentation with the strength and limitations of debating on location as opposed to non-localized in the comfort of residents' apartments.

### 15.4.3   Breaking the Boundaries of Formalized Democracy

Møller and Borrits [16] conducted a project in conjunction with the initiation of a master plan for social reformation in the housing area Frydenlund in Aarhus. Frydenlund comprises 23 four to seven story buildings with a total of 1131 dwellings inhabited by approximately 2500 residents. Frydenlund consists of five housing estates that are part of five different housing organizations. The master plan was supported with funds from the state along with funds from Landsbyggefonden (the national fond for public housing). A number of master plans for social development are initiated regularly for a 4-year period. Housing areas, neighborhoods, are selected based on social indicators such as unemployment, crime, children institutionalized, etc.

While the approaches taken by Heath [7] and Kjeldsen [11] were guided by a strong initial design idea, Borrits and Møller proceeded in a much more "ethnographic" manner by establishing initial contacts to the groups conducting work in two social master plans in two different housing areas. They started out by building trustful relations to the personnel and then gradually approached various groups of residents they could establish contact with.

Møller and Borrits [16] based their project on a loose idea that attachment, sense of ownership and community were preconditions for democratic engagement. Hence, that positive side effect of the social master plan would be broadened engagement in residents' democracy.

The social workers in the master plan group turned out to have established very good contacts with a large group of teenage boys, mostly with emigrant background. "The boys" were connected through a Facebook group that they used to coordinate meet ups for soccer games and that the social worker for the young in the area occasionally used for announcing activities organized by "the master plan". Initially, Møller and Borrits pursued to have a series of workshops with "the boys" where they would design technologies for the neighborhood of the future. However, it turned out to be impossible to engage them in that kind of activity. Instead Møller and Borrits organized a series of soccer-oriented activities with "the boys" and used those activities as platforms for vision building. A number of visions, or wishes, emerged through vision generating activities embedded into the soccer-oriented activities. "the boys" had a wish for having at least one soccer field, among the many found in Frydenlund, with larger goal posts. They, wanted a water post near the soccer field, and not least they wanted a clubhouse.

Møller and Borrits, took some of the wishes and ideas from "the boys" to a meeting with the chairmen of the local committees of the five housing estates in Frydenlund. They wanted to explore how such a set of ideas could be developed to implementation. The first observation in the meeting was that the chairmen expressed a need to find methods for understanding and getting in dialogue with groups such as "the boys", regardless of the fact that it was far from clear which specific estate they belonged to.

In cooperation with the chairmen and "the boys", Møller and Borrits envisioned a system that could be accessed through smart phones (the most used technology by "the boys"), where wishes and ideas could be posted and debated. The system would be a neutral ground where actors like the estate chairs would then go and find ideas and suggest their realization, and detail it further with, e.g. "the boys". The system would support the kind of "idea brokering" that Møller and Borrits did by bringing the idea of the water post to the chairmen and one of them subsequently picked it up and preceded to get it implemented. The system was implemented as a series of mobile enabled web pages.

Møller and Borrits [16] analyse their case and the prototype they develop in terms of Dewey's [4] concept of the public as being oriented towards a common problem. They further use Hallahan's [6] concepts of an aroused versus an active public to describe the positions of "the boys" and the position they would hopefully be able to take with help from the prototype. According to Hallahan [6], the aroused public has high involvement but low knowledge, and thereby few possibilities for action. In contrast the active public has high knowledge in addition to high involvement, enabling a wider range of actions for solving the problem at hand.

In testing the prototype with "the boys", they saw a clear inability among "the boys" to engage in debate. They formulated wishes, but did not comment on each other. Thus, the expected collective creation of a common future did not happen with the prototype. That finding conforms to the experience reported by a social worker coordinating a previous social reformation master plan in another neighborhood that they interviewed. According to the interviewee working with similar groups of teenagers takes a lot of trust building that is immediately broken down if expectations are not satisfied. Democratic action cannot be brought about by means of technology alone. It requires education and trust.

An important insight to take away from this project is that some important groups, such as "the boys", are not given voice in the formalized democracy. New spaces for the involvement of such groups are needed and could be supported by ICT as demonstrated in the project.

## 15.5   Democracy Between Decision and Joint Action

Based on the three experiments it is possible to discuss what residents' democracy really is about. The historical development in the Danish public housing sector has, until 1997 been one of progressively more decision power being given to the residents. Residents have become their own landlords through the democratic structures [10].

### 15.5.1   Democracy Beyond Formal Institution

The three experiments show that the challenges faced by residents' democracy cannot fruitfully be understood merely in terms of the formalized decision-making processes. Challenges such as excessive agenda control, non-inclusive culture, lacking conditions for collaborative creativity, and groups who do not have a formal voice call for a broader perspective.

Residents' democracy is based on community. Joint decisions are made about common property, resources and opportunities for life. When residents enter the estate meeting, they join a community. If participants at the meeting are not talking together in ways so that everybody understands what is going on and can follow the pace of the meeting, it doesn't work. If participants at the meeting know other participants it is easier to be part of the process. If the participants experience a sense of common interests they become better at making good decisions. So, even if public housing democracy is only about decision-making, community and shared interest is a precondition for it. Also, the residents meeting in itself generates community. Residents meet and learn that behind differing views nice people can be found. People talk and chat during the meeting and maybe they meet outside the meeting and continue the conversation.

New ideas do not often come about at meetings, but somewhere else. Aiming to imbed idea development and balancing of views in the democratic structure seems timely.

The residents' meeting has, in its standard form, grown out of the historical consultation rights that residents were granted gradually from 1958 and onwards. Traditionally, ideas for renewal and change have not come from the residents but from management. In our most recent studies of residents' meetings we have observed how the two meeting agenda items that open for debate are sometimes used for formulating a need that the local board then commit to. A specific example was at a meeting where residents were unhappy with their Internet provider and then formed a project group to help the local board develop a good proposal for the next meeting.

In recent debate about democracy, the idea of deliberative democracy, as a practical application of Habermas' "Theorie des kommunikativen Handelns", has become popular, setting rational debate as the corner stone of democratic action. All views are taken into account and through rational deliberation good solutions are reached. A number of different models for deliberative democracy exists and are promoted through a number of organizations. While this Habermas inspired perspective may seem naïve in contexts of hard contradictions and un-balanced power relations, it appears as a way forward in attempting to include more people in the local decision-making processes of residents' democracy and to develop forms of participation that can be more creative.

## 15.5.2  Residents as a Public Sphere

Residents who have been actively involved in residents' democracy for a long time often make a distinction between residents who are part of residents' democracy ("er med i beboerdemokratiet") and those who are not. As if it is a club you can be member of or not. As Levinsen et al. [14] point out, however, we are witnessing a shift from lifetime engagement to case-by-case activism, and thus it does make increasingly less sense to understand residents as democracy activists or non-activists. Hence all residents are part of the democratic body regardless of actual participation in democratic institutions and activities. Residents in a public housing estate are only loosely connected and in most cases do not understand themselves primarily as part of a democratic body. They form a more open association of people that may better be described as a public sphere. Such a notion of a public sphere is closer to Habermas' concepts than the concept of the public inspired by Dewey adopted by Møller and Borrits.

While organized deliberation is possible when the body of residents in an estate acts as a community or members of an organization, the residents understood as a public sphere cannot in the same way be subjected to such orderliness.

The public sphere in an estate can express itself through a variety of formats. Very often it is staged and controlled by the local committee. This control can be problematic for many reasons. Committee control can limit motivation for participation; it can preclude alternative views from being developed, etc. Thus, quite often there will be a need for spaces that are not controlled by the housing organization or by the local committee – a need for neutral ground controlled by an external third party. In recent years Facebook groups have evolved around public housing estates around Denmark. In many cases as channels for the organizations communication to the residents, but in other cases as spaces where ordinary residents can discuss regardless of agendas set "from above". The Facebook group for "the boys" in Frydenlund [16] was a main channel of communication among "the boys" supplementing mouth-to-mouth communication when calling for spontaneous soccer games etc. The youth social worker in Frydenlund also used the Facebook group to communicate and guide "the boys", but in ways that did not contest the group as "the boys" own space.

### 15.5.3   Center and Periphery

Lave and Wenger [13] used the concept of legitimate peripheral participation (LPP) to denote apprentices' involvement into a community of practice in the case of tailor apprenticeship in Liberia. The apprentice begins at the age of five by sleeping on the tailor's bench and would then gradually begin doing tailor work – accepted as a part of the community even if not yet a tailor. The Beboermødeportal [7] supported legitimate peripheral participation, and it seems to be fruitful in the context of ICT-support for inclusive democracy, to discuss the relation between centers and peripheries.

However, in the public sphere of a public housing estate, many residents may not want to leave the periphery. And many residents may want to return to the periphery upon engagement in a specific case or project. Thereby, the one-directional perspective on development embedded in learning perspectives such as LPP is challenged. In the context of estate democracy a perspective acknowledging multiple centers as well as oscillation between center and periphery is needed to fully understand residents' engagement and how to support it. What is center depends on perspective. There are a number of possible centers that it may be interesting to discuss:

- The annual residents' meeting defines a formal center through its formal power over budgets and renewal plans etc. But, as discussed above, the mere right to vote doesn't necessarily imply influence on decisions.
- The local committee is elected and thereby has legitimacy, and very often understands themselves as the elite of the local democracy. Moreover, the local committee has access to information and expertise from the administrative staff. Finally, the committee exercises a large degree of control over the annual residents' meeting. E.g. by knowing how to put forward a formally correct proposal.
- The administrative and technical staff of the organization works professionally and posses knowledge including knowledge about how the public housing sector is regulated through government control. The staff also, to a large extent, holds the power of objectivity because they are not privately interested in the estate.
- Actual activities in the estates such as weekly coffee and cake for women, or monthly common dinners are most often organized independently of the local committee. Such activities may become venues for debate about issues in the estate, and carriers of the estate culture and norms. Thereby, they sometimes become strong informal centers of power.

• Even the value system of the estate can be considered as a possible center. Such value systems of estates can e.g. be related to ordinary cleanliness and good behavior that were central norms for the public housing sector until the late 1960s.

These examples of centers exist as products of power relations, mechanisms of exclusion, and conflicting (or incommensurable) perspectives in general, and they do indeed conflict with each other. While learning is an important aspect of what goes on in residents' democracy as well as personally motivating for many people doing volunteer work in the sector, it is not a sufficient perspective in this context. Experienced democrats may exclude other residents out of lacking competencies in involving others rather than out of a wish to keep them out. Thus, we should not only aim for ICT support for the transition back and forth between being at the periphery, and being at the center, but we should also aim for support for those who have defined themselves as center, to learn better to understand those who do not participate, and those who just want to stay in the periphery. By analyzing center and periphery, we get to understand that centers should not define legitimacy.

### 15.5.4  Overcoming Opportunity Apathy

Based on current challenges in BKÅ and the public housing sector in general, we previously outlined three aspects of overcoming opportunity apathy to support cooperative creativity in democratic action [2].

1. Involving people,
2. Opening the process,
3. Providing views into the possible practical futures.

The playfulness of the above approaches may attract more residents to get involved. The Beboermødeportal [7] provides new ways of letting residents get involved without leaving home. It does, however, limit involvement by requiring residents to create a profile and login. The Beboermening [11] provides easy involvement with predefined issues provided that the residents have smartphones. We speculate that when residents have used time for commenting on an issue, they would be more motivated to continue to participate in the debate. Møller and Borrits [16] took a number of approaches to get various groups to get involved, most successfully the soccer related activities. This points to the classic dilemma about how much sugar coating it makes sense to apply. Their prototype as such, breaks the locus of engagement in the same way as Beboermening, but furthermore invites groups without a formal say to participate.

All three experiments provide openings into the planning of the decision making process. Heath [7] does it in a quite direct way, by rendering the preparation and follow up work visible for all residents in the estate. Kjeldsen [11] does it by providing residents with a channel into the process that eventually leads from an issue to a proposal. The same is the case with the prototype for "the boys" [16].

None of the prototypes in the three experiments provided effective support for the creation of views into the possible practical futures. Indeed the local committee could utilize the [7] or [11] as media for inspiring provocations, but the prototypes do not support that directly. In [1] we outlined a number of examples for how these challenges could be approached in an ICT mediated set up. Asynchronous Future Workshops organized in a web-based medium where residents could go through the critique, fantasy and realization phases over a period of days. Treasure Hunts or Debate Tours, inspired by geocaching and Beboermening [11], could enable groups of residents to explore challenges and possibilities by moving physically in the estate. Web-based Co-development of extreme character and scenarios inspired by [5] could help provide views into possible futures. E.g. how the future estate could accommodate new families like model railway enthusiasts, promiscuous single mothers, or burglars.

## 15.6 Residents' Democracy as an Opportunity for ICT Design

In recent years several experiments have aimed to make participation in residents' democracy more effortless to get more people to participate. There seems to be three directions to take in computer support for residents' democracy.

1. Computerized decision processes such as "e-voting".
2. Simplified access, and support for deliberation.
3. Supporting community building in and around democratic processes.

Over the last decade we have seen a number of experiments labeled as computerized asynchronous estate meetings (e.g. in the housing organization FSB). The premise for such experiments seems to be that the voting process is central, that rational debate could fruitfully be limited to the textual form of asynchronous communication, and that it is more attractive to participate in a computerized forum. These approaches seem to diminish social and community building aspects of the estate meeting, thereby creating an inability to understand democracy as people's collective co-creation of conditions for life. According to the law for public housing, decisions have to be made at the residents meeting, or by means of a electronic ballot. Thus, the experiments that have been made with full-scale electronic residents' meetings have been quite limited. Most experiments comprised of a subset of the Beboermødeportal [7] combined with an electronic asynchronous ballot. The vision of the fully computerized residents' democracy does not seem attractive, not least because voting is not a big problem in residents' democracy.

*Simplified access* is the intention behind estate or organization web pages with resources, meeting minutes etc. It is also the motivation for the many experiments with more understandable budgets etc. we see these years in the sector. The three experiments provide points of simplified access for debating issues, developing proposals and for uttering needs.

Fruitful approaches to simplified access and support for deliberation would most likely be based on an aim to reduce existing barriers and mechanisms of exclusion, spanning between free, uncontrolled debate in platforms residents are comfortable with and know, and structured formats where concerns and views can be analyzed without drowning in chaotic debate. Facebook is where people are and feel at home, but it is not a very good platform for unfolding and analyzing debate, here much more structured platforms like Slashdot and Liquid Feedback seem more promising.

It is, however, not enough to enable and accommodate. As illustrated in the above discussion of opportunity apathy, openings into the space of opportunity are central for true democratic co-creation. The structured forms for computer-mediated creativity discussed above, would be relevant, but also tools for interactive experimentation with "what if" scenarios could reduce the power asymmetries discussed earlier.

In the project with "the boys" [16], we saw that some stakeholders loose interest and motivation if the time between an idea and the implementation of the idea is longer than a couple of days. Thus, the sense of a political or collective decision process, and its subsequent implementation is something that should be supported, e.g. by continuously rendering manifest results visible.

*Supporting community building* in and for democracy is primarily a perspective to be integrated with access and deliberation. It is important to acknowledge that community building, the sense of belonging to, etc. are key aspects of a working local democracy; in digital space as well as in the non-digital. Heath [7] notes that participants in the Beboermødeportal experiment spent relatively long time setting up their profile in the system, but in general the three experiments did not have enough penetration to provide insights into their community building potentials. As discussed above, Facebook groups serve this community building purpose. Current experiments in BKÅ, with estate TV is another example of isolated support for the creation of joint identity in an estate.

The design space for ICT support for democratic engagement is intertwined with social media in general. Because residents do not see democratic engagement in their estate as a defining part of their lives, it may not be feasible to bury ICT support for community building in the estate among minutes and forecasts in a dedicated system most residents never access.

## 15.7  Conclusions

In this paper we have discussed the challenges Danish residents' democracy faces with respect to participation, and we have demonstrated and discussed the potentials of addressing theses issues through ITC based solutions. We do not question the residents' meeting as the center of local democracy, but we point to ways in which ICT can make it easier, more attractive to participate in the decision processes, and we point to ways for including new voices in decision-making. In particular, the public housing sector has a democratic structure where residents' decisions have an actual effect. Thus, the sector can serve as a laboratory for the development of ICT for democracy in general.

**Acknowledgments** I want to thank my students Thomas Heath, Mikkel Kjeldsen, Anders V. Borrits and Christian B. Møller for collaboration and for providing empirical background; Henrik Korsgaard and other colleagues for discussions; people in the housing sector, including Søren Høgsberg, for collaboration and discussions over the last 20 years.

# References

1. Bertelsen OW (2013) Activating the semi-publics of tenants democracy in Danish social housing. Position paper for workshop on participatory publics in conjunction with ECSCW 2013
2. Bertelsen OW (2014) Overcoming residents opportunity apathy in Danish social housing democracy. COOP 2014 Workshop on collaborative technologies in democratic processes. Int'l Reports on socioinformatics, vol 11:1, IISI, ISSN 1861-4280
3. BL (2009) http://bl.dk/om-bl/maalsaetningsprogram-2010-2014
4. Dewey J (1954) The public and its problems. Sage Books, Chicago
5. Djajadiningrat JP, Gaver WW, Frens JW (2000) Interaction relabeling and extreme characters. Proc DIS'00. ACM
6. Hallahan K (2000) Inactive publics: the forgotten publics in public relations. Public Relat Rev 26(4):499–515
7. Heath T (2010) Digital residents' democracy – experiments with a webportal to support housing estate meetings (in Danish). Master thesis, Aarhus University
8. Høilund B (1987) Beboerdemokrati – en håndbog om boligselskaber og boliglovgivning. København, KAB
9. Jensen L, Kirkegaard O. Pedersen DO (1999) Beboerdemokrati og forvaltning i den almene boligsektor. Ideer og praksis. Statens Byggeforskningsinstitut
10. Jensen L (2006) Lokalt beboerdemokrati i den almene boligsektor – baggrund, funktion og udfordringer. Andersen, Fridberg (eds) (2006) Den almene boligsektors rolle i samfundet. SBi 2006:11 Statens Byggeforskningsinstitut
11. Kjeldsen M (2014) Supporting localized democracy, Master's thesis, Aarhus University
12. Korn M (2013) Situating engagement: ubiquitous infrastructures for in-situ civic engagement. PhD dissertation, Aarhus University
13. Lave J, Wenger E (1991) Situated learning: legitimate peripheral participation. Cambridge University Press, Cambridge
14. Levinsen K, Thøgersen M, Ibsen B (2012) Institutional reforms and voluntary associations. Scand Polit Stud 35(4):295–318
15. Lund-Andersen N (2003) Beboerdemokrati – det havde jeg aldrig tænkt på. Interviews med beboere med indvandrer- og flygtningebaggrund om deres erfaringer med beboerdemokrati i Brøndby Strand 2002–2003, Projekt Ny Viden
16. Møller CB, Borrits AV (2014) Activating the aroused: a design oriented study on engagement and participation in a social housing area. Masters thesis, Aarhus University

# Chapter 16
# The Life and Death of Design Ideas

Tone Bratteteig, Ole Kristian Rolstad, and Ina Wagner

**Abstract** The paper explores the question why a design process ends up with a particular result. We analyze a collaborative design process where different stakeholders design an urban site using a participatory design tool. Our analysis is based on Schön's view of design as a process of 'seeing-moving-seeing' combined with the concept of choice from Schütz. Analyzing the case provides an understanding of the ways in which ideas 'move' a design. We describe the dynamics of collaborative design work where design ideas are moved forward or deliberately blocked from being pursued further. We point to how design decisions are interlinked, making it possible to see how some design decisions are more important than others. Our analysis is narrative in character, but we also present a technique for visualizing the 'life and death' of design ideas.

## 16.1 Introduction

Why does a design process end up with a particular result? Why do some design ideas 'survive' and others just disappear during the process? What influences the design result? Understanding how design ideas are created, selected and concretized is interesting for educators as well as for practitioners of design, and for participatory and user-centered design in particular: how do users contribute to design? This paper provides an analysis of a collaborative process of creating design ideas for an urban site by means of a participatory design tool. It provides insights into the role of design ideas in decision-making in design and how the power relations in the design team influence the design result.

Design is often used as an 'umbrella term' for practices in different domains, e.g., architecture, urban planning, product design or software development that are in fact quite diverse and varied. Common to all of them is that they deal with 'wicked problems' [26], problems that are ill-defined and ill-structured. Since the problems

T. Bratteteig (✉) • O.K. Rolstad • I. Wagner
University of Oslo, Oslo, Norway
e-mail: tone@ifi.uio.no; ina.wagner@tuwien.ac.at

© Springer International Publishing Switzerland 2016                                          259
A. De Angeli et al. (eds.), *COOP 2016: Proceedings of the 12th International Conference on the Design of Cooperative Systems, 23–27 May 2016, Trento, Italy*,
DOI 10.1007/978-3-319-33464-6_16

to be addressed are not clear from the beginning, defining and understanding them becomes an important part of the design process. A result of this 'wickedness' is that design processes are open-ended, often exploratory, and highly complex. Designers have to deal with manifold interdependent issues – of form, function, materials, technical requirements, economic constraints, and so forth –where they may have to involve different specialists.

Urban planning is special in some ways: it is of longue-durée, typically spanning a time horizon of up to 20 years, involving stakeholders with different (professional) background and interests, hence prone to controversy and conflict. Complexity in an urban project is due to the large number of stakeholders, each of them representing diverse professional cultures, academic training, and economic logics. The designed artifacts, whether buildings, infrastructures or open spaces, are themselves complex, embedded within more and more sophisticated technologies, offering numerous services, and demanding sophisticated solutions. The problems urban projects need to address are of a multidisciplinary nature [23]. The case we discuss in this paper is particular, as it is about involving citizens in creating design ideas for an urban site. There is a long tradition of participation in urban planning (see e.g., [12]). Typically, collaboration with citizens in an urban project does not focus on specialized 'technical' solutions but on creating a vision that includes citizens' experiences and perspectives. In meeting with urban planning teams citizens may address issues such as connectivity with other places in the city, mobility and accessibility, ambience, recreational facilities, housing types, social, educational and cultural services, and the like [36].

We focus on design ideas as a way to capture designers' 'imagining what could be in the future' on a conceptual level, using metaphors, images, exemplars of solutions or artifacts, such as sketches or mock-ups. Hence, design ideas are about the choices that open up in a design project. Examining how these ideas are expressed, shared, and elaborated helps understand an important aspect of the dynamics of collaborative design, where stakeholders with different knowledge and perspectives meet and a diversity of design ideas will compete. Our study shows that in order to 'survive' a design idea has to be 'put on the table' as a representation (sketch, prototype) or – in collaborative design processes like the one we have studied – be recognized by other design participants. Within CSCW studies of design practices as varied as software development, product design and architecture have focused on the various coordinative practices that design work involves in addition to the representations and artifacts designers produce to align work that is often highly distributed. Our study is a detailed study of a collaborative design process.

The paper starts by looking more closely into some of the previous research on understanding the dynamics of collaborative design work. We then present the case, providing illustrations of the different ways in which 'ideas move design'. While most of this analysis is narrative in character, we will also describe a technique for visualizing the 'life and death' of design ideas. We conclude by examining some of the processes through which design ideas are moved forward – or blocked from being pursued further.

### 16.1.1   Understanding the Dynamics of Collaborative Design Work

Designing is a process, in which problems are set and solutions are found and evaluated. Schön [29], who has followed the projects of individual designers, looks at design work as sequences of 'seeing-moving-seeing'. A 'design move' or 'move experiment' [30] consists of the designers' evaluation of a situation, a move to change it and an evaluation of the move as a step closer to the final result. In this light a design idea is what the move is about: a suggestion for a particular (part of) a design solution to be tested and evaluated through the move. Schön stresses the evaluation part of design moves, what he calls 'reflection-in-action'. Also Goldschmidt uses the notion of design moves, which she defines as 'a step, an act, an operation, which transforms the design situation relative to the state in which it was prior to that move' [15: 89]. A design move results in the change of a representation, be it a sketch, a mock-up or a prototype.

Our notion of design idea is also grounded in what the philosopher Alfred Schütz [31] describes as choices, as design is about creating alternatives to choose from. Schütz sees choices as typical of situations that 'give rise to a decisive new experience' [31: 169]. Choices are based on a combination of projecting in the sense of anticipating 'future conduct by way of phantasying' [31: 162]. Design ideas are possible choices. These choices may be about the vision of a project or about how to implement the vision, developing solutions; they may be more conceptual or technical and detailed (see [3]. Moreover, design ideas are rarely stand-alone. They have repercussions for the design as a whole, and may strengthen or open up for some choices while closing down others. Hence, understanding decision-making in design requires looking at the interrelatedness of the different issues at stake (see [4]).

The focus on design ideas implies an interest in where they come from, how they are expressed, communicated, and shared and how they are selected. One of the insights of studies of collaborative design is that design ideas have to be represented to be noticed and to possibly carry conviction. For example: in a study of design sessions with engineering students Reid et al. [25] emphasize the power of visualizing: just verbalizing a design idea may not be sufficient; it has to be represented visually to be 'seen' and possibly stay; Lim et al. [20] define prototypes as 'purposefully formed manifestations of design ideas'; Vyas et al. [33] highlight collaborative practices of externalizing 'thoughts, of ideas and of concepts on a range of physical media'. Observing architects at work Schmidt and Wagner [28] found that the more complex a design task, the more difficult it may be to represent a design idea and this often results in a diversity of sketches, different scale models, material samples (to illustrate properties), each of which contributes to looking at a design idea from different perspectives and detailing it so that it can be evaluated. Exploring architects' uses of inspirational objects (images, sound, video, animation, 3D objects) for forming ideas, expressing qualities, and for convincing others of the viability and power of an idea Wagner [34] coined the term 'persuasive artifacts'. Cross and Cross [6] emphasize the need for designers to carry conviction for a design idea: 'As well as co-operating in the building and refining of concepts, team members may find it necessary to persuade the others of the value of a concept they particularly favour (usually a concept they generated themselves)' [6: 164]. They also stress the need to make choices between the many ideas that have been proposed.

Design ideas are emerging in what Schön [29] has described as 'reflective conversations with the materials of a situation' [29: 40]. This notion has spurred an interest in the materials designers work with and how these contribute to the formation of design ideas. This is an old idea that has been expressed by designers as influential as, e.g., Vladimir Tatlin, who 'held that design should derive from exploring and exploiting a material's intrinsic qualities, and be considering how it might combine with other materials' [11: 53]. Jorge Silvetti sees materiality as 'a precondition that promotes ideas, creativity, and pleasure in architecture, and it guides us to the loftiest aspirations of theory' (Silvetti, in [22: xvi]). Studying students of architecture at work Jacucci and Wagner [18] explore how their engaging with different materials helps them develop new design ideas. Binder et al. [1] emphasize: 'In design practice, materiality is seen as more than merely a technical property of the materials from which a building or designed artifact is made. It is a source of creativity and inspiration. Designers work out, evaluate, extend ideas through intimate contact with all kinds of materials' [1: 196].

While some authors point at the importance of inspirational resources in the creation of design ideas (e.g. [1, 18]), others examine the relationships between design ideas and creativity. In scientific work '[i]nteresting creative processes almost never result from single steps, but rather from concatenations and articulations of a complex set of interrelated moves' [17: 177–178]. A classic approach to fostering creativity (in design) is brainstorming. The effectiveness of such methods has been contested by experiments suggesting that people may generate more ideas alone than in groups [7]. A study by Sutton and Hardagon [32] at IDEO maintains that 'brainstorms give designers a chance to use, stretch, and learn a wide range of knowledge and techniques, in other words, to experience skill variety' [33: 701]. Goldschmidt and Tatsa [16] argue 'every creative outcome can be traced back to good ideas that started it off' [16: 593]. They also suggest links between ideas to be a good measure of creativity in design:

> If links are indeed important in creative processes, then we hypothesize that the more significant moves, or steps, or ideas in a process have the highest number of links to other moves or steps or ideas. We call the units that are found to possess more than a certain (threshold) number of links with other thought-units critical: e.g., critical moves, or critical ideas'. [16: 595]

The literature and our own engagement with design projects provide us with a basis for identifying and describing design ideas:

- They capture designers' 'imagining what could be in the future' on a conceptual or a solution-oriented level;
- They are the choices that come up in a design project;

- They have to been represented so that others can appreciate and critically evaluate them and they have to carry conviction;
- They often emerge in 'conversations with the materials in the situation' (Schön) and are inspired by engagements with different materials.

Few studies look into the details of how design ideas – choices – are created and selected in collaborative design projects. In Bratteteig and Wagner [5] we have used Schön's notion of design moves to explain how design decisions are arrived at: through processes of creating choices (or design ideas), selecting (deciding which of these ideas to take up), concretizing the idea in an evolving set of sketches and prototypes, and seeing/evaluating the concrete result. Each move is a step towards the final result: the overall vision or goal is the basis for evaluating each of the moves. Our observations of design moves in a collaborative urban planning workshop focus on the process of creating choices, visualizing them, and further developing some of the choices.

## 16.1.2   The Case

The case we present is a full day workshop with seven participants and two facilitators discussing and visualizing how an existing metro station (Blindern station in Oslo) could be redesigned. Hence, the project at stake was a real urban project under discussion. In preparing for its 200th anniversary in 2011, the University of Oslo, together with the metro company, had applied to the city council for funding the rebuilding of the station, and had arranged an architectural competition. The understanding was that the winning architect's drawings constitute the basis for rebuilding the station. So the participatory workshop had a real agenda – to evaluate the plan and eventually come up with ideas for change – and workshop participants were real stakeholders. One of them was from the architect firm that had won the competition for redesigning the bridge across the train tracks ('bridge architect'); a university architect (representing the university management); two students also working for the traffic information company; and students and faculty who used the station daily, representing various interests: a universal design and accessibility researcher, a bicyclist, a sound and music researcher, and a frequent user of the bridge working in a department with units located on both sides of the station. In the end the university did not receive the funding.

The participatory design tool about which we have published widely (e.g. [36]) was a round table onto which maps of different scales of the area could be placed (Fig. 16.1 left). The Oslo workshop was the last of eight workshops in different urban projects, and had a reasonably well-functioning prototype. The workshop participants were invited to view the site, discuss the existing metro station and the winning bridge, and to collaboratively visualize their design ideas by using tokens of different shapes and colors, with which they could associate different types of visual content (e.g., buildings, objects, people) and sound (e.g., café talk,

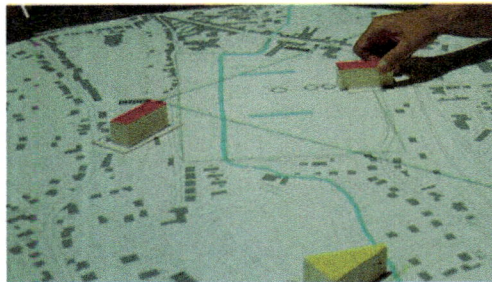

**Fig. 16.1** The PD tool: table with map (*left*) and projection on the wall (*right*) where the placed objects become part of a photographic panorama

the metro trolley stopping and starting, traffic). The content that was made available to them in the form of 'content cards' reflected the concerns the participants had voiced in interviews prior to the workshop: the difficulties for people with strollers or wheelchairs to cross the bridge, especially in winter time; the traffic around the bridge, but also the shortcomings of the present metro station which was seen as 'not welcoming'. The content cards that the designer team provided were partly also designed to stimulate participants' thinking about alternatives. The urban scenes participants created on the map were projected onto a screen where the design ideas could be seen as a more photo-realistic representation of the area (Fig. 16.1 right): in the case of this workshop three photographic panoramas of the metro station area were offered with corresponding maps, from different perspectives. The participants could also 'move' between these perspectives.

In the following section we present details from the design process, which was captured by two video cameras (one mobile and one fixed), complemented by photographs. Screenshots of the situation on the table and the projected mixed reality scenes were captured automatically. We also had the possibility to upload the scenes participants saved as a result of a particular step in building their scenarios, review the scene and listen to the sound. In our analysis we used all this workshop material together with video, which is our main resource (see also [27]).

While other publications about the participatory tool look more into issues of spatiality, representation and hapticity (how the tangible interface of the tool influenced collaborative envisioning, e.g. [37]), in this paper we are particularly interested in the design ideas workshop participants proposed and represented, and how they were received: did anyone confirm the idea, build on it, add to it, argue for or against it? Some patterns emerged and helped us identify several trajectories for the design ideas.

### 16.1.3   Collaborative Design of a New Metro Station

The area that was the object of this workshop includes a metro station, which in this part of the city runs over ground; a bridge for pedestrians and cyclists crossing the

**Fig. 16.2** Photo of metro station (*left*) with the winning architect's 3D model (*right*)

**Fig. 16.3** *Upper row*: newspaper stand at the platform (*left*); platform as information space (*middle*), convenience store turned into café (*right*), *lower row*: sketch of bridge (*left*); placing a stage with musicians (*right*)

track (Fig. 16.2 left), for which a new design had been created (Fig. 16.2 right); as well as the different paths and roads leading to the station. Workshop participants generated different design results for different parts of the area.

One idea that came up early in the workshop was based on the participants agreeing that the existing metro station was not welcoming. The first design move was to place a newspaper stand close to the metro station and, while observing its impact, to change its scale and position (Fig. 16.3 upper left). This led to questioning a building, which is currently used as a small convenience store: maybe it could be turned into a welcoming place and information center. The next move consisted in placing the newspaper stand closer to the building, linking it with sound. Participants returned several times to the convenience store, finally turning it into a café with indoor and outdoor seating (Fig. 16.3 upper right).

**Fig. 16.4** Animated flow leading across the track (*left*); newspaper stand amidst flows (*right*)

The main design task was to discuss and eventually improve the new bridge design. The 'bridge architect' had provided a 3D image of the 'winning bridge' (Fig. 16.2 right). As it was too time-consuming to render, the visual artist in the project team (a painter) made two sketches of it, changing the character of the bridge into something light and open (Fig. 16.3 lower left). Positioning the bridge across the train tracks required some patience. It involves finding the right viewpoint in terms of angle of vision and distance. Alternative bridge designs that had been prepared by the researcher team to help participants probe new solutions were not considered.

Participants started placing flows of people, cyclists and cars on the paths close to the bridge and across it, an affordance of the participatory tool (Fig. 16.4). But an individual design move by the 'bridge architect' made them return briefly to the question of making the area more welcoming. He placed a small stage with musicians representing 'entertainment' between the bridge and the convenience store building.

The flows that were rather prominent in the mixed reality scene drew the attention back to the bridge itself. After a long discussion on how to ensure access to the bridge for people in wheelchairs, as well as the safety of pedestrians on a bridge, which is also used by cyclists, participants turned back to the station and the adjacent building but looking at it from the bridge (with another map and panorama). They agreed that they wanted people to maybe stop at the station, meet there, get information and buy newspapers or coffee – 'so it's a mingling area instead'. The newspaper stand was moved closer to the platform and the 'traffic jungle of pedestrians, cyclists and cars' (Fig. 16.4).

Later the universal access researcher brought the conversation back to the need for an information center. Her idea was to envision it as a quieter place with better lighting, tactile information, maps and dynamic information available. She suggested establishing information posts on both sides of the station, an idea that the 'bridge architect' picked up immediately, saying that they should use the area under the bridge, a move supported by the local resident. He immediately started

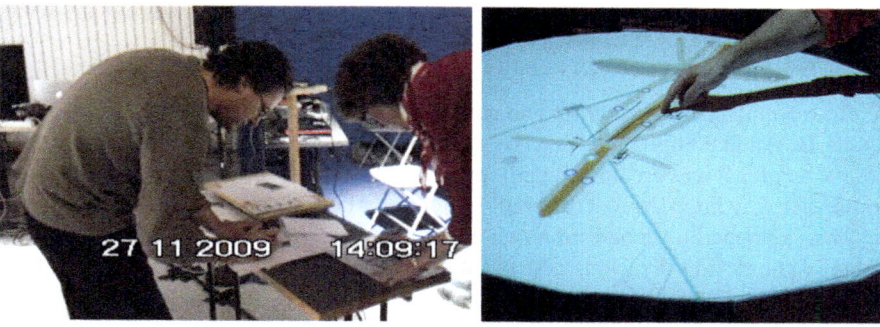

**Fig. 16.5** Bridge architect producing sketch (*left*), placing his sketch on the table (*right*)

visualizing the station as an information space, producing a series of sketches of information devices, such as 3D map of the area, a signpost and a poster wall (see Fig. 16.5 left). He placed these sketches on both platforms, taking great care in placing, sizing and coloring these sketch objects. All workshop participants appreciated the resulting scene (Fig. 16.2 middle) as a main collaborative design result.

## 16.1.4   Ideas Move the Design

Design ideas need support from others to be taken up and further developed, a process by which they often change. However, not all design ideas, even those that are taken up by others, make it into the design result. This also depends on how individual participants manage to place their ideas, concretizing them, and have them accepted. Looking closely into this dynamic makes power issues come to the fore. In urban planning, which is highly political this is an important perspective.

Switching our attention from the design ideas to those that suggested and eventually concretized them, we observed several strategies for influencing the 'life and death' of design ideas. Two of these strategies: blocking ideas by preventing them from being represented visually and further explored and forming alliances, are often used in conjunction. 'Agenda control' [2] is another strategy of exercising of power in a more subtle way: controlling who is invited to the workshop, what is discussed and who decides the topics, which solutions are possible, hence, which problems are defined (and judged relevant) and therefore addressed.

Let us first look at examples of blocking design ideas. Both architects used this strategy several times to prevent ideas that would have impacted the new station area and bridge design from getting seriously considered.

> The universal access researcher repeatedly mentioned the difficulties for wheelchair users to access the bridge, climbing up the hill 'because like it is today you are going up this slope like this and I observed several people, one man with you know very heavy bags and so on and, and he seemed to be too …'.

The 'bridge architect', interrupting her: 'But actually the road that goes to B is steeper than the regulations for a normal new construction'.
Bicyclist: 'So it is an illegal road!' <excerpt 1 from field notes w. transcripts>

Both architects then went into an elaborate argument presenting the new solution as 'perfect' and compliant with the regulations and claiming how all other solutions would be illegal and create a huge impact, destroying the area. In this way a design move that may have led to a different (potentially better) solution was blocked.

This happened a second time, when the universal access researcher questioned some of the design decisions concerning the bridge, and commented that the lack of access ramps or elevators to shorten the distance crossing the bridge from one platform to the other, was not a good solution for people in wheelchairs or people pushing strollers.

The local architect immediately countered: 'Elevators in the outdoors function extremely badly here'.
When the universal access researcher pointed to the example of a well functioning outdoor elevator in the city, he stated: '<The metro company> don't want it, outside elevators, their malfunctioning is … too high'. <excerpt 2 from field notes w. transcripts>

This is also an example of participants forming alliances for and against design ideas. The two architects very often acted as allies, agreeing on and against ideas.

When some participants blocked design ideas, they did this through anticipating restrictions (real and imagined ones), simple lack of interest in an issue or by 'putting the foot down', when their own design ideas were challenged. Practical argumentation was the most used blocking mechanism against any (new) design idea. Very concrete problems concerning garbage or the current owner of the convenience store came up as arguments against a new café. We also heard the metro company being used as an ally against an idea (they will not allow outside elevators) and the more general: 'I don't think the authorities will like it'.

These small examples highlight power issues in design. As design ideas need more than one person to survive, participants sometimes behave in strategic ways. Often the blocking was successful, since both architects used their power/ knowledge [10].

The universal access researcher and the bicyclist also joined forces, making critical comments and suggestions for increased accessibility. Only their strong alliance made the 'bridge architect' include some of their arguments in 'his' solution. This happened, for example, during the long design session about how to accommodate both, pedestrians and cyclists, on the new bridge when the universal access designer and the bicyclist used agenda control as a strategy, insisting on a focus on flows, an affordance offered by the participatory tool. Creating and discussing flows (see e.g. Fig. 16.4) turned out to be particular useful in addressing accessibility issues. When the 'bridge architect' realized that potentially dangerous situations between pedestrians and cyclists could arise, he immediately tried to integrate their arguments into 'his' design. He used his 'power to', putting transparent paper on the map and sketching his new solution whilst talking (Fig. 16.5). The distinction between 'power to' (agency) and 'power over' (dominating others) made by Pitkin [25] is useful for discussing power in design [5] – acknowledging that these two forms of power interact.

In this situation the 'bridge architect' deliberately ignored the participatory tool, resorting to an architect's way of producing an architectural drawing. This pushed the other participants into the position of onlookers. Apart from commenting they could only watch the architect sketching. He made a redesign move based on his 'seeing' the unintended consequences of the existing bridge design, hence blocking a more radical questioning of his design that may have led to a different type of bridge. In this way ideas and arguments against the bridge were transformed into improvements of the original solution: The bridge remained 'on the table'. In this case the 'bridge architect's 'power to' enabled him to maintain his 'power over' the solution.

The workshop was an occasion to see different kinds of power 'at work': the 'power to' of the professional designer to concretize his design ideas in 'his way', circumventing the participatory tool; the different power/knowledges of the participants: architectural expertise, expertise in universal access issues but also practical experience (using the bridge with a bicycle). Both architects used 'normalizing' [10] as a strategy: stressing conventions, regulations, and 'how things are being done normally'. We noticed also blocking, preventing an idea from being taken up as a type of agenda control. The universal access specialist and the bicycle enthusiast were good at breaking the agenda control, insisting on utilizing the potential of the PD tool, looking at flows and accessibility issues.

Design ideas do not flow freely. They are subject to different types of interventions upon which their 'fate' depends. Design ideas that were put on the table, concretized as parts of the urban scene that the participants built, stayed there. However, many of the design ideas brought forward by one of the participants were not noticed by others and just 'fell to the ground'.

### 16.1.5   Design Ideas Influence Each Other

Starting from this short story we now look deeper into how design ideas were put forward, taken up by others, expanded and further developed. The design process is iterative: participants return to the idea many times in the course of the workshop, expanding it. Some design ideas, such as turning the convenience store into a café, lasted throughout the process: they can be seen in the design result. Other ideas, such as the welcoming and information areas, were merged or built on in several rounds by several participants; hence they changed their shape during the process.

According to Flach [8], there are two dimensions that contribute to problem space complexity in an urban design project: first, the number of variables, parameters, and degrees of freedom of a system; second, the nature of the interdependencies between these dimensions. Hence, it is important to understand the consequences of design choices. They may open up new choices but also narrow down the design space, precluding alternative choices. These are not neutral to the design process. Looking into the nature of the relations between the choices – the linkages – helps understand how they create a particular kind of dynamic in a design process. Taking up a design idea (or choice) is a design decision.

The fact that design ideas influence each other has been observed by others studying design work. Goldschmidt [13, 14] seeks to capture interdependencies between design ideas by performing a 'linkographic' analysis. This involves identifying design ideas, evaluating their contributions to a design task, and examining (and quantifying) their links with other ideas, the assumption being that the number of links makes a design idea stronger. This also implies that some design ideas are more influential than others. We can take a step further in analyzing the choices made in a collaborative design project by taking their nature into account, not just 'counting' them. Langley et al. [19] propose to look at decision-making in organizations as 'a complex network of issues involving a whole host of linkages, more or less tightly coupled' [19: 275]. They have identified different types of decision-linkages: sequential, precursive and lateral ones, and developed a whole taxonomy of linkages.

Almost all the choices participants in the urban design workshop made had *sequential* linkages, which Langley at al. define as 'interrelationships between different decisions concerning the same issue at different points in time' [19: 271]: one design decision spurs other, smaller or bigger decisions. *Snowballing* – a series of smaller decisions 'snowballing' into a major one – is a particular kind of sequential linkage. The design moves towards the station as an information center can be considered as a 'snowballing' of small design moves: from the newspaper stand, the stage with music, the café, through the consideration of flows and accessibility issues, to an expanded version of the initial design idea to have the information points on both platforms. In retrospect these steps (and the detours they implied) all 'snowballed' towards the end result.

*Recurrence* – the same or similar situation recurs – is another type of sequential linkage quite common in design work. It can be found in the instances when designers after an unsuccessful move have to go back to a previous state in order to take the design in a new direction. Wagner [35] calls this 'meandering': an oscillating between preliminary fixing and re-opening. An example is the unresolved conflicts of the bridge design (Fig. 16.5), which were recurrently addressed during the iterative process of redesign. Separating the flows of pedestrians (some with wheelchairs, others pushing strollers) from the flows of bicycles (some of them fast and potentially dangerous) was an issue not easy to resolve.

*Precursive* linkages concern decisions that are linked across issues and time where 'a decision on one issue affects future decisions on other issues' [19: 270]. Six different types of precursive linkages can be distinguished: enabling, evoking, cascading, merging, preempting, and learning. An *enabling* decision makes certain outcomes more likely. We noted this in the workshop when the decision to keep working with the existing convenience store by the metro station increased the likelihood of integrating the building in the design – and this is visible in the

**Table 16.1**   Overview of decision linkages

| Sequential linkages | Snowballing | A series of smaller design ideas snowball into a large design idea |
|---|---|---|
| | Recurring | When prior choices have not resolved the issues at stake, a similar decision situation may recur |
| Precursive linkages | Enabling | A decision may remove 'blocks', opening the way for additional options |
| | Preempting | A decision may render other issues irrelevant or obsolete – this can be enabling or constraining |
| | Cascading | A decision results in a series of (often unforeseen) problems that need to be resolved |
| | Evoking | A decision evokes new problems and opportunities |

design result. *Preempting* linkages occur when 'one decision may render other issues irrelevant, obsolete' [19: 274]. In the urban planning workshop preempting linkages were created when design ideas were blocked, rendering other related issues irrelevant, leading to the 'death' of the design idea. One may consider the existence of the new bridge design as a preempting linkage, which made alternative ideas obsolete from the very beginning. The new bridge design remained on the table. It had a similar effect as a technical decision in an IT design project, which already has been materialized in a prototype [5]. The existence of the bridge design also had a *cascading* effect, creating the need to solve a series of complex technical issues. This narrowed the design space with potential alternative solutions being excluded from being considered.

*Evoking* linkages are found when 'one decision may evoke new problems or opportunities'. The decision to explore the traffic flows around the metro station area, led to the discovery of problems, creating *learning* linkages, which in turn provided the participants with the opportunity to redesign the station to resolve the problem. Finally, the *merging* of initiatives and ideas can create larger design ideas: making the area more welcoming was combined with the idea of providing an information center.

*Lateral* linkages are linkages between organizational issues that share resources (*pooled*) or context (*contextual*). Since the design process constitutes the context for most of the design move-decisions we do not discuss them here (Table 16.1).

Looking at the different kinds of linkages helps understand that design ideas do not just 'appear' but have repercussions: new problems may be evoked, alternative solutions precluded or a promising new choice enabled.

## 16.1.6   Visualizing the 'Fate' of Design Ideas

A visual representation of the 'fate' of design ideas is given in Fig. 16.6 [27]. Design ideas are represented as colored circles, with different colors standing for different participants. The circles are individual contributions, merging into pie charts when

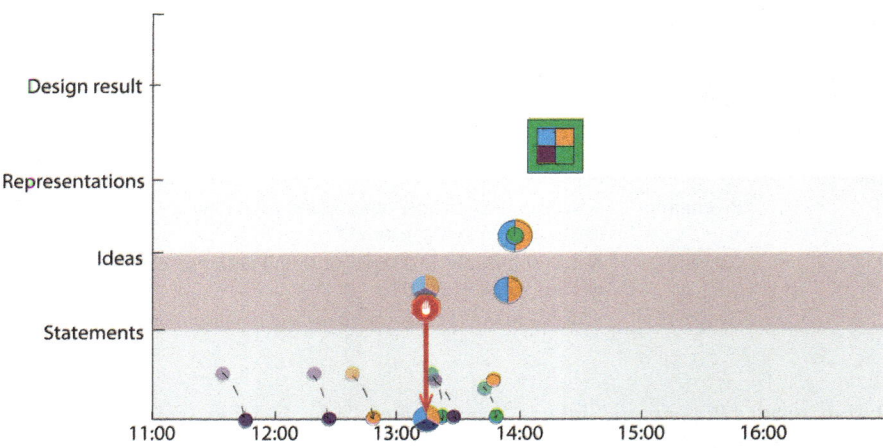

**Fig. 16.6** A representation of the idea development leading to a design result (https://www.mn.uio.no/ifi/forskning/grupper/design/aktuelt/animation-with-text.mp4)

several participants elaborate on the design idea or merging into a new, expanded idea. A circle 'moves up' to become a design idea when it is confirmed by another participant and/or represented visually in the urban scene. Then it may be expanded, resulting in a more elaborate representation and eventually become part of the final design result (the square). A sequence of these graphical representations gives an impression of the dynamics of the design process [27].

The local resident (purple) suggests ideas that nobody takes up. The bicyclist (orange) also provides suggestions, which turn into a design idea when the universal design researcher (light blue) joins him as an ally. However, the local architect (red) stops the idea (see excerpt 2). The alliance 'orange-light blue' adds a design idea (the flow debate), which the architect (green) incorporates into his design (green added to the alliance circle). Later, an alliance between the three and the local resident (purple) ends up with a final design result that stays (square).

Many design ideas fall to 'the ground', for a number of reasons; in fact, most individual suggestions for design ideas in the workshop were just mentioned once and then not followed up in any way. An idea can get left behind when the participants pursue an alternative or competing idea, leaving the idea to slowly fade away: design ideas die when they are replaced by new ideas. Ideas 'die' when no one grabs hold of them; the idea may float around in the conversation for a period of time before it slowly falls to the ground (like in a brainstorming session where a large number of ideas are thrown into the conversation and only those that are represented visually have a chance to 'survive').

In the diagram the density of interactions with a design idea is captured in the form of increasing circle size. A larger circle size indicates a stronger and better-supported design idea. Ideas that are visualized on the table are even stronger: ideas that are a part of the final design result represent the strongest ideas, i.e. the ideas with the highest support among the participants. The final result is represented by a square. Design ideas that were not represented, expanded, contextualized or changed properties ended up as individual initiatives that were not recognized by others or discussed further.

## 16.2   Conclusions

Architectural design has long been dominated by the 'star system' [9], where the planning and detailing work is largely about concretizing the design concept of one architect. Urban planning differs, as the political stakes are high and the issues too complex to be addressed by one specialist only. Bringing stakeholders around the table, as we did in the urban planning workshop we describe in this paper, means that many design ideas are generated. Which of these ideas make it into the vision for an urban site, depends on many factors, some of which we have been able to identify.

Our analysis has looked at design ideas as choices that participants bring to a design session and at decision-making in design as selecting among those choices to further develop them. Following several design ideas that were brought up in the workshop enabled us to trace the different paths these ideas took, from an individual statement to an idea that is taken up by other participants, to being represented (put on the table), and (in some cases) making it into the final design result. In visualizing these paths we could see some of the circles representing design ideas rise and grow, and that the larger a circle and the higher it rose, the more probable it was that it became part of the end result.

The design process we describe was by no means linear. Trying to understand its dynamics, we identified several elements.

Ideas need to find support. Often, this requires that they are 'put on the table', hence visualized. Our analysis confirms previous research on the power of visualizing (e.g., [13, 34]. The participatory tool that was used in the workshop had been designed to give lay participants a voice in a discussion that is normally dominated by experts. Hence, visually representing a design idea by 'putting it on the table' was made easy for the lay participants. However, we also saw how an expert ignored the tool in order to be able to appropriate arguments in favor of his solution.

Another element is complexity and how a design idea may expand into a solution or close the design space. We show how design decisions influence each other: evoking new problems that need to be resolved due to unforeseen consequences; opening up alternative choices or preempting them; several small ideas snowballing into a large one, and so forth. Understanding the nature of decision linkages in design – something which may only be possible in retrospect – captures an important aspect of (collaborative) design work: the consequences of a design move for other moves in the process to a design result.

However, it is not just the specific nature of different design ideas that moves the design process. We also highlighted issues of power: different participants with different power/knowledges form alliances, promoting or blocking design ideas, exercising agenda control. In particular the 'power to' of professional designers allows them act as experts in their own language. Our analysis also points to the power of 'normalizing': the ability to establish or refer to particular norms as the right way of 'seeing' as an important resource in collaborative design work. McDonnell [21] in her analysis of the work of two designers collaborating in software development points at the importance of 'signaling tentativeness' in collaborative design, as well as what she describes as 'encapsulating' a

> disagreement without losing sight of the fact that it exists. The encapsulation does not support the design of the software by data abstraction very well, but does serve the collaboration itself by providing a way of avoiding having to resolve disagreement sufficiently for designing to continue. [21: 61]

The strategies we identified were more confrontational. That workshop participants made use of 'oppositional moves' may have to do with the fact that for some of them (the 'bridge architect' in particular) the stakes in the project were high. In workshops conducted in the context of other urban projects, where participants had more space for imagining and exploring from different viewpoints, we observed more 'collaborative moves' [5].

The case we discuss in this paper is special, since it concerns a participatory tool for collaborative design that provides lay participants with the possibility to make their own design moves. The case demonstrates that there is a number of ways to create design ideas and influence design decisions and hence the design result.

# References

1. Binder T, Ehn P, Jacucci G, De Michelis G, Linde P, Wagner I (2011) Design things. MIT Press, Cambridge, MA
2. Borum F, Enderud H (1981) Konflikter i organisationer: belyst ved studier af edb-systemarbejde (in Danish: conflicts in organisations, illustrated by cases of computer systems design). Nyt Nordisk Forlag Arnold Busck, Copenhagen
3. Bratteteig T, Stolterman E (1997) Design in groups – and all that jazz. In: Kyng M, Mathiassen L (eds) Computers and design in context. MIT Press, Cambridge, pp 289–316
4. Bratteteig T, Wagner I (2012) Spaces for participatory creativity. CoDesign 8(2–3):105–126
5. Bratteteig T, Wagner I (2014) Disentangling participation: power and decision-making in participatory design. Springer International
6. Cross N, Cross C (1995) Observations of teamwork and social processes in design. Des Stud 16(2):143–170
7. Diehl M, Stroebe W (1987) Productivity loss in brainstorming groups: toward the solution of a riddle. J Pers Soc Psychol 53(3):497–509
8. Flach JM (2012) Complexity: learning to muddle through. Cogn Tech Work 14(3):187–197
9. Forsyth A (2006) In praise of Zaha: women, partnership, and the star system in architecture. J Archit Educ 60(2):63–65
10. Foucault M (1982) The subject and power. Crit Inq 8(4):777–795
11. Fredrickson L (1999) Vision and material practice: Vladimir Tatlin and the design of everyday objects. Des Issues 15(1):49–74
12. Fung A (2006) Varieties of participation in complex governance. Public Adm Rev 66(1):66–75

13. Goldschmidt G (1996) The designer as a team of one. In: Cross et al (eds) Analyzing design activity. Wiley, Chichester, pp 65–92
14. Goldschmidt G (2014) Linkography. Unfolding the design process. MIT Press, Cambridge
15. Goldschmidt G, Weil M (1998) Contents and structure in design reasoning. Des Issues 14(3):85–100
16. Goldschmidt G, Tatsa D (2005) How good are good ideas? Correl Des Creat Des Stud 26:593–611
17. Gruber HE (2005) Afterword. In: Feldman DH (ed) Beyond universals in cognitive development. Ablex Publishing Corp, Norwood, pp 177–178
18. Jacucci G, Wagner I (2007) Performative roles of materiality for collective creativity. Proceedings of the 6th ACM SIGCHI conference on creativity & cognition. ACM 73–82
19. Langley A, Mintzberg H, Pitcher P, Posada E, Saint-Macary J (1995) Opening up decision making: the view from the black stool. Organ Sci 6(3):260–279
20. Lim Y-K, Stolterman E, Tenenberg J (2008) The anatomy of prototypes: prototypes as filters, prototypes as manifestations of design ideas. ACM Trans Comput-Hum Interact (TOCHI) 15(2):1–27
21. McDonnell J (2012) Accommodating disagreement: a study of effective design collaboration. Des Stud 33(1):44–63
22. Mori T (2002) Immaterial/ultramaterial: architecture, design, and materials. Harvard Design School/George Braziller, New York
23. Özdirlik B, Terrin J-J (eds) (2015) La conception en question. La place des usagers dans le processus du projet. Éditions de L'Aube, Paris
24. Pitkin HF (1972) Wittgenstein and justice. University of California Press, Berkeley
25. Reid FJ, Reed S, Edworthy J (1999) Design visualization and collaborative interaction in undergraduate engineering teams. Int J Cogn Ergon 3(3):235–259
26. Rittel HWJ, Webber MM (1974) Wicked problems. Man-Made Futur 26(1):272–280
27. Rolstad OK (2014) The life and death of design ideas. An analysis of the Oslo color table workshop. Master thesis, University of Oslo
28. Schmidt K, Wagner I (2004) Ordering systems: coordinative practices and artifacts in architectural design and planning. Computer Supported Cooperative Work (CSCW) 13.5–6:349–408
29. Schön DA (1983) The reflective practitioner. Basic books
30. Schön DA, Wiggins G (1992) Kinds of seeing in designing. Des Stud 1(2):593–611
31. Schütz A (1951) Choosing among projects of action. Philos Phenomenol Res 12(2):161–184
32. Sutton RI, Hargadon A (1996) Brainstorming groups in context: effectiveness in a product design firm. Adm Sci Q 41(4):685–718
33. Vyas D, Heylen D, Nijholt A, Van Der Veer G (2009) Collaborative practices that support creativity in design. Proceedings of ECSCW 2009. Springer, London, pp 151–170
34. Wagner I (2000) Persuasive artefacts in architectural design and planning. Collaborative design. Springer, London, pp 379–389
35. Wagner I (2004) Open planning – a reflection on methods. In: Boland R, Collopy F (eds) Managing as designing. Stanford University Press, Stanford, pp 153–163
36. Wagner I, Basile M, Ehrenstrasser L, Maquil V, Terrin J-J, Wagner M (2009) Supporting community engagement in the city: urban planning in the MR-tent. In: Proceedings of the fourth international conference on communities and technologies. ACM 185–194
37. Wagner I (2012) Building urban narratives: collaborative site-seeing and envisioning in the MR tent. Comput Supported Coop Work (CSCW) 21(1):1–42

# Chapter 17
# "Matters of Concern" as Design Opportunities

María Menéndez-Blanco and Antonella De Angeli

**Abstract**  Public design can be understood as a perspective that follows democratic approaches to design, addresses collective conditions, and supports the formation of publics. In this paper, we present our efforts to engage with a public design perspective in a case study addressing the topic of dyslexia. The paper contributes to the understanding of the process of articulation of matters of concern in public design. In addition, the results can be considered as opportunities for design that can serve as inspiration for other projects addressing the topic of dyslexia.

## 17.1  Introduction

In the book "The reflective practitioner", Schön [15] suggested that design happens in "messy and problematic situations" and, therefore, should not be seen as a systematic approach to solving well-formed problems. He argued that design happens in a space that emerges through the interaction between the designer and the design environment. In this perspective, the design process is defined as a dialog between the designer, the object of design and the environment. Through this dialog, the design environment becomes a "lived landscape" that facilitates the expression of "what can be through the exercising of what is." [17].

This understanding of design as a dialog is consistent with the view of design as contributing to the articulation of matters of fact into matters of concern. In recent years, a small but active part of the design literature has investigated the role of matters of concern in the design process. For example, [1] discussed matters of concern as a way to elaborate on the controversies in participatory design approaches to social innovation and [5] elaborated on design as a way to express

M. Menéndez-Blanco (✉) • A. De Angeli
InterAction Laboratory, Department of Information Engineering and Computer Science,
University of Trento, Via Sommarive 9, 38123 Trento, Italy
e-mail: menendez@disi.unitn.it; deangeli@disi.unitn.it

© Springer International Publishing Switzerland 2016
A. De Angeli et al. (eds.), *COOP 2016: Proceedings of the 12th International Conference on the Design of Cooperative Systems, 23–27 May 2016, Trento, Italy*,
DOI 10.1007/978-3-319-33464-6_17

matters of concern by showing its factors and consequences. In this paper, we present the articulation of matters of concern as part of a project addressing the topic of dyslexia. The results of this articulation process can be considered opportunities for design that can help as inspiration for further research on the topic.

## 17.2   Related Work

### 17.2.1   Public Design

The concept "public design" has been used mainly in fields such as architecture, urban planning and service design to refer to design for public contexts. The concept has been recently introduced to the HCI community by the work of Di Salvo and colleagues [5]. In "The Public Design Workshop", a research studio at Georgia Institute of Technology lead by Carl DiSalvo, technology is used as a tool to articulate issues, contribute to the construction of publics, provide new ways of empowering communities (e.g. homeless community), and stimulate reflection around issues of public interest (e.g. air pollution). In this context, public design is described as an approach that, through issue articulation and problem framing, contributes to the formation of publics understood in Dewey's terms as "a group of people who, in facing a similar problems, recognize it and organize themselves to address it" [4]. These few papers have investigated how design activities can facilitate the formation of publics [11], however further work is required in this direction.

Public design is a relevant perspective to the CSCW community because it deals with collectives, and investigates how they relate to each other and the potential role of technology. Indeed, public design share important characteristics with other CSCW related design perspectives, such as community-based design [16]. However there are also important differences between the two of them: community-based design deals with established communities, while public design deals with the formation of new assemblies of people who face a similar issue and organize themselves to address it [4]. In addition, the concept of community entitles a shared space, being this physical or virtual (as in the case of online communities), and a shared goal and identity [14]. This shared identity is reflected in shared interests and/or practices [14]. On the other hand, publics are heterogeneous and issue-driven [16]. In order to explain this heterogeneity, some authors argue that there is not a public but a multiciplity of publics [4]. As opposed to communities, publics are issue-driven and therefore tend to emerge around controversial issues. These characteristics suggest that adopting a public design perspective entails embracing methods to facilitate articulation of these issues from different actors. In order to address this objective, the concepts of matters of fact and matters of concern seem like a path worth pursuing.

## 17.2.2  *"Matters of Concern" in Design*

In 2004, Bruno Latour elaborated on the concepts of matters of fact and matters of concern and argued that the former refers to issues that claim to report objective conditions, whereas the later refers to "highly complex, historically situated, richly diverse" political and social conditions [10]. Following this line of thinking, he proposed that matters of fact could be articulated into matters of concern. Ever since, the concept of matters of concern has been used in a few studies within the design community [e.g. 1, 2], and in particular in public design [5]. In these studies, the concept is instrumental to the articulation issues, understood as complex situations that involve several actors, or groups of actors, who have different positions with respect to the issue, and to the formation of publics [11]. An important characteristic is that the elaboration of the space of design in terms of matters of concern entails an understanding of design as a process of dealing with issues, rather than solving problems [5]. Some of these studies investigate how technology design can help express matters of concern [5] and some others engage with the concept as a way to analyse, communicate and reflect on relevant actors and controversial issues [2]. Even though the articulation of matters of concern seems to be an important aspect of the design process, these studies do not show how this articulation can be actually attempted.

The contribution of this paper consists in the articulation of matters of concern in the context of a project dealing with the topic of dyslexia. Furthermore, this articulation process can be considered as facilitating the emergence of design opportunities that might facilitate public formation. Finally, the identification of these matters of concern constitutes a contribution of its own since it might be interesting to address them in the context of other projects addressing the topic of dyslexia.

## 17.3  Case Study

The case study deals with the development of a physical and virtual space around the topic of scholastic inclusion, understood as the acknowledgement and facilitation of different ways of learning in a scholastic context, with a special focus on dyslexia. The process of design was initiated by different research activities that were aimed at understanding existing controversies, with an emphasis on the relevant actors and their relationships.

## 17.3.1  *SPAZIOd*

The activities presented in this paper are being developed in the context of Città Educante (2014–2017), a program that aims to contribute to the infrastructuring of a city as a learning place. This vision is an alternative to existing technology-centric approaches of the "Smart City" [7], which tend to focus on system development and data gathering, and often overlook cultural, societal and individual aspects [7]. Città Educante covers three main thematic areas: school/education, society and technology. These thematic areas envision activities that contribute to the development of an active, welcoming and reflective city where technology is seen as a mean and not as a goal. As part of our involvement in the project we have started SPAZIOd. This project wants to address the difficulties that the current educational system faces when dealing with different ways of learning, with a special focus on dyslexia. The choice of starting this project was grounded on the suitability of the topic to the Città Educante program and a personal and professional interest of the researchers involved.

The project is developed in a small region in North Italy, where the local government has an especially powerful position. In addition, the project was timely situated in a moment in which new educational policies mandated a Content and Language Integrated Learning methodology in German and English. This approach prescribes teaching a language and a subject at the same time (e.g. teaching mathematics in German). The trilingual policy was launched in September 2015 and encountered fierce resistance from teachers and parents. A source of controversy was that the project did not make any reference to learners with different ways of learning. These characteristics render SPAZIOd as a case of public design because it addresses a collective condition that involves many different actors that have diverse, and often conflicting, views on the same matter. Interestingly, the conflicting views are not only related to the particular setting of the project but also to the topic of dyslexia.

## 17.3.2   The Dyslexia Debate

In their recent book "The dyslexia debate" [6], Elliott and Grigorenko describe how dyslexia has been a source of controversy for a long time. Even though experts agree that dyslexia relates to a difficulty in decoding and/or producing written language, there is no generally agreed definition, nor shared understanding, of its nature and causes, and little is known on how to address it in practice [6]. This lack of consensus might have raised some skepticism, reaching the point that in 2009 a British Member of the Parliament claimed that dyslexia was a myth invented to excuse poor teaching in schools [3]. In spite of the lack of an agreed definition, there are shared underlying conditions that are commonly considered when doing a certification of dyslexia. These conditions include IQ equal or superior to the average, no physical disability (e.g. visual impairment), adequate schooling and not being at a socio-economic disadvantage [6]. However, certification is not free of controversy either, as it is subject to interpretation and largely affected by the context. This complexity might partially explain the large variability in dyslexia incidence, which ranges from 5–8 % to 20 % [6].

In Italy, the context in which the research reported in this paper is situated, the dyslexia debate has been exacerbated in the last few years due to a recent law. Particularly, the Italian Law 170, approved in 2010, recognizes dyslexia as a "learning disability" and provides a set of criteria for diagnosis, requirements for teachers' formation, didactic instruments and support to families.

In the design community, there are only a few studies that deal with the topic of dyslexia. Most of them present specific design artefacts that support dyslexic children in different activities [8, 13, 18]. However, to the best of our understanding, the topic of dyslexia has not yet been addressed as an example of public design, which understands the issue as a collective condition that might trigger the formation of a public.

### 17.3.3 Method

Several research interventions were carried out to collect data regarding the context. In this paper, we build on ethnographic activities performed by the authors, who participated in several events around the topic of dyslexia (e.g. seminars at schools and meetings organized by a parent group), analysed online data collected from websites and social network groups, and performed eight semi-structured interviews. While being involved in these activities, we realised that the topic entailed an important emotional component, especially for children. Most of the activities involved actors and activities related to children up to 14 years old. For this reason, and based on ethical considerations, we decided not to involve children directly in the initial research activities.

Eight interviews were conducted with a group of parents, teachers, educators and local government officers. Parents and educators were approached due to personal knowledge; teachers were selected based on the recommendation of the two interviewed officers. One officer was responsible for Inclusion and Equality and the other for the implementation of the trilingual policy in schools. The interview script was designed building on the data collected through ethnographic activities. In particular, it addressed potentially controversial topics emerged during the analysis of this data, such as the understanding of dyslexia as well as the certification process and public opinion.

At the end of the interviews, participants were invited to engage in an actor mapping activity. This activity was aimed at identifying relevant actors, understand how they perceived themselves and others, and facilitate the emergence of potential controversies. In public design terms, this activity enabled the identification of potential, or existing, publics and how they related to each other. To fulfill this objective, participants were given ten post-its with the names of the relevant actors, and an empty A3 cardboard. The list of actors was created using the actors who were mentioned during the seminars and meetings. This list included teachers, children, parents, associations, schools, local government, researchers, local health department, and private companies. In addition, participants were provided with a set of empty post-its, if they wished to add any other actor. Then, they were invited to create a map of the topic of dyslexia, with the actors and their relationships, while thinking aloud [19]. They were told that it was not necessary to use all given actors and that they could add new ones as they wished.

All participants but one allowed recording the audio, which included the interview and the actor mapping activity, and using the data for further analysis. Interviews were conducted by one of the authors; an external researcher transcribed the audio recordings. The primary data of the analysis presented in this paper is the interview transcript. The data was coded using Atlast.ti and thematically analysed in two steps [3]. First, one of the authors coded the transcription individually using open codes to identify recurrent themes, such as "certifications take a long time" and "parents of DSA children are usually very proactive". The themes were consolidated through comparisons across the interviews and discussions with the authors. In the second step, the themes were used to further identify central statements in the transcripts. The analysis continued through meaning condensation and interpretation [9], yielding to the identification of different matters of concerns.

We triangulated this data with our notes from the observation of several events. They included a 4-h public meeting organized in Trento by the Italian Dyslexia Association, where two bachelor students shared their University experience with parents, younger students and teachers (in order of frequency of attendance) and a 2-h presentation organized in Madrid by the Madrid Dyslexia Association. We also attended a 2-h presentation hosted by a local school where a local teacher association presented their homework support services offered, and 8 h of meeting of a peer-support parent association. Furthermore, one of the authors had personal experience with the topic [12].

## 17.4  Understanding the Design Space

### 17.4.1  Actors Mapping

During the actor mapping activity, most of the participants created a main cluster formed by teachers, parents and children (Fig. 17.1). In most cases, participants thought that this was the main cluster and placed it at the center of the map. However, for some teachers, the school should be considered the main actor, and therefore placed in the center of the map. In this interpretation, the school was regarded as an institutional and central hub that mediated among different actors and clusters of actors.

Regardless of where they positioned the school within the map, most of the participants embraced the vision of the school as a central hub. Following this line of thinking, they described that the school should act as mediator, facilitating communication between parents and teachers. However, the extent to which this happened in practice was perceived as limited and influenced by a problematic relationship

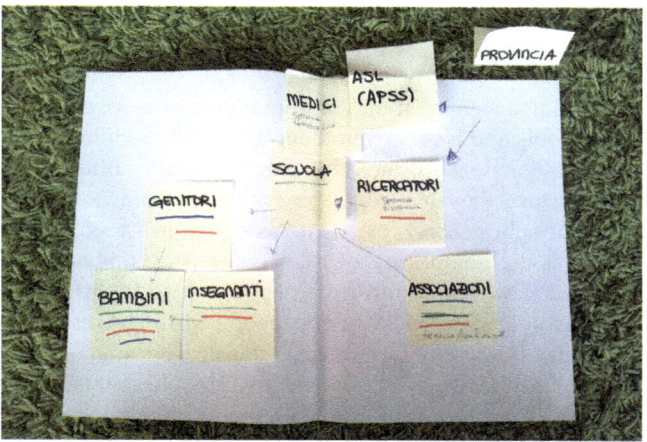

**Fig. 17.1** Example of the actor mapping activity

between parents and teachers. Parents thought that teachers did not understand what dyslexia was, or did not want to understand it, and knew very little about teaching methods and instruments which could support children with dyslexia. On the other hand, many teachers thought that it was difficult to communicate with parents of kids with dyslexia. They complained that there were some parents who did not understand the issue, or overlooked it, and some others who showed an excessive preoccupation accompanied by a little willingness to collaborate. Teachers proposed that there should be a referent in the school specifically dedicated to the mediation between parents and teachers. In their opinion, the special needs representative already present in most of the schools should play this role in the context of dyslexia.

Many times the local government, local health department, associations and researchers were placed nearby and understood as the actors which could facilitate the advancement of different aspects related to dyslexia. This notwithstanding, teachers and parents claimed that at the moment this contribution was very limited. In addition, most of the participants pointed out that the collaboration among these actors was quite limited and complex, there were different understandings of which were the weak points. In general, teachers were critical about their relationship with the officers of the local government and highlighted that they mainly contacted them to request data and to ask them to perform questionnaires but hardly ever to reply to their comments, provide information or acknowledge their work. On the other hand, local government officers were generally quite critical about teachers and argued that they were resistant to change, particularly with respect to the trilingualism project. However, they did not point out any specific communication issue with schools, which might be due to the fact that they claimed to usually communicate with the school principals. These officers also mentioned that they had on-going collaborations with researchers and companies, mainly through research-funded projects. Indeed, they particularly mentioned an on-going project dealing with the topic of dyslexia. Interestingly, some of the activities performed in the context of these projects were the source of teachers' complaints regarding data gathering and questionnaires distribution.

Most of the participants agreed on the importance of associations as mediators among parents, schools and local government. However, both teachers and officers highlighted that associations formed by parents could sometimes hinder this communication because they tended to be critical but did not propose ways to address the criticisms. In general, the term "associations" was perceived as a too general for denoting the complexity of roles enacted by this actor. Even though a few people added new actors, most of them did it to highlight the difference among kinds of associations. Most of the people distinguished between social cooperatives, which offered support services during and after school hours; and parents associations, which were usually perceived as grassroots communities that were born out of the need to improve the communication among parents, schools and the local government.

Some people highlighted that collaboration among the local health department, researchers and teachers was especially important. Some teachers expressed their interest in attending training activities organized by the local health department and researchers. They explained that this collaboration could help teachers, and especially those who played the role of mediators between the school and parents, have a high quality training based on scientific knowledge. Most of the participants left the actor denoted as "companies" outside of the map, stating that they played a minimal role in the debate. In most cases, companies were considered as possible future employers and potential sponsors for activities.

The actor mapping activity highlighted two main findings. In the first place, there is a need for mediators that can intercede among actors, or group of actors. For example, mediators are needed to intercede between teachers and parents. They are also needed between the local government and the parents. The second finding is that there is currently a public information. This public is a grassroots community formed by parents who have a personal interest in the topic of dyslexia.

## 17.4.2  Matters of Concern

### 17.4.2.1  Public Awareness

Most of the people agreed that there is a lack of public awareness regarding the topic of dyslexia. However, most of the tensions were not only triggered by the lack of public awareness but also by the understanding of dyslexia as a disease, or a disability. Parents, teachers and officers felt unease with this understanding and denounced that it was something that needed to be changed. Paradoxically, most of the existing initiatives to improve awareness were addressed to people who already had a personal or professional interest. According to teachers, not knowing or misunderstanding dyslexia became especially problematic when they spotted a child who might have difficulties reading or writing. In their opinion, when this happened parents who did not know about dyslexia became scared, or in denial:

> *I have children in the fourth class of the elementary school that do not have the certification because of the pupil's parents ... there is always a familiar context that it is not the same for all children and in which it is not possible to intervene. I think that as parents everyone tries to do their best for their children, but many times one does not arrive to the point* [Teacher]

Furthermore, teachers also highlighted that that some parents did not want their children to work with dyslexic children because they thought that it might hinder their learning. In addition, parents and teachers mentioned that children with dyslexia were sometimes isolated from their schoolmates. In order to deal with this issue, some teachers claimed to adopt strategies to explain children what dyslexia was (for example, by showing movies which contained references to the topic of dyslexia during scholastic hours) or to privilege activities that minimize the differences between dyslexic and non-dyslexic children, such as learning-by-doing activities:

> *When we do natural sciences ( ... ), we seed the vegetable garden, I make children hoe and touch the ground ( ... ). They live the discipline and not only study it. In this way, the problem of dyslexia, or any other kind of problem, becomes minimal.* [Teacher]

### 17.4.2.2 Practical Information

In spite of the fact that the local government published a set of operational indications for "specific learning disabilities", most of the actors claimed that it was difficult to find practical information about the topic of dyslexia. In general, teachers and parents thought that finding information regarding legal aspects and practices that could support children at school and at home was a difficult task and sources were sometimes not consistent. This issue was especially problematic at the schools, where many teachers complained that there was not a protocol to be followed once it became evident that a child might have reading or writing difficulties:

> *(I get the information) through word-of-mouth because no one explains you anything ... I know everything through word-of-mouth and experience ... I have worked on my own experience because when I need something I become interested on it and I go to the one who knows about it, who at this moment are the special needs educational assistants, they know everything.* [Teacher]

Some schools initiated activities aimed at providing more information. For example, one teacher (who was also the special needs' responsible at a school) mentioned that her school had created a document that summarized the most important legal aspects related to dyslexia and how to apply them in the school context. Even though the document was shared within several secondary schools, it was not publicly available.

Most of the parents seemed to collect complementary information on how to do the certification from different actors, which included teachers, the local health department and private experts such as logopedists and psychologists. In addition, parents of children with dyslexia seemed to become avid information searchers on the Internet. Face-to-face meetings were opportunities for exchanging and confirming this kind of information. For example, one of the parents association organised evening sessions with addresses several aspects that range from providing support (e.g. adult dyslexics which tell their experience) to facilitating the services of experts (e.g. inviting educators that help children doing their homework). Furthermore, there were some experts and companies in the territory that offered presentations in which they explained the details of the certification process, and offered their private services, or presented their technological compensatory instruments. However, none of this information was stored in a form of a shared repository where it could be openly accessed.

### 17.4.2.3 Technological Instruments

Most of the actors agreed on the fact that technology can be beneficial for dyslexic children. Indeed, the Italian Law 170 envisions that children with a dyslexia certification have the right to use supportive technology and foresees financial support to families to ensure so. Interestingly, most of the tensions regarding technological instruments emerged due to a limited access to technology at schools. During the research, references to different kinds of technological instruments emerged. Teachers and officers mainly referred to what can be seen as general technological instruments to support learning, such as a computer room and interactive whiteboards. Parents often referred to assistive technologies, such as the text-to-speech reader and autocorrect spelling, and cognitive training programs specifically designed for dyslexics.

Many teachers complained about the limited technological resources and highlighted that technology did not only help dyslexics but all children. These teachers claimed that the relatively low availability of technological artifacts was due to the limited financial resources, which sometimes generated tensions among parents. On the other hand, officers argued that the technological instruments were available at schools but teachers did not use them. Indeed, a few teachers acknowledged having little technological skills:

> I have very basic knowledge, I am not a native user. I have been born in 1970 so I have started using the computer at the university ( . . . ). I have reached to the [Office] package, and not even, I know a bit of Excel, Word and several browsers. [Teacher]

Access to technology was perceived as paramount by some parents and experts, who argued that computers are for the dyslexic what glasses are for the short-sighted. Indeed, some teachers and parents claimed that children experienced fewer difficulties when they used assistive technologies and cognitive training programs. This notwithstanding, parents complained that when computers were offered to dyslexic children at schools, they tended to be quite old and perceived as something extraordinary. In addition, most of the schools had little technological resources specifically designed for dyslexic and some parents highlighted that people, including themselves, lacked information about the existence and how to use these instruments. Furthermore, the school did not envision specific support for the children to help them learn to use the computer and teachers usually had a limited knowledge of how to use it. Therefore, in most of the cases the family, experts and associations, both in the form of social cooperatives and grassroots groups, were the ones helping children use the computer and identifying available assistive software and cognitive training programs. Unfortunately, this kind of knowledge did reach neither the school nor the teachers:

> When I look around I see parents which have informed themselves, who have children with difficulties and have got information, and they have these kind of [technological] support at home but that at the school usually is not used. [Officer]

Furthermore, excelling in the use of computers seemed to have a positive effect on dyslexic children's self-esteem and, according to teachers, many times they decided to pursue careers in technical topics such as computer science. Several teachers mentioned that once children learned how to use the computer, they became much more skilled with computers than other children:

> Furthermore, they [dyslexic children] become kind of computer experts because they have this instrument only for them, so many times ( . . . ) they become our technicians. [Teacher]

In general, most of the actors perceived technology as important in supporting learning. Initially, it seemed that the main issue was the scarcity of technological resources. However, deepening into the issue it emerged that the problem was not only the availability of recourses but also the awareness of available tools and skills on how to use them. This was particularly important in the case of technology designed for dyslexics. The main actors involved were the children, teachers and parents. Interestingly, this issue had already brought some parents together who, through a grassroots community, organized events where experts helped children using these technologies. Unfortunately, this knowledge remained at a local level and did reach neither the school nor the teachers.

### 17.4.2.4 Emotional Load

Many of the interviewed people mentioned that dyslexic children were perceived, and perceived themselves, as being different. Some teachers highlighted that being dyslexic was a characteristic "*as having curly hair*" but this did not seem to be a general understanding. Indeed, it is interesting to notice that some of them used the term "*outing*" to refer to the moment when dyslexic children decide to make their characteristic explicit to others. To avoid feeling different from their classmates, dyslexic children often renounced to bring their computer to class, and the family sometimes influenced this decision:

> Often they refuse to use these instruments in class because the are afraid of being judged as different, of being offended. ( . . . ) We need to make them [families] understand that using

*these instruments means providing a sense of fairness. Giving these children something that is missing, the instrument that places them in the same condition as others. Because sometimes they say 'but it's better they don't because maybe after they make fun of them'.*
[Teacher]

According to some teachers, not using the compensatory instruments might start a vicious circle: without the computer, children might strive to catch up with the rest of the class and, therefore, increase their frustration and lower their self-esteem. Indeed, feelings of frustration, anger, low self-esteem and sadness came out very often. Indeed, these feelings were usually more intense when children realised that they experienced more difficulties than their colleagues, but did not have yet a dyslexia certificate:

*They are sad children, sad because they feel misunderstood, at the margin of their sociability and often they isolated. They are children that usually stay aside.* [Teacher]

The emotional distress might be influenced by the fact that in the secondary school (age 11–16) most of the times being different seemed to be perceived as a problem and seldom as a value. Very often during the meetings, parents told stories that referred to negative experiences, frustration and incomprehension. Negative experiences seemed to be especially present during scholastic activities and the certification process. Teachers and, in particular, parents elaborated on several specific practices that could stimulate negative feelings (e.g. highlighting errors with a red pen) or positive ones (e.g. making children more participate in practical activities; highlighting strengths).

### 17.4.2.5  Certification Process

Obtaining the dyslexia certification was an important milestone in the familiar and scholastic context. Sometimes parents did not understand why their children experienced so many difficulties at school and described the moment in which they obtained the certification as a relief. In the scholastic context, having a certification allowed teachers to start applying dispensatory and compensatory measures:

*Until the certification does not arrive, in which it says that I am authorized to intervene in a certain way, and even if I have the intuition that the child needs it, until you do not have this damn piece of paper you cannot start doing anything.* [Teacher]

The certification process seemed to be also a source of controversy. Many teachers and parents complained that the process was too slow; giving place to situations in which children who started the certification process at the beginning of the scholastic year had not got the certification until the end of the scholastic year. Teachers argued that the local health department was the bottleneck in this process. Indeed, the time required by the certification process seemed to be significantly reduced when it was lead by a private expert. However, in other cases, some teachers complained that nowadays everyone who started a certification process "*comes back with something*" and that some children who were certified as dyslexic might only need some additional time:

*From my point of view, it [dyslexia] is simply a lack of respect for the time that different children need. ( . . . ) If they would have done one year more at the kindergarten or one year more of elementary school, they would have probably straighten their path.* [Teacher]

From the moment the child had a certificate of dyslexia, the family brought it to the school, which could start applying the measures envisioned by the law, such as the creation of the PEP (Personalised Education Plan). The goal of the PEP was to adapt the scholastic activities to each child based on the specific difficulties observed during the certification process. The PEP was usually created by the school and discussed during a meeting with all relevant actors such as parents, teachers, educators and experts.

In theory, the meeting to discuss the PEP should play an instrumental role towards the alignment among different actors. In practice, parents usually complained that the school was little proactive in providing the PEP, which should also be renewed every year, and that some of them did not even do it. Teachers highlighted that the usefulness of this meeting often depended on the kind of experts involved. In their opinion, experts who belonged to the local health department usually did not participate in the PEP meeting and the certification document was too general, difficult to understand (it was usually perceived as "*too technical*") and lacked practical implications for the school.

### 17.4.2.6   Collaboration Among Actors

In many cases, the relationships among different actors seemed to be problematic. The most critical one, especially considering their role in the issue, was the relationship parents-teachers. Interviews and meetings highlighted several conflicts between these two actors. Some parents felt that teachers did not understand the needs of their children and even wondered whether they were qualified to do so. This conflict was highlighted during the meetings, in which it was very common to listen to personal stories of parents complaining about a particular teacher. On the other hand, some teachers felt overwhelmed by the interaction with parents and criticized their unwillingness to collaborate. Surprisingly, officers thought that parents' opinions, in particular with respect to the trilingualism project, were being manipulated by the teachers, who wanted to the deliberately damage the project in benefit of their personal interest. In addition, officers claimed that the communication with parents did not work and, in their opinion, associations should mediate this relationship:

*Associations should support parents and collaborate with the local government because the associations manage to gather parents' voices, collect their opinions and synthesize them and, therefore, they should be the channel towards the local government. We usually experience a communication parents- local government and parents-public institution . . . . That it does not have much sense, it is not efficient and the system does not learn. And this is a problem.* [Officer]

Indeed, teachers also saw the associations as playing a central role since they could address a broad range of needs. For example, associations were perceived as an actor that can help mediating between different actors (e.g. local government-parents and school-parents), providing information on procedures and available materials (e.g. certification process, legal issues, compensative instruments) and infrastructuring the offer of supporting services (e.g. provide educators, organize home-work groups after school). However, officers and teachers thought that currently some associations were also detrimental since they brought too many complaints and too little proposals.

### 17.4.2.7 Digitalization of Practices

Most of the teachers used the Internet to look for didactic resources, such as media content to show to the students and examples of practical activities to be implemented in the classroom. Many of them identified specific websites or video channels to find material. These activities were usually performed alone and not shared with other teachers. In spite of this interest, there seemed to be also a part of the teachers who show some resistance to technology and argue that it cannot supplement face-to-face and hands-on activities. An interesting case came out during one of the interviews, in which one teacher described how a group of teachers at her school was trying to collaboratively create a virtual space for sharing relevant didactic content. During the interviews, she mentioned that they had not finished yet because, in spite of the fact that the school's IT services helped them with the technical issues, adding content was too tiring and time-consuming.

Even though the lack of time and, in some cases, skills were the main issues hindering the digitalization of practices, some teachers also expressed some resistance to the public exposure that the use of technology and the Internet might entail. For example, one teacher was worried about having English mistakes in the website, particularly due to the fact that the center was a reference point for the trilingual policy. Some teachers thought that such a platform might also be useful for communicating the homework, so children could check it online and would not need to copy it from the whiteboard (a common issue among dyslexic children).

### 17.4.2.8 Precarious Working Conditions

Most of the teachers had a precarious working condition, which included not having a fixed position, moving among different schools and low salaries. Teachers were usually overwhelmed by additional activities such as support for the school, participation in department board and professional development activities. Per year, teachers needed to spend 40 h in additional activities and a minimum of 15 h in professional development activities. An important issue among teachers was an uncertainty regarding which activities would be accepted as "additional activities". Also, they did not have a system that recorded or showed how many hours they had done and how many were missing. This uncertainty created a potentially problematic dynamic: teachers became concerned about doing activities that at the end would not be registered and used to give preference to those activities they know they would.

Most of the teachers perceived the professional development activities as an advantage. However, some of them complained about the way they are sometimes implemented. In most of the cases, complaints were related to the quality of the trainer and relevance of the proposed topics to their personal interests. In this respect, teachers would like to be able to make proposals on what to spend these hours. A few teachers spontaneously proposed including activities that would contribute to the development of SPAZIOd as professional development activity.

### 17.4.3  Discussion

This paper extends the existing corpus of research on the articulation of matters of concern in technology design [2, 5] by showing how their articulation can be attempted. In our experience, an important aspect is that this articulation entails the triangulation of data obtained through different methods, that enables an exploration of the design space at different levels. On the one hand, the observations of different events allowed us to have a general understanding of the complex political and social conditions [10]. On the other hand, through the interviews, we could identify specific issues that were relevant for many people but regarded differently by different actors. Results indicate that these activities are intertwined and, therefore, should not be considered independently, especially when designing following a public design perspective. For example, the data collected through the observations at events were instrumental in the elaboration of the script used during the interviews and the initial actors in the actor mapping activity. In addition, the data gathered during the interviews triggered the further exploration of the political conditions. For example, the interviews highlighted the existence of a project aimed to enable the early identification of potential writing and reading issues, which was grounded on the 170 law and where the local government, companies, research institutions and some schools collaborated.

An interesting aspect of the concept of matters of concern is that it illustrates issues around which publics can be formed [5, 11]. For example, the lack of practical information on legal and procedural aspects mainly relates to parents, experts, teachers and associations. These actors, or some of them, might eventually get together to face the issue and trigger the formation of a public. In addition, the issue of lack of practical information can be addressed by designing a specific artefact (e.g. a digital platform which supports sharing of relevant information among related actors), which can be considered an opportunity for design. These results suggest that the articulation of matters of concern is an interesting concept, but further research needs to be done to understand how it can facilitate public formation and artefact creation. In our experience, an important aspect is to engage with activities that facilitate the understanding of the related actors and their relationships. In our study, the actor mapping activity allowed the identification the important role of the mediators to bring people together. The need for mediators also highlighted tensions among actors, particularly between parents and local government, and parents and teachers. Associations could play the role of mediators although it would be important to differentiate between social cooperatives and grassroots communities.

Finally, the results highlighted issues that can be instantiated as design opportunities worth to be pursued. Although they are situated, we still believe that they can serve as inspiration for research that deals with design related to dyslexia. For example, the lack of information with respect to existing technological instruments specifically designed for dyslexic children can help as inspiration for the creation of a digital platform that supports gathering and transferring this kind of knowledge. In this way, technological artefacts are not used to articulate matters of concern [5], but the articulation of matters of concern inspires the development of technological artefacts. In addition, the controversies emerged due to the misunderstanding of dyslexia as a disease or disability can inspire the organization of initiatives that aim to influence the public understanding of dyslexia. Although out of the scope of this paper, this has been the inspiration for the activities following this research. The main one has been the organization of the first "European Dyslexia week" in Italy, which triggered the design and development of several design artefacts and supported the creation of ties among related actors, such as the local government, schools, parents, associations, research centers and the university.

## 17.5  Conclusion

The articulation of matters of concern can contribute to addressing the "messy and problematic situations" in which design takes place. An especially interesting aspect of the concept of matters of concern is that it facilitates dealing with issues, rather than solving problems. This approach can be an alternative to many of the current approaches to the design of technological artefacts, which tend to focus on solving problems by means of mobile applications or digital services. In addition, the identification of relevant issues might contribute to the formation of publics. In our opinion, the relationship among the articulation of matters of concern, design artefacts and public formation is an interesting one. Previous research has elaborated how design artefacts can express matters of concern; this paper aims to contribute to the understanding of the relationship between the articulation of matters of concern and design artefacts. A potentially interesting research direction in public design would be investigating the relationship between public formation and artefact design.

**Acknowledgments** We would like to thank Maurizio Teli for his comments and participation in the research and analysis. The analysis that has brought to this paper has been possible thanks to the funding granted by the Ministero dell'Istruzione, Universita' e Ricerca through the project "Citta' Educante", project code CTN01_00034_393801.

# References

1. Andersen LB, Danholt P, Halskov K, Hansen NB, Lauritsen P (2015) Participation as a matter of concern in participatory design. CoDesign 11(3–4):250–261
2. Björgvinsson E, Ehn P, Hillgren PA (2010) Participatory design and democratizing innovation. In Proceedings of the 11th Biennial participatory design conference. ACM, pp 41–50
3. Braun V, Clarke V (2006) Using thematic analysis in psychology. Qual Res Psychol 3(2):77–101
4. Dewey J, Rogers ML (2012) The public and its problems: an essay in political inquiry. Penn State Press, Pennsylvania
5. DiSalvo C, Lukens J, Lodato T, Jenkins T, Kim T (2014) Making public things: how HCI design can express matters of concern. In: Proceedings of the 32nd annual ACM conference on human factors in computing systems. ACM, pp 2397–2406
6. Elliott JG, Grigorenko EL (2014) The dyslexia debate, vol 14. Cambridge University Press, Cambridge
7. Greenfield A (2013) Against the smart city
8. Khakhar J, Madhvanath S (2010) Jollymate: assistive technology for young children with dyslexia. In: Frontiers in handwriting recognition (ICFHR), 2010 international conference on IEEE, pp 576–580
9. Kvale S (2008) Doing interviews. Sage, London
10. Latour B (2004) Why has critique run out of steam? From matters of fact to matters of concern. Crit Inq 30(2):225–248
11. Le Dantec CA, DiSalvo C (2013) Infrastructuring and the formation of publics in participatory design. Soc Stud Sci 43(2):241–264
12. Neustaedter C, Sengers P (2012) Autobiographical design in HCI research: designing and learning through use-it-yourself. In: Proceedings of the designing interactive systems conference. ACM, pp 514–523
13. Pandey S, Srivastava S (2011) Tiblo: a tangible learning aid for children with dyslexia. In: Procedings of the second conference on creativity and innovation in design. ACM, pp 211–220
14. Preece J (2000) Online communities: designing usability and supporting socialbilty. Wiley, Chichester
15. Schön DA (1983) The reflective practitioner: how professionals think in action, vol 5126. Basic books, New York
16. Simonsen J, Robertson T (eds) (2012) Routledge international handbook of participatory design. Routledge, New York
17. Telier A, Binder T, De Michelis G, Ehn P, Jacucci G, Wagner I (2011) Design things. The MIT Press, Cambridge
18. Tittarelli M, Marti P, Peppoloni D (2014) Rapping dyslexia: learning rhythm, rhyme and flow in dyslexic children. In: Proceedings of the 8th Nordic conference on human-computer interaction: fun, fast, foundational. ACM, October, pp 865–870
19. Van Someren MW, Barnard YF, Sandberg JA (1994) The think aloud method: a practical guide to modelling cognitive processes, vol 2. Academic, London

# Part II
# Interactive Experiences

The widening interest from research to design in this volume becomes central in the following chapters, which elaborate on experimental interactive experiences that represent, reflect upon and instantiate the conference theme: "Making Together". The Interactive Experiences track welcomed submissions about artistic experiments, digital artefacts or interactive installations that emphasized making and cooperation such as community engagement, civic participation, or collective making and digital fabrication. The track did not only call for submissions which provided fascinating outcomes but also for installations that reflected on how the artefacts were designed and could be enacted in practice.

Considering the cross-boundary nature of this kind of installations, the submission format was accustomed to accommodating both artistic and more academic contributions. All installations submitted a portfolio containing a description of the installation, the technical and logistical requirements and a possible scenario of how it could be implemented within the conference. In addition, authors had the opportunity to write a short paper to extend the portfolio and further unfold, on a more academic level, the lines of inquiry and theoretical grounds instantiated by the proposed interactive experience.

This section presents a total of five accepted papers. Each of the papers represents an individual contribution that must be seen through the lenses of the actual installation and interactive experience enacted at the conference. They explore collaborative systems and collective action on a number of levels, in a variety of contexts and taking widely different forms of expression; from sonification of everyday environments to audiovisual and tactile music-making and engagements with research data, from gamified technology probes for computational thinking to the experience of WiFi through sensorial augmentation. The aim is to facilitate discussions and debate around these themes at COOP as a resonance between the embodied, interactive experiences and academic, critical reflections.

This track would not have been possible without the help and enthusiasm of the authors and reviewers, who offered their effort and time. In particular, we really would like to thank Ilias Bergström, Laurens Boer, Erik Grönvall, Liesbeth A. Huybrechts, Susan Kozel, Fabio Morreale, Oscar Tomico, Niels Wouters and Victor Zappi for their insightful reviews and discussions, which did not only contribute to the particular installations but also to shaping the first ever Interactive Experiences track. Thanks to Antonella De Angeli, Liam Bannon and Patrizia Marti for the inspiring discussions that lead to the framing of this track.

# Chapter 18
# Audio Satellites: Overhearing Everyday Life

**Morten Breinbjerg, Marie Koldkjær Højlund, Morten Riis, Jonas Fritsch, and Jonas R. Kirkegaard**

**Abstract** The project "Audio Satellites – overhearing everyday life" consists of a number of mobile listening devices (audio satellites) from which sound is distributed in real time to a server and made available for listening and mixing through a web interface. The audio satellites can either be carried around or displaced arbitrarily in a given landscape. In the web interface, the different sound streams from the individual satellites can be mixed together to form a cooperative soundscape. The project thus allows people to tune into and explore the overheard soundscape of everyday life in a collaborative and creative process of active listening.

## 18.1 Introduction and Motivation

In this paper we present "Audio Satellites – overhearing everyday life", a cooperative system that allows people to actively listen to their everyday soundscape by mixing together streams of auditory data recorded at different physical locations. Hereby, people can curate a mediated soundscape that expresses an individual or collective perspective on the everyday. The idea of listening to a soundscape normally relates to a passive situation, where people listen to a pre-recorded soundscape or participate in a sound walk in which they are encouraged to listen to e.g. a city soundscape following a predetermined route. In our project, we want

M. Breinbjerg (✉) • M.K. Højlund • M. Riis
School of Culture and Communication, Aarhus University, Helsingforsgade 14,
8200 Aarhus N, Denmark
e-mail: mbrein@dac.au.dk; musmkh@dac.au.dk; mr@dac.au.dk

J. Fritsch
IT University of Copenhagen, Rued Langgaards Vej 7, 2300 Copenhagen S, Denmark
e-mail: frit@itu.dk

J.R. Kirkegaard
Sonic College, University College Southern Denmark, Lembecksvej 7, 6100 Haderslev, Denmark
e-mail: jrk@soniccollege.dk

© Springer International Publishing Switzerland 2016 297
A. De Angeli et al. (eds.), *COOP 2016: Proceedings of the 12th International
Conference on the Design of Cooperative Systems, 23–27 May 2016, Trento, Italy*,
DOI 10.1007/978-3-319-33464-6_18

instead to encourage people to be active listeners in the following two ways. First, the audio satellites can be displaced at free will as long as there is access to a WiFi-network that allows for live streaming of sound from the built in microphones. Second, the different sound streams can be mixed together in real time and listened to by a person through a custom designed web interface. The people setting up the audio satellites and mixing together the audio streams can be the same, or they can have decided to work together, but will most likely be unknown to each other.

The project builds on an ongoing exploration of the collaborative potential in using interactive sound to engage people in living cultural heritage and collective storytelling as a form of community engagement [1, 5]. The research agenda pursued in "Audio Satellites – overhearing everyday life" is to create a more agile system, with mobile listening devices that can be distributed freely indoor and outdoor, and further to add the real time mixing as a collaborative ingredient to facilitate a participatory and active listening experience

In this article we first outline a conceptual framework for how listening through technology can be used as a strategy to engage people in an exploration of their everyday lives. We build on this to introduce the concept of "overhearing" as a central concept for exploring the aesthetics of listening. We then present the Audio Satellites system and related work. Finally, we reflect on the way in which the system can be understood as a cooperative system that allows people to attune to their everyday environments in novel ways through collaborative making and active listening.

## 18.2   Listening Through Technology

Often soundscape recordings are seen as ways to represent or draw attention to the structure or the constituent elements of a given place, but as Murray Schafer noticed any recording is technologically mediated and as such the role of technology and the question of what it means to listen through technology should be considered [8]. As a consideration, we wish to avoid what Yolande Harris calls sonic colonialism, as any de-contextualization of a soundscape from its environment forces us to listen as outsiders, inevitably biasing our understanding, often leading to a pseudo-understanding of a distant location. Harris stresses the importance of considering our relationship to the recorded sounds: the context in which they originate, the place in which we hear them and how our experience is mediated by technology [4]. So how, then, can we make the acute awareness of embodied location present? By playing with ways of listening, e.g. by encouraging listeners to be aware of the displacement in interplay with their immediate surroundings and technology.

Harris suggests the term techno-intuition to encompass the practice of using technology to establish and enhance our relationship to the environment through sound and listening in action [11]. With the aid of sonic technologies and awareness enhancing practices, we can re-experience environments we know and access others beyond our physiological abilities. So rather than considering technology as the antithetical to the environment it becomes a way to provoke a sense of direct involvement and entanglement with it. When we are physically involved in movement and action it provokes an attitude of openness challenging us to expand beyond ourselves as consistent, closed entities. In this way active listening through technology provokes an open attitude that form new sonic relationships with the environments around us, than through passive listening.

## 18.3   Overhearing: The Aesthetics of Listening

Brandon Labelle, echoing Michel Serres, introduces the concept of the overhear as a generative potential forming an essential part of our experience of everyday environments. The overhear is not to be considered as the neutral backdrop (as suggested in the common term background noise/noise pollution), but a necessary ground on which the signal is heard, and therefore a part of the relation and a productive component of all information transmission. The overhear is the horizon that all sounds relate to, in the open space, as there is always sound outside the frame of a specific listening and therefore these multiple perspectives become part of the experience with a promise of the outside. The overheard registers and underlines our spatial surroundings by explicitly connecting us deeper than through what we see and consciously listen to. In this sense, the overhear expands our space or freedom to act [7]. With the concept of overhearing we wish to call attention to the kind of listening strategies that the Audio Satellites system supports. In Danish, the word "overhear" has two meanings. The traditional understanding of the word refers to the situation where we do not hear something that we were supposed to hear due to e.g. distraction. The second and recent understanding refers to the situation in which we hear something that was not meant for us to hear in the first place. In this context, we play on both meanings of the concept in the sense that the system allows people to attune to sounds we normally do not pay attention to e.g. noises or background sounds, to penetrate what Luc Ferrari has called the "domain of secrecy" [3] i.e. tapping into sounds that was not deliberately directed to our attention. In the latter case, issues around intimacy, surveillance and telepresence come forward. As such the system allows, in the terms of Susan Sontag, for both a hermeneutic and an erotic way of listening [9]. In the hermeneutic way, the soundscape becomes "readable". We hear the different sound streams as representations of specific events and places and use them to make sense of what we are listening to. In the erotic approach, the purpose is not to map and identify space and to seek an overview but to affectively sense the sounds heard in all their detail and material diversity and to follow imaginary paths that echo the unruly and "ghostly" nature of sound [2, 10].

## 18.4   The Audio Satellites Concept and Related Work

The project "Audio Satellites – overhearing everyday life" consists of a number of mobile listening devices (Audio Satellites) from which sound is distributed in real time to a server and made available for listening through a web interface – the overHEARD online soundscape mixer. The Audio Satellites can either be carried around or displaced arbitrarily in a given setting. Through a web interface, the different sound streams coming from the individual satellites can be mixed together to form a cooperative soundscape. The soundscape can only be heard in real time, and is not recorded. The proposed soundscape mixer is compatible with current digital devices such as smartphones, tablets and computers.

The Audio Satellite technical platform is based on the Raspberry Pi 2 equipped with WIFI/3G modem and a high quality audio interface. Streaming is done using Darkice and Icecast with a 3G modem. Besides a Linux OS, the Raspberry Pi runs the Jack Audio Server, Pure Data (pd-extended) and Darkice. Dynamic directional microphones are placed at carefully selected places at the site, all connected to a rack mount digital mixing console with DSP capabilities. Via Ethernet based OSC (Open Sound Control) it is possible to control parameters such as level, pan, equalization and dynamic processing (compression/limiting). The output from the mixer is then connected to an audio interface. From the audio interface the audio is sent to Pure Data. From here it is routed via Jack to Darkice that encodes the audio stream to mp3-format and streams it to the Icecast server. The web interface where users can mix the soundscapes contains a player that receives the Icecast streams from the different satellites. The different Audio Satellites are physically constructed for outdoor use and designed to be as maintenance free as possible. The enclosure ensures a moist free environment so the electronics will not corrode or short-circuit. They do not need Internet cable connection as they stream via a 3G modem. However, they do need power. The Audio Satellite status can be monitored and reset via the Internet connection and calibration/adjustment to the audio signal can be done here as well.

The Audio Satellite system continues a line of inquiry opened by the possibility of bridging different geographical locations through sound in real time arising as early as with the invention of telephone and radio broadcasting, understood as forms of listening through technology. With these technologies, the ghostly nature of sound, which allows for "the presence of what is absent" [10], like the voice of a person transmitted from the far end of the world, is accentuated. Today, many projects presenting the soundscape of places around the world can be heard on the Internet based on uploaded sound recordings or live streaming of sound. In the *London Sound Survey* initiated by Ian M. Rawes in 2008, sounds of everyday public life throughout London is collected in order to document the soundscape of London city and how the sound environment changes (http://www.soundsurvey.org.uk). Similarly *radio aporee*, an open and collaborative platform for research on sound founded by Udo Noll, allows people to upload sound recordings as long as they subscribe to a few guidelines (http://aporee.org/maps/). In the *orca-live.net* project, building on the research of Paul Spong, underwater sound is streamed live through a network of hydrophones allowing for e.g. the detection and experience of whale/orca songs. The project relates to the concept of the Nature Network: stations set up in Nature in order to transmit live images and sound to people around the world. All these projects differ from each other by being either curated or collaborative/open and by being archival or live/in real time.

A more explicitly socially oriented project is *Peccioli Radioscape*, which formed part of the Presence Project led by Anthony Dunne and William Gaver, and explored how radio could be used to amplify the sociability of the small rural village of Peccioli. The elderly people of the village were enabled to overhear the social life taking place in the streets, at the market or in cafe's from within their private homes. By placing transmitters with built-in microphones in the landscape, people could tune into the sounds of other people talking and discussing or into the sounds of the rural landscape like bird songs or the sound of splashing water from near by streams.

In "Audio satellites – overhearing everyday life" we share the common ideas of presenting different everyday soundscapes to people using different listening technologies. We wish further to expand the idea by developing an aesthetics of listening based on active overhearing, having listeners mix different sound inputs from their everyday environments. The ambition is to qualify the way people can overhear and attune to everyday soundscapes through technology as active listening.

## 18.5 Conclusion

The aim of the project "Audio Satellites – overhearing everyday life" is to allow people to tune into the everyday soundscape and evoke an active listening approach through a process of participation. The active listening process is facilitated by either controlling both the position and placing of the individual Audio Satellites or by mixing the individual audio streams into a personalized soundscape through the web interface. Active listening as overhearing is to be understood as a process of bodily action, interaction and intentionality. As such, people participate in a creative process of collaborative making that is both situated and embodied, formatted through a complex relation of technological and human agency. This creative process arises within a field of force and flow of material, as suggested by Tim Ingold, where the active listening process represents a form of improvisation with technology, flows and rhythms of sound and spatiotemporal conditions [6]. Hereby, overhearing becomes a process of active involvement, participation and exploration that counters the normal comprehension of overhearing as a passive and unconscious modus.

**Acknowledgments** This research has been funded by Aarhus University's interdisciplinary research centre, Participatory IT, www.PIT.au.dk (project code 10509) and European Capital of Culture, Aarhus 2017. Also thanks to the people at CAVI (Centre for Advanced Visualization and Interaction) for technical support.

# References

1. Amund D, Breinbjerg M, Fritsch JS (2013) Ekkomaten – exploring the echo as a design fiction concept. Digit Creat 24(1):60–74
2. Breinbjerg M (2012) Urban sound interfaces: poetic approaches to media architecture. MAB' 12 proceedings of the 4th media architecture biennale conference: participation. Association for Computing Machinery, New York, pp 43–46
3. Ferrari L (1996) I was running in so many different directions. Contemp Music Rev 15(1–2):95–102
4. Harris Y (2014) Techno-intuition. In: Artistic experimentation in music: an anthology, vol 167. Leuven University Press, Leuven
5. Højlund M, Riis M (2015) Wavefront aesthetics – attuning to a dark ecology. Organised Sound 20(Special Issue 02):249–262
6. Ingold T (2010) The textility of making. Camb J Econ 34(1):91–102
7. LaBelle B (2012) Shared space. Talk at "The Sound of Architecture". Yale University, Philadelphia
8. Schafer RM (1994) The soundscape – the tuning of the world, 2nd edn. Destiny Books, Rochester
9. Sontag S (1961) Against interpretation and other essays. Farrar, Straus and Giroux, New York
10. Toop D (2010) Sinister resonance. Continuum International, New York
11. Yolande H (2013) Presentness in displaced sound. In: Leonardo Music Journal, vol. 23. MIT Press

# Chapter 19
# Gamified Technology Probes for Scaffolding Computational Thinking

Rosella Gennari, Vincenzo Del Fatto, Edona Gashi, Julian Sanin, and Angelo Ventura

**Abstract** This paper advances the idea of gamified probes for scaffolding children's computational thinking, and specifically algorithmic thinking. The paper presents the making of such a probe for a sorting algorithm. The making of the probe was alternated with its evaluation, and realized in the MakerSpace of the University of Bozen-Bolzano through a collaborative interdisciplinary effort of computer-science students and researchers from different research areas.

## 19.1 Introduction: Background and Motivations

In the 1980s, Saymour Papert had conducted computer science studies with children for growing their problem solving skills [4]. Moving from Papert work, Jannette Wing introduced the idea of *computational thinking* as a collection of skills for problem solving used by computer scientists [5]. Pioneering work behind computational thinking can be traced back in the 1950s with *algorithmic thinking*, which requires reasoning on a problem with algorithms.

Several computational thinking approaches to teaching algorithms to children, such as CS Unplugged and specifically algomotricity, require reasoning about algorithms through physical activities, which should help children in developing their mental representation of how algorithms work. Computational devices should be of secondary importance. Such approaches mainly require *experiential learning*: the direct transmission of knowledge should be kept to a minimum, and children should learn by experimenting through the scaffolding of teachers and physical objects acting as probes.

R. Gennari (✉) • V. Del Fatto • E. Gashi • J. Sanin • A. Ventura
Faculty of Computer Science, Free University of Bozen-Bolzano, Piazza Domenicani 3, Bolzano, Italy
e-mail: gennari@inf.unibz.it; vincenzo.delfatto@unibz.it; edona.gashi@stud.inf.unibz.it; julian.sanin@unibz.it; angelo.ventura@unibz.it

© Springer International Publishing Switzerland 2016                                         303
A. De Angeli et al. (eds.), *COOP 2016: Proceedings of the 12th International Conference on the Design of Cooperative Systems, 23–27 May 2016, Trento, Italy*, DOI 10.1007/978-3-319-33464-6_19

In this paper such tangible objects take the form of a *gamified technology probe*, named BALA. This was developed for scaffolding children's comprehension of sorting algorithms through playful activities, as explained in the following.

The idea of gamified probes is rooted in gamification of educational (interaction design) activities for children, advanced in [1] and put to work in [2]. In the 2014 study in [2], such gamified probes acted as design probes: each was endowed with few functionalities specific for the activity. Probes were gamified because they were designed with game design principles and patterns. Those probes were assessed through observations, and inspired the design of improved gamified probes for children, equipped with technology. Technology, in the form of embedded micro-electronics, helped in transparently improving probes' interaction with children and in promoting interaction among children and adults, besides in logging relevant data according to the expected functionalities of probes.

This paper carries over the idea of gamified technology probes for educational activities with learners of different ages. It advances the idea of gamified probes for algorithmic thinking. The paper starts presenting the idea of the BALA gamified probe for sorting, and it explains its making through collaborative design. The paper also outlines how formative evaluation sessions were conducted and interleaved with making sessions, by adopting a lean User eXperience (UX) approach [3].

## 19.2  A Gamified Technology Probe for Sorting: BALA

BALA is a gamified technology probe for the bubble-sort algorithm. See Fig. 19.1. It was printed with a 3D printer, and enhanced with Arduino micro-electronics components and a display. Bubble-sort is a simple sorting algorithm that goes iteratively through a list, comparing each time two adjacent items and swapping them if not ordered. BALA embeds the idea of pair-comparisons, and guides children to sort themselves or objects by reasoning about pairs. The following scenario explains the intended usage of BALA in a primary school. However, BALA can be used with older users, e.g., its design is meant to be usable for all. Therefore the following scenario can be extended to one with older people.

**Scenario: A Class Uses BALA for Sorting**
It is a sunny day and the class of 8-year old children of Edona, a primary school teacher, is ready for their first algorithmic thinking day. Edona asks the class to form a random queue, and shows them BALA. Children look in amazement at BALA: what should the do with the hats at its extremes? Edona says that BALA hats are like Harry Potter's sorting hat: wearing them, two children can know the taller. The first two children in the queue wear BALA hats. Edona asks them to stay still for 5 s, and watch what happens:

(continued)

BALA shows through its display who the taller is and asks children two swap positions. Edona passes now BALA through the queue. At the end of the queue, everybody has tried BALA once, but they are not sorted yet! Children start complaining: they are disappointed that BALA did not sort them. Edona calms down children and explains that BALA may have to be used more than once to sort them; children do so. Now BALA says that no swap is needed, and children realize that the queue is sorted.

**Fig. 19.1** Lean design of BALA

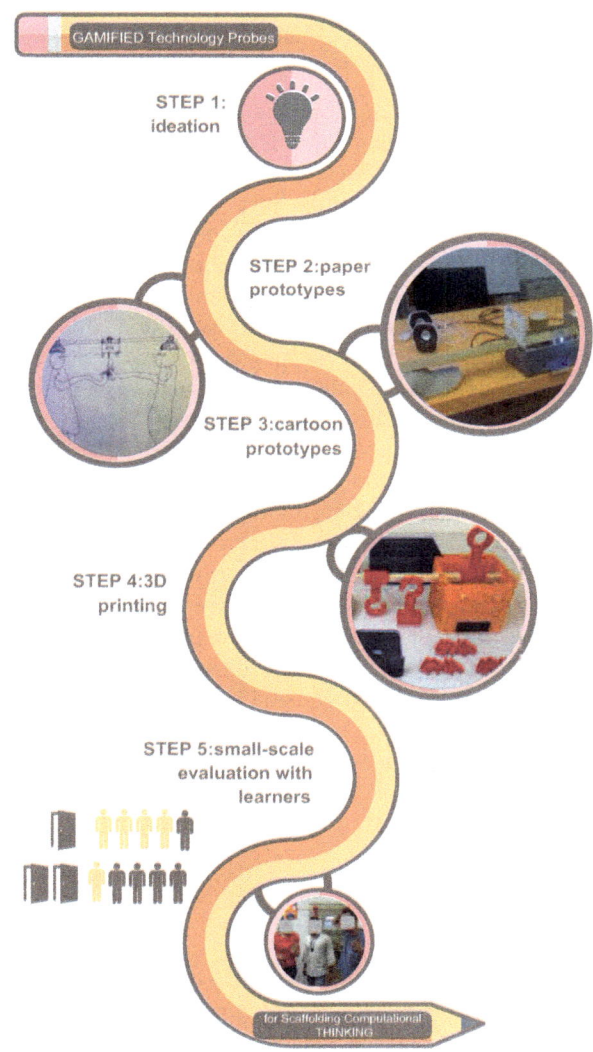

## 19.3   Making and Formative Evaluation of BALA

**Making** BALA was realized in the MakerSpace (makerspace.inf.unibz.it/) of the Computer Science Faculty of the Free University of Bozen-Bolzano. The making team was composed of two students of computer science, an industrial designer, an interaction design researcher and a user experience researcher. The team collaborated throughout the making experience via meetings and prototypes of BALA. Making was alternated with formative evaluation sessions, as in lean UX design. See Fig. 19.1.

**Evaluation** Formative evaluation was of two types, both concerned with children's experience with BALA: (1) an analytic evaluation with experts; (2) a user experience evaluation with children.

The analytic evaluation was an expert review. It consisted of three evaluation sessions, each leading to re-design choices concerning BALA, and involving the user experience researcher, the interaction designer, and the industrial designer. The first session was run on the very first paper mockups and then cartoon prototype of BALA. The second session was for the second BALA prototype, printed with a 3D printer. Experts assessed the expected children's experience with the product, focusing on its usability for children, e.g., affordance issues emerged. The third session was for the latest version of BALA. All experts tried BALA in order to give their feedback on the playability of the product for children. E.g., experts signaled that BALA could have hooks so as to inspire new playful usages of BALA: weighting instead of sorting by height.

The evaluation with children was a small-scale experience evaluation with the BALA version resulting from the last evaluation with experts. It had two evaluation sessions, each leading to re-design choices. The first session was run inside the MakerSpace with three children: two were 8 year old; one was 6 year old. The evaluation aimed at assessing the usability of BALA and whether children enjoyed BALA. It was conducted through observations and interviews. The second session was also run in the MakerSpace with four other children: two 8 year old; one 10 year old and one 14 year old. The evaluation aimed at assessing whether children used BALA as expected and grabbed how bubble sort works. This was assessed mainly through questioning at the end of the experience, concerning whether children were able to transfer the usage of BALA to the idea of sorting objects by weighting them: all children were able to do it.

## 19.4   Conclusions

This paper advanced the idea of gamified technology probes for computational thinking, and specifically algorithmic thinking. Such probes are endowed with specific functionalities, enhanced with micro-electronics, and related to the inner working of the considered algorithms. Probes are gamified in that they should be playful for engaging children in learning. The paper reported on the collaborative making and formative evaluation of the BALA gamified technology probe for scaffolding children's comprehension of the bubble sort algorithm.

# References

1. Dodero G, Gennari R, Melonio A, Torello S (2014) Gamified co-design with cooperative learning. In CHI'14 extended abstracts on human factors in computing systems, CHI EA'14, ACM, New York, pp 707–718
2. Dodero G, Gennari R, Melonio A, Torello S (2014) Towards tangible gamified co-design at school: two studies in primary schools. In: Proceedings of the First ACM SIGCHI Annual Symposium on Computer-human Interaction in Play, CHI PLAY'14. ACM, New York, pp 77–86
3. Gothelf J (2013) Lean UX. O'Reilly Media
4. Papert S (1980) Mindstorms: children, computers, and powerful ideas. Basic Books, New York
5. Wing JM (2006) Computational thinking. Commun ACM 49(3):33. doi:10.1145/1118178. 1118215

# Chapter 20
# Beatfield: An Open-Meaning Audiovisual Exploration

**Raul Masu, Andrea Conci, Zeno Menestrina, Fabio Morreale, and Antonella De Angeli**

**Abstract** This paper presents Beatfield, a musical installation that allows players to explore an audiovisual landscape by positioning tangible objects on an augmented game board. The underlying idea of the installation was the proposition of an artefact that could encourage heterogeneous interpretations. Beatfield had to offer a multitude of interpretations and ways of appropriating the system; there would be not a right or wrong way to play with it. To this end, the design of the installation integrated related work on open-ended interaction, ambiguity, and appropriation with enigmatic aesthetics, ambiguous interaction strategies, and unpredictable mapping between user input and audiovisual output. The results collected from a user study confirmed the potential of the installation to stimulate a variety of different experiences and interaction strategies.

## 20.1 Introduction

In the last decade, the literature in HCI has been broadening its scope of interest from the work environment to ludic activities, music, and other forms of art [1]. This shift caused a redefinition of research objectives. For instance, the strive for obtaining a single and correct interpretation of a design artefact is no longer a universal requirement as open-meaning of artefacts gained importance [7]. As

R. Masu (✉) • A. Conci • Z. Menestrina • A. De Angeli
InterAction Laboratory, Department of Information Engineering and Computer Science, University of Trento, Via Sommarive 9, 38123 Trento, Italy
e-mail: raul.masu@unitn.it; andrea.conci.1@unitn.it; zeno.menestrina@unitn.it; antonella.deangeli@unitn.it

F. Morreale
InterAction Laboratory, Department of Information Engineering and Computer Science, University of Trento, Via Sommarive 9, 38123 Trento, Italy

Centre for Digital Music, School of EECS, Queen Mary University of London, London, UK
e-mail: f.morreale@qmul.ac.uk

© Springer International Publishing Switzerland 2016
A. De Angeli et al. (eds.), *COOP 2016: Proceedings of the 12th International Conference on the Design of Cooperative Systems, 23-27 May 2016, Trento, Italy,*
DOI 10.1007/978-3-319-33464-6_20

309

**Fig. 20.1** Beatfield

a consequence, a number of concepts that HCI traditionally opposed, such as *appropriation* [2, 3] and *ambiguity* [4], were promoted as means to give rise to heterogeneous interpretations of an artefact.

Appropriation is an "improvisation and adaptation around technology" [2], which allows users to adapt the interaction possibilities offered by the system at their own. It can be encouraged by operating on the affordance of the artefact. In the design of new musical instruments, for instance, appropriation strongly relates to interface affordances, and how they are used in musical practice [8].

Ambiguity should be pursued when a design product is intended to be evocative and enigmatic rather than instrumental and explicit [4]. It can be encouraged by a series of design considerations. For instance, the product should expose inconsistencies and cast doubts on the source of information, it can diverge from its original meaning when used in radically new contexts, and it should assemble diverse contexts, as to create tensions that must be resolved.

Appropriation and ambiguity were employed in the design of Beatfield (Fig. 20.1), a musical installation with ambiguous character that was specifically designed to stimulate a multitude of interpretations by promoting appropriation of interaction strategies and objectives [omitted]. Appropriation is fostered by the affordance of the aesthetics of the object and by the way in which the user can interact with it. Beatfield consists of an augmented game board whose aesthetics resembles that of a chessboard; users can interact with it by placing a number of tangible blocks on top of it.

Beatfield can be experienced by a single user or by a group of users, depending on which the experience acquires the character of a collaborative musical interface, an exploratory game, or an immersive unreflective interaction. The interface was evaluated by 21 invited participants. The results confirmed that the interpretations they attributed to the installation were highly heterogeneous.

## 20.2 Beatfield

The design of Beatfield was performed with a series of participatory design activities based on MINUET, a design framework of musical interfaces used to generate design ideas [6]. A number of design solutions have been followed to ensure users to appropriate the installation giving it their personal meaning. For instance: (i) the mapping between user input and audio visual output is unpredictable, (ii) the functionality of the system are pointed out without explaining the narratives of use; (iii) the tangible objects evocate an enigmatic imagery.

### 20.2.1 Architecture

Beatfield is composed of two wooden boxes (Fig. 20.1). The box on the top is an augmented game board called the Radiant$^2$, a tangible interface originally designed as a videogame controller [5]. The surface of the Radiant$^2$ is divided into a $6 \times 6$ matrix. Beneath the opaque top surface lays a number of RGB LEDs; each LED sits beneath a cell of the matrix. Players can interact with the device by placing tangible objects on the surface of Radiant$^2$. The objects are equally divided into two colour, yellow and a blue, and each colour is composed of one *king* and three *pawns* (Fig. 20.1). This physical appearance recalls a standard chess game environment. This choice helps to clarify the standard interaction mechanics (i.e. moving pieces on a board), but it also enhance the ambiguity of the system given that the game mechanics differ from those of chess. The box on the bottom contains a portable speaker (Bose SoundLink2) that allows having a self-contained object where the sound source and the interaction device correspond. The computer that controls the audio and light can indeed be placed on a remote desk, thus it is transparent to the user.

### 20.2.2 Functioning

Each cell of the Radiant$^2$ is associated to a specific rhythmic pattern, which is played every times a *pawn* is placed on top of it. Pieces of the same colour have the same timbre (yellow pawns sound the same, and so do the blue). As opposed to *pawns*, *kings* don't play any sound but have an influence on lights: when positioned on a cell, a *king* lights up three cells with its colour. Those three cells have a rhythmically-alike pattern, meaning that they sound harmonic when they play together. Lights affect the timbre of the rhythmical patterns when a *pawn* of the same colour is placed on top of it. In this case, that specific rhythmic pattern has an enhanced harmonic spectrum. In some cases, when both *kings* are placed on the Radiant$^2$, they could be rhythmically affine to the same positions. In such cases, these positions would light up with green colour (a combination of yellow and blue).

### 20.2.3 *Music Generation*

The music generated by Beatfield is composed of a drone tone (a low, slow sound with *dark* timbre), and up to six rhythmical patterns (one for each *pawn*). Players interaction has no influence on the drone tone. Instead, they can manipulate the rhythmical patterns by placing *pawns* on top of a cell. Each cell of the matrix is associated with a fixed rhythmic pattern. The columns of the matrix correspond to the bar length (i.e. the first column is one quarter bar long, the second two quarters long, and so on up to six quarters); the rows correspond to the number of notes in the bar (i.e. the first row has one note for each bar, the second two notes, and so on up to six notes for bar; Figure). Such configuration allows for a great variety of rhythms, whose density spans from the cell in position [1, 6], which plays six notes for second, to the cell in position [1, 6], which plays one note every 6 s. A global metronome set at 60 bpm for the quarter note synchronises all the rhythms.

Each rhythmic pattern is filled with notes randomly selected from a set of eight notes. The notes that populates this set continuously evolves: every 12 quarters, one note is removed from the set and replaced with a new one. This new note is also transposed two octaves lower and replaces the drone note. All the sounds are synthesised using a FM synthesis model. Blue *pawns* have bell-like low timber, while yellow *pawns* have high bright timber.

## 20.3   Evaluation

In order to assess the potential of Beatfield for stimulating a variety of interpretations, we conducted an evaluation with 21 participants that were especially invited to try the installation. The installation was tested in an historical building in the city centre of [omitted]. Beatfield was positioned on a table located at the centre of an empty room. Participants tried the installation alone or in groups up to three people. None of the players received information about the objectives or the mechanisms of the system.

At the end of the session, which lasted as long as participants wished, they were interviewed by a researcher with a semi-structured method. They were invited to talk about whatever they considered relevant to describe their experience. As one last question, we asked participants: to produce a description of the object and the meaning they attributed to it. Results showed that players interacted with Beatfield using a number of different strategies and gave the system a variety of interpretations. It is worth noting that, in most cases, participants underwent more than a single interpretation and interaction strategy.

Several participants spent most of the session trying to understand the underlying mechanisms of the installation. In other cases, participants focused on meaning making. They wanted to explore the goals of the installation and they tried to find rules they were supposed to follow. Some participants interacted with Beatfield pretending it was a musical controller. They were aiming at creating particular polyrhythmic structures, or manipulating the overall timbre. In some cases, participants explored the visual feedback of the Radiant[2], searching for specific light combinations (in most of the cases they were hunting for the green light), or creating geometrical dispositions of pieces. Other participants, rather than consciously exploring the artefact, abandoned themselves to a free interaction with the installation. They simply followed their instinct, disregarding to spend time understanding the mechanisms of the system but rather enjoying the such open-ended character of the interaction.

Interestingly, when Beatfield was played by groups, two main dynamics emerged. Some of them exhibited *challenging* and gaming attitudes. They spontaneously divided the pieces into two teams of different colours. In these cases, they had a competitive experience, both on the ownership of the pieces and on the light positions. By contrast, other participants showed a *collaborative* attitude. They discussed about the system aiming at cooperatively understanding its underlying functionality, sharing comments and ideas. In some cases, they specifically aimed at creating something they liked as a group, specifically directing their interaction strategies to compose a musical or visual compositions they liked.

## 20.4   Conclusion

For the Interactive Experiences session of COOP 2016 we would like to arrange the installation focusing on the interaction with Beatfield in a public context. When experienced by groups of people, the open-ended character of the installation should stimulate collaborative reflection. With respect to the evaluation with invited visitors, testing the installation in a public context should produce collaboration among visitors simultaneously interacting with it, but also among people that try it at different times. Beatfield will not be reinitialised after each iteration, thus newcomers will play starting from the composition as it was left by previous visitors. It will become a piece of participatory and relational art, in which the art piece has not a final configuration but it keeps evolving with successive modifications of the visitors. As discussed above, the installation offers a number of different interpretations, and no one can be considered correct or wrong. During the interactive experience session such character of the installation should potentially encourage debates among participants.

# References

1. Bødker S (2015) Third-wave HCI, 10 years later – participation and sharing. Interactions 22(5):24–31
2. Dix A (2007) Designing for appropriation. In: Proceedings of the 21st British HCI Group Annual Conference on People and Computers: HCI . . . but not as we know it-Vol 2, pp 27–30
3. Dourish P (2003) The appropriation of interactive technologies: some lessons from placeless documents. Comput Supported Coop Work 12(4):465–490
4. Gaver WW, Beaver J, Benford S (2003). Ambiguity as a resource for design. In: Proceedings of the SIGCHI conference on human factors in computing systems, pp 233–240
5. Menestrina Z, Bianchi M, Siesser A, Masu R, Conci A (2014) OHR. In: Proceedings of the first ACM SIGCHI annual symposium on computer-human Interaction in Play, pp 355–358
6. Morreale F, De Angeli A, O'Modhrain S (2014) Musical interface design: an experience-oriented framework. In: Proceedings of NIME
7. Sengers P, Gaver B (2006) Staying open to interpretation: engaging multiple meanings in design and evaluation. In: Proceedings of the 6th conference on designing interactive systems, pp 99–108
8. Zappi V, McPherson A (2014) Dimensionality and appropriation in digital musical instrument design. In: Proceedings of the international conference on new interfaces for musical expression, pp 455–460

# Chapter 21
# FeltRadio: Experiencing and Participating in WiFi Activities Through Sensorial Augmentation

**Jonas Fritsch and Erik Grönvall**

**Abstract** FeltRadio is a portable technology for sensing WiFi through sensorial augmentation and Electric Muscle Stimulation (EMS). The technology enables its wearer to sensorially engage with the radio waves and WiFi activities that have become an integrated part of our everyday lives. The sensorial engagement changes people's experience of WiFi activities, and allows them to participate in wireless communication infrastructures in novel ways. This is both an immediately embodied activity as it is a new form of social awareness. In this paper, we briefly present the FeltRadio technology and show how it facilitates new forms of critical reflection through sensorial participation in our contemporary experience of wireless traffic.

## 21.1 Introduction

Radio waves surround us but still they remain largely undetected by our senses. Unless we use specifically tuned hardware, such as FM radios, cell phones or WiFi modems, human beings cannot perceive wirelessly transmitted data. FeltRadio is a portable and wireless technology that makes it possible to turn radio signals into visual and tactile stimuli as a form of sensorial augmentation. This way, FeltRadio enables people to experience WiFi as a sensory input.

The FeltRadio technology is a piece of experimental engineering, both exploring new ways of using existing digital technologies as well as new ideas about how these technologies can be used to change our experience of our technologically saturated everyday lives. In our work with developing and testing FeltRadio, we have been inspired by technical experiments with sensorial augmentation [1], work on Electrical Muscle Stimulation (EMS) [2] and theoretical framings on our 'felt experience' of technology [3], the omnipresent reality of 'Hertzian Space' surrounding our use of electronic objects [4], and our experience of 'wirelessness' [5],

J. Fritsch (✉) • E. Grönvall
IT University of Copenhagen, Rued Langgaards Vej 7, 2300 Copenhagen S, Denmark
e-mail: frit@itu.dk; erig@itu.dk

© Springer International Publishing Switzerland 2016
A. De Angeli et al. (eds.), *COOP 2016: Proceedings of the 12th International Conference on the Design of Cooperative Systems, 23–27 May 2016, Trento, Italy,*
DOI 10.1007/978-3-319-33464-6_21

315

all of which we have unfolded in [6]. In this paper, we will focus on how it is possible to frame the FeltRadio technology as a cooperative system that facilitates new kinds of critical reflections through sensorial participation in the invisible technological infrastructures that surround us. We build this frame based on a theoretical exploration and findings from two empirical studies we have carried out, where people have been testing the FeltRadio technology. First, we start with a more detailed description of the design of FeltRadio, and what conditions of emergence for experiencing WiFi we are enabling through the engineering of the technology.

### 21.1.1  The FeltRadio Technology and WiFi Experience

FeltRadio takes the momentary peak signal strength of all radio-signals that it detects in the 2.4 GHz frequency band and can either visualize this signal on a led bar display or translate it to electric impulses that are sent into the human body through electrodes (i.e. adhesive pads) placed on the body using an Electrical Muscle Stimulation (EMS) device. FeltRadio takes the form of a physical box with an antenna and two electrodes sticking out of it. Inside the box there is a 2.4 GHz band-pass filter and a circuit that senses the strength of radio traffic signals and converts it to a variable voltage. This voltage is fed into a microcontroller that, depending on the voltage-level (i.e. the strength of the captured radio signal), controls the EMS-level sent into the body through the electrodes. FeltRadio is designed so it can be carried around in a small shoulder-bag or similar, with the electrode-wires running up to the arm or other body part. The new experience of WiFi (or other 2.4 GHz based radio communications) provided by FeltRadio explores and makes us reflect upon what it would be like if we could sense, and feel, wireless traffic [6] (Fig. 21.1).

The experience of WiFi facilitated by FeltRadio is focused on the immediate, local level of radio traffic rather than a more general 'feel' of WiFi coverage and

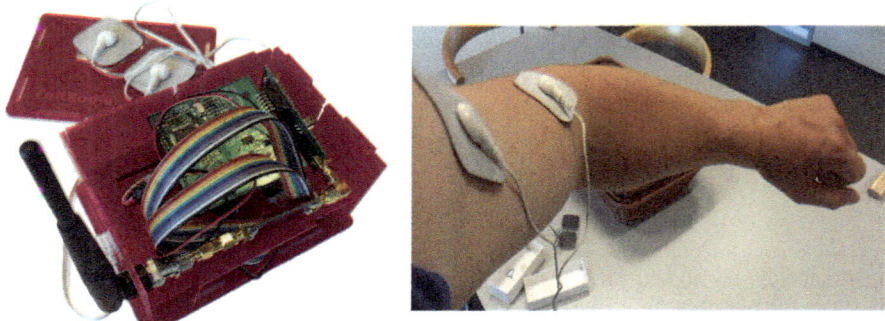

**Fig. 21.1**  Picture of the FeltRadio system and the attachment of EMS pads on a user's arm

as a cloud. FeltRadio takes all signals in a particular radio frequency band and turns these signals into a human perceivable output letting people experience what is going on at a specific frequency band at a specific location and point in time. This means that the experience of WiFi is directly tied to the intensity of wireless activity; somebody – or something – is generating wireless signals within about 20 m from where you are standing. In our work we have mostly been exploring the use of EMS, i.e. using the skin as a receptor. Here EMS is not used to control muscles to create specific limb movement. Rather, it is used to create a sensation, an embodied stimulus (of 2.4 GHz radio activity). The combination of a radio traffic sensing technology and the use of EMS for sensorial augmentation is unique for FeltRadio and that combination is what has motivated our studies so far. In the two case studies conducted, people have been exploring FeltRadio in familiar contexts, like the home neighborhood or the workplace. These explorations have led to reflections on FeltRadio as a technology but also on WiFi, radio and what creates radio traffic. Below, we build on findings from these studies to situate the FeltRadio technology in a cooperative systems context.

## 21.2  Different Kinds of Participation in WiFi Activities

The first was comprised of five people with little technical skills focused on the difference between using LED and EMS as a sensory input and how wearing FeltRadio would possibly impact people's contextual knowledge of their everyday environments. At the same time, we were also interested in findings related to how the feeling of using FeltRadio would be shaped through this contextual knowledge. The second study was comprised of five people with higher technical skills, and was focusing more on unfolding the felt experience of being able to sense wireless technologies, and what kind of sensation people were actually experiencing through EMS in a technologically saturated context of use (the IT University of Copenhagen). We have reported in detail on both studies in [6]. In the two studies, we have focused on people's experience of wearing FeltRadio and resulting reflections. Themes emerging from the studies have concerned general discussions of WiFi in general, of radio and its infrastructures, making sense of what and who 'creates' WiFi traffic and FeltRadio as a piece of interactive engineering. The studies have allowed us to not only understand people's experiences of WiFi through sensorial augmentation but also to better understand FeltRadio as an experimental technology (Fig. 21.2).

From both studies it has become clear that using FeltRadio can both be understood as a very personal, sensorial experience as well as a collective, social experience. According to the test persons, wireless activity is closely related to a sense of sociality, becoming very aware of the social context and what people might be doing to cause the EMS induced tactile vibrations resulting from the increase in WiFi activity. This would either result in people trying to avoid areas with larger groups of people, but some test persons would also seek out people

**Fig. 21.2**  A person exploring
his neighborhood from a RF
perspective with Felt Radio.
The technology is placed in
the shoulder-bag and the
EMS pads are attached to the
person's right arm

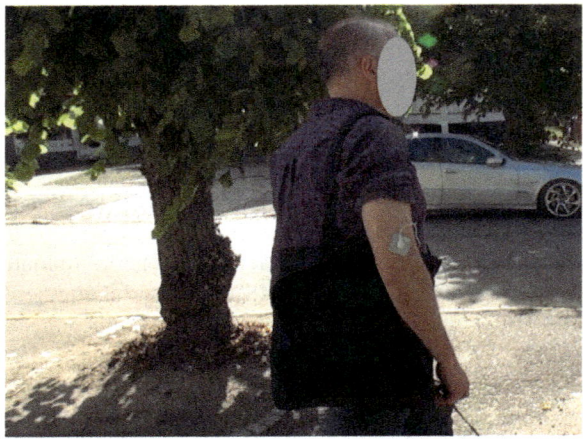

to test the technology. The perceptual trigger of EMS also resulted in the test
persons trying to make sense of the feeling of changes in WiFi activity, making
up stories about what people were doing causing these changes. To a large extent,
these stories were prompted by people's contextual knowledge of i.e. who was
living in a particular house, or what kind of people were gathered in a particular
context. This way, FeltRadio seems to allow for a form of participation in social
experiences strongly influenced by other people's actual or supposed network
activities. Interestingly, experiencing WiFi through the FeltRadio technology has
a distinctly social dimension in addition to the sensorial and embodied stimulation.
The feeling of WiFi activity correlates with a form of social awareness, which is
bodily perceived in a novel way.

In particular in the second exploratory study, the participants would repeatedly
refer to the stimuli provided through FeltRadio as an additional form of sensation,
mixing with their other senses; a sensation of WiFi as a technology but also a
sensation of people and their activities. An interesting finding concerns how the
tactile stimuli provided through the EMS were not only a tactile experience; all
senses would be affected by this new sensorial input. The participants even gave
examples of changes in breathing and heartbeat. Clearly, FeltRadio changes the
parameters for engaging sensorially with people's surroundings as well as people's
own bodily sensations. We are still trying to make sense of this double kind of
sensorial participation, which seems to be an integrated part of the felt experience
of the FeltRadio technology.

In both exploratory studies, people have given feedback on how being able
to suddenly sense WiFi and become more reflective about their participation in
wireless infrastructures might influence their actions on an everyday basis. In study
one, most people said they would use the technology to seek out places with less
WiFi to get 'a break' from the radio waves. In study two, many participants said

they would also use this new form of sensation to seek out places with good WiFi reception. In any case, it is clear that the sensation of WiFi and the reflected participation in wireless infrastructures facilitated by FeltRadio would potentially lead to a change of habits and social actions.

## 21.3   Conclusion: Empowering and Disempowering Aspects of Experiencing WiFi Through FeltRadio

In our studies of people's experience of being able to suddenly sense WiFi, we find it important to critically reflect on the different kinds of participation facilitated by FeltRadio. In both studies we can see that sensing wireless traffic through FeltRadio is a curious experience. This experience can, however, lead to both a feeling of empowerment and disempowerment. A sense of empowerment might emerge from new insights enabled by having access to information that is normally hidden and the ethical and social speculations that may come from this engagement. But a sense of disempowerment can also appear as, in a way, FeltRadio brings to the front our role as bystanders to others' activities and interactions with (wireless) technology. This is closely tied to the use of EMS as well, which registers immediately as a tactile and embodied experience. Through the sensorial augmentation, FeltRadio can make us aware, in a very tangible way, of how our bodies are subject to external stimuli beyond our control.

When looking into the felt experience enabled by the FeltRadio technology, we need to consider the technology's constitutive role in forming basic conditions for our understanding of, and critical reflection on, the relation between (digital) technologies, social action, sensorial participation, and participation in – and exclusion from – different communities through the lens of empowerment and disempowerment. From the studies it seems clear that there is no straightforward answer to how this is experienced by the participants. More studies are needed to shed further light on the relationality of the WiFi experience.

The findings from the FeltRadio project clearly indicate that this technology can be considered as a cooperative system, changing people's everyday sensorial engagement with and social awareness of the world. Making perceivable the hidden infrastructures as something you can sense and act upon is one step towards a critical reflection on the workings of these forms of participation. In the future, we are planning to set up longitudinal studies to better explore how the experience of using FeltRadio might develop over time.

**Acknowledgments** We would like our colleague Anna Vallgårda for her participation in the FeltRadio project. We would also like to thank Erika S. Panduro, Ian V. A. Kjær, Sara A. G. Nielsen, Sofie A. B. Calundann and Troels Madsen for their work with FeltRadio. Finally, we like to thank all our study participants.

# References

1. Linden J, Rogers Y, Oshodi M, Spiers A, McGoran D, Cronin R, O'Dowd P (2011) Haptic reassurance in the pitch black for an immersive theatre experience. Paper presented at the proceedings of the 13th international conference on Ubiquitous computing, Beijing, China
2. Farbiz F, Yu ZH, Manders C, Ahmad W (2007) An electrical muscle stimulation haptic feedback for mixed reality tennis game. Paper presented at the ACM SIGGRAPH 2007 posters, San Diego
3. McCarthy J, Wright P (2004) Technology as experience. MIT Press, Boston
4. Dunne A (2008) Hertzian tales: electronic products, aesthetic experience, and critical design. MIT Press, Cambridge, MA
5. Mackenzie A (2010) Wirelessness: radical empiricism in network cultures. MIT Press, Cambridge, MA
6. Grönvall E, Fritsch J, Vallgårda A (2016) FeltRadio – sensing and making sense of wireless traffic. In Proceedings of Designing Interactive Systems (DIS) 2016, Brisbane, Australia, pp 829–840

# Chapter 22
# Listening to the Walkable City

**Max Willis and Melissa Cate Christ**

**Abstract** This paper describes the creation, experience and assessment of a soundscape installation, conceived and undertaken as a contribution to the research project "Hong Kong Stair Archive: Documenting the Walkable City". It examines the use of audio recordings and their presentation in a three-dimensional sound-field installation to provide an additional layer of data, analysis and interactivity to the investigation of pedestrian urban environments. This installation combines culturally and socially definitive sounds, photographs, architectural drawings and introductory texts to draw attention to the unique qualities of walking spaces and their use context, participatory nature and importance to life in the modern city.

## 22.1 Introduction

*Listening to the Walkable City* is a stand-alone constellation of audio and computer equipment arranged in an exhibition space and supported by original drawings, photography and text from an ongoing research project in Hong Kong that investigates urban environments and pedestrian walking areas. The proposed interactive experience engages people in the research material collected in the project entitled, "Hong Kong Stair Archive: Documenting the Walkable City". The project uncovers the social, cultural and historic aspects of the 'walkable city': those parts of the urban environment that are dominated and shaped by people and their social interactions. *Listening to the Walkable City* is conceived and undertaken as a contribution to the larger research project by introducing the collection and processing of audio recordings as a way to provide an additional layer of data, analysis and interactivity to the investigation of pedestrian urban environments. The presentation of the sound

M. Willis (✉)
Semantics and Knowledge Innovation Lab (SKIL) Telecom Italia, Trento, Italy
e-mail: max@maxwillis.net

M. Cate Christ
School of Design, Hong Kong Polytechnic University, HKSAR, China
e-mail: melissacatechrist@gmail.com

© Springer International Publishing Switzerland 2016                    321
A. De Angeli et al. (eds.), *COOP 2016: Proceedings of the 12th International Conference on the Design of Cooperative Systems, 23–27 May 2016, Trento, Italy*,
DOI 10.1007/978-3-319-33464-6_22

of these environments in an immersive, ambisonic, surround-sound installation aims to transmit the sense of place and ambiance from one context to another, in this case the Hong Kong soundscape to the Trento setting.

The intention of *Listening to the Walkable City* is to activate the experience of the Hong Kong soundfield from two perspectives: (1) the imitation of natural-world acoustic dynamics enabled by the ambisonic technique provides a realistic orientation to listeners, and enhances their engagement with the research material through immersion in a digitally mediated, physical environment; and (2) the creation of a relaxed, playful, social atmosphere within the installation encourages visitors to participate and discuss, further facilitating their engagement with the research materials.

## 22.2   Soundscape and Ambience

When listening, the multitude of sounds in an environment are encountered and processed as one sensation, a phenomenon referred to as tonal coalescence [12]. A soundscape provides this multitude of sounds, for example, the cacophony of a busy urban space or the equally complex but tranquil acoustics of a rural setting. Yet a soundscape is defined not only as an environment of sound, but also as its perception and understanding by an individual or society. The listener is at the center of the field of a soundscape or acoustic ecology [11]. Similarly, the pedestrian is central to the particular environments transposed to this installation. The information provided by the sounds, and their arrangement in the installation environment, places visitors in the virtual space both contextually and acoustically. Entering into the installation, the visitor is immediately immersed in and becomes central to the content of the soundscape. The acoustic immersion is achieved though a unique implementation of ambisonic audio spatialization in MAX/MSP, an interaction programming interface. In the ambisonic space, audio sources can be stationary, or can move dynamically through the space. This dynamism of sound replicates the natural listening situation for participants who enter into the installation's sphere of influence.

The character and nature of an environment, human-centered or otherwise, can be referred to as its ambience, which is a complex matrix of sensations encountered as a whole. Sound is uniquely capable of communicating ambience, as opposed to light, smell or temperature alone, as it can be recorded, arranged and replayed for analysis [10]. In everyday experience, voices and activities are major contributing factors to the character of sonic environments. Likewise, spatialization and localization by way of sound are fundamental to engaging with the surrounding environment. Although within a digitally facilitated media space this engagement with sound is restricted [7], the proposed installation is melding media space with a real environment.

In *Listening to the Walkable City*, sonic attributes form an ambient backdrop which communicates the prevailing spatial practices and cultures that inhabit the space being represented. However, the experience of a sound is mediated, facilitated by the listener's relation to the sound and their ability to contextualize the auditory experience [8, 9]. As the time and place that this installation represents, and the socio-cultural information it communicates, may not be immediately apparent to all audiences, it is necessary to provide some visual and textual background to help create a frame of reference for listeners. The sound environment is therefore augmented with images and text related to the listening experience and the Hong Kong stair environments. These materials are presented indirectly, discontinuous from their position in the soundscape, as the primary aim of the work is to draw attention to the auditory qualities of urban pedestrian spaces.

## 22.3  Interaction and Participation

The focus in discussions about interactivity has long been technology-oriented [4], examining engagement with audiences through digital artifacts. However, emphasis is currently shifting from interactivity's technological facilitation to its perceived modes of interaction, such as its aesthetic, ludological and more frequently, empowerment modes [1]. While the level of interactivity has often been gauged by a given work's similarity with face-to-face communication, deemed to be the ultimate frame of reference for the interactive, this may not always be an applicable paradigm for imagining and examining interactivity [5]. One perspective is that the activities associated with interactivity "expand the boundaries of audience engagement in the unfolding of the work and the correlated process of meaning-making, thus promoting new participatory roles and practices" [3]. Modes which assess to what degree the work facilitates this expansion can be a more accurate measure of the interactivity of an installation.

As a soundscape is comprised of a complex interrelation between sounds space and the listener, so the ambisonic sound-field that we create is an interrelation of digital artefacts, analog signals, equipment, and the exhibition space. At the center of this is the visitor, without whom the installation, it's content and context has no meaning. This space becomes a performance similar to that of the real environment [6], actively acknowledging the visitor as participant and performer. Voice, as we have mentioned, is our paramount contribution to the sonic environment. To enact a vocal participation in our soundscape installation, and return to participants a sense of their own place within the environment, a simple technological interactive system using a microphone is introduced. Participants can speak into the microphone, and hear, from within the soundscape, conversations in Cantonese and Mandarin recorded on the stairs in Hong Kong. Alternatively, the microphone audits the installation environment, and as noise levels rise among the physical participants, so too do voices become louder and more numerous in the virtual environment. The Chinese voice, possibly unintelligible to many who visit the installation in Trento, Italy, provides a commentary on the collective production and experience of language and noise in the urban sonic environment and can lead to reduced listening [2], regardless of its semantic content. This simple technical implementation that triggers sound files based on audio level analysis augments the installation's other inherent modes of interactivity with a playful form of participation whereby the vocalizations of the audience contribute to both real and virtual soundscapes.

## 22.4 Assessment and Outcomes

Listening to the Walkable City is focused on examining the soundscape installation as a transmission of particular research outcomes. Therefore, in order to discover what the installation adds to the public reception of the urban environmental research, a qualitative evaluation approach based on an open sorting methodology will be used to gather feedback as to visitors' attentions, interests and attitudes concerning the experience.

Feedback will be collected in the form of a survey, taken either textually or using hand-held audio recorder, not on exiting the installation, but during the experience. In this case, direct access to participants' thoughts and ideas while they visit the installation will be of greatest value to the research. The design of the questions is meant to extract specific positions as well as open-ended intimations of the experience. Sample questions include: What sounds can you identify, or seem familiar?; Can you determine in which direction the street is located?; Where in the installation space do you feel the most comfortable?; What thoughts or emotions does the experience evoke?; Does the experience revive a particular memory?; Can you imagine you are actually in Hong Kong?; Can you make any associations between these heritage spaces in Hong Kong and those in your own city?; and Can you describe any similarity or differences to other walkable urban environments?

Additionally, a significant amount of data will be gathered through audio and video analysis. This can be examined quantitatively to determine how long each visitor spends in the space and where in the installation they go and spend the most time. This audio-video analysis can be approached qualitatively to address questions such as: How do visitors interact with each other?; Does the microphone interactivity attract attention and stimulate activity?; and Does the social interaction between participants encourage their engagement with the materials?

The performance of the audio questionnaire, the observation of the participants and the correlation of these datasets will enable categorization of the interactions and engagements and begin the formulation of an overall view of the installation's reception by the participants in relation to the presented research.

## 22.5 Conclusion and Development

The process of developing, assessing, refining and redeploying an installation as a means of communicating research outcomes is itself an iterative design process. Through this process, more concrete research questions can be formulated to determine how better to implement the immersive, interactive, multimedia environment to express and extend our research. This line of inquiry leverages creative activity and playful, social interaction to open academic inquiry to the public. The interactive arts serve here as an invitation for recipients, as participants, to engage, to interpret and become active meaning-makers. Thus the work contributes not only by expanding our understanding of sonic interaction and soundscape installation, but by investigating and testing new and engaging means to share and digest research outcomes.

**Acknowledgments**  Special thanks to the COOP 2016 organizers and reviewers, especially Maria Menendez Blanco and Jonas Fritsch for their invaluable assistance. The Hong Kong Stair Archive project is supported by a grant from the Research Grants Council of the Hong Kong Special Administrative Region, China [Project No. (PolyU274002/14H)].

# References

1. Barry M, Doherty G (2016) What we talk about when we talk about interactivity: empowerment in public discourse. New Media Soc. Feb 2
2. Chion M (1994) Audio-vision: sound on sScreen. Columbia University Press, New York
3. Jacucci G, Wagner M, Wagner I, Giaccardi E, Annunziato M, Breyer N, Hansen J, Jo K, Ossevoort S, Perini A, Roussel N, Schuricht S(2010) ParticipArt: exploring participation in interactive art installations. In: 9th IEEE international symposium on mixed and augmented reality 2010: arts, media, and humanities, ISMAR-AMH 2010 – proceedings, pp 3–10
4. Spiro K (2002) Interactivity: a concept explication. New Media and Society 4(3):355–383
5. Kwastek K (2013) Aesthetics of interaction in digital art. MIT Press, Cambridge
6. Lefebvre H (1991, 1974) The production of space. Blackwell, London
7. Paterson N, Conway F (2013) Situated soundscapes: redefining media art and the urban experience. Leonardo Electron Almanac 19(1):122–134
8. Sarah P (2009) Doing sensory ethnography, vol 143. SAGE Publications Ltd, London/Thousand Oaks, pp 13–15
9. Saldanha A (2009) Soundscapes. University of Minnesota/Elsevier Ltd., Minneapolis
10. Thibaud J-P (2011) A sonic paradigm of urban ambiances. J Sonic Stud 1(1) (http://journal.sonicstudies.org/vol01/nr01/a02)
11. Truax B (2000) Soundscape composition as global music (sfu.ca/~truax/soundescape.html)
12. Zuckerkandl V (1973) Sound and symbol. Music and the external world. Princeton University Press, Princeton

# Symposium on Challenges and Experiences in Designing for an Ageing Society. Reflecting on Concepts of Age(ing) and Communication Practices

**Markus Garschall, Theo Hamm, Dominik Hornung, Claudia Müller, Katja Neureiter, Marén Schorch, and Lex van Velsen**

## Description of the Theme

Practice- and user-oriented design approaches, e.g., user centred design (UCƆ) or participatory design (PD), have built a canon for IT projects aiming at product development for the ageing society. However, there seem to be still many blind spots, which are simply overlooked or taken-for-granted, when reflecting on IT design projects from either a bird's eye or micro perspective. This symposium is devoted to creating a space for reflections on projects from both perspectives in two separate tracks.

M. Garschall
AIT Austrian Institute of Technology, Innovation Systems Department,
Business Unit Technology Experience, Vienna, Austria
e-mail: markus.garschall@ait.ac.at

T. Hamm • D. Hornung • C. Müller
IT for the Ageing Society, University of Siegen, Siegen, Germany
e-mail: theodor.hamm@uni-siegen.de; dominik.hornung@uni-siegen.de;
claudia.mueller@uni-siegen.de

K. Neureiter
Center for Human Computer Interaction, University of Salzburg, Austria
e-mail: katja.neureiter@sbg.ac.at

M. Schorch
Information Systems and New Media, University of Siegen, Siegen, Germany
e-mail: maren.schorch@uni-siegen.de

L. van Velsen
Roessingh Research and Development, Telemedicine Cluster, Enschede, The Netherlands
e-mail: l.vanvelsen@rrd.nl

© Springer International Publishing Switzerland 2016
A. De Angeli et al. (eds.), *COOP 2016: Proceedings of the 12th International Conference on the Design of Cooperative Systems, 23–27 May 2016, Trento, Italy,*
DOI 10.1007/978-3-319-33464-6

Track A addresses the discussion of and reflection on *images of age and ageing from a meta-perspective*. The focus will be set on the social construction of concepts of ageing, and how these are being framed in (taken-for-granted) theories of age and ageing, from deficit- to activity-oriented stances [10]. In this track it is the goal to take a deeper look at how images of ageing are present in different stakeholders'/participants' heads [11, 13]. At the same time, we aim at the deconstruction of their impacts on the design of artifacts as well as on the formulation of IT project objectives themselves: A bandwidth of themes is possible from ethnographically derived self-images of older adults and related attitudes and appropriation processes of and towards IT products [3, 5, 6] to questions of how individual research interests shape the projects themselves (i.e., the formulation of needs, requirements, research targets, and so on) [5, 14].

Track B focuses on *communication practices in UCD and PD projects*, which are widely established practices to focus on users' needs [1, 2, 7, 9]. Both approaches require clear and inspiring communication among all members involved, particularly the end-users. While there has been a variety of research on best practices and pitfalls during UCD and PD approaches, particularly with regards to older adults (e.g., [2, 4, 8, 12]), communication issues in this context are barely addressed. However, creating and fostering an open, clear and inspiring mode of communication is crucial for generating innovative, ground-breaking technology. The main goal is to discuss and reflect upon notions, best practices, and recommendations for successful communication to better address user requirements throughout the development process, when working with older adults. We aim at developing principles and guidelines that support the communication process among engineers and designers.

# References

1. Abras C, Maloney-Krichmar D, Preece J (2004) User-centred design. In: Bainbridge W (ed) Encyclopedia of human-computer interaction. Sage, Thousand Oaks, pp 445–456, 37(4)
2. Ellis RD, Kurniawan SH (2000) Increasing the usability of online information for older users: a case study in participatory design. Int J Hum-Comput Interact 12(2):263–276
3. Fitzpatrick G, Ellingsen G (2012) A review of 25 years of CSCW research in healthcare: contributions, challenges and future agendas. In: Comput Supported Coop Work (CSCW)
4. Lindsay S, Jackson D, Schofield G, Olivier P (2013) Engaging older people using participatory design. In: Proceedings of CHI'12 human factors in computing systems, pp 1199–1208
5. Müller C, Hornung D, Hamm T, Wulf V (2015) Practice-based design of a neighborhood portal: focusing on elderly tenants in a city quarter living lab. In: Proceedings of CHI'15, pp 2295–2304 (CHI 2015 Honorable Mention)
6. Müller C, Neufeldt C, Randall D, Wulf V (2012) ICT-development in residential care settings: sensitizing design to the life circumstances of the residents of a care home. In: Proceedings of CHI'12, May 05–10 2012, Austin, USA
7. Muller MJ (2002) Participatory design: the third space in HCI. In: The human-computer interaction handbook: fundamentals, evolving technologies and emerging applications, L. Erlbaum Associates, Hillsdale, 1051–1068

8. Newell A, Arnott J, Carmichael A, Morgan M (2007) Methodologies for involving older adults in the design process. In: Universal access in human computer interaction. Coping with diversity. Springer, Berlin, pp 982–989

9. Norman DA, Draper SW (1986) User centred system design: new perspectives on human-computer interaction. L. Erlbaum Associates, Hillsdale

10. Östlund B (2004) Social science research on technology and the elderly – does it exist? Sci Stud 17(2):45–63

11. Sijis et al (2015) Expanding mastery into futures. On involving old people in participatory design. Submitted paper

12. Schorch M, Wan L, Randall D, Wulf V (2016) Designing for those who are overlooked. insider perspectives on care practices and cooperative work of elderly informal caregivers. In: ACM conference on computer supported cooperative work 2016

13. Wigg JM (2010) Liberating the wanderers: using technology to unlock doors for those living with dementia. Sociol Health Illn 32(2):288–303

14. Wulf V, Müller C, Pipek V, Randall D, Rohde M, Stevens G (2015) Practice-based computing. Empirically-grounded conceptualizations derived from design case studies. In: Wulf V, Randall D, Schmidt K (eds) Designing socially embedded technologies in the real-world. Springer, London

# Contextual Collaboration: Where Automation and People Meet

**Nicole Perterer, Verena Fuchsberger, Manfred Tscheligi, Astrid Weiss, Volker Wulf, and Klaus Bengler**

## Theme of the Workshop

This day-long workshop focuses on collaboration with autonomous systems and in automated environments. Due to trends towards autonomous driving and smart industrial automation (e.g., Internet-of-Things, cyber-physical systems), individuals are more and more surrounded by (semi-) autonomous systems. The way humans collaborate with each other in these automated environments or with autonomous systems and how they experience the interactions is of great interest for researchers and practitioners, for instance, in the car context (e.g., [5], [10]).

Research has demonstrated that context-sensitive designs are central for a unique situation-specific user experience (UX) (e.g., [1], [2], [6-8], [9-12], [13]), requiring an exploration of novel interface techniques as well as an understanding of contextual collaboration.

N. Perterer • V. Fuchsberger • M. Tscheligi
University of Salzburg, Sigmund-Haffner-Gasse 18, 5020 Salzburg, Austria
e-mail: Nicole.Perterer@sbg.ac.at; Verena.Fuchsberger@sbg.ac.at; Manfred.Tscheligi@sbg.ac.at

A. Weiss
Vienna University of Technology, Gusshausstraße 27-29, 1040 Vienna, Austria
e-mail: Astrid.Weiss@tuwien.ac.at

V. Wulf
University of Siegen, Kohlbettstraße 15, 57072 Siegen, Germany
e-mail: Volker.Wulf@uni-siegen.de

K. Bengler
Technical University of Munich, Boltzmannstraße 15, 85747 Munich, Germany
e-mail: Bengler@lfe.mw.tum.de

© Springer International Publishing Switzerland 2016     331
A. De Angeli et al. (eds.), *COOP 2016: Proceedings of the 12th International Conference on the Design of Cooperative Systems, 23–27 May 2016, Trento, Italy*,
DOI 10.1007/978-3-319-33464-6

However, the researchers' focus is often primarily on immediate effects of autonomous technology, on particular acceptance and control issues related to autonomous technology (e.g., [3], [14]), or on interactions between a system and a human (e.g., [4]). Human-human collaboration related to autonomous systems or environments have not been directly addressed in research yet.

## The Goal and Purpose

This workshop aims to address these challenges to initiate an in-depth discussion of present and future scenarios (e.g., close collaboration with robotic co-workers, semi-autonomous driving), which are envisioned to highly impact human-human as well as human-system collaboration. The topics of interest include:

### Impact of Modern Automation Technology on Collaboration

- Which roles and tasks may users have? What do these roles and tasks imply for collaboration? (e.g., human in the loop or joint interaction; human-human interaction or human-machine collaboration)
- What privacy, safety, or security issues are emerging?
- How do users experience collaboration via and with (semi-) autonomous systems?
- What aspects of the users' experience are affecting collaboration? (e.g., trust, joy of use)

### Methodology, Measurements and Design Techniques

- Which challenges impede investigating collaboration in (semi-) autonomous contexts (e.g., regarding methods and measures)?
- Which methods and measures are appropriate?

### System Design Fostering Collaboration

- Which challenges and constraints does interaction design face when designing for collaboration in (semi-) autonomous environments?
- What interaction paradigms are appropriate or needed to support collaboration in automated environments and with (semi-) autonomous systems?

The workshop offers a platform to share and learn from each other's experience, discuss challenges, opportunities, constraints, and further advance the dissemination of CSCW knowledge within these domains (e.g., factory, car). The outcome of the workshop will be a list of challenges provided as a white paper after the conference.

# References

1. Brown PJ, Bovey JD, Chen X (1997) Context-aware applications: from the laboratory to the marketplace. Pers Commun IEEE 4(5):58–64, http://dx.doi.org/10.1109/98.626984
2. Chittaro L, Buttussi F, Zangrando N (2014) Desktop virtual reality for emergency preparedness: user evaluation of an aircraft ditching experience under different fear arousal conditions. In: Proceedings of the 20th ACM symposium on virtual reality software and technology (VRST '14), pp 141–150
3. Flemisch F, Bengler K, Bubb H, Winner H, Bruder R (2014) Towards a cooperative guidance and control of highly automated vehicles: H-mode and conduct-by-wire. Ergonomics 57(3):343–360, http://dx.doi.org/10.1080/00140139.2013.869355
4. Hayes B, Gombolay MC, Jung MJ, Hindriks K, De Greeff J, Jonker MC, Neerincx M, Bradshaw JM, Johnson M, Kruijff-Korbayova I, Maarten S, Shah JM, Scassellati B (2015) HRI workshop on human-robot teaming. In: Proceedings of the tenth annual ACM/IEEE international conference on human-robot interaction extended abstracts (HRI'15 Extended Abstracts), pp 255–256. DOI=http://dx.doi.org/10.1145/2701973.2714396
5. Meschtscherjakov A, Tscheligi M, Szostak D, Ratan R, McCall R, Politis I, Krome S. Workshop: experiencing autonomous vehicles: crossing the boundaries between a drive and a ride. In: Proceedings of the 33rd annual ACM conference extended abstracts on human factors in computing systems (CHI EA'15), pp 2413–2416. http://dx.doi.org/10.1145/2702613.2702661
6. Obrist M, Reitberger W, Wurhofer D, Förster F, Tscheligi M (2011) User experience research in the semiconductor factory: a contradiction? In: Proceedings of the 13th international conference on human-computer interaction (INTERACT'11), pp 144–151
7. Perterer (Gridling) N, Meschtscherjakov A, Tscheligi M (2012) I need help! Exploring collaboration in the car. In: Proceedings of the ACM 2012 conference on computer supported cooperative work companion (CSCW'12), pp 87–90
8. Perterer N, Meschtscherjakov A, Tscheligi M (2015) Co-navigator: an advanced navigation system for front-seat passengers. In: Proceedings of the 7th international conference on automotive user interfaces and interactive vehicular applications (AutomotiveUI'15), pp 187–194. http://dx.doi.org/10.1145/2799250.2799265
9. Siewiorek D, Smailagic A, Hornyak M (2002) Multimodal contextual car-driver interface. In: Proceedings of the 4th IEEE international conference on multimodal interfaces (ICMI'02), pp 367–373. http://dx.doi.org/10.1109/ICMI.2002.1167023
10. Wagner M, Koopman P (2015) A philosophy for developing trust in self-driving cars. In: Meyer G, Beiker S (eds) Road vehicle automation, vol 2, Lectures Notes in Mobiltiy. Springer, Switzerland, pp 163–171
11. Weiss A, Mirnig N, Bruckenberger U, Strasser E, Tscheligi M, Kühnlenz (Gonsior) B, Wollherr D, Stanczy B (2015) The interactive urban robot: user-centered development and final field trial of a direction requesting robot. J Behav Robot 6(1):2081–4836
12. Wurhofer D, Meneweger T, Fuchsberger V, Tscheligi M (2015) Deploying robots in a production environment: a study on temporal transitions of workers' experiences. In: Proceedings of the 15th international conference on human-computer interaction (INTERACT'15), pp 203–220
13. Zhang D, Adipat B, Mowafi Y (2009) User-centered context-aware mobile applications—the next generation of personal mobile computing. Commun Assoc Inf Syst 24(3):27–46
14. Zimmermann M, Bauer S, Lütteken N, Rothkirch IM, Bengler K (2014) Acting together by mutual control: evaluating a multimodal interaction concept for cooperative driving. In: Proceedings of the 2014 international conference on collaboration technologies and systems (CTS'14), pp 227–235. http://dx.doi.org/10.1109/CTS.2014.6867569

# Infrastructuring Collaboration

**Giacomo Poderi and Michela Cozza**

## Workshop Theme

Derived from the Latin *cum* (with) and *laborare* (to work), collaboration means the act of working alongside someone to achieve something. Framed in contemporary society, such a definition emphasises the power of collaboration for achieving purposes that would be challenging for a person alone. However, the collaboration is far from being spontaneous and this is why it deserves the experts' attention. How to support collaboration in design field was the theme of a full day workshop that we organised on the occasion of the 12th International Conference on the Design of Cooperative Systems. The purpose was to engage participants in a discussion about collaboration while developing a discourse on *infrastructuring*. Such a term emphasises the complexity of activities that occur over-time in socio-material-technical contexts [1]. By applying the Open Space Technology (OST) [2] the workshop grounded on the question: "What should we consider for infrastructuring collaboration in design/-ing?" The participants were invited to reflect on the conditions for collaborating today, that is how to infrastructure [3] collaboration in different domains while experiencing an infrastructuring process.

G. Poderi • M. Cozza
Department of Engineering and Computer Science, University of Trento, Via Sommarive 9, 38123 Povo 2, Trento, Italy
e-mail: giacomo.poderi@unitn.it; michela.cozza@unitn.it

© Springer International Publishing Switzerland 2016                   335
A. De Angeli et al. (eds.), *COOP 2016: Proceedings of the 12th International Conference on the Design of Cooperative Systems, 23–27 May 2016, Trento, Italy*,
DOI 10.1007/978-3-319-33464-6

## Method

The workshop was conducted according to the OST approach that operates under four principles and one law [2]. The four principles are: "whoever comes are the right people", "whatever happens is the only thing that could have happened", "when it starts is the right time", and "when it's over it's over". The law is known as the Law of Two Feet: if you find yourself in a situation where you are not contributing or learning, move somewhere where you can. The workshop agenda was set by the attendees according to their interest and desire to see it through. Organizers acted as facilitators while fostering the creation of discussion groups. Each work group was invited (strongly urged, but never commanded) to write an "Instant Report" about the content and the results of its discussion. A standard format was supplied by the organizers/facilitators. All Instant Reports were collected in a final document, and made available to all participants by the end of the day.

## Final Remarks

An OST meeting happens in time and space, and although the requirements are minimal, they are important as this workshop proved. There is no "perfect", "ideal", or generically optimal space and time for an OST [2]. The real question in such initiatives is one of appropriateness to the people and the task.

## References

1. Karasti H (2014) Infrastructuring in participatory design. In: Proceedings of PDC 2014, 06–10 Oct, Windhoek, Namibia, pp 141–150
2. Owen H (1997) Open space technology: a user's guide. Berrett-Koehler, San Francisco
3. Star SL, Bowker GC (2002) How to infrastructure? In: Lievrouw LA, Livingstone SL (eds) The handbook of new media. Social shaping and consequences of ICTs. Sage, London, pp 151–162

# Exploring Data-Work in Healthcare:
# Making Sense of Data Across Boundaries

Enrico Maria Piras, Federico Cabitza, Gunnar Ellingsen, Claus Bossen, and Katie Pine

**Abstract** The workshop focuses on data-work in healthcare in the light of increasing to re-use and re-circulation of data for clinical, managerial, governance and research purposes. Firstly, consumer health informatics has enabled lay people and patients to collect, manage and share health and bodily parameters. Secondly, healthcare managers and policymakers are interested in accessing health-data generated from various IT systems and artifacts in order to evaluate performance and quality, redesign services and allocate funding. Once generated for clinical reasons, health-data are now expected to flow across institutional boundaries and are re-used and re-purposed. This requires additional or new kinds of work in order to disentangle data from the context of its production, and aggregate, analyze and present it in meaningful ways. Topics of interest include, but are not limited to data standardization, re-use of data; design of artifacts and infrastructures; politics of "algorithms"; new forms of data work, visualization of healthcare data.

E.M. Piras
Fondazione Bruno Kessler, Trento, Italy
e-mail: piras@fbk.eu

F. Cabitza
Università degli Studi di Milano-Bicocca, Viale Sarca 336, 20126 Milano, Italy
e-mail: federico.cabitza@disco.unimib.it

G. Ellingsen
Arctic University of Norway, Tromsø, Norway
e-mail: gunnar.ellingsen@uit.no

C. Bossen
Aarhus University, Aarhus, Denmark
e-mail: clausbossen@dac.au.dk

K. Pine
University California, California, USA
e-mail: khpine@uci.edu

© Springer International Publishing Switzerland 2016                                    337
A. De Angeli et al. (eds.), *COOP 2016: Proceedings of the 12th International Conference on the Design of Cooperative Systems, 23–27 May 2016, Trento, Italy*,
DOI 10.1007/978-3-319-33464-6

Data and information have long been a central concern in studies of IT systems in healthcare, since they are an essential part of how coordination, cooperation, and communication are accomplished between co-operating occupations and units in healthcare. These systems have typically been produced by and for clinical and administrative personnel, the producers and primary consumers of the data managed through those systems.

However, two new trends are emerging. Firstly, consumer health informatics has provided laypeople and patients with tools to collect, manage and share bodily parameters, whose measurement once required medical equipment and expertise. The envisioned potential of these data to inform healthcare research and measure quality and outcome of treatment and care has generated much interest and efforts to link and integrate data from the civic, public sphere with clinical data.

Secondly, healthcare managers and policymakers are increasingly interested in accessing and reusing health-data generated from various healthcare IT systems to evaluate performances, redesign services and allocate funding. This may both shape how new ICT systems in healthcare are designed, for instance through increased efforts of structuring the content as well as an increased concern among clinicians how the data they have collected will be used for a range of different purposes.

Accordingly, the landscape of healthcare data-work is undergoing a great transformation. Once generated for strictly clinical reasons, health-data are now increasingly expected to flow across institutional boundaries to be re-used for purposes different from the ones that led to their generation [1]. This circulation of information may require new hybrid technologies [2], additional or new kinds [3], as well as to aggregate, analyze and present it in meaningful ways [4], not to mention that some actors may claim ownerships and restrict its circulation [5].

This workshop focuses on the challenges and the complexities involved in making sense of health data as different actors, in different times and under diverse constraints use them for various purposes.

Topics of interest include, but are not limited to: data standardization or re-classification across institutional boundaries, re-use of clinical data; design of artifacts and infrastructures; politics of "algorithmic" data interpretation; new forms of healthcare data-work, including new occupations, visualization of healthcare data.

# References

1. Pedersen R, Ellingsen G (n.d.) The electronic patient record – sufficient quality for clinical research? In: ECIS 2011 Proceedings. Paper 274
2. Cabitza F, Simone C, De Michelis G (2015) User-driven prioritization of features for a prospective InterPersonal Health Record: perceptions from the Italian context. Comput Biol Med 59:202–210
3. Berg M, Goorman E (1999) The contextual nature of medical information. Int J Med Inform 56:51–60

4. Bossen C, Groth Jensen L, Witt F (2012) Medical secretaries' care of records: the cooperative work of a non-clinical group. In: Proceedings of the ACM 2012 conference on computer supported cooperative work. ACM
5. Piras EM, Zanutto A (2014) "One day it will be you who tells us doctors what to do!". Exploring the "Personal" of PHR in paediatric diabetes management. IT People 27:421–439

Printed by Printforce, the Netherlands